The Union Street Bakery

THE UNION STREET BAKERY SERIES (BOOK 1)

MARY ELLEN TAYLOR

Chapter One

MONDAY, MARCH 22, 2010, 3:30 AM
ALEXANDRIA, VA

Life can turn on a dime. It's a common cliché, and I'd heard it often enough. People die or move away. Investments go south. Affairs end. Loved ones betray us. Stuff happens.

In the light of day, I've always been able to acknowledge that life's bad curveballs are out of our control. I mean come on, who really wants cancer? Who expects lightning to strike a plane and send it plummeting into the ocean? And ladies, how could we really have known that Mr. Say-All-the-Right-Things was such a schmuck?

Bad things happen to good people. When I'm at the office carving into my to-do list, sharing a joke with friends, or running at a breakneck pace on the treadmill, I understand this concept. I really do.

However, ask me those same questions during the darkest time of night when there's nothing to distract me, and my answer won't be as philosophical. Without life's diverting whirl and buzz, my rational logic quickly surrenders to shadowy emotions that lurk and wait to strike. When alone, the promise of control whispers that happiness is mine for the having only if I work very, very hard. *Hold on tight. Run fast. Work hard. Dress right.* If I can do everything right then maybe, just maybe, the herd, the clan, friends, coworkers, or whomever, will keep me close.

When I was a kid, this gut feeling translated into socks and lunch boxes. In grade school I believed that if my socks matched my dress, if I carried the right Barbie lunch box, and if I made all A's, I'd be accepted by friends, teachers and family. I just knew if I could be perfect, I'd somehow be more deserving of . . . love. This obsession with belonging followed me from grade and high schools, college, and into the professional world. No detail was small enough to be managed. No problems were too insignificant to obsess over. My therapist once said, "Life listens to no master." Sound advice that I really wanted to embrace but never quite managed

And so, I did what I did best and focused more attention on all the details, no matter how tiny, believing that somehow, I would remain a step ahead. I'd earned a master's degree in business administration, a Chartered Financial Analyst certificate and quickly established myself as a rising star in a Washington, D.C. money management firm. I also spent wisely and invested in my company stocks. Donated to the SPCA and the United Way. I had friends, a sublease on an apartment with sweeping views of Rock Creek Park and jam-packed purposeful days that left little time for worry or second-guessing. Having done everything right, I fully expected that circumstances would never turn on any damn dime, and my life would not only be filled with love, but that the flock would always embrace me.

And then the chief financial officer of our firm swaggered up to the stock market's metaphorical poker table holding two of a kind and bet most of the chips. The house, however, held a royal flush, and with its better hand swiped the company winnings off the table. I, along with a few others, suggested hysterical she became. She'd called her mom shortly after midnight and begged to go home.

She'd never slept over again.

I'd always feared the future, but I'd never been afraid of whatever dwelled in this house. In fact, whoever was here was more like an annoying friend than foe.

You are not lost. . .

"Want to bet?"

The temperature plummeted, and the scent of honeysuckle permeated the air. *Follow the stars.*

"Is that the best you got? What the hell does that mean?"

Follow the stars.

I waited, listening for specific details, but heard only the sway of the wind through the trees outside my window.

For generations, my parents' town house had not only been home to the family but to the family business as well. Long before I was born, the building's first floor and basement were dedicated to the Union Street Bakery, which has been owned and operated by a McCrae since 1852.

Below my window stood the bakery's sidewalk café furnished with a collection of bare wrought-iron tables. The tables' umbrellas along with the potted red geraniums had been pulled in last night, as they had been every night for as long as I could remember.

The trees lining the land between the garden, and the Potomac River hadn't bloomed or filled with leaves so I could still see the lazy waters meander past. Lights from the Maryland side winked back. Soon green foliage would blossom, fill the empty branches and blot out the Wilson Bridge, which joined the shores of Virginia and Maryland, and the development on the north side of the river. And this corner of Union Street would then feel as if it had slipped back to the time of carriages, cobblestone streets, schooners, and the first whispers of the Civil War.

The first McCrae of the clan's American branch, Shaun McCrae, had been an Irishman known for a quick temper, a mind for business, and the devil's luck in cards. He'd settled in Alexandria in 1842, coming to America with his daughter when his first wife died in the potato famine. He'd found work on the docks, and for a few years, his life slipped into the shadows. And then, in 1851, city records mentioned that Shaun McCrae was the new proprietor of the McCrae's Bakery, later to be known as The Union Street Bakery. His specialty was sea biscuits or ship's bread, a hardy cracker that fed sailors who labored on the barges, schooners, and other ships docked in Alexandria's thriving harbor. Seaman, and later, Confederate and Union soldiers, drawn to the thriving seaport talked about McCrae crackers and biscuits with reverence.

In 1865, Shaun married his second wife Sally Good, a young girl from Ohio. She became his partner in every sense and some said her eye for commerce rivaled his own. They passed the business to their oldest son, and he did the same when he retired. Ever since, a McCrae had operated the business. And now I have returned to the city to do what so many of my clan did before me: to bake bread.

I pushed open the window, closed my eyes, and inhaled the honeysuckle-laced air. The twisting, twining vine had bloomed a month early this year, and reminded me of the day my birth mother kissed my cheek on a crowded Saturday afternoon at the bakery. She pushed a plate of butter cookies toward me and whispered, "Be a good girl. I'll be back soon."

Even though I was three, I had sat patiently nibbling my cookies, watching red sprinkles pepper my yellow skirt, waiting and expecting my mother to return. In those days, time always felt like forever, but I was used to waiting for my birth mother, so I didn't panic or cry. It was Sheila McCrae, the young hippie bakery shop owner with five- and three-year-old daughters of her own who had noticed I had sat alone and that the CFO retrench. Back off. Don't expose us so much. Unmoved by logic and seemingly imbued with confidence, the CFO raised the bet on the mortgage market. This time he held a straight—better, but not enough to beat the house's royal flush.

The staggering loss knifed into the firm's investment accounts, which quickly started hemorrhaging. No matter how hard the investment team and I tried to stop the bleeding, we could not. Soon, clients bailed. The CFO resigned. And finally, in a New Year's Day panic, the firm's big boss sold our investment shop to a larger bank, which quickly declared all the members of the investment team obsolete.

One second, I was at my desk talking to a client, assuring him that my investments, though battered, remained tied up with the company like his. And in the next, the new CFO had me in his office and was spouting phrases like: *This is no reflection of you, Daisy. We respect what you did. . .* Before I had time to shake off the shock, I had to stumble through a maze of gray cubicles toward the elevators, the buzzing fluorescents mingling with the whispers of coworkers. Tucked under my arm was a single box holding a plant, a framed picture of my parents standing in front of their bakery, a black mug, and my two diplomas. Someone had called out their best wishes to me, but I was too stunned and too humiliated to turn. The elevator doors opened, and I woodenly stepped into the car. In a blink, the doors closed on the last decade of my life.

Now, as I sat on the edge of the pullout sofa in my parents' attic room and watched the shadows dance and sway over roughly hewn ceiling beams, I wondered for the hundredth time what I could have done differently to stop the explosion that rocked my life. I had seen the CFO's moodiness deepen daily and had felt the weight of his stress. I had known something was wrong but had assumed his plight was personal, not professional. I should have pushed through my own worries and spoken to him privately. I should have muzzled my insecurities and demanded to see his trades. I should have stood up on my desk and screamed, *Houston, we have a problem!*

But I didn't do any of those things. I kept my head down, basically obsessed with trimming trees while the forest burned.

"Damn." I swung my legs over the side of the sofa to the cold wooden floor. My toes curled and my heart drummed faster against my ribs as I stared at the fortress of crates, boxes, and suitcases crammed into the attic room. Beyond the barrier, my road bike leaned against one wall, stacks of books piled high on the floor, and my laptop rested on an old sewing table. All my worldly goods had been wedged into boxes and trash bags and stowed in every available corner.

I dug long fingers through my black hair and then pressed the heels of my hands to my forehead.

Though I might not have always loved my job, I had done it well and it had rewarded me with success and pride. Never had I once thought that the job was *me* or *I* was the job. We were two separate entities.

But as I raised my gaze to the moonlight streaming into the room's single window, I had to concede that the job had wormed into my identity like sprawling ivy vines, which over time, slowly and carefully had burrowed into the mortar, brick, and foundation of my life.

With the job gone, I was left damaged and marked like bricks stripped clean of ivy. I was lost. Adrift. Who the hell was I if I wasn't Daisy-S-McCrae-vice-president-Suburban Enterprises?

Panic scraped at the back of my head and made my skin crawl. It would be so easy to just scream and cry at the utter futility of this mess. But I'd learned at a very young age that crying never solved anything, nor did it calm the chaos.

"Damn." I stared at my toes and the chipped red polish from a two-week-old pedicure.

Finance jobs in the area were few and far between in recent months and with each new *no, not now, overqualified, underqualified*, my sense of helplessness grew. Never in my life had I worked so hard and received so many rejections.

Soon, showers and a clean change of clothes had stopped being an everyday thing. My appetite vanished. I avoided friends and family. I couldn't seem to untangle the net that had me trapped.

My cell phone, sitting on a makeshift moving box-turned-nightstand, shrilled an alarm that cut through the silence and startled me. I quickly shut off the glaring noise and checked the time. Three twenty-one.

I could barely think or function, and yet it was time to get up. Tears welled up in my throat, and as much as I wanted to pull my sleeping bag over my head and hide, I didn't. I swallowed. No tears. Daisy McCrae did not cry. How did I get here?

Here was Old Town Alexandria, Virginia. My new—but I have been quick to say, temporary home—was the top floor apartment in my parents' 120-year-old brick town house. It was the room I'd shared with my sisters as a kid, where I'd played dress up, dreamed of my birth mother, and traded secrets with imaginary friends. It was ground zero, square-one in my life, and I was back.

Oh God.

Dropping back against the lumpy mattress, I pulled the sleeping bag over my head. The money I'd invested with Suburban was all but gone, the furniture that filled my apartment was gone, my designer suits and Prada heels were in storage, my mail now forwarded to a four-by-five-inch P.O. Box in Alexandria. In a blink, I became the loser unemployed kid living in the attic.

"Maybe if I lay very still, I'll really wake up and find that the last few months have just been a nightmare."

I waited, hoped, prayed for a miracle even as the spring in the sofa mattress poked my backside and my mind shouted, *Get up! You've got promises to keep.*

I'd never broken a promise in my life, ever. And that quirk was why I'd always been careful about making them. "Shit!"

I sat back up, tossed aside the sleeping bag and again swung my legs over the side of the sofa bed. Groping fingers found my worn sweatpants and a faded University of Richmond T-shirt, which thankfully I'd laid out before bed. Shrugging off my nightgown, the cool night air hit my bare skin and sent a chill through my body. Cursing my life, I quickly slipped on my clothes.

Bare feet went begrudgingly into worn clogs as I pulled my crooked ponytail free and combed fingers through my wavy hair. I weaved through unpacked boxes toward the moonlight streaming into the window that overlooked Union Street in Old Town. It was a clear night and the stars twinkled.

I had never felt more lost or alone.

You are not lost.

The whisper-soft words rattled in my head now as they did the night prior when I first climbed the stairs to the attic. I'd not heard the voice in years. Most might have fretted overhearing a voice, but it was as familiar to me as the house's clanging pipes, flickering lights, and squeaky floorboards.

You are not alone.

"Go away." My voice was gravelly and rough with sleep.

Hearing myself respond out loud reminded me of the time I had a friend sleep over when I was a kid. Millie had heard me talking to someone she could not see, and when I'd told her the house had a ghost, she'd tried to laugh it off, but I could see the worry take root. That night, as the shadows swayed and my room filled with the steady familiar sound of footsteps on the attic stairs, she'd freaked. I tried to calm her with assurances that the ghost was good, but the more I spoke the more hysterical she became. She'd called her mom shortly after midnight and begged to go home.

She'd never slept over again.

I'd always feared the future, but I'd never been afraid of whatever dwelled in this house. In fact, whoever was here was more like an annoying friend than foe.

You are not lost...

"Want to bet?"

The temperature plummeted, and the scent of honeysuckle permeated the air. *Follow the stars.*

"Is that the best you got? What the hell does that mean?"

Follow the stars.

I waited, listening for specific details, but heard only the sway of the wind through the trees outside my window.

For generations, my parents' town house had not only been home to the family but to the family business as well. Long before I was born, the building's first floor and basement were dedicated to the Union Street Bakery, which has been owned and operated by a McCrae since 1852.

Below my window stood the bakery's sidewalk café furnished with a collection of bare wrought-iron tables. The tables' umbrellas along with the potted red geraniums had been pulled in last night, as they had been every night for as long as I could remember.

The trees lining the land between the garden, and the Potomac River hadn't bloomed or filled with leaves so I could still see the lazy waters meander past. Lights from the Maryland side winked back. Soon green foliage would blossom, fill the empty branches and blot out the Wilson Bridge, which joined the shores of Virginia and Maryland, and the development on the north side of the river. And this corner of Union Street would then feel as if it had slipped back to the time of carriages, cobblestone streets, schooners, and the first whispers of the Civil War.

The first McCrae of the clan's American branch, Shaun McCrae, had been an Irishman known for a quick temper, a mind for business, and the devil's luck in cards. He'd settled in Alexandria in 1842, coming to America with his daughter when his first wife died in the potato famine. He'd found work on the docks, and for a few years, his life slipped into the shadows. And then, in 1851, city records mentioned that Shaun McCrae was the new proprietor of the McCrae's Bakery, later to be known as The Union Street Bakery. His specialty was sea biscuits or ship's bread, a hardy cracker that fed sailors who labored on the barges, schooners, and other ships docked in Alexandria's thriving harbor. Seaman, and later, Confederate and Union soldiers, drawn to the thriving seaport talked about McCrae crackers and biscuits with reverence.

In 1865, Shaun married his second wife Sally Good, a young girl from Ohio. She became his partner in every sense and some said her eye for commerce rivaled his own. They passed the business to their oldest son, and he did the same when he retired. Ever since, a McCrae had operated the business. And now I have returned to the city to do what so many of my clan did before me: to bake bread.

I pushed open the window, closed my eyes, and inhaled the honeysuckle-laced air. The twisting, twining vine had bloomed a month early this year, and reminded me of the day my birth mother kissed my cheek on a crowded Saturday afternoon at the bakery. She pushed a plate of butter cookies toward me and whispered, "Be a good girl. I'll be back soon."

Even though I was three, I had sat patiently nibbling my cookies, watching red sprinkles pepper my yellow skirt, waiting and expecting my mother to return. In those days, time always felt like forever, but I was used to waiting for my birth mother, so I didn't panic or cry. It was Sheila McCrae, the young hippie bakery shop owner with five- and three-year-old daughters of her own who had noticed I had sat alone and unattended for too long. She called for a search that quickly became frantic.

I remember Sheila's husband, Frank McCrae, talking to the police, the social worker speaking to me softly, and me screaming bloody murder when they tried to lead me away. I'd shouted. "No! Mama!"

Sheila McCrae had pulled the social worker aside and told her I could stay at the bakery if I wanted. Some compromise had been struck and Mrs. McCrae had told me I could wait for my mother. Finally, I stopped crying. They'd coaxed me inside, found a change of clothes for me, and fed me supper. I sat awake in bed, clutching the sheets, still hoping my mom would return. Finally, I'd drifted to sleep.

My birth mother never came back that night or the nights that followed. The police launched a search. The river had been dredged. There'd been newscasts and articles that flashed my picture and the few statistics the McCraes had coaxed from me. But no one had come forward with information on the Abandoned Bake Shop Baby.

I had only vague recollections of my birth mother: the scent of peppermints, the feel of her fingertips as she brushed hair out of my eyes and the husky sound of her voice as she sang her one and only lullaby, "Rock-A-Bye-Baby." The police never found or discovered her identity. I gave my birth mother the made-up name of Renee because it sounded very exotic. But the name Renee was as much a part of my imagination as the images I had created of her. With no facts to anchor Renee, her story and likeness often shifted when I daydreamed. A destitute woman. A movie actress. A spy. But no matter who she was or what she looked like, she loved me, and deeply regretted leaving me behind.

Sheila and Frank McCrae, even before the Commonwealth terminated Renee's parental rights, effortlessly wove me into their family. The McCrae family formally adopted me almost a year to the day Renee left.

Both of my new parents did their best to make me feel loved in their home. When Mom dispensed candy, each of her daughters got five pieces. When Christmas rolled around, we each had six wrapped presents under the tree. We bought back-to-school supplies at the same time, and in elementary school we each ended up with the same style backpack and the same white Nikes. But in my mind, I was a dark stray thread that was a little too off color to fully mesh with the delicate Irish McCrae linen.

As I stared at the patio, a rush of anger flooded my body. Whenever I go back to the early years with Renee, I become frustrated that I can't remember more than cookie sprinkles on my yellow skirt. When Renee left, she took critical pieces of my life with her. My sisters have their The-Day-You-Were-Born birth stories. They know their grandmother suffered with breast cancer and that the heart disease that plagued our dad is a threat. They know they inherited Mom's fair skin and Dad's blue eyes. But I had no medical details, and I don't know who gave me my dark hair or my raspy voice. When Renee left, she took my history with her, and she created in me a jigsaw puzzle with missing key pieces. Almost complete, but not quite.

What could a three-year-old have done to deserve being ditched?

You are not lost.

"Shut up." I sucked in a deep breath as a therapist once advised. More honeysuckle filled my lungs, and I longed for the high-rise office with its sterile, computer-controlled air that held no hints of the past. Like it or not, I was back home. To live. And to bake bread. It was also not lost on me that I'm not a real McCrae. And I felt a little like a fraud.

"Daisy! Daisy! Are you awake?" My sister, Rachel, pushed through my bedroom door, two cups of coffee in her hands.

Rachel was only three months older than me, but we were as different as night and day. Rachel had the McCrae clan's coloring: strawberry blond–cool looks, pale skin, blue eyes, and hundreds of freckles. Like our parents, Rachel was eight inches shorter than my near six-foot frame; and like Mom, her sunny disposition drew people as easily as honeysuckle summoned bees.

"Ready to start your first day?" A neat ponytail accentuated her freshly scrubbed peaches-and-cream face. And of course, she was smiling. Rachel was always smiling.

I tossed a final glance at the night sky. "Day? You're kidding, right?"

Rachel laughed as she crossed and handed me the steaming cup of coffee. "Welcome to the world of a baker. You remember Dad climbed out of bed at three every morning when we were kids."

"I guess." Dad had rattled around the kitchen each morning, cursing and trying to make his coffee. I often got up, found the coffee beans, and set the pot to brew as we sat and listened to the gurgle of the machine. After he filled his cup and drank his first sip, he'd kiss me and then shoo me back to bed.

I stared into the dark depths of my cup, knowing I wouldn't be going back to bed and that I had a three-cup minimum before I'd function at full speed. "It's one thing to know someone was up early, but it's quite another to be the one who is actually awake and operational."

"Henri has been in the kitchen since midnight." Henri, who originally hailed from the Basque region of France, had worked for Dad for over twenty-five years. Every night, Sunday through Friday, Henri clocked in at midnight to fire up the bakery's stoves. He mixed dough and shaped loaves until his shift ended just before seven. I only had vague recollections of him leaving each morning just before the store opened, a cigarette dangling from his lips, flour coating his black shoes and several loaves tucked under his arm. Henri had always been a bit of a ghost to me. The thought of working side by side with him was jarring.

"Working until three in the morning was the norm when I had deadlines for the firm but rising at this unholy hour is different. It breaks all the laws of nature. I can't believe you've been doing this alone for the last year."

Rachel shrugged, and I imagined worries rolling off her shoulders like rain from a duck's feathers. "It hasn't been so bad. I'm up and have the bulk of my work done before the kids wake up. And remember Margaret is scheduled to open the storefront at seven."

According to the new plan, I would work in the bakery kitchen with Henri and Rachel, and then at seven, our other sister, Margaret, would arrive to work the front counter while I retired to the bakery office to sort the paperwork. Rachel would hurry upstairs to her second-floor apartment to get her twin five-year-old daughters up and dressed for school. Once the girls were out the door, Rachel had to head back downstairs to work in the shop, which she'd keep open until three.

Rachel's late afternoons were split between the bakery and doing more kid-related things—soccer, dance, and God only knows what else. Mom promised that the new plan would run like clockwork.

Clockwork.

Right.

This entire family hadn't had many clockwork days in recent years.

Six years ago, when our parents retired, they moved into a town house across the street, which they'd bought in the eighties and had been renting out. They also turned over the bakery to Rachel and her new husband, Mike. Mom and Dad were near seventy by then, and Dad's heart had given him some fits in the form of minor heart attacks. The changing of the guard seemed a natural, logical switch. I had just gotten a big promotion at work, and my sister and her husband had happily taken over the bakery. With my parents safely retired, my association with flour, hot ovens, and waiting on customers promised to slip happily into the past forever.

A year later, Rachel and Mike's twins, Ellie and Anna, came screaming into the world seven weeks early but, in the long run, perfect. Rachel and Mike were thrilled. Mom and Dad beamed. Even my older sister, Margaret, had seemed happy with her PhD studies at William and Mary. We had all found our place in the world. And then, thirteen months ago, Mike had suffered a brain aneurysm while he'd been icing cakes. He died before the ambulance reached the hospital.

The family rallied. I had made a loan to cover Rachel's cash-flow problems and Mom and Dad had stepped in to run the bakery. Margaret came home for a few weeks and kept the register running. And Rachel hid in the kitchens, pouring her grief into endless confections. She often said the girls and baking had saved her sanity.

Unfortunately, the routine my parents had managed so well for most of their youth soon overwhelmed their aging bodies. Dad had suffered another minor heart attack, so Rachel approached Margaret and asked for help. Margaret reluctantly agreed, believing she could work in the bake shop and finish her dissertation in her spare hours. I sent money, more than happy to part with cash so I could keep my distance.

The family and bakery limped along for another year, but the schedule didn't really work. Margaret lost more and more time from her dissertation, and Rachel's weight and vitality waned.

Last Christmas, I came home on the heels of a bad breakup, only half listening to Rachel and Dad exchange heated whispers over selling the bakery. Mom had whipped mashed potatoes into a fine, gooey paste all the while reminding us it was the holiday, and we damn well better act nice to each other. But it had been a grim gathering. The bakery, it seemed, might just have to close.

But then the McCrae's Irish luck came calling. A week and a half later, I lost my job. Though I had hopes of landing something before my three months of severance pay expired, I had quickly discovered employment prospects for the crewmembers of Suburban, a.k.a. the SS *Titanic*, were slim to meager.

Last week had marked three months of unemployment and the end of severance. Mom had summoned me home for a family dinner. I'd gone expecting that she'd ask for more money. I didn't have a lot left after the company's crash, but I'd been ready to offer what I had. Instead, Mom had been all smiles, and she'd been serving her deadly daiquiris. I really should have known better.

Mom's daiquiris had stealthily unwound the tension normally knotting my gut and lowered my guard when she'd offered me the job of bakery manager. I'd been too buzzed and too at peace for my own good to say no. I agreed to manage the bakery and work with Rachel—until I found something better, of course.

Like rabid dogs, my parents and sister had named a salary and offered living arrangements before I sobered. I'd thrown a blowout going away party for my unemployed work friends, and then my family had moved me from my D.C. apartment back to Alexandria.

I really appreciate this, Daisy," Rachel said.

I sipped coffee, remembering Rachel brewed it too bitter

for my taste. "Hey, family helps family. And we'll find you someone who can help on a more permanent basis soon."

"Right."

I pushed through mental cobwebs and searched for Dad's old schedule. We had almost four hours before the bakery opened. "So, we mix the bread dough first?"

"Just like in the days Dad ran the business, Henri has mixed the dough, and then we help him shape the remaining loaves and rolls. Bagels next, and cakes after that so they can cool while we bake the cookies."

"Great." I gulped more coffee. "Let me pee, and I'll be right down."

"Sure." Rachel nodded but didn't leave. "It really will be nice working with you."

"Should be great." Still, Rachel hesitated, which triggered an awkward need in me to fill the silence. "Are Mom and Dad going to help this morning?"

"No. They want us to go it alone. Dad's not been feeling great." She sipped her coffee and frowned. "And you know Mom never worries when you're around."

"Mom worries about everyone."

"But she worries less when you're here. You're the rock."

"Maybe Mom also knows today won't be easy for me and avoiding my moodiness."

"You moody? Never." The unexpected sarcasm made us both laugh. But when the laughter trickled away, the darkness regained footing.

Rachel sensed the shift in me, just as Mom always did. And like Mom, Rachel got that wounded look in her eyes. It hurt Rachel and especially Mom when I cringed when they hugged too tight or kissed my cheek. I've long wanted us to be closer, but I'd come to believe that I don't know how to really love. I care about people, worry about their welfare, but an invisible barrier has always kept me separate from the world.

Despite the distance or perhaps because of it, I became fixer of all things McCrae. Need a picture hung, a ride, or furniture moved? Call Daisy. Need a little money? Call Daisy. A babysitter. . . yup, Daisy is your go-to gal.

I glanced up at Rachel, and I realized she wasn't going anywhere despite bruised feelings. "I can pee by myself, Rachel."

"Oh, yeah, right. I know. Curse of small kids," she said, stepping back. "I'm always lingering in case I'm needed."

Which reminds me, you cut up my food last night."

Rachel's laugh held a hint of apology. "Sorry."

And still, she didn't leave.

I pulled the rubber band from my hair, finger combed it, and then gathered it into a smoother ponytail. "Really, I can pee on my own." Rachel traced the rim of her cup and with each turn of her finger her smile faded. "Daisy, I know you don't want to be back. I know this has really got to suck for you."

I smiled but sensed it looked more like a grimace. Faking nice has never been one of my specialties. "Am I that obvious?"

"You are—to me. I think you fooled Mom and Dad well enough."

"They wanted to be fooled. It was easy."

Fresh tears glistened in Rachel's eyes. "I'm sorry."

"For what?"

She wrung trembling hands. "For not being able to keep this place afloat by myself. If I could, you'd be somewhere else."

"Come on, Rachel, don't cry. I hate it when you cry." I half expected Mom to bust through the door. "Daisy, did you make your sister cry again?"

"And yeah, I'd be somewhere else. I'd be in an apartment I

can no longer afford, and I'd still be jobless. You did me the favor."

"You don't believe that."

"I do."

"Keep saying it out loud and you might believe it." Rachel swiped away a big, fat tear. "Stop crying."

"You know me. I cry over spilled milk."

"Hey, this could be fun." A small lie that supported the greater good wasn't so bad, was it?

"It's just since Mike died, I've been doing so much by myself."

"No more worries. Daisy to the rescue." I had the sinking feeling that my temporary arrangement with the bakery had just been extended.

"Just remember the baking gene skipped me. You'll need to tell me what to mix. I can burn toast."

That seemed to buck her up a bit. "Who knew flames could shoot that high out of a toaster oven?"

"Don't forget the flaming cheese when I cooked pizza from scratch." As a teen I'd gained a reputation as a terrible cook. The description had stuck, and though I really had improved over the years no one in the family had really noticed. In their mind I would forever be Daisy, burner of all things edible.

A laugh eased some tension from her shoulders. "Right."

"Hey, I know my fractions, and I can add and subtract. You stay close for the finesse part of the work, and I'll do the heavy lifting. Between the two of us we're a decent baker."

I can do that." Rachel swiped another tear and straightened her shoulders. Hints of her trademark smile reappeared. "I can do that. I can do that."

"See? All better." I patted her on the shoulder, but my hand was stiff and my touch a little too hard. "Now, Rachel, please leave because I really, really have to pee."

Chapter Two

MONDAY, MARCH 22, 2010, 4:00 AM

Henri, a short willowy man with stooped shoulders, kneaded the gooey dough with gnarled fingers as he randomly dusted his mixture with more flour. What looked haphazard to me was not arbitrary to Henri. Like any master baker, Henri read dough as easily as I read the paper. Too much water? Too humid? A bad batch of flour? Henri knew.

When I was a kid, I had been fascinated that he'd never used a written recipe or measuring cups. I would stand in the corner just a little afraid to talk to the silent man who never mingled with the family and watched him dump his ingredients into the large mixing bowl. I once screwed up the courage to ask him how he knew what to do when. For a long moment he didn't answer or move his gaze from the dough, and then he'd shrugged and said, "*Je sais.*" I know.

"Henri," I said, clearing the gravel from my voice and trying not to sound like he still intimidated me. "*Que pasa?*"

He raised his gaze, and his brow arched as he stared at me. I half imagined he was glad to see me, and then he grunted a greeting before returning to his dough.

Others might have been offended by Henri's abrupt, almost rude response. But I wasn't. In fact, I drew comfort from it. So many people have changed on me, disappointed me, or let me down, but never Henri. I can always count on Henri to worry more about his dough than polite "Good Mornings."

I sat my cup down on the large stainless worktable and picked up a white apron hanging from a hook. As I slipped the apron over my head and crisscrossed the ends around my waist, I had a moment of pure panic.

God, please tell me this is a joke! I was not unemployed or living in my parents' home or working in the family business. I had not gone full circle into a brick wall. Had I?

"I know that look," Rachel said as she slipped on her apron and tied a crisp bow in the front.

I couldn't even muster a fake smile this go-around. "You mean the look of blinding panic."

"Exactly."

Over the years I'd surrounded myself with people who didn't really know me, so it was a little unnerving now to be around someone who knew me a little too well. "I won't bolt. I made a promise. I'll see it through." Gritty determination laced the final words as if someone had just yanked a thorn from the bottom of my foot.

You know we've all bet on how long you'll last." She smiled but her eyes harbored a hint of desperation that broke my heart a little and ensured I would not run this time.

Casually, I moved toward the small stainless sink, turned on the hot water, and pumped soap from a dispenser. I washed my hands. "No huge surprise there. Dad turns everything into a bet or a race."

Rachel stood beside me and washed her hands. "You do have a reputation for frequently changing jobs and boyfriends." Her tone projected her simmering worry and fear.

"So how do the betting odds look?" I grabbed a freshly laundered towel from a stack, dried my hands, and tucked the towel under my tied apron strings. Through the course of the day, I'd use a dozen towels like this one, not only drying hands, but also wiping down countertops or cleaning dishes.

"Mom says a month. Dad says two. Margaret says two days."

"Two days?" My older sister and I have been oil and water since day one. She was six when I was adopted, and for reasons I can't explain she always resented my presence. "That's wishful thinking on her part."

"You know Margaret. She was ruler of the house until you came along. You usurped her authority at every turn."

"I enjoyed rattling her cage." Even if this place burned to the ground this morning, I would stay onsite working for more than two days if only to spite Margaret.

"You think?"

Margaret was a problem that I didn't have to face until seven a.m., and for now I refused to consider the battles to come. "What kind of bet did you place?"

"A year."

That's optimistic." I didn't even try to hide the surprise. If I'd bet, I'd have wagered three months, tops.

"This is a good place for you, Daisy. You just don't believe it yet." I grunted, Henri style. "You really think I'll last a year?"

"I think you'll last longer. This is where you belong." A sheepish smile undercut her light tone. "Plus, I'll need a good year of solid help to get myself together."

My mind suddenly tripped back to my first days at the bakery. It couldn't have been long after Renee left. I'd been crying. So, lost. And Rachel had gotten out of the twin bed next to mine and given me one of her Barbies to hold. I hadn't wanted the doll. In fact, I think I threw it on the floor.

But I'd never forgotten that she'd tried.

I don't know if I belong but if it takes a year to get you settled, it takes a year. I said I'd stay until you found real help, and I will."

Damn Barbie.

Shoving aside the sharp prick of emotion, I focused on the workroom and took a moment to look past the shine of the stainless. Neat as a pin didn't hide the room's age. The state-of-the-art equipment my parents had installed thirty years ago now looked dated and tired. *Rode hard and put away wet* came to mind. "How's the equipment running?"

"It gets the job done." Rachel moved toward the large industrial refrigerator and pulled out an armload of butter.

"That doesn't answer my question."

"Sometimes I have to tinker and cajole to keep the motor running on the big mixers, but they still keep spinning."

Closer inspection revealed nicks and scratches in the stainless patina. A dent in the side of the large mixing bowl was evidence that it had been dropped, and I could imagine Rachel single-handedly hefting the bowl. Full of dough, it easily weighed over a hundred pounds. The image fueled my guilt at not having done something earlier. "We should get someone in here to have a look at the equipment?"

Henri grunted but didn't raise his head.

"Is that a yes or a no, Henri?" I asked.

Rachel hoisted a thirty-pound bag of flour. "It's a yes. But repairs cost money."

"It may be necessary, no matter what it costs." I glanced at the ovens used for baking cakes, which looked to be in decent shape. But a glimpse at the brick oven was another matter. This was the oven we used to make our breads because it added a flavor few other bakers in the region could match. It was what distinguished the Union Street Bakery bread from the stuff on grocery store shelves.

Chunks of mortar were missing from the oven's sides, and the cast iron door was rigged closed with a wooden spoon.

In a low voice, Rachel added, "Henri doesn't want to learn how to use a new oven. He likes his oven."

"Does Henri not speak for himself anymore?" I whispered.

Rachel's gaze was so serious. "He never talks when he bakes, don't you remember?"

My gaze flickered from the stone oven to Henri, who'd always seemed strong. Now when he turned sideways, I could see how slim he'd become and that the perpetual hunch in his shoulders looked more like a hump.

Henri and his stove didn't have as much time as Rachel hoped. Like the mixer and the oven, I sensed he was hanging on only for Rachel.

One last gulp of coffee wasn't nearly enough fortification, but I set down the cup. "God help me, I'm going to work. You said bread first?"

Rachel grinned. "Then bagels, cakes, and cookies."

Two hours later, I stood in the center of the basement bake shop covered in flour. My back ached from hefting bread dough from the industrial mixer and the repetitive motion of forming more bagels than a single human should have to produce in a day.

Rachel looked cool and composed as she hummed, as if a great weight had been lifted from her shoulders. Even Henri looked a bit younger and a little less bent than he had hours ago.

I realized that the invisible burden had been lifted from their shoulders and placed squarely on mine. Everyone really believed that my presence was going to save the day. God help us all.

My dough-shaping efforts were a sad attempt compared to Henri's and Rachel's practiced efficiency. My work was the work of a novice, not a bakery rescuer.

I didn't want to be a savior. I wanted my air-conditioned office back with the door that closed so easily. I wanted to look out the window that overlooked the bustling street in D.C. I wanted to run and hide. But this was my family. . .my *only* pack. And the idea of letting them sink terrified me more than working here.

"This is God's curse," I said, tossing another round of dough on a sheet.

Rachel arched a brow. "What do you mean? Together we move four times as fast as I did with Dad."

Using the back of my forearm, I brushed aside wispy strands of hair from my eyes. "I can't believe you do this every day."

"It's not so bad once you get used to it. And in time, you'll see that all we do here has a real Zen quality."

The last time I'd heard talk like that was when I'd paid money for a yoga retreat. After a few hours of deep breathing and chanting, I'd slipped out the back door and gone home to have a beer. "Zen. Shit."

Henri grunted.

Rachel laughed and hummed as she opened the large stainless refrigerator and pulled out several more pounds of butter so they could warm and soften before mixing. "You'll see the art once you've tasted the bread. In fact, you will stop hating bread once you've tasted USB bread."

"I don't hate bread. I love bread. I had a bagel a few months ago." The markets had rallied, and it appeared Suburban would survive. The bagel had been my mini celebration. "Bread just doesn't love me back."

"How can you say that? Of course, it loves you. You've turned your back on bread because you are rebelling against this place."

"It's not a rebellion thing. It's a jeans-that-have-grown-too- tight-to-zip kind of thing."

Her eyes sparked with challenge. "Did that bagel taste as good as mine?"

"No. Too doughy, as I remember."

Her gaze narrowed as she seemed to flip through the baking process. "No doubt they rushed the cooking time."

"I didn't double back and question them."

"You should have. Always good to know what the competition is doing."

"They aren't my competition."

"They are now."

Responding to that comment suggested I was really a baker, and I had not made that leap yet. "At the time, I never gave any thought to the lady behind the bagel counter, or the poor slob locked in the basement grinding the bagels out."

Rachel's laugh rang clear and bright. "And now you are that poor slob."

"I'm in hell."

By seven, the earthy fragrance of freshly baked bread perfumed the shop. The front display cases burst with breads, cookies, and pies. The place was transformed from a dark cold space to a warm inviting retreat that beckoned those who passed. Rachel had done this. She had brought the sunshine.

Rachel flipped the closed sign to open as I wiped the flour from my palms onto my apron. I should have been enjoying this moment of peace sandwiched between the morning baking and the rush of the day's first customers. But butterflies chewed at my gut with ravenous voracity. At Suburban, I'd shouted down my fair share of brokers, consultants, and traders and never broke a sweat. So why was I so freaked now?

I moved out to the patio. I opened the umbrellas, wiped off the tables and chairs, and pulled out the planter. The dewy street was quiet, but the nearby rumble of trucks and honk of horns told me the city was awake. I remembered that our first customers, if they weren't waiting outside for us to open, arrived minutes after opening.

Our regular customers had deep ties to the area. Many lived in the historic town houses that lined the narrow cobblestone streets or worked in the retail shops that dotted the blocks near the waterfront. A good many had grown up starting their day with Union Street Bakery bread. Dad had said the number of customers had dwindled in recent years because the lure of low-carb diets and inexpensive grocery store bread had hit USB like a one-two punch.

I moved back into the store and stood directly behind the counter, where it felt just a little safer. I hadn't stood behind this counter since the summer before college, seventeen years ago, and I wasn't looking forward to doing it today. In a small community like Old Town Alexandria, comments about my return, which I'd no desire to field, would be unavoidable.

I retied the strings of my apron and smoothed my hands over my hips as Rachel pushed through the saloon doors. "Where is Margaret? I thought she was supposed to work the front counter."

"You know Margaret." Rachel, her baking done, looked relaxed and content, as if she'd had great sex. "Always late."

I squared an order pad with the edge of the counter and then gently drummed my fingers over the register keys. "Has she ever been on time a day in her life?"

"Doubtful." Rachel moved toward me, pulling off her apron.

"She'll be here soon. Until then, you can work the register just like you did back in the day."

"I've spent the better part of the last seventeen years

blocking out the hours I worked in the bakery." In my former bakery days, all I could do was dream of better places to live. "I don't remember anything."

"It's like riding a bike. You'll pick it right back up. I've posted the prices by the register for quick reference. Now, I've got to get upstairs and wake the girls. They're going to be late for school if I don't."

Shoving aside unreasonable panic, I nodded. The girls needed their mother more than I did but that didn't ease the tension coiling my gut.

"Sure. Fine. Go. Leave me to the wolves. Where's Henri?"

"He left five minutes ago, three baguettes under his arm."

"Great." I was alone.

Rachel's brow deepened with renewed tension. "Hey, if you want me to stay..."

I shoved out a breath. "No, no. The girls need you. I can do this."

Rachel nibbled her bottom lip. "You're sure?"

"Very. I'm just being dramatic."

She nodded. "I have confidence you can man the ship."

"Remember my last ship, the SS *Suburban*, sunk."

Rachel grinned, and then vanished up the back staircase to her apartment. I stood in front of the counter, my shoulders back and my body tense. The cupcake clock on the wall behind me ticked as the cappuccino machine on the counter gurgled and hissed. I drummed my fingers and considered dashing around the counter to clean the front window. But that would mean leaving the safety of the counter, so instead I knelt and readjusted already military-straight pastries in the case.

Maybe no one would come right away. Maybe Margaret would show and . . .

The bells on the front door jingled as the door opened.

I was so relieved to hear the bells. I smiled, determined to swallow all the nasty Margaret curses I'd readied. I just wanted her here so I could escape back to the kitchen or the office.

I stood, but instead of Margaret I saw my first customer since high school enter the shop.

She was a burly African American woman wearing a white nurse's uniform, and she was pulling a wheelchair. With practiced ease, the nurse spun the wheelchair around to reveal a very elderly woman sitting hunched forward, her head slightly bent, and her right hand drawn up in a *C* shape. The old woman wore a yellow dress that all but swallowed her thin frame; a pillbox hat, which covered thinned, short hair that looked as if it just been styled; and her white gloved hands draped a small rectangular purse. A blue crocheted throw blanket warmed her legs.

I knew the old woman from back in the day, and though I couldn't recall her name, I remembered she had a taste for sweets. Cookies? Pies? No, sweet buns. A half-dozen every single Friday. But it was Monday, not Friday.

I stood a little straighter and offered my best Rachelesque smile. "Welcome." The word sounded so rusty. I cleared my throat. "Welcome to Union Street Bakery."

The wheelchair-bound woman raised her head at the sound of my voice. She studied me as if she were sizing me up. "As I recall, you swore you'd never be caught dead behind that register again."

The direct clear voice didn't jive with the withered body that looked so painfully fragile. "Excuse me?"

The old woman's clear, bright gaze was as powerful as her voice. "Last time I saw you here, you screamed and hollered like a baby. Said you'd never come back."

My last day in the bake shop hadn't been one of my finer moments. A woman had come into the bakery, and I'd sworn she was Renee. *My Renee.* As she'd sipped coffee on the sidewalk cafe, I kept staring, certain we shared so many similarities. Dark hair. Slim, tall build. Wide-set eyes. She even was eating sugar cookies like the ones my Renee had given me that last day.

A bundle of nerves and tension congealed in my belly and when she rose to leave, I'd panicked, feeling I was about to lose my one and only opportunity to meet my birth mother again. I was certain she'd not recognized the three-year-old that had now morphed into a seventeen-year-old. So, I had gathered up the courage, introduced myself, and asked her if she was my birth mother. She looked at me as if I'd lost my mind, but I'd been too emotional to read her expression and so I kept babbling.

"I'm Daisy. And I'm still at the bakery." I even hugged her.

Her body stiffened like forged iron, and she anxiously glanced around looking for someone to help her. "Really, kid, I don't know you."

She smelled of Chanel and fresh soap. "You left a daughter here fourteen years ago. That girl is me. I was three at the time."

Fear had given way to pity in the woman's gaze as she pried herself from my arms. "Honey, I've never been here before. Really."

"My name is Daisy. I was three when you left me."

"No, honey," she'd said softly. "That wasn't me."

With growing horror, I'd realized my terrible blunder. Shame had burned so hot in my throat I thought I'd pass out.

"You cried like a baby," the old woman said.

Refocusing on her, I exhaled the breath I'd been holding. "Really?"

Gnarled fingers picked at the edges of the caftan. "Stirred up a real scene."

Mom had been summoned from the back and had crossed straight to me. As she'd apologized to the woman, she'd tried to calm me, but the more she spoke in soothing whispers, the louder I'd cried.

"Who could just leave a kid like that?" I'd wailed into Mom's sweatshirt. Carefully the woman had backed away from the table and the nearby faceless customers' chatter had grown unnaturally silent.

"I don't know, baby. I don't know. But it had nothing to do with you."

Sloppy tears rolled down my face. "It had everything to do with me."

I realized that day that I had been waiting for Renee since she'd abandoned me. I'd been ready to turn down offers to go to college in hopes she'd return and explain her absence in a way that excused everything. I was waiting for her to tell me she loved me.

In that moment, I'd realized Renee was never coming back. Daily fears and hopes of seeing her had been brewing inside of me for as long as I could remember, and I knew then that if I didn't leave, those fears and hopes would eat me alive. My survival depended on me getting out of town and away from Union Street. So, I'd grabbed my scholarship to the University of Richmond and ran, swearing never to return.

I slid not-so-steady hands over the apron covering my hips, and I straightened. "You were there that day."

"I was."

Just my luck. "You've a good memory."

The comment pleased the old woman. "People think I can't remember, but I remember it all. The body is failing but my mind is as sharp as a tack."

Great. She'd used her super-sharp memory to recall the second worst day of my life. I cleared my throat. "What can I get for you?"

Her eyes narrowed. "You remember my name?"

"No."

The woman grunted. "You're young. You should remember."

Annoyance teased the back of my skull. "I don't remember."

She coughed, and for a moment struggled to get her breath. Her nurse leaned forward, gently patted her on the back, and whispered something in her ear, but the old woman waved her away. "Margaret always greets me by name."

"Sorry."

With shaking bent hands, the woman opened the retro purse and pulled out a petty-point change purse. Her hands trembled as she struggled with the purse's clasp. Finally, she clicked open the squeaky hinges and dug out a ten-dollar bill. "You said only a sucker would work behind that counter."

I glanced at the cupcake clock on the wall: five minutes past seven. When did we close for the day? Three? "I'm only here temporarily. I'm helping my sister."

She smoothed out the rumpled bill. "I heard you lost your job."

"I'll get another one." *Keep smiling. Keep smiling.*

"Looks like you got one."

When Margaret showed her pert little face, I was going to kill her.

Very, very slowly. "May I take your order?"

Her gaze searched the display case now crammed full of cookies, apple and strawberry tartlets, cakes, and all manner of breads. "Six of those sweet buns."

I was right about the sweet buns. Too bad I'd not called it out loud before she ordered. I'd always liked the look of surprise on a customer's face when I remembered their favorites.

The nurse leaned forward. "Mrs. W., you know what the doctor says about sweets. Ain't no good for your sugar."

W. Wentworth. Welbourne. Williams. I couldn't capture the name.

Mrs. W. waved her away. "I'm ninety-nine, Florence. How much longer you think I'll live anyway? Now bag those sweet buns, Daisy."

She spoke my name with force as if to say, *I remember you.* Unsettled by the sound of my name, I ducked my head, grateful for a task, and concentrated on arranging six sweet buns in a white pastry box that I carefully sealed with a gold sticker embossed with Union Street Bakery. "That'll be nine dollars."

The old woman raised a trembling, bent hand and offered me a deeply creased bill. She wrapped bony fingers around my wrist when I reached for it. Her touch was cold, but she possessed unexpected strength. "I dreamed about you last night."

I stiffened. "What?"

"I dreamed about you." Clear blue eyes pierced right through my skin, making me feel as unsure as I did that last awkward day in the bakery.

Bravado stiffened my spine. "How could you have dreamed about me? You haven't seen me in seventeen years."

Narrow shoulders shrugged, but her gaze didn't waver. "Dreams don't worry about time. They come when they come."

I pulled my hand free. "I'll get your change."

She fisted gnarled, pale fingers. "Don't you want to know what I dreamed about?"

"No."

"Your loss, Daisy." Mrs. W. ripped the seal on her bakery box, lifted the lid, and pinched a piece of sweet bun. She popped it in her mouth, and for a moment closed her eyes as pure pleasure softened the lines in her face. Finally, she opened her eyes. "You were strolling down by the river with your mama and that little imaginary friend of yours. What was her name?"

My hands trembled a little as they hovered over the register keys. "What are you talking about?"

"The dream."

"I told you I didn't want to know."

As if I hadn't spoken, "What was her name?"

"I don't remember." *Susie.*

"You don't know your mama's name?"

"Oh, I thought you meant my little friend." Irritation snapped.

"My mother's name is Sheila."

"Not that mama, the other one."

For a few long tense seconds, I was stunned. "No one knew the other one." I cleared the rasp from my voice, which had suddenly turned unsteady. "She abandoned me."

"I remember her." Mrs. W. pinched another bite of sweet bun. "I just always thought you'd remember her name."

I'd not spoken aloud about Renee in years. "Why would I remember her name? I was three when she left."

"Three's old enough to remember."

The headline in the *Alexandria Gazette* had read: "Abandoned Bake Shop Baby."

"You're remembering the articles in the paper. Mom said the town talked for months about me."

"I remember the articles. And I remember you with your mama."

"Mrs. W.," the old nurse said, her tone low and warning. "Best we get going. This young lady has got work to do."

Mrs. W. waved a bent hand. "Not yet. I'm not finished."

How could a crazy old woman know my birth mother? Surely if she'd read the articles and seen Renee she'd have come forward to the police.

Shifting my gaze to the keys on the register, I punched

buttons. In my haste, I hit the wrong keys, which required more keypunches as a fix. I tossed in a few silent curses aimed directly at Margaret before the damn register dinged and the drawer finally popped open. I dug out a single and leaned over the counter toward the lady. "One dollar is your change."

Mrs. W's eyes narrowed. "I saw you. You and your Mama, plain as day."

The certainty in the old woman's voice was more evidence of senility, I was sure. "Really?"

For a moment she closed her eyes, her breathing grew very deep, and I thought she might have nodded off. "You ate peppermint sticks by the docks."

The peppermint reference caught me off guard because I'd always associated peppermint with Renee. I laid her change on the counter. "If you saw us, why didn't you say something when the articles ran? The police searched everywhere for her."

Leaving the question unanswered, she reached out, scraped the rumpled bill toward her and tucked it in the change purse nestled in her lap. "Funny I should dream about you after all this time."

Hilarious. The tightness returned to my throat. "The police kept requesting any information. Why didn't you come forward?"

Mrs. W. shook her head. "I didn't have anything to say to the police."

"Because you didn't know my birth mother." I needed to convince myself this woman was confused. "You just think you remembered."

"I knew her."

"It's time we get going," the nurse said. "This young lady has her work to do."

"You won't forget me, Daisy," the old woman said.

"I doubt it, Mrs. W." The old woman had ensured my first day back was as miserable as my last day seventeen years ago.

"Good." With the sweet buns resting on her lap, Mrs. W. raised her hand, and her nurse turned her chair. When they reached the front door, she craned her neck toward me and winked.

"That dream was a sign."

I could care less about signs. "Did you know my birth mother?"

The nurse shook her head. "Baby, she's old. She's lived so much life, sometimes past and present get all jumbled. Don't listen to her foolishness."

The nurse's words silenced my next question. I was arguing with a senile old woman. She was confused. Old. She had no answers. "Sorry."

Mrs. W. took another bite. "Signs let us know when things are going to change."

A few unladylike words danced in my head, begging to be spoken. "I've surpassed my quota of *change* in the last few months, Mrs. W., so I'll pass on anymore."

Laughter sparked in her old eyes. "Baby girl, you're just warming up."

The black woman turned the wheelchair. "That's enough out of you, Mrs. W. Leave this poor girl alone." The nurse pushed her toward the entrance. Despite my anger, I hurried around the counter and opened the front door. Bells jingled as the old lady and her nurse moved over the threshold. I stepped outside to make sure I wasn't needed.

"Do you think she could be right?" I said to the nurse.

Florence shook her head. "She's old, baby, and she's been mighty restless lately. Just let it go. And tell your mama we appreciated the bread last week. You got a good mama, baby, and that's all that matters."

As they walked away, a river breeze carried the thick scent

of honeysuckle. I folded my arms around my chest and watched until they disappeared around the corner.

A good bit of my bluster eased, but without anger to occupy the space, sadness filled in the creases. As I moved back toward the bakery, I had the sinking sensation that life had again turned on a dime.

Chapter Three

MONDAY, MARCH 22, 2010, 11:00 AM

Your other mama. The words buzzed around my head as I stood on the sidewalk outside the bakery. The old lady couldn't have known Renee. No one had known my birth mother. The nurse had as much said that Mrs. W. was crazy. Old. Confused. Senile.

I dug deeper into my bag of logical explanations, hoping if I scraped out enough, my heart would stop knocking against my ribs. A stronger river breeze flapped the edge of my apron, making the well-washed white cotton flutter against my faded jeans.

According to lore, the cops had done a complete sweep of the city in search of Renee after I'd been found. They'd gone house to house and alley to alley. Police diving crews had even searched the Potomac River bottom. In the end, they'd found no trace of Renee and had concluded she hadn't been in town long enough to make an impression on anyone. The press had been all over the story. Everyone knew about me. It had never occurred to me that someone might have seen Renee with me and never spoken up to the police. To remain silent at such a time would have been unthinkably selfish and cruel.

And from what I could remember of Mrs. W., she had never been cruel. Prickly, yes. Outspoken, you bet. But I had flickering memories of her always making a point to ask me about school or work at the bakery.

I'd not thought much about it at the time, but now considering her latest comment, I began to wonder if she hadn't been nursing some guilty conscious. Maybe she had known Renee. Maybe.

No, no, no! Mrs. W. was confused. She was older than dirt and was born before the invention of airplanes. She'd somehow mixed the old newspaper articles up with a drama she'd seen on television or maybe another story she heard long ago. Of course, with so many memories crammed into her skull, it made sense that time would scramble and deposit them in the wrong places.

Surely Mrs. W. meant no real harm. She was just befuddled. Not everything was personal.

So why, as I stood in the open bakery door, did unshed tears clog my throat? For thirty years, I had honed and practiced the art of running and hiding from the past, and I'd almost begun to believe I'd mastered the task. But now, all that experience had abandoned me. Mrs. W's hapless comments had ignited an unresolved anger that now flickered and smoldered in a soul so littered with dried tinder that it threatened to erupt into an inferno.

I'd morphed back to the little girl with cookie crumbs on her skirt and a note in her pocket that read: "Take Care of My Daisy."

"I told Mom you'd abandon us by lunchtime. I never figured you'd bolt five minutes after opening."

Margaret's caustic tone startled me. So lost in old, familiar worries, I never heard her approach. That alone was unsettling. Margaret was sneaky. I always kept my guard up around her.

Like Rachel, Margaret had a fair complexion, blond hair, albeit a little dirtier, and rosy cheeks. Margaret was short; however, her bones were thicker and sturdier than Rachel's and calories clung to my oldest sister like rats on a drowning ship. She scowled more often than she smiled, and no one ever had used the words *cheerleader* and *Margaret* in the same sentence.

From her shoulder dangled a well-worn leather satchel purse she'd bought in Greece a decade ago. Its fringes brushed full hips clad in faded jeans tucked hastily into water-stained brown boots. The black T-shirt under her jean jacket read: *Those who do not remember history are doomed to repeat it.*

Damn.

I'd bet money she'd chosen that shirt on purpose. Margaret had a talent for pissing me off. Most days I'd have dreaded the anger but today I was grateful for it. In my book, furious always trumped scared.

"Glad you could join us." I moved back into the bakery, purposely letting the door close between us.

As I walked back toward the register, the bells rattled hard as Margaret yanked open the door. "Do you always have to be such a bitch?"

"It's what I do best." Grateful the tremor in my gut hadn't reached my voice, I barricaded myself safely behind the register, and I smiled back at Margaret. "Get your apron on. We've got customers coming, Princess."

Margaret looked over her shoulder and saw two women in suits reaching the front door. She swallowed whatever nastiness she'd readied and dashed behind the counter to dump her purse and get her apron. Margaret might be late, and she might be a pain in the ass, but she understood that the customer was always, always first. It was the golden rule at the Union Street Bakery. Dad and Mom had made it clear that without the customers we would all be on the street.

My sister had a PhD in history and was some big-deal kind of scholar when it came to the history of Greece, but the paycheck from this bakery buttered her bread—no pun. The current job market didn't have much use for scholars of ancient Greek history. The best she'd been able to do was a twenty-hour-a- week job at Alexandria's Historic Cultural Center. The job didn't enhance her chances of landing a gig teaching Greek history, nor did it pay her electric bill, but it nourished her curiosity for all things old and dead. Without her income from the bakery, Margaret couldn't have afforded her biannual trip to Greece, where she could dig in the dirt searching for her precious bones and bits of pottery. Even though she acted like she'd been doing the bakery a favor when hired, Mom had said she needed the store as much as it needed her.

For the first time in a long time, Margaret and I found ourselves drifting on the same leaky lifeboat, which required us both to bail as fast as we could if we didn't want to sink. And so, our quibbling tucked away, we both waited on customers side by side for the next couple of hours. My plans to slip to the back when Margaret had arrived had quickly vanished when I realized it would take both of us to service the morning customers. There were plenty of regulars but a good many folks today had stopped to see me.

"Daisy McCrae, I heard you'd come back to town, but I thought it was a lie." The comment came from Tammy Fox, a gal I'd gone to high school with. She still had long blond hair, big green eyes and a sinfully small waist. As pre-teens, we played soccer in middle school together. She'd been the forward and I'd been the goalie. Mom took us on a tournament trip once, and I spent the whole weekend listening to people mistaking her for the McCrae and me for the friend. I quit soccer shortly after that trip. By the time we hit high school, I was all about making perfect grades and Tammy was all about cheerleading, showcasing her double-D breasts, and landing the quarterback.

I wasn't a gawky teen any longer. I was grown up and, until a couple of months ago, a career success. I knew I'd get back into finance eventually. So why did I feel like I had just tripped out of middle school as I stared at Tammy, who was pushing a high-end stroller with a cute three-year-old version of herself? Maybe because Tammy looked like she'd just stepped out of a salon and her little mini-me daughter's fat face and goofy grin could charm just about anybody. Or maybe it was the rock on her left hand, which rivaled the sun's brilliance.

"Yep, I'm back." A couple hours of work and I was already getting better at faking a smile. "How are you these days, Tammy?"

She held up her left hand as if I might have missed the rock. "Married with a baby."

"Congratulations. You must be so happy." When Margaret glanced at me, her eyes bright with amusement as if she had caught the whiff of sarcasm.

"I am." Tammy ordered a dozen cookies and three loaves of bread for dinner with her husband, Hunter. I pictured Hunter to be tall, broad shouldered with a lantern jaw. Tammy had always liked the big ones.

I wrapped the cookies in a box and the bread in long, slim bags. "Here ya go."

Tammy took her goods, met my gaze, and tried to look upset. "So, I heard you lost your job."

I wasn't going to lie. That would have been beyond pathetic. But after three months of being out of work, I was getting tired of explaining what had happened at Suburban. "I did. And now I have a new one." In that moment it felt good to know I did have a job. I might be underemployed in a temporary gig that was the last job I'd ever want, but it was a job, and I had a story.

Gold bracelets jangled on her slim wrist. "I never thought you'd come back." And in a stage whisper added, "I thought you hated it here."

My grin widened as I planted hands on my hips. "And yet here I am. That'll be twenty dollars."

Margaret nudged my shoulder and grinned at Tammy. "We were lucky to get her."

I smiled at Margaret, knowing she was lying but still grateful for the backup.

Tammy handed me a credit card. "So, are you, like, baking the bread?"

"That I am." The muscles around my smile were starting to cramp and, as I handed back the charge card and slip, I wished she'd just vanish. As she signed, the gel tips of manicured fingers winked in the light. "Did I hear you were seeing someone in D.C.? Someone who knows whoever you were dating knows Hunter, I think."

I was aware that Margaret's ears had perked up. "Hard to say. I dated around."

Tammy tucked her credit card in her Gucci wallet. "He was in finance. I thought you two had a steady thing."

"I'm a serial dater, Tammy. And most of the guys were in finance."

Despite the dodge, I knew who she was talking about: Gordon Singleton. We'd dated for nearly a year. He'd asked me to marry him. But that was a story I'd not told my family.

Tammy tucked the bread bag in the back of the stroller. "I'll have to ask Hunter. He'll know the man's name."

"Good luck with that." There were parts of my life at Suburban I'd hoped to leave on the other side of the Potomac.

"You know, we really should have lunch. I'd love to catch up and hear all about your life."

"That would be wonderful."

Margaret coughed and it sounded a little bit like bullshit. "What a cute baby you have."

Tammy glowed. "Her name is Katie. She's nine months."

On cue, the kid gurgled, smiled, and revealed three teeth. Like her mom, Katie already knew how to work a crowd.

"Really cute," I said.

Tammy and I smiled, promised to have lunch, and then I watched her push her baby out the front door.

Margaret finished restocking a tray of oatmeal cookies and closed the glass case. "What the hell kind of name is Hunter? I'm picturing a guy in a loincloth running around with a bow and arrow." The jab was her attempt to make me feel better.

In an odd way I appreciated Margaret's words. "It's a fine name, I suppose."

"I'd never name my kid Hunter. I mean, if you had a second boy, what would you name him? Gatherer?"

That prompted a smile. Rachel joined us just after ten thirty. She reported that the girls were off to school. She apologized for being late; she'd forgotten about a parent-teacher conference. Anna, one of the twins, had mixed it up on the playground with another kid and a meeting had been called.

The three of us continued to work. Margaret handled the register, and Rachel and I filled orders. The morning quickly becomes a busy blur of customers, breads, and confections.

The more questions I fielded about my return, the more practiced my answers became. By eleven thirty, my story had grown from a stumbling string of mutterings to a well-crafted tale. In Margaret's and Rachel's evolved version, I had forsaken the cold corporate world because I'd come to realize my true passion: owning a small business. I'd grown up with baking so coming home proved to be the perfect fit. My sisters enhanced and embellished the fable with each telling. According to them, I'd not only left the corporate world but had turned down a West Coast job—which might have been true if I'd been willing to leave the area and had applied for the job when I'd heard about it.

Throughout the morning, my nervous energy demanded to be fed. Each time I took a near-empty tray back to the kitchen, I'd snuck bites and nibbles of broken buttery confections, hoping to soothe frayed nerves and a tense stomach. As I downed my tenth crumbled chocolate chip cookie, I told myself that tomorrow would be different. Tomorrow I'd be back on my rigid eating plan.

When I'd left the bakery after high school, I'd been twenty pounds overweight and hopelessly addicted to sweets. Away from my parents' home and the constant *drip-drip* of emotional water torture of waiting for Renee, however, my appetite had vanished. By spring of my freshman year of college, the twenty pounds were gone, and I thought that I'd finally won whatever battle had raged inside me.

By twelve thirty, the morsels that had calmed my nerves had done little to nourish me. My stomach grumbled and I wondered if the pizza shop around the corner still delivered.

"Anybody want pizza?" I asked.

Margaret handed a white pie box to a woman, sealed with a USB sticker, and smiled. "It's just past noon."

"In the baker's world it's late afternoon." I glanced at the clock. "Dear God, I'd been up for over nine hours."

"The pizza is rank," Rachel said. "Eat a bagel."

I peered into the bin of bagels Rachel had just pulled from the oven. They were the misshapen ones I'd made. Despite their less than perfect shape, their smell was enticing. Sure, I'd been eating broken cookies all morning, but one bagel would not be the end of me.

"Go on," Margaret said. "You know you want one. Besides, they're just a little too lopsided to sell."

"Of course, they'll sell," Rachel said. "And this is a big day for you, Daisy. Live a little."

No more coaxing was required. I rooted out the ugliest cinnamon raisin bagel I could find. This was a big day, after all. And, as I'd already promised, tomorrow I would be back to my normal egg-whites-and- salad routine. "This afternoon I've got to get by the grocery and buy eggs and cheese so I can have a real breakfast tomorrow."

I bit into the bagel. My blood pressure dropped as the soft dough— the perfect right blend of raisins and cinnamon— melted in my mouth. Henri's genius had trumped my unpracticed hands.

Rachel smiled as she handed a bag of bagels to three teen girls. When they left, she released a contented sigh. "Doesn't it give you gals satisfaction to know that we are the staple in so many of our customers' lives?"

Margaret pulled a stack of one-dollar bills from the register drawer and started to arrange them face up. "It makes my heart flutter."

Rachel tossed an irritated glance at Margaret. For an instant the tired cheerleader could cheer no more. "Can't you at least pretend you care, Margaret?"

Margaret looked at her, no hint of apology in her gaze as she shrugged. Now that the customers had gone, we were no longer the united front. "Do you have to care so much, Rachel?"

Rachel's eyes widened with hurt. "This is our life, Margaret." Margaret rolled her eyes. "*Your* life, Rachel. Not mine. Not Daisy's." Rachel looked at me as if searching for support.

I shrugged as my stomach grumbled and I tore the bagel in half.

"She's right, Rachel. This is what you love. It's what we do. Given the choice, we'd all have different lives."

"How can you not love this place?" Rachel demanded.

Margaret tipped her head back as if swallowing an oath. "Give the Pollyanna crap a rest, Rachel."

"I do love this place. It's my home," Rachel said.

"Your husband died here," Margaret said. "And it's sucking the life out of you."

Rachel straightened and her face paled. "This place is holding me together."

"B.S.," Margaret countered. "It's ripping you apart. In fact, I'm starting to think the whole damn place is cursed."

Tears welled in Rachel's eyes. If the cheerleader lost it, I feared we'd all go right down the drain. "I need to get into your office, Rachel, and have a look at the books. Margaret, you hold down the front while we review the ledgers."

Rachel simply nodded, too emotional to speak.

"Why do I always have to work the front?" Margaret shoved the bills in the drawer and closed it with a hard *clang*.

"Because you can't add or subtract," I said. "And neither can Rachel. I'm the math genius. But if we find ancient pottery fragments buried under the desk, I'll give you a call."

"Bite me," Margaret said.

Her frustration gave me a measure of satisfaction. At least for now she'd back off and be quiet.

That satisfaction lasted all about thirty seconds—the time it took me to walk down the hallway into Rachel's small office. I flipped on the lights and immediately stopped short. The old roll top desk that had been with the bakery for more than a hundred years was covered in piles and piles of bills, papers, letters, and junk mail. I could barely see the new laptop I'd bought for Rachel last Christmas. The gift had been in response to her laments about organization and misplaced paperwork.

My stomach took such a ferocious leap that I feared no cookie or bagel would calm it.

"Rachel. What happened?"

Rachel moistened her lips. "I know. I know."

I moved to the desk, picked up a bundle of unopened mail, and flashed back to my final months at Suburban Enterprises. "When's the last time you were in here?"

"A week ago. Maybe two?" All her morning's joy had drained away.

I turned one envelope over. past due was stamped in red to the left of the bakery's mailing address. Several other envelopes shared the same label. When we were kids, Dad often juggled cash flow like a master. He always wrote the must be mailed by date in the upper- right-hand corner. When the day arrived, he'd press a stamp over the date and mail it. He prided himself on never missing a deadline. "Has Dad seen this?"

What little coloring she'd gained vanished. "God, no. Please don't tell him. He'll have another heart attack."

No arguing with that. Dad would die if he knew the Union Street Bakery was developing a reputation as a bad account. "He hasn't been down here?" I tossed the envelopes on the desk.

She rang her hands. "He's been bugging me for weeks. He wants to see the books. I keep telling him he's micromanaging, that he needs to trust me to run the business."

"But you're not." There was no softening the statement.

Tears welled in Rachel's eyes. "The kitchen side I can do in my sleep but this stuff. . .I hate it."

Margaret's quip about this place being cursed rang in my head. Adrenaline raced through my veins, and I pictured myself hopping on my bike and peddling away. "I can't believe you've kept Dad out of here."

She slid trembling hands over her hips. "Last week he threatened to come down here and bust down the door."

I rubbed the tight muscles on the back of my neck. "What stopped him?"

"Mom said you were coming to work at the bakery and that you were taking over the books. That calmed him right down." She sounded so small and afraid. "You and he are wired the same. Margaret and I are more like Mom."

I met her gaze. "A week ago, Mom didn't know I was returning to the bakery. I only agreed three days ago."

Rachel's eyes widened a fraction as if she realized she'd just confessed to a crime. "Did I say a week? Maybe it was just a few days."

I felt a bit like the wild dog that had been cornered by crazed torch-wielding villagers. "Rachel, you are the crappiest liar and Mom is a master manipulator."

Blue eyes widened. "I'm not lying."

"*Please.* I know Mom. She's been hatching her evil plan for weeks. She called me a month ago and asked me to lunch but I said no. And so, she tried again with her daiquiris."

Rachel attempted a smile. "Don't tell her I spilled the beans."

Hands on hips, I glanced at the mess on the desk and released a long sigh. "What's the point? Like it or not, I don't have a job or anywhere else to go."

She fumbled with her apron strands still tied in a neat bow. "If you did, would you be here?"

I smoothed long fingers over my head. "Honestly, no."

Rachel nodded, as if appreciating the honesty. "If you could be anywhere, where would it be?"

"Back in my old life."

"Join the club. I'd give just about anything to get my old life with Mike back."

The offhand comment sobered me. I'd lost a job. She'd lost her husband and the father of her children. As much as we'd both liked to have gone back, that door had closed forever for us both.

There was only forward.

Rachel sniffed. "Mom should have been more honest with you." That prompted a laugh.

"Maybe. But the truth is, I lost my job, and I was sitting at home feeling sorry for myself. I've no one to blame but myself."

"The market blew up. You didn't have anything to do with that."

"Looking back, I can see that there were warning signs. I should have paid closer attention."

I believed now in my heart of hearts that if I'd been more vigilant about watching the details, I could have stopped the mess at Suburban. The crap between Gordon and me had temporarily screwed up my judgment. I deliberately shifted my attention to the stack of letters under the desk. I couldn't fix my life, but I could fix this mess.

Rachel frowned. "I should have bugged Mike more about seeing the doctor. I knew he was getting headaches."

I rubbed the back of my neck. "You couldn't have known."

She shook her head. "But I knew he was tired. I wanted to help him more, but the girls just ate up so much of my days."

"He was a baker working eighteen-hour days and he wanted you taking care of the girls."

"But—"

I held up my hand. "The pathologist said he was born with the faulty vessel. You had no control. And even if he'd gotten all the sleep he needed, he would have still died."

She folded her arms over her chest. "I know."

"You had nothing to do with his death."

Rachel swiped away her tear and studied me. "So, if you can cut me slack why can't you cut yourself slack?"

For a long moment I didn't say anything. "I'm different."

"How so?"

"Never mind." I picked up a stack of unopened bank statements.

"Do you have any idea how much money you have in the bank?"

Her gaze dimmed. "Not exactly. But I made a three-thousand-dollar deposit on Saturday."

I pushed papers off the laptop. "I set up the online banking account to pay your bills. Have you been using that?"

She started wringing her hands again. "I couldn't find the password. And I couldn't remember what you'd told me about what to do. It was easier just to write checks."

"You could've called me."

"I felt like an idiot."

"Mother of God." The words carried the weight my frustration.

Breath expelled from her clenched teeth. "I knew you'd be pissed."

"I passed pissed a week ago when my lease came up for renewal and I knew I couldn't commit." No, right now I just felt as if I were drowning.

A wan smile tipped the edges of her lips. "Any second now, I expect you to blow a gasket and run screaming from this bakery."

A plane from nearby Reagan National Airport rumbled over our heads as it banked over the Potomac. I wondered where it is going. A choppy, awkward laugh escaped me. "Where would I go, Rachel?"

Her gaze was direct, unnaturally serious. "You're smart. You can make a living anywhere."

In time I would find something. In fact, I could have taken that auditing job with the bank in New York or that temp accounting job. But I'd said no, hoping better would come along. And then Mom had called, plied me with alcohol, and reminded me that this bakery was all Rachel and her girls had left. "If this boat is going to sink then we'll ride it down together."

She swallowed as her delicate fingers lost a bit of their tension. "You mean it?"

It was going to take more than one bagel to get me through this mess. "I said I'd stay."

She grimaced. "That was before you saw this."

"This mess doesn't freak me out. This is something I can handle. Numbers I know."

"Really? It's not too much?"

"I've seen worse, I'm sure." Where, I couldn't say.

"Thank God." Tears welled again in her eyes. "Let me help you sort this."

"No!" The word came out in a hard rush. "Just point me toward the most recent pile."

She tugged hard on a loose apron thread and twisted it around her index finger. "I think it's the one on the right."

"The one weighted down with a bag of flour."

Rachel retrieved the flour, holding it in her arms as if she were protecting a child. "Yes."

"What's with the flour, Rachel?"

Her face brightened. "This is the most awesome flour I've ever used. It's organic and milled about forty miles from here."

I was almost afraid to ask. "Why is it on your desk?"

"As a reminder to me to ask you if we can afford it. It's more expensive than the brand we're using now. But it's so worth the extra money. Even Henri grunted his approval when I showed it to him."

I stared at the white bag with the red star emblem and blue stripes. "But you don't know if you can afford it?"

"We're barely in the black, I think. I hope. That's why I can't fix the ovens. Or buy a new mixer or water heater."

I did my best not to sound like a schoolteacher. "You'd buy new flour over fixing the equipment?"

Rachel clung to her bag of flour like it was a small child. "I want to, but I haven't."

"Good. And for the record, the answer, for now, is no." Hope glimmered in her gaze. "But that could change, right?"

"I don't know." As I glanced again at the stack, I feared I'd be happy if I could pay the electric bill.

"Ask me about dough and I can tell you how long it's been rising, if the flour is organic, or if the texture will be right. Give me five butters, and I'll tell you where they came from. Sugars, I know. Anything food I know. Money and numbers make me want to cry."

Staring into her watery blue eyes, I couldn't hold onto any residual irritation. "It's going to take hours, if not days, to sort this out. But I will, but you need to worry about customers and keeping Margaret out of my hair."

She straightened her shoulders. "I can do that. But I can help you, too. I kind of know where the bodies are buried, so to speak."

Even surrounded by the chaos, I felt oddly in control. Numbers didn't judge nor did they have hidden agendas. They were what they were. "Don't you buy supplies Monday afternoon like Dad did?"

"It can wait a few hours. But I'll need to place an order by four." She moved toward the desk to reach for an invoice.

I shifted to the right and blocked her path. "When we are in the bakery, you can boss me around all you want. But when you are in this office, I'm boss. I'll do the bills, and then I'll let you know how much we have for supplies. This isn't going to be easy, Rachel."

Tension melted from Rachel's shoulders, and she hugged me. "That is such a deal. Thank you!"

I patted her awkwardly on the back and squirmed free. "Let's hope you'll stay this happy."

"I so will."

"Good. Now get out of my office." And just because I was feeling charitable in my new domain I said, "Besides, how bad could it be?"

Famous last words.

It was a favorite expression of my mother's, which she'd uttered after one of us kids made a dumb promise or pledge. *Don't worry, Mom, I can hold the crystal vase and not break it. God, Mom, Mike and I aren't kids . . . we know how not to get pregnant. How bad can it be?*

How bad? Like bad. Like some vendors hadn't been paid in months and were now threatening to cut off supplies if they didn't get paid. Like quarterly taxes were due soon. Like we weren't on a leaky rowboat but the SS *Titanic*.

It didn't take a brain trust to know the bakery needed an infusion of cash. For a few seconds, as I sat in the office alone, I was aware that the building had grown quiet. The bakery had closed for the day, and I felt alone. I thought about calling Dad. It made sense, after all: This had been the business he'd lovingly nursed and worried over for five decades. He'd want to know.

But he didn't need to know. Not yet anyway. He'd done his tour of duty in the kitchens and office. He'd suffered heart attacks. And Mom had said she was afraid for him.

Like it or not, it was my turn to carry the weight and fix this mess. I had only one real option, and I dreaded it.

Fearing too much analyzing would make me hesitate, I picked up the old black rotary phone on the desk and dialed. On the third ring I heard a gruff, "Brad Foster."

"Brad, it's Daisy McCrae." Brad was one of the few remaining friends I had from Suburban.

"Daisy." He drew out my name in a long lazy string, and I imagined him leaning back in his leather chair and staring out his picture window over downtown D.C. "How's it going?"

"Going pretty well, as a matter of fact." I didn't go into a long dissertation about my life over the last three months but said easily, "I'm managing my parents' bakery."

"The one on Union Street?"

"The very one."

"God, I love that place. Every time I'm in Old Town I stop by and get one of those carrot cake cupcakes. They really are a sin."

"We like to think so," I said easily. "My sister Rachel is a goddess in the kitchen."

"Damn, Daisy, I wish I had the stones to walk away from finance and just do something creative like running a bakery."

"It's a dream come true." I glanced toward the heavens, hoping God wouldn't strike me down.

"So, you're getting up in the middle of the night and mixing the dough and stuff?" The words carried a wistful, almost nostalgic tone.

"That's me. White uniform, hair net, flour on my shoes and all."

"Damn. I'm jealous. I always had this dream of being an ice road trucker." He sounded genuine.

In the computer screen I caught the barest hint of my reflection. My hair sprung out of my ponytail. There was a pencil tucked behind each ear and flour smudged my face. "You watch too much History Channel."

"Maybe. Maybe," he said chuckling. "So, what can I do for you?"

Jump or dive. Now or never. I blew out a breath. "I need to sell the remaining stocks I have in Suburban."

"Daisy, you and I both know the timing on this sucks." His voice's dreamy quality vanished under reality's harsh glare. "You'll lose a bundle."

I pressed fingertips to my forehead. "I know. Believe me, I know. But I need cash."

"If you can hold on for a couple of months, you could have twice what you do now. The market is rallying."

"I know. But a couple of months from now won't do me any good. I need the dough to make dough."

The lame joke didn't stir any laughter. "There's no way you can wait. Do you have any other cash reserves?"

I smoothed my hand over a pile of bills and then thumbed through them. "No."

He sighed into the phone. "The markets are closed now, but I can sell first thing in the morning and have money wired to you tomorrow."

"Great. Thanks."

"I wish I could talk you out of this."

"Like I used to say, in for a penny, in for a pound."

"Hey, so you're doing well?" Dropping his voice, he injected concern I didn't want.

"Living the dream, baby." My chair squeaked as I leaned back and turned from the stacks of bills.

"You should come by the bakery sometime. I'll treat you to a carrot cake cupcake."

He chuckled. "I just might do that."

My smile felt tight and unnatural. "Great. Would love to see you."

"I'll get that money right over to you, Daisy."

"Thanks, Brad."

I hung up and laid my head on my desk. The sale would likely net me about ten to fifteen thousand dollars. Two months from now I might have gotten three times that amount, but like I'd told Brad, it was now or never. Those stocks were the last of any kind of nest egg for me, and the cash from their sale would buy the bakery thirty or so days. I was now officially flat broke and shackled to the business.

I breathed deeply. "What have I done?"

"Daisy, Daisy!" My mother's singsong, baby way of saying

my name had me lifting my head from the computer screen toward the office door.

Sitting up, I pulled my ponytail free, combed hair with my fingers and knotted it. "In here, Mom."

Mom was an older, much plumper version of Rachel and Margaret. Her short blond hair remained light—but that was thanks to peroxide and not nature. Deep lines wrinkled her forehead and the corners of her eyes. And for as long as I could remember, she'd worn bright red lipstick and an oversized blue T-shirt, which she thought created a trimmer silhouette.

I tossed my thick, black-rimmed glasses on the desk, minimized the screen, rose, and stretched the stiffness from my back. I glanced at the clock and realized it was nearly six.

"I came to check on you, honey."

"And she's got Dad with her," came my father's deep baritone voice. Dad stood about several inches taller than Mom. He claimed to be five foot ten but that would have been on his best day years ago. Stooped shoulders now robbed him of an inch or so. Mother Nature had taken most of his thick hair, and a razor took care of what remained. A white T-shirt hugged his round, hard belly and allowed gray chest hair to curl over the V-shaped neckline. He looked a bit like an old Irish American version of Mr. Clean.

Mom set a turkey sandwich on whole wheat bread with chips and a pickle on my desk. You've got to be starving."

I crunched on a chip. "Yes. Starving. Thanks."

Dad set an unopened can of diet soda next to the plate. His gaze lingered on the desk, searching, and I knew he wished he'd brought his reading glasses. The lines in his forehead deepened. "So, what's the damage? How has Rachel done with the books?"

I'd razzed my sisters in a heartbeat when it was the three of us. In fact, growing up I took great pleasure in pointing out their mistakes to them. But for reasons unknown to me, if they screwed up so badly that Mom and Dad had to get involved, I covered it up. “Not bad at all. I’ve been able to jump right in.”

Never mind the fact that my finances had officially tanked.

Dad glanced sharply at me as if trying to determine the truthfulness of my words. “You sure? Rachel is a great baker, but she can barely add two and two.”

“No worries, Dad. Really. I’ve got it under control.” The lie tripped so easily off my tongue.

Mom grinned and hooked her arm in my father’s. Some would see it as a loving gesture, but

I knew Mom. She was bracing to drag him out of here, if need be. “See, Frank, I told you the bakery was fine. Rachel did a good job. And now Daisy will make things even better.”

“No worries, Dad. Really. Rachel did a great job holding it together.”

Dad straightened, not yet swayed. “Mind if I have a look at the books?”

Mom tightened her hold.

“I do mind, Dad. I’m just getting this sorted to my way of doing things, but I’m not at the point I can talk about it without getting a little turned around. Give me until month’s end, and we’ll have a major discussion.”

“A couple of weeks?” He arched a brow, but the worry faded a fraction, as if just having a deadline was a relief.

“That’s not so long, Frank,” Mom said.

“It’s fifteen days, Sheila.” He was a man who had spent his life measuring everything: ounces, minutes, dollars, and days.

“We’ll go over it all,” I promised.

Dad grunted. “Did Margaret show up on time?”

“Right on the dot.” Five minutes late was right on the dot in Margaret time.

His gaze narrowed. “How did the baking go this morning?”

"Clockwork." I knew the word was a favorite of my mother's.

Mom grinned. "See, Frank? All good. Clockwork. The display cases in the front of the shop looked like you'd just about sold out."

"We had a very busy morning. Margaret said my return generated some curiosity in town. It accounted for a few sales."

"Did your friends give you a nice welcome home?" Mom prompted.

"I think a lot of folks were curious about my return after my dramatic exit years ago. And a few knew I'd lost my job." People don't watch the Indy 500 to see cars go in circles. They watch for the big wrecks.

Mom frowned. "No one cares about any of that, honey. That is already a lifetime ago."

"Mrs. W. remembered. And she made a point to mention it."

"Mrs. Woodrow?" Mom said. "Good lord, I'm amazed she made it by. She's been in bed for months. We thought we'd lost her last week."

Woodrow. Mabel Woodrow. That was her name. The lost name had been niggling at me since morning. "She came by and shared all kinds of crazy stories."

"Well, she's an old woman, honey," Mom said. "She speaks her mind a little too much."

"I think her memory is a little off."

Dad shook his head. "I'm amazed the woman was here at all."

"I spoke to Florence and Mrs. Woodrow last week when I dropped off bread and told them you were moving home. That perked Mrs. Woodrow up a bit. I need to make a point to get by and see her."

Mom had told Mrs. W. last week that I was coming back. That explained the visit. "She looked spry today."

Dad scratched the back of his head. "Did she get the sweet buns?"

"She did."

"I can't believe Florence let her buy the sweet buns," Mom said. "The woman's been a diabetic for years."

"Florence tried to stop her, but Mrs. Woodrow wasn't hearing of it. The old lady might be batty, but she knows what she wants."

"She's been like that since I was a kid," Dad said. "She'd set her mind to something and that was that. No one changed it."

"I sort of remember her, but not much. What's her story?"

"She's lived in the same house all her ninety-nine years. Her brothers and sisters moved away, but she stayed put. Married when she was young, but he was injured in World War II. He died a few years later. Family money has kept her afloat ever since."

I remembered what she'd said about my birth mother. Batty or no, she'd seemed so clear about Renee.

It would have been so easy just to ask my folks about Renee, but the last time I'd brought my birth mother up to my parents, it hadn't gone so well. Mom had told me to ask whatever I wanted, but her eyes went all soft and gooey like she'd burst into tears. Feeling like a real traitor, I'd dropped the subject almost as fast as I had brought it up.

Besides, I had enough in the present to worry about. My real job was gone. My real savings were gone. And I'd thrown my lot in with one sister who couldn't add a column of numbers and another who'd rather have her head in ruins. Whatever nonsense Mrs. Woodrow had spouted shouldn't have ranked on the priority list. And still. . . the mention of Renee had triggered memories. No one had mentioned my birth mother in years. I guess they figured I'd forgotten. But I hadn't forgotten. I just didn't know who to talk to about it.

Just my luck. The one person who might be a resource was a crazy old bird. I could go right now or even tomorrow and visit Mrs. Woodrow's house and ask her about Renee. I could. And I would, soon. But for right now, my plate was filled with this bakery and the shambles of my life. Tossing in a birth mother search was more than I needed now. As much as I wanted to know about Renee, I didn't have the energy to deal with her right now. But I would.

Soon . . .

By the time I climbed the staircase to my room, the cupcake clock chimed ten times. Bone tired, my body ached, and my head throbbed. Sorting the books had been just as complicated as I'd feared. I should have taken it a bit at a time, but I'd been unable to move away from the desk until I really understood what was happening with the bakery's finances. The bottom line appeared to be that we weren't generating enough business based on number of employees versus number of goods sold. Today's flood of customers had been an anomaly.

Most days, business was at least 30 percent less. Since firing a sister wasn't an option, the bakery needed to find ways to cut inventory and market. From what I could tell, we were totally dependent on walk-in traffic, and the only catering we did was around the Christmas holidays. We needed more catering. More weddings. Maybe even a deal with a high-end grocery store willing to carry our bread.

In my room, I kicked off my clogs, tugged off my clothes, and dropped them in a pile by my bed before slipping on a flannel nightgown. As much as I'd have liked a shower, I just didn't have the energy. I brushed my teeth, splashed water on my face, and climbed into my sleeping bag on the lumpy sofa.

One moment I was aware of closing my eyes and the next, I tumbled immediately into a deep sleep.

I dreamed of two little girls laughing.

"What game do you want to play today? It's your birthday so you can choose!" The little girl's smile was so wide, deep dimples burrowed into her cheeks.

I sat cross-legged on my bed staring at Susie. The little girl wore her hair in tight, neat braids secured with blue ribbons that teased the tops of thin shoulders covered with a starched white dress. Susie had a light mocha complexion that soaked up the sun in the summer. Like me, she was about twelve.

"I don't want to play a game."

Susie frowned. "Why not? You always want to play? I know you love I Spy." Susie tapped her finger to her lips. "Let's see, I Spy something blue."

"No." My mood had been sour since I'd risen, and no amount of coaxing would draw me out. My mom had grown frustrated and grumbled about me being selfish. "I don't want to play."

Susie cocked her head. "Why are you such a Sour Sally on your birthday?"

I folded arms over my chest, trying to understand the anger that stalked me today. "I don't know."

Susie leaned forward and in a singsong voice said, "There's always a reason. Tell me."

When I didn't answer, Susie rose from the bed and started to dance around the room. "Tell me. Tell me. I won't go away until you tell me, Daisy McCrae!"

Frustrated, I watched Susie twirl and twirl as she sang. Susie had been the only one today who wanted to understand my moodiness. She'd been the only one who didn't wonder why I was so ungrateful.

Finally unable to stand the pesky tune, I blurted, "I don't know when my real birthday is."

Susie stopped dancing and came back to the bed, tucking her legs under her lace skirt. "Of course, you know. Today is your birthday."

"It is not."

"Of course, it is! You are so silly."

I shook my head. "Nobody knows my real birthday. Margaret told me my parents made up my birthday when I was adopted. May 12 is just a story."

"Margaret is a sour mean puss."

"But she's right. No one knows."

"Except Renee," Susie said.

"Except Renee."

Chapter Four

MONDAY, MARCH 22, 2010, 11:00 PM

"Did you find it?" Mabel asked.

The old woman leaned forward in her wheelchair, tugging nervously at a loose thread on the edge of her blue crocheted blanket. She and Florence were in the back spare room of her town house, a room she'd not been in in more years than she could count.

Even as a bride, she thought the room dreary. And now it seemed danker and darker than ever before. She could have lived with the smell of dust and mothballs or tolerated the overhead light that spit out only a miserly bit of brightness or even the tasseled velvet floor-to-ceiling curtains, which blocked the sun and views of the river. She also didn't care so much about the piles of newspapers and boxes, old furniture, and knickknacks that covered most of the floor. All that was part and parcel of an old house.

No, what she hated most about this room were the bad memories. Every square inch of the room was soaked in sadness. Of death. This room had been her husband's when he'd been so sick. Her Henry had suffered and eventually died in this room over sixty years ago.

Florence Tillman glanced up from the deep wooden trunk filled with dusty clothes. Stirred-up dust made her sneeze. "I'm looking, Miss Mabel. I'm looking."

Mabel leaned forward in her wheelchair, hating the craggy edge of desperation burning through her body. "Well, look faster. I don't have a lot of time. She's already told me I don't have many more days."

"You talking to spirits again?"

"Don't matter who. She's right: I'm out of time."

Mabel had never figured after all the living that she'd done that she'd be so fearful of crossing over. Maybe it was because she'd always prided herself on control and of taking matters into her own hands, just as her grandmother had taught. She'd spent many hours with her grandmother learning, not only listening to stories that sounded more like fairy tales but also learning the value of grabbing destiny when it was elusive. *Be anything you want but don't be no fool, Mabel Ann.*

And so, Mabel had never feared taking life by the horns. When she was twelve and the copperhead snake invaded her mama's garden, she didn't scream or squeal like her sisters; instead, she'd gotten her pa's ax and cut its head right off. When her husband started having fits of anger after he'd been wounded in the war, she didn't reach out to anyone. She went to the medicine cabinet. A few drops of laudanum in Henry's morning coffee kept him even and steady for the last few years of his life. And when her no-good great-niece had come looking for drug money, she'd turned her out onto the street, refusing to hear the girl's sob stories.

Like a vigilant gatekeeper, Mabel Woodrow did what she had to do to keep life moving forward, just like her grandmother had done.

Whereas her grandmother had been cursed with regret, Mabel didn't have any damn regrets for the way she'd lived her life. She'd done what she'd done. Life was what it was. And only the weak fussed and fretted over spilled milk.

With the time left in her life ticking down day by day or perhaps hour by hour, she'd come to see that the Lord meant for her to fix something before she left His Earth. She'd never go so far as to say any kind of penitence for her actions. She'd done what needed to be done, but she was willing to concede that perhaps a bit of mending was in order.

"It's in the bottom of the trunk," she said. She twisted the edge of her lap blanket tighter.

"I heard you the first time." Florence's words snapped with irritation.

"Move that wide bottom of yours so that I can see into the trunk."

Florence straightened and turned her full attention to her employer. "Now, if you want to drag your bony ass out of that chair and look for yourself, I'm more than willing to sit on the sidelines and criticize while you hunt through fifty years of mold and dust."

Old eyes narrowed to priggish slits. "Don't you get smart with me, Florence Tillman."

"Don't you be bossing me, Mabel Woodrow. We are way beyond that now. Now, you going to be nice?"

"You going to move a little faster?"

Florence shook her head. "I swear I wonder why I stayed with you all these years."

Mabel clicked her false teeth. "Because you like me."

Florence shook her head and went back to digging as Mabel settled back into her chair, irritated and frustrated that so little time remained for this important task. She'd put one ball in play over a month ago but had begun to fear that her efforts would fail. This would be her last chance. "Fine."

Florence snorted and returned to digging in the trunk again. She tossed out an old quilt and a stack of newspapers onto the floor beside her. "Beyond me why you got me hunting and digging through all these dusty old trunks. I swear it's those damn sweet buns you ate this morning. The sugar has diddled with your mind and made you a little crazy."

The sweet buns had not been the culprits. She'd barely taken a bite or two. Food didn't much interest her anymore. Nothing much except this last task interested her.

The cauldron of worries had been stirring for months with each new dream that came to her. And last night's dream had been the clearest and most vivid of all, once again churning up matters she'd buried long ago. The dream had made her rise early and demand that Florence take her first to the bakery and then to her lawyer's office.

"It's in a box," Mabel said. "And the box is wrapped in fabric."

"You told me that twice already. I just wish you could remember which trunk and what kind of fabric."

"How many books could there be?"

"Quite a few."

Mabel glanced around the dusty room at the three other trunks that Florence had unpacked, searched, and repacked. Her grandmother had given her the book and bade her to keep it close and hidden until the time was right. "It's got to be in that one. It's the last wooden trunk, and I know I put it in a wooden trunk."

Florence dug through more layers of clothes. "I don't think . . . wait a minute." Her lips flattened with determination, and then she pulled out a book wrapped in a faded blue calico fabric. "Is this what you are looking for?"

Nervous energy snapped through Mabel's withered limbs as Florence rose and laid the box on her knees. Mabel's hands hovered over the book. She'd not felt such a tremor of excitement in years. It had been so long since she'd seen it, so long since she'd even thought about its significance.

She tugged at the twine that held the fabric but quickly discovered her aged hands couldn't breach the bindings.

Florence shooed her hands away. "Hold your horses. You're going to break a finger. I got my nail clippers in my pocket." She fished the clippers from her jacket pocket and easily clipped the twine. The brittle twine popped free as if it had been waiting to be released for years.

Mabel's hands shook as she watched Florence peel away the fabric and then faded newspaper dating to 1922, the year she and Henry married. When she'd removed all the layers, she found the small leather-bound book, which wasn't much bigger than her outstretched hand. Though scuffed and worn, the leather exterior appeared whole and true.

Gently, Mabel ran her hand over the fabric covering the book. Carefully, she opened it, amazed how time had faded the ink in the last eight decades. She flipped to a page and marveled at the precise handwriting she'd not seen in so long. *To S. With love, J.*

Mabel closed the book. *S.* Dearest S. Dead so long and yet if Mabel closed her eyes, she could see her now smiling as the two churned butter. Mabel smoothed gnarled, bent fingers over the soft texture of the cloth cover.

Seeing the inscription magnified her regret and made it hard for her to pull in a breath. Tears glistened in long dry eyes.

"You'll see that she gets this," Mabel said.

Florence sat beside her. "Why on Earth do you want her to have it? Makes not a bit of sense."

Mabel smiled. "She'll figure it out. She's a smart one. Just promise me that she'll get this."

The blanket on Mabel's lap had slipped and Florence tugged it back into place. Carefully she tucked the edges under the seat of the wheelchair cushion. "I'll deliver it first thing in the morning."

"Don't tell any of my damn relatives about it. Those nephews of mine might see some value and take it. I don't want it getting mired in my estate. And if she needs anything, you see that she gets it."

Florence softened the edge in her voice. "Miss Mabel, you can give it to the child yourself. I'll take you straightaway in the morning."

Bent hands, lined with veins and wrinkles, gently stroked the book. "I don't think I'll be seeing morning."

Florence frowned. "Now, don't be talking like that."

"I'm nearing a hundred, Florence. I've had a good run but it's time for me to leave."

Florence's gaze softened. "What are you going to do if you wake up in the morning and you're still kicking?"

"I won't be." She raised a brow and met her old friend's gaze. "But if I am, I'll deliver the book myself."

Florence nodded. "That's more like it."

Mabel closed the book. "Just promise me, you will see that she gets it after I pass."

You aren't going to pass for a good while."

"*Promise* me."

Florence stared at her a long moment, and then she nodded. "I promise."

Mabel eased back in her wheelchair and closed her eyes. She sat so quiet and still that Florence thought she might have died then and there.

"Mrs. Woodrow."

The old woman nodded but didn't open her eyes. "And the second letter?"

Florence patted the old woman's arm. "I mailed it four days ago, like I said."

That prompted a resigned smile. "Good."

Chapter Five

TUESDAY, MARCH 23, 2010, 3:30 AM

The alarm bellowed like an army drill sergeant jarring me awake. Blindly, I reached for the phone, pressed the dismiss button, and dropped back against the pillow. I lay very still for a moment or two, savoring the warmth of the covers in the chilly room. Hoping I'd set the alarm for the wrong time, I rolled on my side and peered at the glowing numbers on the phone's display: three twenty-nine. Damn.

Yesterday, adrenaline had prodded me through the day. Much like the first day of school, the entire experience felt like one big novelty. Today, however, reality hit home with a painful force, making me yearn more for what I'd had at Suburban.

A year ago today, I'd been living in Gordon's neat, clutter-free, brand-new condo. Unlike my current digs, Gordon's place boasted all that was modern. Polished chrome fixtures winked in the overhead light, and his pipes didn't rattle when I turned on the hot water tap. A soft beige carpet covered the floors, and there wasn't an uneven, creaky hardwood floor to be found. No drafts chilled me when I slept, and direct and indirect lights offered generous illumination, unlike my attic room's miserly bulbs.

Most mornings at this hour we were where any sane people would be—in bed. Gordon would be lying beside me, nestled close against me. I liked the feel of his coarse chest hair tickling my skin, and the feel of his erection flickering to life and pressing against me. He'd wake, kiss me on the shoulder, my neck, my ear . . . The heat would rise in me, swift and hot, and I'd roll over, wrap my arms around his neck and kiss him on the lips. His touch would gain urgency and his kisses would travel to my chin, the hollow of my neck, my breasts . . .

In those warm, cocooned moments, the barriers dropped, pretense vanished, and the chaos stilled.

After we'd made love, we'd drift back to sleep entwined in each other's arms. Most mornings when my alarm sounded at six, Gordon would already have showered, dressed, and left for work. I'd lie in bed, his scent still clinging to my body until I'd reluctantly rise and step into the shower.

Now as I lay on the sofa bed, the heavy weight of loneliness settled on my chest, crushing the breath in my lungs and conjuring an ache in my throat. I stared at the play of shadows on the peeling plaster ceiling. Weighted by fatigue and sadness I wondered if I'd ever feel light again. I'd not really spoken to Gordon since last October. I'd been packing the last of my clothes and moving for good out of his apartment. He'd come home early and surprised me. That meeting had been awkward and tense, choked with barriers and pretense. We'd continued to work together for several more months, but we'd skillfully avoided each other.

Shit.

Another failure.

Another regret.

I rolled out of bed, flipped on the lamp by my sofa bed, and swiped away a stray tear. The cold wood floor prodded me to move so I quickly slipped on yesterday's jeans, a fresh T-shirt, and my clogs, which were still dusted with flour and smelling of cinnamon and sugar.

Suddenly, the chaos that awaited me in the bakery didn't seem so daunting. In fact, I welcomed it. At least in the bakery I didn't have time to think.

I shoved aching fingers through my hair and padded toward to the bathroom, negotiating around the untouched boxes and bags, brushed my teeth, tied back my hair, and splashed warm water on my face. I was halfway down the attic staircase when Rachel rounded the corner, two cups of coffee in hand. Her smile wasn't the 100-watt perky kind that was trademark Rachel.

Accepting the cup, I studied the shadows under her eyes and reminded myself that she was only thirty-four, a widow with two small children and a business that teetered on ruin. "Rough night?"

She shrugged as if to say all was well, but the gesture was stiff. "Ellie is getting a cold. She didn't sleep well."

My long fingers wrapped around the mug, greedily siphoning the warmth. "Where is she now?"

"She finally fell asleep about an hour ago. With luck, she'll sleep for a few more hours. I doubt she'll make it to school today. I've already told Mom, and she's gotten into my bed with her."

I sipped the coffee, bracing for the java's bitterness and much needed jumpstart. When I'd been little and afraid, Mom would get into bed with me, lie beside me, and in her soft voice, spin fairy tales that transformed the shadows into wonderful characters in rich stories. Now when I remembered those moments, I pictured Mom rising at the crack of dawn to help Dad in the bakery. She'd never complained about exhaustion but there could have been no escaping it with three children and a business to run.

"Mom will take good care of her."

The worry in Rachel's eyes faded a fraction, but there was no hiding the guilt of a mother who couldn't be there for her sick child. "I know."

"What about Anna?"

"She's fine." Rachel drank her coffee and shook her head as if she were trying to figure out a puzzle. "That kid is like you. She has got the constitution of an iron horse."

It was a bit odd that my niece and I were so much alike. She'd inherited my olive complexion from, I guess, her father's side, and like me enjoyed books, strawberry ice cream, and saying the occasional expletive. At thirty-four I'd learned when to hold my tongue; Anna, however, at age five had yet to understand that teachers didn't appreciate frustrated kindergarteners dropping the *S* word. More than once, Rachel had been summoned to the principal's office to deal with the latest Anna event.

"I take no responsibility for anything genetic when it comes to your kids. Of course, if their behavior is stellar, then we'll chock it up to Auntie Daisy's nurturing."

Rachel laughed. "Duly noted."

We moved downstairs to the first floor and then the basement. "Did you order your supplies yesterday?"

"I did," Rachel said. "We'll have our regular delivery tomorrow, but I think the driver will want to talk to you. He's going to need a check."

The money from Suburban should hit today and if the vendor held the check a day or two the wire would clear. "Did the vendor give you any trouble?"

"Oh, no, Ike is always so nice to me. But he was just adamant about getting a check."

"How much?"

"Fifty percent."

I did a rough calculation. Fifty percent equated to about

one thousand dollars. The money from my liquidated stocks was not going to last long. “Okay.”

“On the bright side, Chase Sugars was all smiles yesterday.”

“That’s because I sent them enough money to get our accounts updated. We owed them a chunk of change.”

She looked shocked. “I could’ve sworn I sent them a check.”

“You did. Four months ago.”

She chewed her bottom lip. “So do we have enough to cover the bills?”

“We do for this month but we’re going to have to hustle to make up ground for next month.”

The sparkle returned to her gaze. “Business was great yesterday.”

“Let’s hope the novelty of my return continues.”

We found Henri at this mixer, stabbing the risen dough with his finger. I’d learned long ago that if you poke a floured finger into the dough and the hole doesn’t collapse, it had risen enough and was ready to be kneaded. He frowned as he stared at the dough, studied the indention a moment or two, and then turned his attention to a batch of cookies.

“The dough is slow today,” he muttered. “It is too cold.”

Rachel sipped her coffee, hurrying to the row of hooks on the wall that held our aprons. As I slipped my apron over my head, I recognized the worn cotton smells of something freshly laundered. Sometime during the evening hours Mom had taken the aprons, washed, and returned them. The simple gesture teased a smile from me.

I crisscrossed the apron strings and tied them in front. “So, we shape the dough?”

Henri grunted. “The dough needs a few more minutes. It’s Tuesday. We do croissants on Tuesdays. Shape the croissants.”

"Right." There were daily staples we offered—sweet buns, carrot cake, cookies, and pies. But we had certain specials each day of the week. Tomorrow was walnut wheat raisin bread, and Thursday was Asiago bread. But I didn't remember beyond that. I moved to the large refrigerator and pulled out the "books"— squares of dough folded over and over smaller rectangles of butter mixed with flour. Rachel had prepared today's books yesterday, mixing and rolling out and folding the slabs twice. This afternoon she'd chop walnuts and soak the raisins in rum in preparation for tomorrow.

By the time I rolled out the book for the third time, there were thirty-six layers of butter and flour ready to rise and puff to life. If I'd learned anything about working in a bakery it was that good pastry could not be rushed. Dough needed time to rest and chill before it would really respond to the baker's touch. I laid the book on the wooden work surface, unwrapped it from the plastic and grabbed a rolling pin. A flick of the wrist and Henri and Rachel could dust the dough with just the right amount of flour. Not enough and the dough stuck to the rolling pin. Too much and it would end up tough. It was a delicate, practiced touch I'd yet to master.

Though I couldn't toss the flour with their precise flourish, I knew not to overdo. Soon I had the book rolled out into a long rectangle, had squared off the rough, uneven edges and cut away a long strip from the topside. This strip would be cut into squares for chocolate croissants, and the remaining rectangle would be cut into triangles, which I'd stretch and shape into crescents. My efforts weren't perfect but better than yesterday, and I sensed in a few days I'd be able to move much faster.

The three of us work quietly, each focused on a specific task. By seven, the chilled kitchen had warmed and smelled of butter and cinnamon. Henri had his baguettes and grunted a good day to us as he left through the back door. The shop opened at seven, and as expected Margaret breezed through the front door ten minutes late. She was either too tired or too distracted to make any comments, however, so I let the "Glad you could join us, Princess" crack pass.

I realized how little I knew about Margaret's life. Since I'd moved away to college, I'd lost track of her. I knew about the dissertation but couldn't say much about whom she dated, what she did for fun, or whom she'd befriended. It occurred to me that when we saw each other on birthdays or holidays we were polite for Mom's sake, but we'd not gone out of our way to ask each other too many questions.

I'd never given our distance much thought when I'd been in D.C., but now as I glanced at the dark circles under her eyes, I wondered what she did after work.

"Are you doing all right?" After so many years of benign indifference I didn't know how to undo the tangle of silence.

"Great."

"You look rough."

She shrugged. "Back at you."

While Rachel dashed upstairs to check on Ellie each hour on the hour, Margaret and I worked efficiently together through most of the morning.

Most days the stream of customers was steady until about one p.m. Yesterday had been heavier than usual and today was looking to be just as busy. At times, it took all three of us to fill the orders.

But because we didn't offer a lunch menu, most folks found other places to eat the midday meal. A lunch crowd could be a big source of income but right now I didn't have a clue how we could pull it off.

By one, Rachel had slipped upstairs to check on Ellie and Margaret had vanished into the back to grab coffee and a few cookies. I snagged a croissant and taken a seat on a stool behind the counter. With each bite I calculated fat grams, carbs, and calories. How long before the weight piled on my hips? A day, a week? Maybe running around the kitchen in the morning had offset the extra consumption?

Yeah, and maybe Mom still had my fat jeans from high school. Tomorrow, I really had to get my food act together.

When I heard the front bells clatter, I wiped the crumbs from my lap and stood. My grin froze when I saw the black nurse who'd wheeled in Mabel Woodrow yesterday. I tensed, half expecting the old lady to show and half dreading she wouldn't. One way or another, I had to talk to her about Renee.

I searched around the nurse for Mrs. Woodrow. "Can I help you?"

The older woman moved toward the counter. Her face looked pinched and ashen, and her eyes rimmed in red as if she'd been crying. "Miss Mabel asked me to give you something."

"Is everything all right?"

The old woman sniffed. "Miss Mabel passed early this morning."

My mind jumped to the sweet buns she'd eaten yesterday. Had they thrown her into a diabetic shock that killed her? Right on the heels of that thought, I selfishly thought about Renee. Mabel Woodrow was my fragile, if not tentative, connection to Renee and I had killed her with sweet buns.

In a blink I was irritated, saddened, and even a tiny bit relieved that I'd not have to deal with the situation. "I'm sorry."

The older woman sniffed again. Like yesterday, she wore her salt-and-pepper hair in a tight bun. Small wisps framed her round face, which for the most part, was wrinkle-free. "It was her time.

She had a full life."

The words sounded hollow and clichéd—all the things

people say when an older person dies—and I doubted the words were a comfort. Mom had called this woman Florence but to use her given name felt disrespectful. "My name is Daisy McCrae. You are?"

The older woman tightened her grip on her purse straps. "Florence Tillman. I was Miss Mabel's housekeeper and nurse for forty years."

Forty years. A lifetime. "I'm sorry for your loss, Mrs. Tillman."

Mrs. Tillman sniffed and pushed her pudgy hands into the folds of her dark coat. "I didn't come here to boo-hoo on your shoulder."

Grief had spawned the bitter tone and I let it pass. Grief had devastated Rachel when Mike had died. Her personality had transformed in a matter of minutes from a laughing bright woman to a snappish shrew. We'd all feared she'd never smile again. But slowly, over time, she'd come back to us. "Then why did you come?"

She pulled a package wrapped in gingham out of a large black purse, which dangled from the crook of her arm. "To give you this. Miss Mabel wanted you to have it. She sensed the end was coming, and she didn't want this getting tied up in the estate."

I glanced down at the package, which I now realized was a book. It smelled of dust and age. "A book?"

Mrs. Tillman snapped her purse closed. "It's a journal. A very old journal at that, so mind that you take care of it."

In a heartbeat my thoughts jumped to Renee. "Did it belong to my mother?"

Confusion darkened her eyes. "Mrs. McCrae? No, it didn't belong to her."

Frustration and anger gripped me. I glanced around, fearing one of my sisters or mothers would overhear. "No, I meant my birth mother. Miss Mabel said yesterday that she saw us together a long time ago. I thought she might have known her."

A deep wrinkle furrowed Mrs. Tillman's forehead. "I don't know anything about that. All I know is that Miss Mabel talked a lot of nonsense toward the end, and that she wanted you to have that book. She had me searching most of yesterday afternoon through every trunk in the spare room for it."

I glanced down at the gingham, faded with age. "Why me? She didn't even really know me."

"Like I said, I don't know the particulars. Miss Mabel had a mind of her own, and she had her mind set that I should give you this." She started to turn. "Now, I need to be going. I've a funeral to plan."

I didn't know what to say to her. Thank you. I'm sorry. Let me know if I can help.

None felt genuine. "I'll let my mother know."

Mrs. Tillman nodded. "Your mama is a good woman, Daisy McCrae. And she loves you. Don't you ever forget it."

Why would she say such a thing? I knew Mom was a good woman. I loved her. Appreciated her. "Yes, ma'am."

Mrs. Tillman lumbered toward the front door. "Funeral is on Monday at Christ Church. Miss Mabel wanted to be cremated so there won't be no graveside service."

"I'll tell Mom."

She stared at me long and hard. "Thank you."

After she vanished out of sight, I sat down on my stool and laid the wrapped book in my lap. For a moment, I didn't remove the fabric, fearing what I'd find. My hands hovered over the knot, trembling just a little before I took a deep breath. The fabric was brittle and frayed on the ends but the knot securing it was surprisingly tight. I wedged my fingernail into the knot and dug until it loosened enough for me to pry the ends free.

My breathing swallowed and my heart raced as I gently peeled back the red fabric. Even without opening it I knew Mrs. Tillman was right: It was old. Very old. The tattered book had a worn spine and frayed edges.

I opened the cover, wincing as the old spine creaked in protest. The yellowed first page was brittle, and blank except for an inscription written in an old-world style that had me visualizing the author dipping the nib of a pen into an inkwell. The inscription read: *To S., With Love, J.*

S. as in Susie. For a heart-stopping moment, I pictured the little girl I'd dreamed of for so many years. Of course, the S. could have been S. as in Sam, Sarah, or Simon. But my thoughts had tripped back to Susie, no doubt, because I'd been dreaming about her again.

The letter could have referenced a thousand different names, but still the coincidence had me shifting on the stool. I ran my hand gently, even reverently, over the cover page. The unshakeable sense that I was reaching into the past washed over me.

"What's that?"

I was so engrossed in the journal that I didn't hear Margaret approach. "It's a diary, I think. Mrs. Tillman just gave it to me."

Why would Mrs. Tillman give you a journal?" Genuine curiosity softened Margaret's typically imperious tone.

I traced the *S.* with my fingertip. "She said Miss Mabel wanted me to have it." I glanced up at Margaret. "Miss Mabel died last night."

Sadness snapped in Margaret's eyes. "What?"

A sigh shuddered through. "She died in her sleep."

"Shit. Does Mom know?"

I shook my head. "I just found out a few minutes ago myself."

Margaret sunk down on the stool beside me. Her shoulders slumped forward, and she reminded me of a balloon that had suddenly popped and gone flat. "Damn. She's going to be upset. She'd planned to visit her today. Hell. I'm upset. I liked that old lady."

Guilt niggled me. I hadn't liked her. Even back when I was a teenager, I didn't like the way she stared at me. "I barely knew her. Other than yesterday, I hadn't seen her in almost twenty years."

Margaret didn't hide her surprise and disappointment. "Miss Mabel was here? I never saw her. We always make a point to talk."

Lifting a brow, I shrugged. "You were late. She came before you arrived."

"Shit." Margaret rubbed the back of her neck, coaxing tension away. "I wish I'd been here. She'd not been out of her house in months, and then she came here, and you saw her."

Margaret usually didn't seem to care much about anything, and for her to care about the old woman was a surprise. "Were you two close?"

"When I came back to Alexandria five years ago, I was working on my dissertation on ancient Greek women. I had all my research, but I just couldn't get the work to flow. The Archaeology Center had just hired me and asked me to write an article on Mabel. I did, and found I really liked the woman. So, I kept going back and talking to her. We talked a lot about the city and how it used to be. I also talked to her about her parents and grandparents. You know me and history. She seemed to really love talking about her grandmother. I've got notes and recordings of those talks. I should dig them out."

I tried to envision Margaret sitting in the old woman's home, speaking softly and balancing a cup of tea on her lap as she tried to take notes. "Frankly, Margaret, that's a match I can't picture."

"She inspired me to change my dissertation. I've left ancient Greece behind and am now focusing on Alexandria."

"Which explains why you've not gotten your PhD yet."

"Yeah. But I'm okay with that. Mabel was nearly one hundred. She knew so much about this town. She was a treasure of information. Hell, her grandmother was born in 1840. *Eighteen freaking forty*. But I really liked her. She had a take-no-prisoners kind of attitude about life, and I liked that."

"Did she tell you much about the city?"

"Sure. She told me all kinds of things about what it was like to live here. Her grandmother came to town at the very end of the Civil War."

"Did she tell you much about herself?"

"No. In fact, she was tight lipped about her own life. Every time I asked about her past, she said she wasn't interesting and that I should let that sleeping dog lie."

"Did you look up her records and trace her family?"

"No. She didn't want me to pry, so I didn't."

"Very un-historian of you."

"Tell me about it." Margaret folded her arms and shook her head.

"Now that's she's gone, I guess I'm free to dig as much as I'd like."

"Have at it."

Margaret glanced at the journal. "You know, she always asked about you."

"Why? She didn't even like me."

"She liked the idea of you doing well." Margaret cocked a brow. "You piqued her interest, I guess."

"I wonder what she thought about me losing my job and then stumbling back home to work."

"Mom told everyone you were coming back home because you were one of those huge successes who wanted to turn her back on corporate America and return to her roots."

"Ah, much like the story we spun yesterday."

"Great minds think alike."

I chuckled and rubbed my eye. "Corporate executive to bakery shop manager. I guess on paper my downward move could be seen as a spiritual thing."

Margaret kept glancing at the book. "She said you were like one of those gals who opens a B&B or a winery."

"Mom can put a good spin on anything." I followed her gaze to the journal, which was far more interesting than my descending career. "So why give me the book? It makes no sense that Miss Mabel didn't give it to you."

"I couldn't agree more." A bit of frustration had crept into my sister's voice. "Can I see that book?"

"Sure."

Margaret took the journal; immediately her demeanor changed from sadness and confusion to reverence. Gently, she opened the book, wincing a little when the spine creaked, and studied the yellowed, brittle pages. Blue eyes sparked with joy. "Holy shit."

"What?"

"This book appears to be a handwritten journal, written mid-nineteenth century. Shit. Shit.

Shit. Have you read past the first page?"

"No. Mrs. Tillman just gave it to me. What is the big deal?" It's old and rare, and I could appreciate that on some level but honestly the book wasn't of real interest.

Margaret's face flushed with excitement. Her hands trembled slightly when she closed the book. "We shouldn't be handling this with our bare hands. The oil from our skin isn't good for the paper."

I'd never seen Margaret so excited, and it made me wonder why my heart wasn't racing. I rose and grabbed two sets of fresh plastic gloves. I handed her a set and slipped on mine. "I'll hold the book while you put your gloves on."

Margaret hesitated, as if I'd just asked her to feed her first-born child to the wolves. "Be very, very careful."

Amused by her angst, I thought about pretending to drop the book but decided that was immature even for me. "Margaret, I think I can hold a journal while you put on gloves."

She studied the book with a mother's loving eye. "You have a heavy hand, Daisy."

True. My fingers were not only long but also strong, and I was famous for breaking stuff—vases, door handles, electronics, you name it, I'd broken it. "Be nice or I'm going to take my journal away and not let you read it."

Margaret blinked. "You can't shut me out of this, Daisy. This is so huge. It's the kind of find I've been waiting for . . . well, for a long time."

I tugged it from her fingers. "Yes, I can." The weight of the journal seemed to increase as I cradled it on flattened palms. "If it's such a big deal, then why did Miss Mabel want me to have it and not you? You are the history geek."

Margaret's eyes glistened. "She must have made a mistake. Maybe she was just confused, and she really wanted me to have the book."

No! The journal is yours.

The words resonated in my head, loud and clear.

Instantly a protective urge rose and filled every nook of my body. Mrs. Tillman had given the book to me. She'd not been the least bit confused. "Mrs. Tillman was very clear, Margaret. She said Miss Mabel wanted me to have the book."

As if I hadn't spoken, Margaret reached for the journal ready to retake possession. I drew back. "You can read it, but you will not run this show. The book is mine."

Margaret gave me her best you've-got-to-be-kidding glare. "I'm a trained professional, Daisy. I have a PhD—well, almost as soon as my dissertation is finished—in archaeology. You do numbers, Rachel bakes, and I do old documents. This is *my* thing."

"No argument here, Margaret. But this book was given to me for a reason. And until I understand that reason, I'm hanging on to it."

Margaret stared at me, annoyed; her palms outstretched as if to say *give it*!

Margaret was three years older, and the balance of power in our relationship had always been skewed in her favor, which likely explained why I was always trying to tip the scales. But now, for once, the power had shifted to me without my intervention. And I'd be lying if I didn't say I was enjoying this moment. "Say it."

Blue eyes twinkled with a mixture of annoyance and hunger. "Say what?"

"Say the book belongs to Daisy." I enunciated each word carefully.

She arched a pale brow. "You're being a child."

Maybe I was being childish. Responsible, levelheaded Daisy was acting like a kid. But this book was mine. It was history that Miss Mabel wanted me to know. And seeing as I didn't have all the pieces of my own personal history, the urge to guard this book was surprisingly powerful.

I shrugged. "I know. Say it."

Margaret, born to parents who'd loved her since the day of her conception, and who could trace her lineage back hundreds of years, simply didn't get it. "You're a twit."

"Maybe." Mutinous silence hovered between us. Margaret waited for Daisy the peacemaker to gallop onto center stage and relent. But that Daisy wasn't available today. In her place remained cranky bitchy Daisy, who didn't want to share.

Margaret shoved out an annoyed breath. "The book belongs to Daisy."

"Good." I made a ridiculous show of straightening my shoulders. "Now we can read it."

"Read what?" Rachel appeared from the back.

"Miss Mabel asked Mrs. Tillman to give her a valuable historic document, and now Daisy is playing games with me. She won't let me look at it."

"It's mine," I said. "I call the shots."

Rachel laughed. "You sound like Ellie and Anna fighting over the *Hannah Montana* CD."

The comment hit home with both of us. Miss Mabel had died, she'd given me this journal for a reason, and I was pretty sure it wasn't to stir up an argument between Margaret and me.

"Lock the front door," I said. "We'll take the book in the back and lay it on the table."

Margaret nodded, more excited than I'd seen her, well, ever. She hurried to the front door, flipped the open sign to closed, and threw the dead bolt.

Rachel shook her head. "I haven't seen Margaret move that fast in years."

Margaret shooed us toward the back. "Shut up and get moving."

In the back kitchen, the worktable had been cleaned after the morning baking, but Margaret laid out a clean apron on the work surface. Margaret, who normally slopped coffee on her shirt and left a trail of crumbs behind her wherever she walked in the bakery, made sure the towel lay perfectly flat and the edges were straight.

"Jeez, Margaret, I'm starting to think there should be a chorus of angels singing."

Rachel giggled.

No hint of humor glistened in Margaret's gaze. "Honestly, it wouldn't be out of line."

I laid the book on the towel. "Okay, then. Let's have a

look." I reached for the book cover, but Margaret shooed my hand away.

With fingertips, she delicately lifted the cover and first page. The ink had faded only a little and reading the first entry was remarkably easy.

October 12, 1852

My name is Susie. I am a slave.

Births and deaths aren't always recorded for slaves, but I do know that today is my birthday. I am twelve.

Mama tells me I was born on a cold day. The trees hadn't budded, and an icy rain fell as she'd labored with the midwife in our attic room. She said it was a long, hard birthing, which just about wrung every bit of strength from her.

For most of the night, she said she cried and wailed as her muscles bit and scratched at her insides. She was about to give up when I came out squawking and crying and covered in a fine white powder. She'd said the pain vanished in a blink, and she was filled with joy and sadness. The joy came from her heart, and the sadness came from the knowing that I would be a slave like her.

Master and his wife were out of town when I was born, and when they came home, they made a point to see me. Master's wife often tells me that I was much pinker and whiter than she'd imagined.

"Holy crap," Margaret said. "If this is real, do you have any idea what a find this is? In 1852 only a handful of slaves could read and write."

"I thought there was more education in the African-American community," I said.

"There was, before 1848." When her gaze met my blank stare she added, "Until 1848, Alexandria was a part of the

District of Columbia, which was a haven city for runaway slaves. The city was progressive for its time when it came to education. And the city had a growing population of free blacks. Long story short, however, in 1848 the City of Alexandria seceded from the District of Columbia and joined Virginia."

"Because why?"

"Slave trading was a booming business in Alexandria. The slave traders and businessmen knew it was a matter of time before the district outlawed slavery. They knew Virginia had no such plans, so to protect their business interests, they joined Virginia."

"Just like that?"

"No. In fact, it was a big political fight. Huge. In the end the business community won its bid to join the Commonwealth."

"When was slavery outlawed in the district?" Rachel asked.

"Eighteen fifty." Margaret frowned. "White Virginia owners had always been worried about insurrection among the slaves. Reading, which fostered independence, wasn't considered a good thing, so it was outlawed. Educational opportunities for African Americans in Alexandria ended in 1848."

This was a remarkable, rare find. I understood that. Appreciated the significance. But I had no idea why it had been left to me.

"You said Mabel wanted you to have this, Daisy?" Rachel asked.

"Yeah."

Rachel shook her head as she glanced between Margaret and me. "Why? Daisy, you barely knew Miss Mabel. It just makes no sense."

The edge sharpening her words made me feel like an outsider. I felt a little offended. "I did know she liked sweet buns." I leaned forward on my elbows and stared at the neat, childlike handwriting.

"Sweet buns are hardly the basis for a relationship," Margaret said. "I spent hours and hours with her. We talked endlessly about the city and her grandmother."

I appreciated Margaret's logic. This time yesterday I couldn't even remember the old woman's name, and today I was in possession of a 150-year-old journal. "I have no idea why she gave me the journal."

Chapter Six

TUESDAY, MARCH 23, 2010, NOON

My name is Susie. I am a slave.

As I read the words on the first journal page, the hairs on the back of my neck tingled. Energy pulsed through my body. I had the sense that I was becoming reacquainted with an old friend. That I'd somehow knew this girl who'd written these words over 150 years ago. I was not like Margaret, who believed in the past life/karma theories. I believed that life was only about the living, and you have what you have right here and now.

And still I stared at the yellowed pages with the scripted letters written in fading ink and wondered why I felt such a steely connection. The service bell on the front counter dinged once. Twice. And on the third ding I glanced up, more than vaguely annoyed. I closed the book. "Margaret, can you go see who's out front?"

Margaret slid the book from my fingers before I thought to tell her no. "You go see. I want to look at the book."

As much as I wanted to ignore the bell, the bakery couldn't afford to turn away any business. I handed Margaret the journal, rose, and crossed to the front door.

The closed sign blocked the view, but I could see it was a man.

Flipping the lock, I opened the door still distracted by the journal. "Can I help you?" The words absently tumbled out of my mouth as I smiled but didn't quite make eye contact.

"Daisy?"

I looked up to the sound of a very familiar voice. Standing in the doorway was Gordon. Gordon Singleton. My Gordon. Lover. Ex-fiancé. "Gordon."

"What are you doing here?" The rasp in his voice still roughed up my name in a way that made my breath catch.

He wore faded jeans, a blue turtleneck, and loafers. He'd lost weight and toned up since I'd seen him last year, and he'd let his banker-short hair grow so that it skimmed his collar. Sun had darkened milk-white skin to a deep bronze and added highlights to his hair.

I blinked. Once. Twice. "It's my parents' bakery."

Aware that I wore no makeup, that an old scrunchie barely held my hair in a wild topknot, and that flour and pink cream cheese icing covered my shirt and clogs, I straightened my shoulders.

The last time he'd seen me I'd been in a black tailored suit, cream silk blouse, and Prada heels. He'd been angry and had called me a cold bitch.

I yanked off my engagement ring and set it in the center of the bureau. The gold-and-diamond ring caught the light above and winked.

I'd hoped to have my bags packed and be out of the apartment by the time he gotten home. Gordon rarely got in the door before eight, and it was only seven. I should have come home earlier but there'd been a meeting at the office, and I'd gotten tied up. Now as I glanced at the clock, tension coiled in my stomach. I should have been out of our apartment by now.

I shoved more underwear and bras in a suitcase already

crammed with a haphazard collection of jeans, suits, running clothes, and whatever else I thought I might need until I could return. I'd have left it all behind, but I didn't have the time to replace it all.

Cramming the top down, I clicked the latches on the suitcase and pulled it toward the front door. I'd be out of our apartment in a few seconds and Gordon would be in my past. Keys scraped against the lock on the other side and the door opened. Gordon stood in the doorway. Tall, his broad shoulders slightly stooped. His gaze went to my face and then to the suitcase.

"This shouldn't be a surprise," I stammered.

But the look on his face—a mixture of hurt, anger and frustration—told me surprise barely covered it.

"Did you take the day off from Suburban?" He glanced into the shop slowly as if he weren't sure if he should turn and run or stay.

"The investment team was fired. You didn't hear?" The lighthearted edge didn't soften the words as I'd hoped. "You were always in the know about the comings and goings in town. You didn't hear?"

His gaze held mine, searching. "I don't keep up with the finance world anymore. I barely read the paper these days."

I scraped a stray, annoying wisp of hair from my eyes. "You'd have had to have been on the side of a mountain not to know. It's been in all the news."

Gordon had always had his ear to the ground. Little happened in the D.C. financial world without him knowing. He'd been an information junkie. In fact, that is what I'd called him when we'd fought one of those last times. *There's never time for us.* Of course, sharper, more complicated emotions had been simmering that day, but neither one of us could have put them into words. In fact, I doubt that I could even now.

He slid his hands into the back pockets of his jeans. "I've been on a cross-country bike trip for the last four months."

"During the winter?"

The corner of his mouth lifted. "I never did things the easy way."

My Gordon wouldn't have done anything without a plan and risk assessment. This Gordon was a stranger. "I find that hard to believe."

His stance was casual, open, but there was the slightest edge of apology lurking behind his dark eyes. "What did I have to lose?"

Gordon Singleton had been CFO of Suburban. He'd been the one who, just months after I'd left him, had played the losing poker hand and destroyed the company.

He couldn't have changed that much. He'd been even more addicted to work than I'd been. "You've let it all go?"

"It let me go, remember?" Defensiveness lingered behind the words.

"Right. I'm sorry." Why was I apologizing? I doubt either of us was interested in a postmortem of Suburban or our relationship, and to explain the move home felt akin to climbing a mountain. "Well, the digest version is that I've decided to reconnect with my roots. I'm running my parents' bakery."

His gaze skimmed my face, and for an instant it almost felt like fingertips brushing my skin. "How long have you been here?"

I folded my arms over my chest. "A few days."

He glanced past me into the bakery, and then back at me again. "You look like you belong here."

I laughed. "You're joking."

The hardness in my voice had him cocking his head a fraction. "No, I'm not. You look good here."

Another laugh stuttered past my lips, but I felt angry, annoyed, and oddly flattered. "I don't know if I'd go that far."

Silence settled, and for a fleeting second, I savored the deep hue of his tan, the scruff of blond beard on his chin and the faint *V* dip of his shirt. He looked good. Real good.

Gordon arched a brow. "Are you going to let me inside or not? The sign says you're open until three."

"Oh, right, yeah sure. We had a little excitement and closed for a few minutes." He didn't ask about whatever had come up, and I didn't offer. Better not to get too well acquainted, as my mother used to say.

Rachel and Margaret had moved up to the counter and stared shamelessly at the two of us. They had picked up on the change in me. Leave it to a sister to see what others don't.

"Welcome to Union Street Bakery." Margaret's grin was too bright to be real, and as Gordon moved to the counter, I rolled my eyes.

"Thanks."

Margaret's smile broadened. "My name is Margaret. I'm Daisy's older sister."

Rachel cleared her throat. "My name is Rachel, the other older sister."

"Sisters?" He looked at me, didn't say a word, but I imagined the thoughts tumbling in his head. So, this is the family you never wanted to talk about.

It was hard to explain without sounding foolish. But I'd rarely discussed my life here in Alexandria, and when I talked about my family, I suggested they lived far away. When I'd left for college and then taken the job in D.C., I'd left the bumbling, sad bakery Daisy on the south side of the Potomac. And I guess I feared mentioning the bakery too much might somehow allow the old Daisy to return. Not so logical, but it had worked for the most part.

Hand extended, he moved away from me to the counter and shook their hands. The air around me lost its charge and I released the breath I'd been holding.

"My name is Gordon Singleton." His trademark deep baritone still had the power to command a room.

"Welcome, Gordon," Rachel said.

"What can we do for you, Gordon?" Margaret's voice sounded softer, and I could have sworn she was blushing.

After a hesitation, he said, "I need to order some kind of dessert."

Margaret nodded. "Well, you've come to the right place. We are all about dessert."

I listened as Rachel explained the difference between the confections. They spoke about Gordon's renting retail space and his having a kind of open house for potential financiers. He tossed out an address, also on Union Street, and I realized that my ex-fiancé was now my neighbor. *My neighbor.* The words tangled in my whirling thoughts, and I wondered if I'd jumped from the frying pan into the fire.

"What flavors and confections work best for wrestling money from potential investors?"

Everyone laughed, but all I could think about was that Gordon was setting up shop in Alexandria, and we were going to see each other weekly if not daily.

This was so not good.

I wanted to suggest a cake laced with arsenic, but Gordon and my sisters decided on a cookie tray.

"So how on earth do you know Daisy?" Margaret asked.

I glanced at her, saw the gleam in her eyes, a mixture of curiosity, sexual attraction, and payback for the journal.

Gordon glanced at me, clearly surprised. The smile that played on his lips reflected hurt, not humor. "You never told them."

Heat rose in my face. I could launch into the whole Old Daisy doesn't mix with New Daisy, but at this moment the lines were so blurred. "Why are you here, Gordon?"

"Didn't you just hear? Ordering pastries. Opening a bike shop."

"But you live in D.C." My voice sounded like sandpaper.

"Not anymore. Like I just said, I'm opening a bike shop in Old Town."

This was the perfect storm of disasters: job loss, parents' house, and now the return of the ex-fiancé. "Great. That's great. But I've got to say, I never thought you liked bikes that much."

He glanced briefly beyond me to the street outside. "Back in the day I rode a lot."

When he'd had a few beers, he'd talk about his cycling days. I listened and always marveled at how different we were when it came to the past and present. He longed for the past and I ran from it.

He hated thinking about the present, and it was all I cared about. "I know. I *know.* I just thought you'd left that behind."

He shrugged. "No rule that says I can't double back. You should know that better than anyone now. I'm guess this is where you got your start."

"Right."

Margaret came around the counter. "Daisy has bad manners even on a good day." She reached for the pencil stuck behind her ear as she pretended to search for an order pad. "So how do you two know each other?"

Gordon released a long breath. "From D.C. The finance world is small."

Margaret arched a brow, as if waiting for more. None came. "You seem to be good friends."

"We were. *Are*, I hope." He glanced at me, smiled.

I smiled but had no words to back it up. Suddenly, *I'm sorry* burned in my throat. I'm sorry I never told him about my family. I'm sorry I couldn't trust us to work. I'm sorry I ran. But all the apologies remained unspoken.

"We deliver," Margaret said finally. "So, when is this shindig?"

"Eight days. Next Tuesday."

"We'll get it done for you. And Daisy will drop off the trays."

"Thanks," he said. His gaze was a quagmire of longing, shock, and anger. "See you next Wednesday, Daisy."

"Right."

The bells on the front door jangled and echoed in the bakery long after he left.

"I swear," Rachel said. "If you don't tell me every single detail about Mr. Delicious I am going to bust."

Margaret laughed. "Who'd have ever thought Daisy would have a guy like that."

Annoyance snapped at my heels. "What makes you think there was ever anything between us?"

My sisters laughed. Hard.

As Margaret swiped a tear from her eye, she leaned forward and said, "Because he looks like he could eat you right up. I was ready to make a move myself, but it's clear he only sees you."

I swallowed a comment, knowing whatever I said would simply fuel my sisters' digs. "It doesn't matter what we were. We are history." That should have put an end to it; but history had started a nasty habit of biting me in the ass lately. I marched into the kitchen and carefully wrapped up the journal.

"Hey, don't you want to read it?" Margaret asked. All traces of humor had vanished from her voice.

"I've had all the history I can stomach for today."

"Then why don't you let me take that pesky book off your hands, and I'll take it back to the center, where I can read it carefully. I'll have a full report for you in the morning."

"No. Sorry. I don't want to deal with anything extra right

now." A counselor had once told me that negative emotions collected in us like droppings in a litter box. If I didn't keep the box scooped and I let the emotions build up, the stench would drive me out of the house. My litter box had driven me out of the bakery seventeen years ago. And out of Gordon's life.

I realized my litter box was still full.

And I still didn't know how to scoop it out.

Chapter Seven

WEDNESDAY, MARCH 24, 2010, 3:30 AM

I was in the center of a cornfield. The stalks were tall and thick, and everything was so green and so identical. I began to push through the thick stalks, which brushed against my skin. The air grew hotter, heavier, and was so suffocating that panic rose into my chest. I moved faster and faster, hoping if I could just keep moving, I'd find my way home. But all I saw were stalks, which now scraped against my face and arms. Dread thickened with the foliage until finally, I couldn't put one more foot in front of the other. Helpless, I stopped and buried my hands in my face.

"Mom." The word rose in my throat but remained unspoken.

And then a little girl's unexpected laughter drifted and danced on a cool breeze, skimming the top of the stalks. Like wind chimes or the jingle of Christmas bells, the joyous sound soothed the ache in my chest.

I swiped fingers over my moist cheeks. "Hello?"

More laughter drifted and floated around me. "Daisy. Daisy. Daisy."

I searched the dense field. "Where are you?"

The little girl giggled. "Star bright, starlight. I wish I may. I wish I might."

I listened, but I saw no sign of her. "I can't see you."

And then she emerged from the stalks. She wore a simple blue cotton dress that brushed knobby knees and tight braids that accentuated bright skin and shining green eyes, the color of spring grass. "Daisy. Daisy. Daisy."

My name had a singsong quality that coaxed away the remaining loneliness. "Who are you?"

"You remember me, don't you?"

"I don't."

She giggled. "Look closer."

Her round face was familiar, and in a flash, I remembered.

The alarm shrilled at 3:30 a.m. on day three, and I jerked awake and sat bolt upright in the bed. Brushing the hair from my eyes, I stared into the darkness and struggled to get my bearings. My heart pounded and for a terrifying moment, I didn't recognize anything. As the seconds ticked by, my rattled brain cleared and identified what was now becoming the familiar. The unpacked boxes, the garbage bags full of clothes, and the books that I'd yet to unpack.

I was still in the attic, and it was yet again dark outside. Always up before dawn, a baker's life was bathed in shadows.

Swinging my legs over the side of the bed, I buried my face in my hands. As I rubbed the sleep from my eyes, a breeze from the window blew cold gusts across the back of my neck. A shiver snaked down my spine.

Shuddering, I rose and shuffled in socked feet across the wooden floor toward the window, ready to secure the latch when I discovered it was locked tight. I searched for a hole or crack, knowing old homes shift, separate, and often give way. But this window was airtight. Fresh caulking proved Dad had been in the room recently, mending and fixing.

How many things had Dad had to fix and tinker with over

the years to keep this home and business afloat? I'd not given his puttering much thought until yesterday when the new hot water heater in the kitchen went on the fritz. I'd stared haplessly at the round heater for several minutes and all but begged it to start working again. No hot water meant no clean hands, which meant trouble with the health department. I'd thought about calling Dad but had been determined to keep him out of the loop and away from stress as much as possible.

Finally, frustrated and angry, I'd whacked the heater once or twice with the flat of my hand. To my great relief the heater had started to hum again. I'd accepted the miracle, which would buy me time while I searched for a warranty. I had the sinking feeling that whatever underlying problems lurked inside the steel drum would return. I ran my hand over the windowpanes one last time. Secure. Whatever chill had found its way into the room had come from somewhere else. For a moment my skin prickled and puckered, and I had the sensation that I wasn't alone. It was almost as if someone was standing right behind me, just centimeters away. My heartbeat quickened, and I turned around and searched the dark. Of course, I was alone.

Turning from the window, I moved back toward my bed. I had enough real problems on my hands to worry about. Phantom gusts of air and dark tingly sensations would have to move to the back of the line. The dough waited. Dressing and then slipping my feet into worn clogs, I started toward the bathroom. As I reached the sink, another breeze blew across the room and the skin on the back of my neck tingled more. I glared back at the window, but the curtains lay still against the panes. I was alone. I could see that with my own eyes. But still I got the sense that someone was there, lurking in the shadows, staring at me.

Since I was a kid, the stairs leading to the third floor had squeaked and groaned with each footfall. I'd always considered the quirk my personal early warning system. Like NORAD, the missile defense system in Colorado, my creaking steps warned when sisters and parents approached.

But this sensation was different. It burrowed down to my bones.

For several seconds I stared into the shadows, waiting—for what I didn't know. The inky darkness danced and swayed along the edges of the wall, moving in time to an imaginary song I couldn't hear. I leaned closer, squinted, waited. My heart thumped. And then at the edge of the darkness, I saw the outline of a man.

Most would have freaked at such a sight, but for reasons I couldn't explain I stood my ground. The man's black hair was combed back and accentuated dark and expressive eyes. His partial grin revealed crooked, small teeth. His dark suit appeared hand tailored as did his shirt and vest.

He shook his head.

I shook mine. "Do I know you?"

He stared as if assessing me. And for reasons I could not fathom, I sensed I came up short in his book.

I dug my fingers through my hair. "What's this about?"

He eased toward me, assessing.

"This is about the journal?"

He nodded.

"I didn't read it last night. I was too tired and annoyed. I suppose you're here to tell me not to read it."

The man's expression darkened, and the shadows around us thickened. The walls undulated and moaned, and suddenly the air in the room smelled of rotting eggs.

Fear dug into my gut and triggered a set of worries I never had considered. I'd never been afraid of any bump or squeak in the night in my attic room, but I was now. "Just leave."

For seconds, maybe minutes, we stood staring at each other. And then in the next instant, he was gone.

My heart thumped in my chest as my breathing quickened. I felt as confined and afraid as I had in the cornfield.

The shadowy man's essence was filled with enough anger and fury to send fear snaking up my spine. Several books piled high on a table tumbled to the floor, making me jump. This presence wanted me to leave.

A sane person would have gotten the hell out of the attic. But I was too tired and annoyed to heed common sense. "Get the hell out of my room. When I leave, it'll be on my terms."

My hoarse whisper bounced against dark walls and seemed to boomerang back to me.

"Get the hell out of my room."

I clenched chilled fingertips and swallowed. Seconds ticked as watching eyes stared at me.

"Beat it."

The air thickened and then in a blink cleared. Whatever it was, was gone. The shadows lightened as the clouds covering the moon drifted away.

For a second I wasn't sure what to think. My heart was pounding, and my hands were sweaty. I'd never felt unwelcome in this house, but I did now.

* * *

Ike, the deliveryman, stared at the Union Street Bakery check I'd just handed him. "How many days do I have to hold it?"

In his mid-forties, Ike had a thick muscled body created from years of heavy lifting; dark, thinning hair, and a square face. His brown scuffed boots were clean, his uniform crisp, and his belt buckle shone. Judging by the body language, I guessed he was ex-Army or Marines.

"You could try to cash it tomorrow, but waiting two would be best," I said.

"You do understand that your sister hasn't paid a bill in months."

"Her last check to you was December 1 of last year. I know she's way behind on the bills, Ike. But I'm not my sister. I'm back to run the business and see that our bills get paid on time."

He raised a brow.

"I know how to run a business. That check will be good in two days, and we will be making our payments on time going forward."

"How do I know that?"

"My dad never stiffed you."

"Your sister has."

"You won't be officially stiffed anymore when that check clears. She's just a mess when it comes to the office."

He flicked the check against his open palm. "I got bills to pay, too. I can't carry you anymore."

"You won't. The money is good by Friday, Ike. I swear."

He studied my dark, bold signature. "I don't know."

I'd been in a few bargaining spots before when the odds weren't in my favor. At this point, I guessed he might need us as much as we needed him. "Then give me the check back, Ike. I'll find another supplier."

"Good luck. The word is out that Union Street Bakery is a sinking ship."

I looked at him as if he were a multimillion-dollar investor. "Whoever said that is wrong. We might have had a bad patch but we're on the upswing. We've been here over 150 years, and we'll be here another hundred."

He shook his head as a grin played with the edges of his mouth. "You got balls, Daisy."

"I like to think so, Ike."

He studied me and then looked down at the check again. Finally, after a heavy pause, he neatly folded the check and tucked it in his breast pocket. "If this check bounces, I'm coming back."

"It won't bounce." I held out my hand. "And you know where to find me. I'm not going anywhere. Believe me."

He wrapped long rough fingers around my hand. "Your dad's handshake was always good enough for me."

"And you'll see mine is, too."

He nodded. "I can see you are a chip off the old block."

I helped him unload the flour, butter, sugar, and other necessities, gave him a freshly baked pie and watched him drive off with a fifth of the money I'd invested in the bakery.

Still, for the first time in a few days, I thought I just might be making headway. With smart, careful management, I just might turn this ship around and make a success of it.

After the morning rush, Mom pushed through the shop's front door. Sheila McCrae always prided herself on making an entrance. It wasn't enough to walk into a room, she had to make a *statement*.

Me, I could cheerfully have slipped in and out of any venue unnoticed and be perfectly happy. Not Mom. No entrance was too small for a show. Margaret also liked the attention. If her work weren't garnering her accolades, then she'd seek out negative attention—like showing up late to work with a shitty attitude. Either way, Margaret found a way to get noticed.

And though tragedy had pulled Rachel from center stage, she'd been head cheerleader in high school. Before Mike's death, she'd entered cooking contests and longed for a feature spot on the Food Network. Given a little time, Rachel would tap back into the inner showman that I didn't possess. I'd always attributed our differences to genetics.

Mom was wearing her rhinestone reading glasses, baggy jeans, and a T-shirt that read *Runs with Scissors*. Mom did a half step and shuffled toward the counter as she hummed.

She cleaned a smudge from the display case with the hem of her T-shirt and inspected the trays. A frown creased her forehead, and I imagined her mentally rearranging the baked goods. Part of me was miffed that she was checking up on me and another part touched. Good or bad, she was always there.

"It looks like you gals had another good morning," she said.

"Not bad," I said.

She peered into the display case and frowned. "The sugar cookies could use a little straightening."

I looked down. "They're fine."

"Maybe just a little tightening up." She started to move behind the counter when I shook my head.

"Mom."

She smiled. "What?"

I blocked her path. "What are you doing?"

"I'm going to tweak the sugar cookie display."

"No."

"It will just take a minute."

"No."

She pouted. "Daisy, I worked in this bakery before you were born."

I sighed. "And now it's my turn."

"Yes but—"

"Have you seen Mrs. Tillman?" I asked. "How are the funeral plans progressing?"

She tossed a fleeting glance at the sugar cookies one more time and then stepped back. "She told me Mabel wanted a simple ceremony. I wish I'd visited her more, but life just got away from me."

Her expression had lost its spark. "Florence said Mabel was being cremated."

"She told me. And the service is at Christ Church on Monday."

"By the way, we're all going." Her tone had turned firm.

"We are?"

"Yes. All the McCraes will sit together."

"What time?"

"One p.m."

"We'll have to close the bakery early. Why don't I just stay behind and keep the place running while you, Dad, and the girls go."

"Don't even try to worm out of this, Daisy Shelia McCrae. We go together, which means if we close early, so be it. Mabel was a good friend, and we owe her that much."

"I'd hate to lose the revenue. The budget is tight."

"A few dollars won't make that much of a difference to us. No, we all go, Daisy. I've even spoken to Henri, and he's meeting us at the church."

"Sure. Fine."

Mom smiled, a bit shocked and pleased that I'd agreed without an argument, which was a rare occurrence indeed.

Margaret pushed through the kitchen door. "What's doing, Mom?"

"The usual. Did you sell lots and lots of bread this morning, ladies?" Margaret glanced at the cupcake clock as she pulled off her apron.

"We did well. Not setting it on fire but well."

Rachel emerged from the kitchen. "Hey, Mom. Thanks again for helping with Ellie yesterday."

"Anytime." Mom's gaze drifted between Margaret and Rachel and then settled on me. "All my girls together. I'm so proud." I groaned. Margaret shrugged. Rachel smiled.

"Are we doing all right?" Mom asked.

"Working together or financially?" I asked.

"Both."

"The McCrae sisters are a well-oiled machine," Rachel said.

Margaret and I snorted.

"You girls aren't fighting, are you?"

"No," Rachel said.

"Daisy, are you getting your sea legs back, so to speak?"

"Doing well, Mom."

"You're sure?" She looked worried as she searched my gaze.

"Very."

"Really?"

"Yes." There was no missing the hint of strain in my voice now. Mom, to her credit, knew just how far to push before I lost my temper. "And how's the till looking?"

"You just asked. We're fine."

I could deal with Mom when we steered clear of emotions and focused on business. Business I understood. We only ran into trouble when she started worrying over me. *You look too thin. I don't want you to worry but. . .* That's when I got a little crazy. She never quite accepted that quiet is a comfortable, natural state for me.

The rhinestones in Mom's glasses caught the afternoon light, twinkled and drew attention to the deep lines etched by her eyes. "Sounds good, honey. I know you know what you're doing."

I stared at Mom, waiting for a joke or a song or some outrageous story about her knitting club. But she simply smiled meekly at me.

"Shit, what's wrong, Mom?" I asked.

Mom blinked. "Why should anything be wrong, Daisy?"

"Because you're too quiet. You always have a comment, joke, or show tune to sing. You stopped when I asked you not to rearrange the case. And you're not pressing for specifics about the money."

"Honestly, Daisy, you read too much into everything." Mom glanced into the display case. "Did you make your molasses cookies today, Rachel?"

Rachel folded her arms over her chest and met my gaze. "I did. But you don't like them."

"Your dad loves them. I thought I'd get him a few."

"Dad is on a diet," Margaret interjected.

My sisters and I worked as a pack when we were on the hunt. And right now, Mom was our target. She knew something, and she wasn't telling. Mom always told and blurted. She'd never met a secret she'd wanted to keep.

"I thought I'd treat Dad to some cookies," she said. "He's been doing such a good job with his diet."

"All the more reason he shouldn't be eating sugar, Mom," I said. "What gives?" Rachel demanded.

"Nothing." Her eyes widened as if to add an air of innocence to the word.

"Mom, please," Margaret groaned.

"I've receipts to enter," I added. "Spill it."

Mom slid her hand into her back pocket and pulled out a letter. "I don't want you to worry. I know you're a worrier, and I don't want to add to your plate."

"I'll worry regardless."

"Mom, just blurt it out!" Margaret's voice snapped with impatience. "We are all big girls."

"You always did say it was better to rip the Band-Aid right off," Rachel said.

My mind skidded from one disastrous scenario to the next. Dad's heart. Balloon payment. Foreclosure. All the above. "Mom, if you don't start talking, I'm going to blow a gasket."

"Is it Daddy?" Margaret said. She sounded weak and scared. "Is his heart, okay?"

"No, no, your father is fine." Mom flicked the edge of the envelope with her thumb. "I received a letter a few weeks ago. I ignored it because I thought it was a bad joke. But I got another letter yesterday. It was certified. I had to sign for it."

The muscles by my left eye began to twitch. "It's the bank."

"No. Not the bank. Honestly, Daisy your whole focus is on money." I rested my hand on my hip. "It does make life a little easier, Mom." Mom was a lot like Rachel and Margaret. She was all about the creative side of life. She'd learned to care about money, but she'd never rivaled Dad in that department. Probably because Mom grew up in a normal house: two parents, two brothers, and no great tragedies to mar her perspective on life. She had a joy of living that could drive me crazy but also had kept me from really turning inward to wallow.

I was more like my father: Fancy ideas were fine and good, but the bottom line was if you didn't have the dough, it didn't matter. Dad's own father had died when he was just fourteen, and he'd put dreams of school aside and come to work in the bakery with his mother. By the time he was eighteen he was working eighty hours a week here. He had seen the bottom fall out of his life and understood it could happen again.

Renee had instilled in me that same lesson when she left. I might not have detailed memories of that afternoon but the fear that it could all fall apart had never left me. Money at least gave the illusion that happiness could be controlled, invested, and grown.

"What does the letter say, Mom?" A bit of impatience had crept into my voice.

"It's addressed to me, owner of the Union Street Bakery." She tightened her grip on the envelope as if she could seal its secrets in. "It's from a woman named Terry Miller."

"I've never heard the name," I said.

"Me either," Margaret said.

Rachel shook her head no.

Mom shoved out a breath and, in a rush, said, "She says in her letter that she visited this café thirty years ago. She said there was a young child left at the bakery. She said she knows the girl's birth mother."

In the *whoosh*, all coherent thoughts tumbled out of my head. There was the *tick-tock* of the cupcake clock on the wall behind me. The *drip, drip* of the coffeemaker and the thunder of my heartbeat rumbling in my ears. "Can I see the letter?"

The utter calm in my voice was astounding to me. I should have been ranting, screaming, jumping up and down at such a colossal moment, but I held onto the calm like a life raft.

Mom hesitated, then handed over the letter. "It's typewritten, but she signed it." I dug the letter out of the envelope. The paper's crisp folds reminded me of the way I creased my letters. Carefully, I opened it.

Dear Mrs. McCrae,

I see from the local directory that you and your husband own the Union Street Bakery. The listing does not say how long you've owned the bakery, but I was hoping you could help me. I visited the bakery thirty years ago. There was quite a bit of confusion the day I visited when a young child was found. Over the years, I have often thought about this child, and I'm interested in discovering her fate. I believe I know the child's birth mother. If you can help, I can be reached . . .

Sincerely,

Terry Miller

I reread the page at least three times before the room's deafening silence nudged me to look up. My mother and sisters were staring at me. They reminded me of deer caught in a car's headlights: wide-eyed, stunned, and anxious.

"Do you think she's my birth mother?" Handing the letter to Margaret, I let her, and Rachel read it.

"I don't know," Mom said.

"She doesn't admit to it."

Mom frowned. "No, I suppose she wouldn't."

"That would be admitting to a crime," Margaret added.

Rachel stared at the letter shaking her head as she read. "Why else would she ask about you?"

"I don't know."

Rachel carefully refolded the letter. "My girls are only five. I can't imagine leaving them alone for ten minutes, let alone just walking away from them. What kind of woman just walks away?"

Margaret uttered a curse. "I always forget you're adopted."

That surprised me. "You do?"

Margaret arched a brow. "You can be a pain in the ass, but you've been and always will be a McCrae. This woman doesn't change that."

I wished it were that simple. I wished I could just toss the letter and accept the fact that I did have a pretty good life. Yep, there'd been a few bumps/mountains to deal with lately, but the foundation Mom, Dad, and my sisters had given me were rock solid. In my brain I knew that. But it was my heart that was the stubborn holdout. Logical arguments and sane reasons why I shouldn't care about the woman who had left me just didn't make much headway with my heart.

"I wonder why she's looking for me?" I wanted to tread carefully. This was my family, and as much as I groused about them, I didn't want to hurt them with all my unanswered questions.

Mom set her jaw as she did when she was hurt. "I don't know. And honestly, I don't care. I know she might have been the woman who gave you life, Daisy, but I've been wanting to get my hands on her for more than thirty years."

The anger took me off guard. "Why?"

"Daisy, I've always prayed that you never remember the day I found you. I really do. Because it was not a good moment in your life."

We'd never really talked about that day. We touched on it a couple of times but that was a very long time ago and the story was always sugarcoated. *The day was lovely. You were nibbling on your cookies. You were such a happy girl.*

"What happened that day, Mom? And let's skip the *Father Knows Best* version."

Mom pulled off her glasses and stared into the lenses. Carefully, she wiped a smudge with the edge of her T-shirt. My sisters and I stared and waited. That day was as much a mystery to them as me.

"The bakery was packed. We were slammed, as a matter of fact. Rachel and Margaret were with your dad's mother, who was here for the weekend because it was the Easter rush. I knew I wouldn't have time to work and take care of you girls, so you were upstairs with your grandmother."

Mom and my grandmother had always been cordial but there'd been a distance between them as if they both were trying to ignore something unpleasant that had happened between them years ago. Grandma was kind to me, but I always felt like an afterthought to her.

"Of course, she was thrilled to take the girls. And I was angry and resentful. God rest your grandmother's soul, but she had a habit of making me feel as if I fell short. It gave her great pleasure to know I needed her help."

"I'm sorry, Mom," Rachel said.

Mom put her glasses back on and tried to smile. "I'm not sure where that came from."

Rachel gave Mom a hug. "It's okay. We get that Grandma had a different side."

We'd veered off the main path and were wandering toward a rabbit hole that would lead to nowhere. "Mom, about that day."

Mom sighed. "We were slammed, I was missing my girls, and I'm running around the café picking up plates and trash. I saw you sitting at the wrought-iron table by the fence. The honeysuckle was in bloom. Anyway, I noticed right away that you were alone. I stopped and glanced around the patio expecting to see your mother lurking close by. You know, dumping trash but still with one eye on you. But I didn't see anyone, and you looked quite upset."

"You said I was smiling."

"I only told you that, honey. Your little face was drawn up tight and your fingers in little fists. You didn't have a proper coat on, and your socks didn't match. So, I hovered and waited for another minute before I set my dishes down and went to talk to you. I asked you your name and you told me Daisy. When I asked about your mother, you said she was coming back soon."

I had no memory of that moment, save for the scent of honeysuckles and the sugar cookie sprinkles on my skirt.

"I asked if I could pick you up, and you said yes. You were as light as a feather and your legs were so chilly. You didn't feel like Margaret or Rachel. You didn't have their energy. Their weight. Their alertness. My heart broke. Dad came out about that time and saw us. I filled him in, and he called the police. They came right away and started a search."

"They never found her."

"Not a trace. There were folks in the café who remembered seeing her. Some said she had brown hair, was tall and thin and very young. Others said she wore a red sweater and had blond hair. The police told us later that eyewitness testimony was unreliable."

"You never told me that."

"It was all hearsay. And they never found anyone like her, so I thought they were just wrong."

"You said once the social worker tried to take me."

"She did. By then you'd fallen asleep on my shoulder. When you startled awake and saw the social worker, you started to scream. I'd never felt such sadness. I asked then and there if I could just keep you. I didn't even ask your dad because I knew it was the right thing to do." A wistful smile teased the edge of her lips and her expression transformed to one of pure love for my father.

"When the social worker started to argue, Dad intervened. He said you would be staying with us and called a friend of his in the district attorney's office. In the end you didn't leave."

She cleared her throat. "I gave you a bath that night and put you in one of Margaret's sleepers. You were already too tall for anything that belonged to Rachel. We fell asleep in the La-Z-Boy together."

Sudden hot tears stung the back of my throat. I'd spent a lifetime driving my mother crazy and confounding her on many levels but if not for her and dad. . .I wanted to lean over and hug her and tell her how much I really did love her. But the emotion got all tangled up in fear and hurt. A moment passed before I could speak. "You never heard from this Terry woman."

"No, I never heard from her. And the *Alexandria Gazette* ran several articles on you. It was never printed that we adopted you."

"Why?"

"That was my request. Of course, our friends and family knew, but I had this fear that if the information were printed, this Terry woman, or whoever she was, would just show up and take you. Silly, but I worried about that a lot when you were little."

"You never told me."

"I didn't want my worry to become yours." She tugged at the edge of her T-shirt and straightened her shoulders a fraction.

"You said there was another letter?"

"I burned it."

"Because it was vague enough that it could have been written with information from one of the old articles. And I didn't want to upset you."

"I wish you had."

She frowned. "Well, you've got the letter that really matters."

"Have you told Dad?"

"Not about the first letter, but he opened this one. He said you're a big girl now, and we should leave it up to you to contact her when and if you wish."

"Why isn't he here now?"

"I told him to let me handle it. I know Dad is like you. Emotions don't agree with him."

I couldn't fault him for that. And if not for him, Mom may have burned the second letter.

Curiosity warred with a deep sense of loyalty I had for my family. All those nights of longing for Renee a.k.a. Terry. All the unanswered questions about my past. All the hurt. This Terry woman could fill in so many pieces.

I folded the letter, skimmed my fingers along the crease, and tucked it back in the envelope. "I don't need to talk to her."

That wasn't true. I did need to talk to her. But I wouldn't dig for answers at my family's expense. I made a show of walking to the large trash can in the café, tearing up the letter and dropping the bits into the can. "I've got enough going on in my life right now. Terry can just wonder."

Calling her "Terry" gave me a bit of much welcome distance. In my mind she was Renee, not Terry. I *knew* Renee. I'd loved and missed Renee. Terry was a stranger.

Margaret shook her head. "You're making a mistake, Daisy. You need to call her."

"*Why?*" The word sounded as if it were torn from my

body. "Why do I want to see a woman who left me to fend for myself when I was just a baby?"

Margaret's expression held a hint of pity. "Because she's a piece of your puzzle, and you need her."

"I don't need her!" Too much anger leaked into the statement.

"I don't mean *need* in the sense of *Need*." Margaret's tone sounded adult and careful. "But there are basic considerations here. Like medical information. What if cancer runs in your birth family? You might be a McCrae in every sense of the word but genetically you're different."

"Thanks."

"Oh, stop being a drama girl about this," Margaret said. "This Terry chick might have valuable information for you."

Rachel laid her hand on my shoulder. Small fingers projected surprising strength. "One day you might have children of your own and you'll want to know."

"I'm on the no-kid plan, remember?" That point had been another bone of contention between Gordon and me. He'd dreamed of six children whereas I couldn't quite summon the excitement to replicate my unknown DNA. He'd never seen the logic, and I'd never been quite able to fully explain.

Rachel shook her head. "You have nothing to lose."

"Rachel," I said, "I'm holding on by a thread right now. I've lost my real job, my health insurance and my apartment, and my ex-fiancé just walked into the bakery yesterday."

"Your what?" Mom blinked.

"You were going to marry him?" Rachel exclaimed.

"Shit, Daisy," Margaret said.

"Never mind about Gordon. That's another day's drama. Long story short, guys, I don't have the reserves to deal with this woman now. I've got a full plate."

"But that plate might empty in the next few months," Rachel said. "When Mike died, it was all I could do to tie my shoes and brush my teeth. The idea of planning made my head hurt. In time though I not only managed the basics, but I could think ahead. That day is coming for you."

"My thoughts aren't going to change on this. I'm not calling her, and if she sends another letter then return it unopened. I don't care."

"Daisy," Rachel whispered. "Let us help you. Let me contact her."

"No!" And then more calmly, "No. I don't need any help, Rachel." I enunciated each word with cutting directness. "Honestly."

She shook her head. "Yes, you do."

Unable to summon another fighting word, I stormed across the bakery toward the front door. Nothing mattered right now. Not the letter, my family, not even the journal. All I wanted was fresh air to fill my empty lungs. I needed space. Silence. "I'll be back soon."

"Where are you going?" Mom said.

"Out. I'll be back."

Mom opened her mouth to say something else, but Margaret silenced her with a look. "Mom, not now. Daisy, we'll see you soon."

"Right."

The air outside had turned cooler, and the wind had picked up. Thick clouds promised rain. I crossed the outdoor café, wanting to put as much distance between it and me. The bakery was the last place I needed to be, but something tugged at me, and I stopped.

Hugging my arms around my midsection, I turned and stared at the uneven brick sidewalk now covered in a thick green layer of pollen. The pollen came every time this year, coating everything as it brought renewal, stirred allergies and created an endless need to dust. When I was a kid, I'd been the one to sweep the pollen. Now as I studied the faint coating of green dust on the patio, I realized Mom had been keeping up with it this spring. In the days since my return, I've been too busy to even step foot on the patio.

Stupid to care about the damn patio, but it made me wonder how much of my life I would miss because I'd be slavishly working in the bakery's basement or some new financial office.

A sudden urge rose in me. I wanted to pack my Toyota and just start driving. I'd always wanted to see Nova Scotia and Seattle and New Mexico. There was so much I wanted to do but work at Suburban and now the bakery kept me tethered.

Why couldn't I just break free and run away?

Because as much as I'd like to have packed up my car and driven as far away as I could from the bakery and Renee, I wouldn't. Yes, the bakery and I were shackled together because of finances and promises made, but it was more than that. I really was not so different than I was when I was seventeen. I may have crossed the Potomac to work but basically, I had lingered in the Washington, D.C. area because I was waiting for Renee's return.

And now she had.

And now I didn't want to see her.

A year ago, I'd have been in a better place to handle the letter. A year from now, I'd be back on my feet. But now. . .I was off balance, wondering who I was and how I was going to help support my family. Renee could not have picked a worse time.

I walked up and down the street, dressed in my jeans, sweatshirt, and flour-dusted kitchen apron. The air was chilly, the clouds above thick and dark with rain. I moved down Union Street toward Founder's Park, a small, grassy area that bordered the Potomac. It was less than a couple of blocks wide, but it was a welcome bit of nature in the city. Today, there was an ancient tall sailing vessel, a schooner I suppose that moored at the Queen Street dock. At one time there'd have been dozens of ships just like it in the harbor but now the ship was an odd, out-of-place visitor that no longer belonged.

On warmer days the park would have hosted children and tourists. But the cold and threat of rain had driven everyone inside.

Sitting on the park bench, I stared out at the water. The water rose and fell in short choppy waves. A sailboat, its white sails full of wind, passed by. The boat's captain had his face to the wind.

I was jealous. He looked so free. And I felt anything but free.

I wasn't sure how long I sat on that bench. I think I'd have stayed all night—but then a fat raindrop plopped down on the seat beside me. Another and then another fell. The sky was about to open. And as much as I wanted to remain, I had to get back. Like it or not, I had a life that needed tending.

Halfway back up the street, the rain started to fall faster and faster and by the time I reached the shop, I was soaked. Water dripped from my sweatshirt, my hair, and my eyelids. My shoes squished and slurped with each step. It was past three and the front café was quiet. The shop was closed for the day. The front window sparkled, the floor swept, and the display case cleaned out and ready for tomorrow's baking.

I'd forgotten how peaceful the place could be at this time of day. This morning had been chaos and tomorrow would bring the same bedlam but for now it was so orderly and perfect. When I was a kid, I'd snag several cookies that had not sold, and I'd slip into the closed café after school and just read. Breathing deeply, I had to concede the bakery wasn't all bad. It did have its moments.

I moved past the trash can toward the counter. There was a blue plate sitting on the counter, which held two carrot cake cupcakes. A smile teased my lips as I moved behind the counter and picked up a cupcake. Carefully, I peeled away the baking paper and bit into the moist cake, savoring the bits of raisins, carrots, and the cream cheese icing. Rachel knew her carrot cake cupcakes were my cure-all.

Halfway through the cupcake, I glanced toward the trash can.

Shit. I'd made such a show of ripping up and tossing away the letter. At that moment I really didn't want anything to do with it or the sender. But now that a little time had passed, I wasn't sure of anything. What if . . .?

The trash bags should have been dumped in the Dumpster in the back alley. It wouldn't be too hard to dive in and find the bag.

I glanced toward the back door, which led to the alley. "Damn."

No, look. It's still here.

The feeling made no sense and still I set the cupcake down on the plate, glanced around the café, and out to the street to see that no one was watching. Then I moved toward the can, half hoping it had been dumped and half praying it had not. I peeked inside the lid.

The can was full and untouched. The other can was empty and had a fresh garbage bag liner but this one was as I left it.

Mom and my sisters. They hadn't dumped the trash, and, knowing them, they'd have left the can untouched and un-dumped for days. They knew that eventually, despite protests, I'd want the letter.

I lifted the lid and found the pieces of the letter lying on top. Carefully, I collected, folded and then shoved them into my back pocket. The bulk pressed into my backside as I crossed the café and ducked behind the counter to wash my hands in the sink and grab the cupcakes.

In my room, I sat on my sofa bed and ate, uncaring of

calories or protein exchanges or how much exercise it would take to mend the damage. I just didn't care right now.

I spotted Susie's journal sitting on the center of my unmade bed. I didn't remember leaving it there.

Dealing with anyone's past life or secrets right now felt too overwhelming. I just didn't want to deal.

Quietly, I picked up the book, which felt heavy and awkward in my hands. I carried it to a small box of books that remained packed in a copy box and stowed in a dim corner. I pulled off the lid and gently set the journal on the stack. I dug the torn letter from my back pocket and laid it in the box as well. The journal had been hidden for over 150 years and Terry has waited thirty years to write her letter. Leaving it unread a little longer wouldn't matter in the big scheme of things.

I closed the lid and backed away, carefully and slowly as if I'd just witnessed a great car accident. "Not today, ladies. Not today."

Sinking down onto the mattress, I barely noticed the squeak of the bedsprings or jab of the spring in my fanny. Already the mattress and I were becoming far too familiar with each other.

I plucked the last cupcake from the plate and bit into it. Carefully I peeled the pink paper from the cake and then gently licked icing from around the edges. Though it was my second cupcake, it still tasted as sweet and sinful as the first.

It also tasted of denial and fear.

At best, eating was a temporary fix. I knew, like the journal and letter, my problems waited for me, like specters in the shadows.

But for now, I was willing to settle for some sweet denial and benign procrastination.

Chapter Eight

SATURDAY, MARCH 27, 2010, 9:00 AM

Over the next few days, the bakery's hectic pace made it easy to almost forget Terry's letter and Susie's journal. Gallons of buttercream blended with endless columns of red and black numbers and temporarily quieted the jabbing thoughts during the daylight hours. On Saturday, Brad Foster, my pal from Suburban, pushed through the front door of the bakery. He wore a pink polo, collar popped up, ironed jeans, and shiny loafers without socks. This morning I'd managed to brush my teeth and hair and was feeling snappy until I saw him. I longed for the days when I wore pressed jeans, heels, and makeup.

I tossed him a bright smile as I came around the counter and gave him a hug. The soft scent of Armani aftershave drifted around me. "Brad. What a nice surprise."

He hugged me back. "You smell like cinnamon."

I tucked a curl behind my ear. "Hazard of the trade."

"I like it."

"What brings you to my neck of the woods?"

"Had to see how the other half is living. Plus, I told you I'm addicted to those carrot cake cupcakes."

I waggled my eyebrows. "They're still as great as you remember."

"Good. Set me up with a dozen."

I strolled around the counter. I was the only one manning the fort today. Rachel had a kid thing and Margaret had a cemetery tour that she'd been planning for months. It took some hustling to get the customers served this morning, but I was amazed at how fast I'd settled back into my bakery groove.

Pulling a box from under the counter I reached for the first cake. "A dozen cupcakes, Brad? You won't be keeping that girlish figure of yours if you eat twelve."

"I'm having a party this evening. It's for Dan, the account rep who got laid off last month. He bought a one-way ticket to Alaska and is starting over."

"Wow. Alaska." I pictured snowcapped mountains, cold, and elk. "That's bold."

"Tell me about it."

I carefully aligned each cupcake, knowing presentation was almost as important as taste.

"You said you wanted to be an ice road trucker. Ever considered joining him?"

He laughed. "I talk a mean game, but I'm too much of an office boy. You hear Roger moved to China?"

Mention of Roger had me cringing. I never liked that guy. "Yeah. Teacher, right?

"Yeah. Looks like I'm going to leave the bold moves to you, Dan and Roger."

Bold moves were often born of desperation rather than a quest for adventure. "That's nice you're giving him a party."

"Thought the cupcakes would be a nice surprise. It will remind him of what he's leaving, plus it will give me a chance to let folks know how you are doing."

I carefully folded the cupcake box closed and tucked in the

flaps. "I doubt any will ask, Brad. The Suburban blow up is already old history."

"Don't count on it. Gordon's fuckups were spectacular. Legendary. Everyone felt like you really got reamed."

My hand stilled for a moment. It was one thing for me to bitch to myself about Gordon but to bad mouth him to others, especially chatterboxes like Brad, didn't set well. "It wasn't all Gordon."

"Hey, I know you two had a thing, but the guy f-ed up."

Brad hadn't done the closed-end fund sector any favors in the last six months. Word was he'd had significant losses. I thought about Gordon down the street in his bike shop and understood now why he didn't bother with newspapers or contacts with the old world.

"One day I expect we'll open a dictionary and see the word *Surbanized*. Meaning to blow up or destroy. You were right to dump him when you did. Did you ever hear what happened to the guy? He just fell off the radar."

Carefully, I placed a gold USB sticker on the box. I'm sure Gordon didn't need my protection from the likes of Brad. Gordon was fully capable of taking care of himself, but I did feel something for the guy. Soon enough, folks would know about his new business. "I've got my hands full with my own life, Brad. That will be thirty dollars."

He pulled out two twenties and laid them on the counter. Buffed nails caught the morning light, and I found myself curling my own dried and cracked fingertips away from him.

"So, are you loving this place?" he asked.

"It's a lot of work, but it has its moments." I made change and placed it in his palm.

He stepped back and scanned the cupcake clock and the display case filled with goodies. "I should try something like this. Maybe not as extreme as Brad's move north but I should do something."

I wondered if he saw the walls needed a paint job, small crack in the display case glass, and the cupcake clock was ten minutes slow. "Are the new Suburban owners making noises about more changes?"

"No. They seem happy to keep me and the remaining skeleton crew around."

"So, you're not under the gun."

"No, thank God." He looked at me. "I mean, I'm not as adaptable as you."

"You might surprise yourself." *Especially if you get fired.*

He accepted the box. "I just might try something new one day."

"Well, if you do go into business for yourself, the new paycheck just might give you sticker shock." I'd doled out paychecks yesterday to Rachel and Margaret but had held mine so the money could go toward the plumber who'd come to look at the water heater.

"Yeah, got to be rough. You were making good dough before."

"They say you can't put a price on love, and they are right."

He laughed. "Don't suppose you'd be interested in another job in finance."

"Who's asking?"

"I heard Simon Davenport is looking for finance people."

"Really?" He was a new developer on the scene and had offices near Old Town. "I've heard he's a ballbuster—not that that is necessarily a bad thing."

"He's got one of the few growing businesses in the area."

"You should apply."

"I did. Didn't get the job." He grinned. "So much for my big stab at independence." The faint scent of his Armani after-shave mingled with the aroma of confections. "But he might have something for you."

"A job with Davenport would put you back in the old grind, just like the old days."

"Yeah." I couldn't decide if that was good or bad. "Thanks again." He lowered his voice a notch. "Did you get your money okay?"

"I did. Thanks."

He studied the café, and again his gaze grew wistful and lost.

"Hey, if you need more help financially, I could help you out." I held up my hand. I was flattered, hurt and pissed all in a flash.

"Thanks, Brad but we're good. Things are really clicking along now."

That night, a hot bath eased my strained and tired muscles and sent me into an initial deep, drug-like sleep. These blissful hours were as close as I came to peace. Sleep lately was short lived, and never lasted until the alarm clock.

At two a.m. I sprung up fully awake, my heart racing, the panic rising in my chest hot and furious. When I'd been at Suburban, and it was all falling apart I often woke in the middle of the night. In this witching hour, my mind revved on overdrive, and I thought first about the business. Had we sold enough the day before? Was the new sound in the oven just a rattle that comes with the temperature change outside or was it a harbinger of something more sinister? Was I too abrupt when I said no to the lady with red hair who'd wanted a wedding cake in two days?

And then I thought about Simon Davenport. If Davenport was hiring, could I juggle working with him and the bakery? Margaret juggled. God knows Rachel juggled. Why couldn't I?

I turned on my side, adjusted my pillow, and curled up in a C-shape, staring out the window toward the bright stars. The daily worries gave way to older ones. With a one-two quick-step, my brain jumped back to the long-ago day in the bakery when I'd sat alone, half-eaten sugar cookies on a plate and red sprinkles dotting my yellow skirt.

"Damn." I rolled on my side and readjusted sheets, vowing never to drink coffee after three p.m. again.

Why had Terry written now? Thirty years and now she wanted to connect? Was she dying? Did she need a kidney? Was she sorry? Of course, I had no answer, but right now stewing was preferable to knowing, which might bring more pain than I could handle.

"Why haven't you read my diary?"

"Because it's next to that woman's letter, and I don't want to see it."

A presence in the room gained strength, and I felt a warm breath on my ear, and the tap, tap of her finger on my shoulder. I smelled honeysuckle.

"Read it."

"I don't have time to read your book."

"You are avoiding me."

"Leave me alone."

"Not until you read my story." She pinched my arm. Hard.

I flinched and rubbed the flesh, amazed that it hurt so much. My brain buzzed and ticked through the details of the coming day as I glanced at the clock hoping it read 3:44. Nope. It read 2:44.

No wait. It's Sunday. I don't have to be anywhere. Crap.

Irritation snapped. I had hours of more sleep to enjoy. I needed sleep. I needed to shut down. I laid back and closed my eyes. I did deep breathing exercises. Counted sheep. Punched my pillow and rolled on my side. But nothing coaxed me back to sleep. I was too jazzed.

"Read my diary!"

"Leave me alone."

"Not until you read."

Muttering a curse, I sat up and clicked on a side table light and padded over to the box I'd not opened in three days.

I reached inside for the journal, careful not to let my fingers skim Terry's letter. I was still not ready to open that Pandora's box, but I could look at the diary.

Sitting back on my bed cross-legged, I gently open the front cover.

To S. With love, J.

Over 150 years and so many lifetimes separated me from S and J. I still didn't understand why Mrs. Woodrow would want me to have this mystery. Clearly the old woman had made a mistake. Better to just read the journal and give it to Margaret.

I knew your mama . . . your other mama.

The words clanged and rattled in my head. If only the old lady had lived a few more days. Then I could have taken Terry's letter to her and asked more questions: Was Terry my mother? Was she the woman you saw me with all those years ago? If only Mrs. Woodrow had mentioned my other mother's name. Just a name would have clarified so very much. If only...

I glared at the journal, which I now associated with the letter. There was no logic in this thought process. One had nothing to do with the other. But that didn't make it any easier for me to separate the two.

I opened to a random page.

It's hot work by the stove in the cookhouse behind the master's house. This morning, I was put in charge of making breakfast for the house. Even as I struggled to coax the embers to life and bank the fire, I was grateful I knew how the oven worked. Mistress says I am of good use to her for the first time ever and that I might be worth keeping.

I burned my arm on the cast-iron pan as the flat cakes cooked. The injury stung something awful even after I rushed outside and pumped cool water on it. The cakes burned and, nursing my burn, I had to scrape hard to get them off the pan's bottom.

When Mama got home long after the sunset, I followed her into the kitchen and showed her my burn. I wanted a bit of sympathy, a hug, or praise for the work I did in the master's house. But she had none to spare.

I cried and wailed and tried to show Mama my burn again and again, but she wasn't the least bit kind about my injury.

In fact, the red burn that slashed across my forearm seemed to make her angry. She says Master will have more reason to sell me if I am so clumsy around the stoves. And if the wound were to go sour, I could lose my arm or die.

Then she did unwrap my bandage and looked at the burn. She promised to find herbs tomorrow and make a poultice.

When I repeated what the mistress said about me being of use, she tossed me a bitter smile.

"Make no mistake, girl, she would sell me or you in a heartbeat. The woman has not liked either of us since the day she first stepped over the front threshold."

I pressed for her to explain but she would not. She slumped in the wooden kitchen chair and in silence ate her hard tack smeared with bacon grease. Whatever had happened that day had drained her of all energy and vigor. I asked her about her day, but she said it was none of my concern.

For the first time, my mama looked old.

The kid had been having trouble with her mother. Not what I needed right now. I replaced the journal in the box, dressed, and headed downstairs to the bakery. Fuck it. It was

Sunday but there was always work to be done. At least I knew I could get a little peace of mind working.

To my surprise, I found Henri standing by the large mixer, lovingly feeding flour into his dough. I nodded a greeting to him. He grunted back. Stumbling over to the coffee machine, I filled a USB mug and sipped. Hot and strong, the coffee gave me a much-needed boost. "You know it's Sunday, right?"

"Oui."

I pressed the warm mug to my temple and closed my eyes as I ticked through the day's tasks and listened to the *whirr* and *thump* of the dough mixer. "Why are you here?"

"Baking helps me think."

"Ah." Who was I to argue? We were two peas in a pod. I moved toward a pallet of newly delivered supplies. Sugar, rye flour, and even some of that organic flour Rachel had lusted over at the beginning of the week. I could do inventory. It would save Rachel and me time tomorrow. I set my mug down, content to let Henri bake while I assembled and organized.

We worked in a companionable silence for a half hour before he spoke. "Your sister can't do this alone."

I was shocked that he had spoken a complete sentence. I didn't think he'd ever said so many words to me before.

I turned and found him still hunched over his mixer, his gaze squarely on the dough in the industrial stainless bowl.

For a moment I paused, not certain I'd heard correctly. "Did you say something?"

His downcast gaze didn't flicker, but he raised a gnarled hand to the mixer's speed control. It slowed so he could be better heard. "She's creative, perhaps one of the most talented bakers I've ever known. But no businesswoman."

"I know. Believe me, I know." I didn't approach him because it still felt odd to be having a real conversation with Henri. Most days it was: "Hey!"

Grunt.

"Thanks!"

Grunt.

"Have a good evening."

Grunt.

He grabbed a handful of flour and sprinkled some into the mixer. "So, you will stay?"

I took a tentative step toward him. "For now."

After a moment's hesitation, he said, "I will be leaving soon. The time has come for me to retire."

My mouth dropped open, and then I snapped it closed. "What?"

"I am leaving." His voice didn't waver, and I knew the decision was firm.

I closed my eyes, torn between begging him to stay, wishing him well, and wondering how much more could go wrong. "When?"

"Two months. June."

At the rate the bakery was going, I wondered if we'd have the money to stay open that long. And a part of me was glad Henri would be gone so he didn't have to see the bakery fail.

If we made it to June, I was not sure how we'd make it without the bread. Summer sales were always higher and there'd be no getting by without Henri.

All these thoughts clanged and rattled like the chains of a ghost but all I heard myself say was, "Thank you for staying this long."

He glanced at me with red-rimmed eyes. "I stayed for your parents and Rachel."

"I know."

He sniffed and straightened a fraction. "But you are here now."

Laughter rumbled in the back of my throat. "Everyone keeps saying that."

He shifted a squinting gaze at me. "You will fix things."

I sipped my coffee and wondered if this kind of news warranted an Irish coffee.

"That's asking a lot."

He shrugged.

The utter calm in my voice truly amazed me. "I don't suppose you know of a baker I could hire?"

He turned back to his dough, his stooped shoulders telegraphing his age more than ever. "I will think about that."

"Great." I gulped the rest of my coffee and finished putting away the supplies. I found my way to my office, which now had some semblance of order. I spent the next half hour online, checking our accounts. Ike's check had cleared and still the bottom remained in the black, if only just barely. Two days ago, I'd asked Margaret to really start tracking what sold and didn't sell before she hauled the day's leftovers to the food kitchen. We needed to separate our moneymakers from our duds.

My request had prompted Margaret to roll her eyes and grumble but so far, she'd kept an accurate tally. I hoped in the next two weeks to have a snapshot of what sold and what didn't.

With Tax Day looming, I had gotten on the phone a few days ago with the bakery's accountant. He'd told me he'd filed an extension for the bakery, confident that we had not turned a profit, and had said that I could take the next month gathering all the paperwork. It appeared Rachel's tax system involved dumping receipts in the desk's bottom drawer. I was able to excavate through the receipt layers like an archaeologist at a dig and entered them in my favorite spreadsheet program. Slowly I was piecing together the last year's finances. Each day I dug a little deeper, hoping I'd hit the drawer's bottom.

My cell on my hip vibrated, and I checked the time. Three thirty.

The alarm was always set. As Dad used to say, "A baker never sleeps."

I shut it off and went back to work. It was just after seven when I'd made a second pot of coffee. Henri had finished his random baking, and I'd managed to pull together the tax receipts.

When I heard footsteps behind me, I turned to find Rachel. She'd washed her face and pulled back her hair. I handed her coffee. She sipped it, a moan of gratitude rumbling in her throat as she took a second. "When did you become a morning person?"

"I'm pretty sure it's a fluke. In fact, you just might find me in the fetal position around two o'clock this afternoon."

"You just might find me curled beside you." She closed the door softly behind her. Secured on her hip was the baby monitor she kept in the bakery in case the girls woke up.

So why are you moving so slow?"

"Dreams of Mike. I dreamed again he was alive."

She'd had those dreams a lot in the months after his death. Mom had told me she often woke up crying and disoriented. "I'm sorry."

"Sometimes the dreams are so real I can smell the scent of his skin and feel his knuckles skimming my cheek. When we were married, he always brushed my cheek before he left for the bakery and told me he loved me. Last night I could have sworn his spirit was here."

Color warmed her cheeks as if the statement embarrassed her.

I cocked a brow. "Please tell me he's not haunting the place."

She blinked as if that were the last comment she expected. "Why would you say that?"

I glanced toward the ceiling. "This place seems to be full of odd energy."

"What kind of energy?"

"Hard to say."

Her gaze narrowed. "You deal in numbers, facts, and figures. You're not making sense."

I pinched the bridge of my nose and wondered if I were more rested if I'd have started this conversation. "I think two ghosts in one house are quite enough."

"Two ghosts?" Now she was smiling.

It was good to see her smiling, and I didn't feel so much like a fool for voicing my thoughts. "That's right. Two. A good one and a bad one."

Really?"

"Yep."

She leaned forward, cradling her cup. "Do tell."

"I could swear I've felt two ghosts." I sounded insane but let's face it, I was insane for tackling this bakery manager job. "I know this sounds pretty odd."

She raised a brow. "Reminds me of when you were a kid, and you'd sit in the corner of our bedroom and chat with someone."

"Who?"

"Beyond me. But I think you introduced us once."

I grinned. "Did I?"

"Yep. Her name was...Sally...Sara...I think it started with an S."

"Susie."

"Yeah, that's it. And according to you, she'd lost her mother like you'd lost yours. I told Mom but she said she figured it was just your way of coping with the big changes you'd gone through."

I didn't say anything for a moment. It could easily have been explained away as a childhood fantasy. No one would have blamed me. I wouldn't have blamed myself. But it wasn't a fantasy. That much, I was sure.

"You said two ghosts."

"Yeah. One good and one bad. The bad one doesn't like me so much. He wants me to leave."

Rachel cocked her head. "What did you say to the ghost to make him mad?"

"What makes you think it's my fault? It could just be a bad ghost."

She dropped her voice a notch. "Daisy, you have a talent for irritating the living like no one I know. I love you, but you can be prickly. Stands to reason you've found a way to hack off a few dead people."

I laughed. What was there to deny? I did have a sharp tongue. "It's a talent. What can I say?"

Monday morning was a replay of last Monday. Rachel and I worked in the bakery with Henri, and Margaret stumbled through the front door ten minutes after seven. I'd given up expecting Margaret to arrive on time. Ten minutes here or there didn't matter as much to me as it had that first day. Quirks went hand in hand with this business. Besides, Margaret really was great with the customers. She not only knew all by name, but she remembered their likes and dislikes. And new customers to the store, tourists, visitors or businessmen, quickly felt as if they'd been Union Street Bakery customers for years, thanks to Margaret. So, I let the ten minutes roll.

Rachel, with her pastries and kitchen, was content. Left to her own devices, she'd never enter the bakery office again. And other than her daughters, I'd started to wonder if she cared much about the outside world.

Rachel created, Margaret greeted, and I managed. Between the three of us we made a whole baker. It all felt kind of normal and manageable.

Yet rumbling under the surface of all this calm was Henri's plans to retire, which he'd only discussed with me, the oven that needed coaxing and the water heater that kept tripping the breaker. I also was going to have to have a sit down with Rachel and discuss the menu. We had key items, though delicious, that were time consuming to make and expensive. If they'd been selling well, I'd have let it ride but so far, the molasses cookies, pumpkin bread, and peanut butter bars had to go. Rachel thought of each item as one of her babies, and she would not be happy.

No matter how smooth the waters, there were always sharks under the surface waiting to snap.

I'd forgotten that Mabel Woodrow's funeral was today until Mom breezed into the bakery at eleven and reminded me. Margaret and Rachel had remembered but the detail had never taken root in my brain.

"I can't believe you forgot," Margaret said. "Groovy hair, Mom."

Mom has been to the salon to get her hair done in a style that was a little too formal for my tastes. She gingerly touched the side of her up-do. "Thanks, honey."

A customer entered the shop, and we all grinned. Margaret greeted while Mom followed me to the register.

"You need to go."

"I'm busy. Cut me some slack." I wiped my hands on my apron and punched the Sale button on the register. The drawer popped open, and I started to pull out extra cash for the afternoon deposit. "I kind of thought I'd just hold down the fort."

"No. You're coming." She glanced to a woman wearing a business suit who was ordering sugar cookies, smiled and lowered her voice. Oddly, Mom was more threatening when her voice was low and controlled. "Mrs. Woodrow's funeral promises to attract half of the city. The pews for the one o'clock church service will fill quickly, so we need to leave early."

"Where's the service?" I asked as I arranged all the bills face up.

Margaret handed the lady her change and tossed me a glance that shouted, "Moron!"

"Christ Church," Mom said. "I told you that. And Dad has decided that the McCrae clan should gather at the bakery thirty minutes beforehand and walk the five blocks to the church."

"We won't get a seat," I said.

I considered reminding Mom that she and Dad were in their seventies and didn't walk that fast, but I decided not to go down that path. "Shit."

"Daisy, manners."

"Fine. I'll be ready."

It was a warm spring day and being outside should have been a treat, but I was already feeling the exhaustion creeping into my limbs. I should have slept late yesterday. Or taken a nap. But I'd worked on quarterly taxes most of the day. I'd need a double shot of espresso before I headed upstairs to shower.

After the morning rush, I snuck back to my office and worked on supply orders and arranged the few catering contracts Rachel had signed. By the time I glanced up at the clock I realized I was totally out of time and had to run upstairs for a quick shower.

Stripping as I moved across my apartment, I dropped my clothes and dashed to the bathroom. I turned on the shower and as the water heated, I brushed my teeth. When steam rose, I jumped into the shower, expecting to stay seconds, but the hot spray tempted me to linger. Heat and the steady beat of water worked tension and fatigue from my muscles, and I couldn't help but close my eyes. For a moment my mind drifted.

She wrapped long fingers around my small hand, and I had

to hurry to match her long strides. My feet hurt and the air was cold. All I wanted to do was get back in our car and sleep under my blanket.

"Daisy, you need to hurry. If we're late, the old lady won't see us."

My eyes snapped open and immediately I shut off the water. The memory was so real and tangible it felt like I'd just tripped back in time. Who the hell was the woman speaking to me?

Squeezing my eyes shut, I willed the memory to replay but no amount of coercion, begging, or pleading would bring it back.

"Damn it." I shut off the water, shoved wet hair out of my eyes, and snatched a towel off the hook on the bathroom door. Dry, I dashed naked across my bedroom, and dug panties and a bra from a garbage bag crammed full of clothes I'd yet to unpack. I scrambled into my undies, reached for another bag and dug through layers of clothes, wishing I'd taken some time to unpack. Why was it that I could drop my savings into the business, commit to finding a replacement for Henri, but couldn't unpack?

By the time I'd started to rummage through the second bag, a bead of sweat had formed on my upper lip. I muttered curses until my fingers brushed my favorite simple black slacks. Next, I hunted for a clean white shirt, which I discovered was badly wrinkled. More digging produced a black sweater to cover the worst of the wrinkles.

I brushed my damp hair out, slicked it back in a neat bun at the base of my neck, and secured it with a large clip. Makeup remained nowhere to be found so I settled on dark sunglasses.

Three months ago, I'd never have dared go to work with a wrinkled shirt or a makeup-free face. But my life was no longer my own and vanity had taken a hit for Team Daisy.

"Daisy, are you ready?" Rachel called up from the second floor.

"I just need shoes." I tossed off the lid to the box marked *Shoes* and dug out a pair of kitten heels as well as a red scarf. Shoving swollen feet already accustomed to clogs into the heels, I hurried down the stairs.

Rachel stood with my two nieces. All three looked so pulled together. Rachel had washed and dried her hair and it now curled nicely above her shoulders. She wore a black suit, a yellow silk handkerchief in the breast pocket, white knit top, hose no less, and heels. The girls sported matching yellow dresses that had white bows around the waist. White patent leather shoes and lace socks completed the look.

This was the first look I'd had of the girls since I arrived. I'd heard them run past my office door a couple of times, but I'd been too busy to say hi. I'd promised myself that when Sunday came, I'd take them to the park, but they'd been playing, and I'd been doing taxes. I was starting to understand now why we hadn't seen so much of Dad when we were kids.

"Boy, you girls sure do look fine," I said.

Ellie smiled sweetly. "Thank you."

Anna studied me with eyes that hinted of an old soul. "Your shirt is wrinkled."

"Shh," I said. "Don't tell Grandma." I buttoned the sweater up to the top and looped my long scarf around my neck. "There, is that better?"

Ellie nodded yes. Anna shook her head no.

Both girls giggled, and we headed down the stairs. Halfway down, I said to Rachel, "How do you do it? You are so together."

She smoothed her hand over her skirt. "This is what I wore to Mike's funeral. It's been in the closet untouched, and Mom took the girls shopping yesterday."

The mention of Mike made me sorry I even asked about

the clothes. I didn't want to upset Rachel or bring back reminders of that very dark time. The mood leading up to Mike's funeral had been so different. We'd all been numb, walking around trying not to show our sadness for Rachel's and the girls' sakes. The kids had been about three and a half and they'd not really understood what was happening though each saw the tension in their mother's eyes. By the end of that day, Ellie couldn't stop crying. And Anna had been so angry she'd refused to put on her pajamas until I'd offered a chocolate bribe.

When we'd buried Mike, a cold rain had drizzled, and the February air was cold and raw. When the casket had been lowered into the ground, we'd all just turned and driven back to the bakery. All the McCraes had sat in the front café. I'd been the one who went behind the counter, made coffee, and scrounged the cookies Mike had baked just two days earlier. Our lives had turned on a dime. And no amount of planning on my part or Rachel's could have stopped it. Downstairs, we found Mom, Dad, and Margaret in the front café. Margaret wore a black peasant dress with a brightly colored vest, Mom had pinned a bright blue pin to the lapel of her pantsuit, and Dad wore a red tie. Wearing a hint of color to a funeral was a McCrae family tradition. We wore black to symbolize the sadness of the life lost and the color to recognize the gifts that the departed had brought to us all. I can't say exactly what gifts Mrs. Woodrow had brought into my life but

I had to concede that ninety-nine years of living was no small feat.

"Chop, chop, girls," Dad said. He clapped his hands, winked at Ellie and Anna, and the McCrae unit departed. While Mom, Margaret, Rachel, and the girls lagged a little behind, my normally quick pace started to put distance between us. Dad caught up to me. "I'm still good to see the books?"

"Two weeks."

"Thirteen days. You going to be ready?"

I tossed a wide grin. "I was born ready, Dad."

He did his best to keep his tone casual. "If you don't want to wait the two weeks, we can do it tomorrow."

"Nope. Two weeks is good." I adjusted my scarf. "Don't you just want to let go and rest a little? If this last week has taught me anything, you deserve it." He snorted. "Retiring is a bit like severing an arm."

"Letting go of the bakery? You're kidding."

"Just wait. You'll see. It works its way into your blood."

"Not mine."

He raised a brow. "What did you do on your day off?"

Frowning I glared at him. "I worked, but only because I needed to get caught up."

He chuckled. "That's what I said at first."

"I'm different."

"Not so much, kiddo."

Mom snaked up behind Dad and patted him on the back. "Tell me you are not talking about the bakery."

"No harm in that, Sheila," Dad said.

We walked as a group the five blocks to Christ Church. A brick- and-wrought-iron wall surrounded the pre-revolutionary church and a grove of trees shaded the courtyard from the busy street. Raised beds were filled with bright flowers, and the heavy scent of boxwoods hung in the air. Sandstone grave markers eroded by time and weather dotted the yard. Margaret once said that over time many of the graves had lost their markers, and the ones that hadn't succumbed to weather's blurring effects.

We arrived just as a very large group of mourners gathered at the back door. When they didn't move forward, Mom whispered, "I knew the church would be packed."

"She knew everyone," Dad said. He shifted his shoulders

and his jacket stretched tight across his back. He'd had this same suit since the seventies and though Mom had bugged him about getting a new one, he refused. According to Dad, there were better things to buy. Water heaters and mixers came to mind.

Finally, the group ahead was able to move inside, and we found a standing spot in the aisle near the pulpit. The church's interior was ten degrees cooler than outside.

"Does anybody see Henri?" Dad asked.

I scanned the room and spotted Henri across the room in a back pew. He stared ahead, his shoulders back and straight. "Looks like he got one of the last seats in the house."

"Good," Dad said. "I know his back has been bothering him."

Gauging by the tone of Dad's voice, I sensed he knew more about Henri's health than I'd first thought. "Should I tell him we're here?"

"No," Dad said. "He'll insist on giving his seat to Mom or one of you girls. Let's leave him be."

The priest stood in front of the altar wearing his finest vestments, and the soft murmurs in the church ceased. Behind the priest, two dozen choir members, dressed in red robes, smiled serenely at the crowd.

"There must be two hundred people here," Mom said.

Dad shook his head. "Honestly, I'm surprised there aren't more people."

Including my birth mother? The thought clanged in my head as I scanned the crowd again. Did Miss Mabel really know her? Could the two women have known each other well enough that Renee or Terry would attend the funeral? My heart thumped a little faster, and I couldn't decide if I was angry or excited.

If we're late, the old lady won't see us.

As the minister cleared his voice and began to speak, I

found myself tensing. I recognized a lot of the people. They were bakery customers, high school friends. or folks I passed regularly on the street. I could recall some names but most I couldn't have summoned without prompting.

I searched beyond the inner ring, hoping that perhaps Renee or Terry or some woman who looked like me might be standing back, perhaps even searching for me. But hats and dark glasses obscured most of the distant faces.

A breeze carried the strong fragrance of the gardenias draped around the pulpit.

A large black-and-white picture of Mabel Woodrow had been placed at the front of the church. The photo appeared to have been taken when she was in her twenties. White organza and dark curls framed a heart-shaped face, and her smile enhanced a clear, direct gaze filled with energy and vitality.

According to the priest, Mabel had been born in 1910 to a working-class family. She had two older brothers, attended the area high school, and unlike her brothers, attended two years of college. In 1922, she'd married Henry Woodrow, an Alexandria man of privilege and means who had chosen the military as his career. They traveled the country, moving from military base to military base and by all accounts were a happy couple, even though their marriage was never blessed with children. At the outbreak of World War II, Henry was stationed in Italy and Mabel went to live in the Alexandria house that had been left Henry by his parents. During a battle in northern Italy, Henry had suffered a head trauma from shrapnel, and when he returned home, he was never quite the same. Mabel cared for him until he died six years later.

Mabel had lost her two brothers to heart disease in the last two decades, but she'd remained active in her niece's and nephew's lives. Up until the last few years, she'd dedicated herself to volunteer work, splitting her time between different children's charities. Everyone, it seemed, loved her.

She'd been all but invisible to me when she'd come into the shop last Monday. I'd not seen past her wrinkled skin and gray hair or my own fears and frustrations. Now as I looked at the picture, I glimpsed an interesting woman who'd lived nearly a century in a house only three blocks from the bakery. Until this moment, all I'd known about her was that she'd liked sweet buns and could ramble about my other mother.

The choir sang "Amazing Grace," and the piercing notes of the organ rumbled through the pipes and filled the sanctuary. The scent of gardenias weighed heavily in the stone church.

As if Margaret had heard my thoughts, she whispered, "She loved gardenias. I brought her one for her birthday last November."

"I bet she liked that," I said absently.

"She seemed to." Margaret sighed, no hint of anger in her. In fact, I detected a little sadness when she said, "Beats me why she gave you that journal."

"Me too." I glanced out the small side window beside me at the headstones. "Do you think S or J could be buried here somewhere?"

Margaret shook her head. "I doubt S is buried here. If she were a slave and had managed to live and die in this town, she would have been buried in Freedmen's Cemetery or another African American cemetery—and that's assuming she even died in Alexandria."

"Where's Freedmen's Cemetery?"

"Off Washington Street. They put in a memorial park there a couple of years ago and did some archaeological work. Some of the cemetery was destroyed by development and most of the gravestones were lost."

"What about J?"

Margaret glared at me. "Let me read the book and maybe I

can figure out who J was. Then I might know. Have you even read it yet?"

"No."

"God, Daisy why?" Her voice raised a notch.

Mom shot us both a look. We were in our thirties, accomplished for the most part, and Mom could still reduce us to a couple of twelve-year-olds with a single glare.

I winked at Mom and joined in on the song's chorus. When Mom dropped her gaze back to her hymnal, I whispered to Margaret, "I will soon. I promise. Did you ever find your notes or tapes of your interviews with Mabel?"

"Not yet but I only have a couple of more places to look. It's odd I can't find them. I'm normally good about organizing historical stuff."

Mom cleared her throat. That ended all conversation.

"Ladies and gentlemen, we are here today not to mourn but to celebrate the life of Mabel Ann Samson Woodrow." For the next forty- five minutes, folks climbed up into the wineglass pulpit and shared stories about Mabel, who'd been one of the first women in the city to own a car. She'd also run for office, written for the local paper, championed literacy centers, and marched in the sixties' civil rights rallies.

She'd had such a rich and full life, and yet I'd not really *seen* her the day she'd come to the bakery. She'd been a frustrating annoyance. A guilty sigh rushed from my lungs. I couldn't do anything for Mabel, but I could at least read the book she'd given me.

"Are you around this evening?" I asked Margaret.

Margaret looked toward Mom and then me. "Yeah. Why?"

"I'll bring the journal. We can read it together."

Dark eyes brightened. "Done."

Chapter Nine

SATURDAY, MARCH 27, 2010, 6:00 AM

Margaret lived in a basement apartment located in a narrow town house on Prince Street. The building had loads of charm: windows that stretched from hardwood floors to ten-foot plaster ceilings, fireplaces with carved mantles, and rooms trimmed with ornate crown molding. The place was a sublease from some professor on sabbatical in Greece. A real find, Margaret had always said.

To me, the space was dark and dank. The low ceilings, the exposed brick walls, and the wide pine floors made the place feel cold to me, whereas they charmed Margaret. I couldn't stand that the place was below ground level, and her single street-facing window offered only views of the sidewalk and passing feet. The building, built by a sailing merchant in the eighteenth century, was loaded with history and that meant more to Margaret than the place's unbeatable rent.

As I moved down the four steps to her front door, balancing my purse in one hand and burgers and shakes in the other, it struck me that we'd both been banished—me to the attic and she to the basement.

Loud music drifted through the door. I knocked on the door.

Once. Twice. By the third time, the music dropped, and footsteps clicked on the interior's pine floors. Locks released and unlatched, and Margaret opened the door. "I didn't think you'd ever get here. What took so long?"

Shoving the food tray into her hands, I moved past her. "I came as quick as I could. There always seem to be details in the office."

She slurped one of the milkshakes. "Don't tell me. That business stuff gives me a headache."

Shrugging off my jean jacket, I draped it over an overstuffed chair upholstered in a red-checked print. "Seems it gave Rachel one, too. You've both done a fine job of ignoring the business side of things."

Margaret sat the food on a coffee table. "It's just not my thing. And I told Mom and Dad that from the beginning. Me Worker bee, you Queen bee."

"Very funny."

The small living room was furnished with an old couch covered in a quilt, a coffee table made from an old door, and two red winged back chairs. The furniture arrangement was nestled in front of an unusable brick hearth, which was filled with unlit votives and topped with a gilded mirror that caught the scant light trickling down from the street. Bookshelves crammed with more books than most libraries owned stood shoulder to shoulder over a cranberry wall.

Margaret sat cross-legged on her sofa, and I took one of the wing chairs. "Thanks for the grub. I'm starving." She unwrapped and then bit into a sandwich. "So good."

"It's a new sandwich place on King. I'll admit to doing a little recon thinking one day they might want USB to supply their bread."

"Thinking ahead. I like that." She picked a pickle off the

sandwich and ate it. "So, is balancing the books really that bad?"

I unwrapped my sandwich and smoothed out the wrapper. "It's a hornet's nest for sure, but I've untangled it for the most part. The tricky part will be getting us from red to black."

"Does Dad know?"

"He does not, and don't tell him because I think I can salvage the mess."

She dabbed a paper napkin on the corner of her mouth where a splash of mustard had parked. "I won't tell Dad a thing if you promise me one thing."

"I'm not sure I like the sound of that."

She met my gaze. "You need to promise that you're not going to quit."

I hesitated, waiting for the punch line. When none came, I said, "I thought you were the one who bet I wouldn't last two days."

She slurped her shake. "Seeing as I've lost the bet, you might as well stay." She glanced at her sandwich. "Are you thinking about leaving?"

"Believe me, it has crossed my mind many times. But no, I'm in it to win." Setting down my sandwich, I wiped my hands, dug out the journal, and set it on the coffee table. "Here ya go."

"I was trying to be polite and not ask but I was about to bust."

"I guessed as much."

Margaret set down her burger and wiped her hands on her napkin.

"You read it?"

"Just a page or two."

"How you can hold off not exploring such a treasure is beyond me. I've fantasized, plotted, and planned about sneaking into your room and reading it. What took you so long?"

I bit into my sandwich. "I've been busy."

"It's that letter, isn't it? From that Tracy woman."

I pulled a pickle from my burger and laid it on the wrapper I'd stretched out on the coffee table. "Her name is Terry. And I don't care about her."

Margaret stirred her shake with her straw. "Please. I saw the look on your face. You looked like you'd been punched in the gut."

I picked at the edges of my burger. "Can we not talk about the letter?"

"We need to talk about it. Mom, Dad, and Rachel are afraid of upsetting you; I, however, am not the least bit afraid."

That startled a laugh. "So, I've noticed."

"Don't you at least want to know if she's your birth mother?"

"I don't need to know her." The words stumbled off my tongue and

landed flat. "I have a mother."

"You can bullshit yourself but do not bullshit me. I know you love Mom, but I know you're curious about this Tammy chick."

"Terry."

"Whatever. She owes you answers. Like when your real birthday is and does cancer and stuff run in the genetic line."

"I've lived this long without that information. I can live longer without it."

She set down her milkshake. "I remembered when you'd cry as a kid on your birthday."

Tension and sadness fisted in my gut so tight it was all I could do not to double over. "Do you want to talk about the journal or not?"

"I do. But I'm more worried about that letter."

"You're more worried about the letter from a stranger than a journal from the 1850s. Now who's in denial?"

Margaret released a sigh. "It's pointless to talk about the letter, isn't it?"

"Yes."

She wiped her hands on her paper napkin. "Then let me first tell you what I found."

"Yes. Believe it or not, I'd filed them in my office. I never file anything in its proper place because I just know where I keep stuff. But I'd filed the tapes."

"How many are there?"

"About ten hours. I had a chance to listen to the first tape, which runs an hour. Want to hear a little bit?"

"How does this relate to the journal?"

"Wait and see." She dug a tape recorder out from under the couch.

"Ready?"

"Hit me."

She hit Play.

My grandmother was born in 1840 right here in Alexandria. She never talked much of her own childhood, but she did once mention a friend of hers named Susie.

"No shit," I said.

Margaret stopped the tape. "I know. I just about shit a brick when I heard it."

"Play on."

Margaret pressed Play again.

My grandmother often spoke of this young friend of hers who was a young slave, born to an enslaved woman from Loudoun County. The girl had heard that her mother had been a pretty woman. Fair skin, pale green eyes, and high cheekbones had turned many heads, both white and black. The slave from Loudoun was intended to be a gift to her new master's fiancée, whom he'd be marrying within the year. At first the master had treated his slave fairly, but as the months passed his taste for the bottle became apparent. When he drank, his mood shifted from jovial to sullen. They never spoke of what happened in those early days but just after the master's marriage to his wife, folks in town notice the slave was with child.

"Read between those lines. The guy raped her," I said. Margaret nodded.

The slave gave birth to a healthy girl with a hearty appetite. From her birth, the slave baby thrived and both mother and child often received extra looks or stares from black and white folks alike because they were so handsome. Let me also say that the mother was known in town for her baking skills, and many would have gladly bought the mother for her kitchen skills, but her owner had refused all offers. The master's refusal to sell fueled all kinds of rumors that didn't please his wife. After the slave mother, however, suffered her burns, folks no longer cooed but shied away from her.

About this time the master decided to lease his slave to a local baker. No one ever had asked the slave if she wanted to work in the bakery; she was expected to obey. So, the mother and her three-year-old daughter began daily treks to the bakery for a twelve-hour shift. This leasing arrangement went on for almost fourteen years and though the baker paid generously for her services, the slave woman never saw a penny of the money she earned. All earnings went to her master and his gambling debts.

"What a dick," I said.

"Tough times," Margaret said.

Each morning before dawn, mother and child would make the three-block walk to the bakery. In the bitterly cold months, the duo would don every stitch of clothing they owned to ward off the biting winds from the Potomac. The little girl often said how she hated these mornings and how she longed to stay in her attic room nestled on her pallet under her blankets. But her mother had convinced the master to let the girl to tag along so that she could learn baking skills that would one day be of great value. Mother would often say to her child that the coldest days on the street were safer than the master's house. Only when the child became a woman herself, did she realize her mother feared her master and his wife.

And so, they made their morning predawn treks in the dark. The girl spoke of shoes that were too large and a sole that wobbled when she walked. There'd been talk of sending the boot to the cobbler, but the sole was never fixed. To make the trek more arduous, the girl's hand-me-down calico dress's long hem was forever catching on the boardwalk's roughest planks. So, as she hurried to keep pace with her mother, she was forced to lift one foot high, hold her skirt up, and clench her button-less threadbare coat closed with her other hand.

"Poor kid."

Margaret paused the tape. "It wasn't common to invest money in slave clothes unless they worked in the front of the house and were on display, so to speak."

"Shit."

"I know."

"So is it kind of weird that Mabel is talking about a slave, and she had a slave journal."

"Interesting, isn't it. But let's not assume. Mabel never

mentions family names in her talks with me and Alexandria was a huge slave trading port at the time so we could be dealing with two different girls."

"Yeah, but . . ."

"We need evidence."

I shrugged. "What's the deal with the boardwalk?" I asked.

"At the time there was a long boardwalk that ran along Union Street. From the boardwalk there were massive piers and warehouses, which housed all kinds of businesses. The area was a bustling place in the 1850s." She hit Play.

The girl often spoke of how fearful her mother was of not only her master but of whites in general. She feared being late to work, she feared ruining a batch of biscuits, and she feared saying the wrong thing. Mother and child had both heard tales of other slaves in Alexandria being sold to traders in the Deep South.

Mabel paused; it sounded as if she took a sip of water.

The girl, like all slaves, feared the Deep South, which was filled with cotton plantations and fancy houses. Slaves who went to the South often were subjected to backbreaking work, brutal conditions, and a drastically shortened life.

Margaret stopped the tape and fast-forwarded it. "She talks a little about the city and the ships, and commerce of the time, the railroad, and the pressure to keep up with the Port of Baltimore before she gets back to Susie." She hit Play again.

When the little girl turned ten or so, the baker, a widower, reported that his own daughter had been stricken with measles. Friends and church members stayed clear of the house, fearing the illness. The slave girl's owner, seeing an opportunity for income, proposed to the baker that Susie could sit with and tend the daughter. The baker, relieved to have a caregiver for his child, agreed and so the girl became nursemaid to a child not more than a year or two older than she. Many had believed both girls would perish but the slave girl nursed her charge with care and never got sick. Both survived, and the girls became fast friends during the months-long convalescence.

"Help me out here."

Margaret shut off the tape. "Shoot."

"This girl was born to a slave, but her father was a free white man.

"Why wasn't she free?"

"It was the mother's status that mattered. If she was a slave, all her children would be slaves regardless of the father's position."

"I thought that relations between master and slave went on a lot. I would think the wife of that time would accept it."

Margaret arched a brow. "Would you like knowing your new husband was sleeping with a teenaged girl who lived right under your roof?"

"Point taken."

"History may change but emotions don't."

I frowned. "How did Susie's mother get so badly burned?"

"Hard to say. Kitchens were a dangerous place in those days." She sighed. "I want to dig deeper, and I'm hoping the journal will tell me who owned Susie. If I can figure that out, then maybe

I can link the tapes to the journal. And if I can do that . . . I might finally have a dissertation that I can sink my teeth into."

I'd not seen Margaret this excited in a very long time. "You said there are more tapes."

"Yes. They don't all have to do with the slaves, but I'll listen again to be sure."

"Well, the journal is all yours. Have at it." I'd taken the time to wrap it in cloth and then slip it into a gallon-sized zip-top bag. Preservationists likely would have cried their outrage at the book's treatment.

Nodding, Margaret wiped her hands again on her napkin and jeans and pulled a set of cloth gloves from her pocket. "Smart move."

"Do you always carry cloth gloves?"

"Not always." She grinned and then took the book and reverently held it between her palms. She studied the first pages. "Looks like everyday life."

"So, no great epiphanies."

She arched a brow. "The epiphanies are in the everyday notes. How people lived, what they did during their regular lives is what fascinates me. I'm only concerned about the big moments in history when they affected everyday life."

"I don't care about piecing history together. I just want to know what happened to Susie."

"Why?"

"I don't know." Staring at the worn book, I tried to picture the little girl who had held it more than 150 years ago. "I just feel like I need to know—that I'm supposed to know."

"Supposed to know? Why?"

Somehow talking to Margaret about my ghostly/imaginary friend sounded ludicrous. "Your guess is as good as mine."

Margaret gently turned the pages as she scanned the scripted words. "The journal only covers a year. And then it just ends."

"There are a lot of blank pages remaining. Why would she just stop?"

"Back then, who knows? Maybe she died. Maybe she was sold. Could be a lot of things."

Her frown deepened as she read more. "I doubt things went well for her."

"Why would you say that?" I was really rooting for this kid now.

"It was 1852. She was a slave. A female. The cards were stacked against her."

"Do you think you can find her?"

When Margaret sat back on her couch, her cheeks were flushed with excitement. "Let me read all the entries and see what I can figure out."

"But you can find her."

"That's one hell of a needle in the mystery haystack."

It wouldn't take much to get Margaret to bite on this job. This kind of detective work was what she lived for. "So, you're saying that you can't find her?"

Margaret stared at the journal, her gaze a mixture of excitement and joy. "Please. You are dealing with the master when it comes to this kind of stuff. I'll find her."

Waking ten minutes before my alarm was becoming the norm. My eyes popped open, and my mind was sharp with a maddening clarity. It could just as well have been the middle of the day and I could have been sitting at my desk at Suburban. Only I was being weighed down by a sleeping bag and backstabbed by a sofa spring. Both were reminders of where I really was, and that realization drained the spark of energy from my bones. And suddenly all I wanted to do was go back to sleep.

I blinked, rolled on my back, stared at the cracked plaster of the ceiling and practiced the deep breathing my therapist had mentioned to me on several occasions. I'd not seen Dr. Myers in five months, and I did miss his calm, sane approach to life. Like so many other luxuries, he was another casualty of my job loss and vanishing benefits.

"Daisy why do you feel like you have to fix the world?" Dr. Myers said. "I don't know. I just know it needs to be fixed."

In and out I breathed. One. Two. Three. Seconds passed. I breathed more, but nothing happened. The clock read 3:22. One minute had passed.

"I am the glue," I said to Dr. Myers.

"What do you mean?"

"I'm the one who must keep my family together."

"Why is it your job to keep the family together?"

"I don't know. I've always felt in charge of keeping Team McCrae on task."

"Margaret doesn't fret over the details. Rachel doesn't get mired down in this burden."

I shrugged. "I guess because I can't lose another one."

"Another what?"

"Another family."

He stared at me directly. "Daisy, you're not the reason your birth mother walked away. You could not have stopped her."

"Maybe if I'd been a better kid, she'd have stayed."

Annoyed at the thoughts, I rolled on my side, hoping to look out the window and catch a glimpse of the stars and moon. Instead of light, I saw a dark figure standing by my bed.

I bolted upright and tensed. It was the other one. The bad one had returned.

The figure had no defined face or structure, but I knew it was a man. And though he stared toward the window, hands clasped behind his back, he was here for me. He possessed great patience . . . and great anger.

I blinked, hoping he was the residue from a dream I'd already forgotten. He would vanish once I stopped clinging to the warmth of my bed and let the morning cold bring me to full consciousness. I shoved long fingers through my hair, cleared my throat, and stood slowly. The sleeping bag dropped away, and the cold floor made my toes curl. "I'm awake now. You can go."

But he didn't fade, even as a chill puckered my skin with gooseflesh.

The figure didn't turn or speak, but continued to stare, the silent sentinel. No words were uttered, and I tried not to let crushing fear take root. "You're the one who was here before. You were angry."

He didn't acknowledge my comment.

"So, you want to tell me what this is about? Or better yet, who you might be?" My hoarse whisper cut through the morning stillness and sounded a bit ridiculous.

My bike started to rattle and shake and then fell to the ground. Books flew off the shelves.

Stomach churning, I glanced toward the door. "What the hell is this about?"

Silent and still, the figure continued to stare forward and without a word spoken I knew he wanted me to leave. *Get out.* I could almost taste his impatience.

"When or if I leave, it will be on my terms, not yours."

And then in a blink, he faded, like a cloud caught in a heavy wind, scattering and fading so quickly that I would have doubted his presence if not for the tumbled bike and books.

Heart racing, I dug fingers through my hair. No threats or declarations were needed to rattle my cage.

I hurried toward the window where he'd stood. The air was cold and the glass icy to the touch. I padded back toward my bed and clicked on the side lamp. I winced at the light and waited as my eyes slowly adjusted and focused. My back and shoulder ached from sleeping on the sofa and I felt scared and annoyed. The alarm on my cell shrilled and I quickly grabbed it and shut it off.

The presence of this ghost left me with a clear message: *Tread carefully.*

Chapter Ten

TUESDAY, MARCH 30, 2010, 9:00 AM

Tuesday morning, Gordon stood in the center of the bike shop surrounded by dozens of unpacked boxes. The store wasn't slated to open for a couple of weeks, but at the rate he was going he'd be lucky to make the deadline. He wanted to hire help to finish with the unpacking and the stocking of inventory, but he flat out couldn't afford it.

The front money he'd sunk into this business represented the last of his net worth, and he'd be damned if he'd borrow a dime to make this dream happen. He'd invested and lost fortunes in the last year. His decisions, which he'd thought so sound and solid at the time, had lost untold amounts of investors' funds, jobs, and ultimately the company. He'd fucked up so much.

Too many nights he'd lain awake in bed staring at the shadows dancing on the ceiling, bargaining with God for a reprieve. *Take whatever you want from me. Just get me out of this fix. You can take my sight if you can save the others. You can . . . if only . . .*

The bargaining, worrying, and gut-wrenching panic had

gone on for nearly a year. And in the end, God had not swooped in and saved him. God had left him out on a limb as if to say, you made the mess so you can clean it up.

He could argue that everyone who entered the stock market assumed risk. It wasn't like investing in a bank account. It wasn't safe. But after so many years of wins and gains, he, like everyone else, had forgotten just how easily and cruelly the market could turn. Too much success had allowed them all to lower their guards.

He'd left Suburban knowing the owners could sell to buyers who could infuse enough cash in the company so that the employees would have severance and his client's accounts would not be completely gutted.

He'd paid the price for his choices—both professionally and personally. He'd kept the "patient" from dying, so to speak, but the "cure" had caused untold pain and suffering that would never be forgotten.

When he'd left Suburban, he'd sold what he had. Car. Condo. Art. Furniture. Basically, whatever he could find a market for, he sold. In the last decade, he'd made millions and spent and lost millions.

As he'd ridden cross country, pumping his pedals, staring at asphalt and dodging cars for four months, there'd been time to work his body to exhaustion, talk to the demons, and beg for forgiveness. He'd slept in bad motels, churches, the homes of random family members and friends.

His body had gotten stronger on the trip. He'd argued and talked to the demons until he was hoarse, but forgiveness was something that still eluded him. No matter how many miles he put on the road, he still would be the guy who blew up Suburban.

Scraping together the bits of money that remained after the trip, he'd had just enough for a year's rent on this place and the remodel job. The marketing plan would be word of mouth and beating the pavement.

The bells chimed and he turned to see Daisy walking into his shop.

She'd twisted her dark hair up into a curly topknot. Clogs, faded jeans, and a Union Street Bakery T-shirt had replaced her trademark sleek heels and suits. Her body still snapped with energy, but it didn't feel as frenetic as he remembered. Since her Suburban days, she'd put on a few pounds, but he found the extra curves appealing.

She carried a large white box tied with a red bow and marked with a gold sticker. "I have your order," she said.

For a moment, he didn't know what she was talking about. And then he remembered: He'd gone by the bakery hoping to see someone who could tell him something about her. All he'd known about Daisy's past was the photo of her parents standing in front of the Union Street Bakery.

When he'd come face to face with Daisy, he'd been stumped. Caught short. So, he'd placed an order. What had he said? Investors coming by the shop?

"Right on time," he said. No investors were coming.

"We aim to please." She set the box down on the front counter and handed him a sealed envelope. "Your invoice."

"Thanks. Can I drop off a check tomorrow?"

"Sure." She glanced around the shop. "This is a surprise."

He found himself analyzing her tone.

Was it a good surprise or a bad one? "Time to start over."

She skimmed her fingers over the chrome handlebars of a beach bike. "Ready or not, right?"

"Your job at the bakery isn't a new start?"

She shrugged. "More like back at square one."

She was a hard woman to know. She kept her barriers fully intact every waking minute as if she expected an attack. When he'd first met her, he'd been intrigued by her coolness and drawn to the challenges she presented. Most women he'd met fell for him easily. He was the golden boy with the golden touch and women flocked.

But not Daisy. Never Daisy. She seemed to have cared less if he lived or died when they'd first met. She was focused on work and work alone. And for several years, they'd worked side by side. He'd dated other women. She'd dated a couple of guys. And their paths had just never crossed.

And then they'd been at the Christmas party a year and a half ago and he'd been just buzzed enough to ask her why she'd never hit on him. She'd laughed. And walked away.

And of course, he had followed and asked the question again. "Why don't you hit on me?"

There'd been a hint of glitter in her makeup. "Because you expect it."

His reserve was relaxed. "What if I wanted to ask you out? Would you say yes?"

Boredom, not interest sparked in her gaze. "Ask and you shall see." He'd felt so clever, as if he'd breached the outer shell. "Well?"

"Well, what?"

"Will you go out with me?"

She sipped her wine and glanced around the room as if she was on the lookout for someone more interesting. "Where?"

"I don't know."

She paused, the glass just below her lips. "I guess you assume that most chicks will gladly go out with you."

His ego had taken the first jab then. "Most do."

She sipped her drink, making him wait. "I don't do half-assed requests."

"I'm asking you out," he said, as if those words had been explanation enough.

"Really? Because I'm feeling a little like sloppy seconds." She

shook her head. "I don't like sloppy seconds, so if and when you want to ask me out like you mean it, I might consider it."

And she'd walked away, not even bothering a glance back in his direction. Two days later, he showed up in her office with tickets to a concert and dinner reservations. She'd agreed to go out with him. Their relationship quickly exploded with great sex. Within a month of their first date, they'd moved in together.

Now, Daisy glanced around the shop at the collection of boxes, her gaze searching and critical. "Looks like you've got work ahead of you."

"I do. But I'm glad for it. Feels like I'm really doing something these days. Not just pushing paper anymore." He didn't want to talk about himself.

His interest was in her. "Do you still have that bike I gave you?"

"I do. Though I've not ridden it much."

"Bring it by; I'll tune it up for free."

"Thanks." Absently, she spun a bike wheel.

"When did you move back into town?"

"A couple of weeks ago."

He half waited for her to ask him about his return and when she didn't, he said, "I've been back about a month. Kind of odd we'd both end up here."

"Not for me. I grew up here."

That was part of the reason he'd chosen Alexandria. He'd sensed that if he'd opened his shop here that sooner or later, he'd see her. "So, are you here to stay?"

A small smile tugged the edge of her lips. "I'm out of here as soon as I can get help for Rachel."

"Oh."

"You don't happen to know anyone who would like to work long hours at the bakery for free, do you?"

He tried not to smile. "No. Sorry."

She shrugged. "If you do, let me know. Until then I'm stuck."

"I'll keep my ears open."

"And if you need more cookies, let us know. We deliver."

"Thanks."

She started toward the door. It was almost like when they first met.

Him curious, her aloof. It didn't matter that they'd lived together for six months, talked of marriage, made love. He could almost say they'd landed back at square one.

But they'd never really see square one again. There was nothing fresh or new about their relationship now. It was tarnished and piled high with baggage. He could have kept playing cat-and- mouse, but they weren't in middle school. And he was too old to play games. "Do you ever think about me?"

She turned and faced him. Curling wisps of hair had escaped the topknot and framed her face. She looked younger without makeup. "I try not to."

He folded her arms over his chest, unable to let this go. "But you do?"

"Sure." She shoved out a sigh. "We had a good thing for a while." Anger he'd long buried under so many other emotions clawed to the surface. "I never figured being engaged would scare you so much." She was silent for a moment. "I didn't realize how bad I was with long-term commitments until then."

"You've never made a long-term commitment?"

"Never. I dated you longer than I dated anyone else."

He leaned toward her. "You're the one who first mentioned marriage."

She nodded, glanced at the ceiling and then at him. "I know. I know. I thought if I could do it with anybody it would be with you. But I'm not so sure it's in my DNA to marry."

"That sounds like bullshit."

She swiped a stray strand from her eyes. "Nothing lasts forever, Gordon. Nothing. I realized that to promise love and fidelity forever was foolish and unrealistic. I couldn't make a promise I couldn't keep and knew it was better to just cut ties. Believe me, I did us a favor. Five or ten years down the road, when it all blew up, it would have been more painful."

He offered a wan smile that likely showed more bitterness and hurt than joy or acceptance.

"Anything can last if you want it to."

A bitter smile tips the edge of her lips. "Wanting, praying, hoping, working, is never enough.

Believe me, I know."

* * *

Do you think about me?

Gordon's words lingered in my head for days, revisiting and buzzing around at the most inopportune times. Why would he ask me something like that? We'd been over for almost a year, which was longer than when we were together.

His question had caught me off guard like a right hook to a glass jaw. *I try not to.*

As I sat back in my office chair, the words were an admission that I had thought about him. And I had. I did. A lot. What I hadn't told him was that not thinking about him was much like stopping a moving train. It couldn't be done, no matter how hard I tried or no matter how much I wanted it. And when we first broke up, I didn't have the energy to stop the rumbling thoughts that just bowled right over me. In those weeks and months, all I could do was curl up on my rented couch and cry. I'd left him and yet I'd felt abandoned. Had I expected him to follow? That had been one of Dr. Myers's questions when I'd sat on his couch sobbing.

Finally, memories of Gordon had lost their sharpness and eased into a dull ache. In the last few months, thoughts of him still could be prickly but they no longer knocked the wind out of me. They'd become like buzzing bees, and I'd learned if I was very careful, I could swat them away without being stung.

Do you think about me?

It was the question I'd wanted to ask him for almost a year. But I never had, and I never would. The wounds were nearly healed, and I didn't want to open them again.

"You wanted to see me?" Rachel asked.

"Yeah," I said, straightening. "We need to talk about the bakery product list."

She stiffened. "What about it?"

I reached for my spreadsheet. "I've had Margaret tracking what sells and what doesn't."

She frowned as she took the seat next to my desk. "I noticed that."

"We've got to cut 15 percent off the menu. And based on the numbers, I'd say we must cut the pumpkin bread, molasses cookies, and prune tarts."

Her face paled. "So, you're going to cut just like that?"

"No. You're the baker so it makes sense that you should decide. I'm just reporting what products are the least productive."

Rachel folded her arms over her chest. She shook her head. "We can't cut anything."

"Why not?"

"Because it's all great stuff."

"I agree that it all tastes amazing. But we need to cut costs. We can't support an expanded menu right now. Period."

She shook her head. "No."

"Rachel, why are you so upset? This is business."

Tears welled in her eyes. "Those were selections that Mike added. He was very proud of them."

I had just stumbled into a minefield. "Don't you think Mike would be looking at these numbers now?"

"This whole place would be different if he were here."

"But he's not, honey. We've got to decide."

"Not me. I can't cut."

I pulled off my glasses. "Well, if you don't want to cut menu items, we could always buy less expensive ingredients such as margarine."

The latter amounted to sacrilege in Rachel's mind, and predictably, her mouth dropped open and her eyes spit fire. "What!"

"I don't like it any better than you, Rachel, but we must cut something. The overhead is too high, and seeing as I can't cut staff, I've got to look at the menu or the ingredients."

She rose to her feet her fists clenched. "This is bullshit, Daisy. You have no right to mess with Mike's and my bakery."

I knitted my fingers together and kept my voice low. "Why are you so upset?"

"You're cutting into my life now. And I resent the hell out of it."

Fatigue, irritation, and my own insecurities had me rising to her challenge. "I wouldn't be doing this if you'd managed it properly. But you've damn near driven this place into the ground, and Mom and Dad have brought me in to fix it and I am going to fix it."

Her lips thinned. "I can't believe you're being such a bitch."

"I'm treating this place like a business, not a day-care center where the kids get to play with any toy they want. If we don't make changes, we won't survive."

She raised her chin. "When Mike and I ran this place, we made the menu work."

"Did you? That's great." I refused to mention that I'd had to make the bakery a loan eighteen months ago after Mike's death because the numbers were hemorrhaging even then. "Rachel, Mike is gone, and it's my job to clean up the mess."

"This is bullshit."

I'd never seen Rachel so emotional or upset. "Grow up, Rachel. Choose what needs to be cut or I will."

"I could quit."

"Really? And where would you go? Face it, sister, we're all shackled to this place, and we better start bailing because the boat is going to sink if we don't. Do you want to move and take Ellie and Anna from their only home?"

Tears glistened in her eyes. "No, of course not."

"Then start making decisions."

She studied me. "Is this what you were like at Suburban?"

"At times." I put on my glasses. "I'm not having fun here, Rachel. Not my idea of an ideal day."

"Fine."

"Fine what?"

"I'll cut 10 percent."

"Fifteen."

"Fine!"

She stalked out of my office in such a huff I couldn't decide if I should laugh or cry. Rachel and I had always gotten along, and I was surprised by her reaction to my request. "Shit."

Another knock on the door had me turning to find Mom. Crap.

Not now.

"Have you read the letter yet?" Mom's voice reverberated from my office door.

I focused back on the bakery ledgers, hoping somehow if I looked at the numbers long enough, she'd disappear.

"Daisy."

"Mom, I must finish my work."

My work. My invoice piles. My office. Somehow in the last

ten days, the work and space had become mine. The tasks and space no longer felt foreign or like a shoe that didn't fit. Bit by bit, paper by paper, as I organized Rachel's chaotic mess, I made the space and duties mine. Rachel might have fought tooth and nail for her menu, but she no longer asked if she could help me sort through papers as she'd done the first days. Now she simply placed her receipts in my new inbox and tiptoed out.

Oddly, I'd organized it just as I had my desk at Suburban Partners: computer just right of center, calendar to my left, and pending files stacked like stair steps to my right.

Mom didn't leave. She waited and hovered, relying on a lifetime of wearing me down with her stare.

"Mom, I'm right in the middle of balancing the accountings." And Rachel is pissed, and I don't need this right now.

"You're always busy. Every time I've tried to talk to you in the last couple of days, you hide behind work."

The air in my office suddenly felt old and stale. "I'm keeping the place going, Mom. It's not like I'm goofing."

Mom's stance was unflinching. She wasn't going anywhere. "I get that honey, but you need to read that letter."

I tossed down my pen. "You sound like Margaret. And Rachel."

"And Dad. But he's not saying it to your face. We want you to read that letter."

"Why?" The word telegraphed more meaning than it should. *Do you want to get rid of me? Don't you really love me? I thought I was a real McCrae.*

"Honey." She dropped her voice a notch. "Don't you want to know what happened and why?"

My chair creaked loudly as I swiveled abruptly toward her. "What exactly do you think I'll learn? Say the woman is my birth mother. Say she's legit. What would I say to her: 'Bitch, how could you leave a three-year-old alone in a crowded café?

How could you just walk away from your kid?'" Anger coated each syllable.

Mom nodded. "That would be a good start. But of course, you could leave out the bitch part."

"Why? She's a bitch."

Mom eased into the seat next to my desk like a homesteader staking a claim. "For one, I raised you better than that. And two, she might not be a bitch. She might have been a scared kid."

My throat tightened with tears. "Mom, you and Dad *raised* me. You didn't have to step-up, but you did, and though I don't say or show it much, I know you did a good job. I don't see the point in talking to this Terry chick."

Mom ran her finger over the edge of my desk, brushing away the dust. "You need to face her, honey. She's been a demon in the shadows too long."

I thought about the real demon in the shadows that had visited me twice. "A demon in the shadows? Have you been watching Oprah again?"

"No. Well, maybe a little, and maybe I picked up a thing or two about adoptions and maybe I even read a couple of books on adult adoptees."

"Why?"

"For the same reason I read about young widows and single girls in their late thirties who only care about history. Because you are my child, and I care about you."

"Mom, I appreciate your efforts. I do. But I did get shitcanned three months ago, and I'm kind of back to square one career-wise. Kind of a stressful time for me. I don't need more drama, especially from a woman who abandoned me."

She patted my knee. "I don't agree. You need this. You need to talk to this woman. You are *off*, and I don't see any signs of it getting better."

"Like I just said, it's been a hell of a year."

"You've been off long before you lost your job. Since last summer."

When I broke up with Gordon. When I realized I wasn't destined for long-term love. I folded my arms over my chest and leaned back. "I'm not off."

She sighed. "Just read the letter. And if you won't do it for yourself then do it for me."

"You? Why?"

Mom pulled a picture from her pocket and handed it to me. It was taken of me when I was about three and a half. Dark curly hair framed my round face, and I sported a purple backpack, hand-me-down red shorts, a Scooby-Do T-shirt, and white sneakers.

"That was taken six months after you came to live with us. It was your first day of preschool. You were so damn proud of that backpack that you slept with it for the three nights leading up to school. Even on your first day of school, the teacher said how smart you were."

Tears tightened my throat. The only thing I remembered about that day was a pair of toy binoculars in the classroom. I fell in love with them and wore them all day.

Mom cleared her throat. "When I turned to leave you that day, you panicked. You ran to me, grabbed my legs, and started crying."

I didn't remember.

"I kept promising I'd be back, but you wouldn't hear of it."

I traced the halo of curls around the little girl's face. That little girl smiled a lot because she needed people to like her. On some level, she understood if people liked her, they'd keep her around and that she'd be safe. Somewhere along the way she grew up and stopped smiling. She turned prickly, determined to scare off those who might be worthy of love.

"What did you do?"

"I sat in the hallway just outside your room. The teacher agreed to keep the door open so you could see me."

"You sat there the whole time?"

"All three hours. And every five or ten minutes, you would get up from whatever you were doing and look out at me. I remember you wore those goofy binoculars around your neck the whole morning."

"How many days did you have to do that?"

"Four. By the last day, you'd stopped checking."

"I didn't know that."

Mom slid small fingers into her jeans pocket. "I need to know why Terry left you. I need to know why she'd just walk away. I want to find a reason to forgive her."

Heaviness settled in my chest. "I'll think about it."

"That's a, yes?" she persisted.

"It's a maybe."

As she opened her mouth to argue, Margaret appeared in the doorway.

The excitement on Margaret's face mirrored the little girls in the picture. "You're not going to believe what I've found."

I was almost afraid to ask. "What?"

"Information on Susie."

Chapter Eleven

TUESDAY, MARCH 30, 2010, 2:00 PM

"I read the journal twice," Margaret said. "Incredible."

"What happened?" I leaned back in my office chair, grateful to see Margaret. The calvary had arrived and saved me from Mom's questions.

"What are you two talking about?" Mom asked.

"The journal Miss Mabel gave to Daisy," Margaret said.

Mom arched a neatly plucked brow. "Mabel gave Daisy a journal?"

I filled her in on the details, which only seemed to make her frown deepen. "Why would she do that?"

"We've no idea," Margaret said.

"Mom, did Mabel ever say anything about me?"

Mom shook her head. "She showed an interest in all my girls."

"Did she ever say anything about my birth mother? Did she ever mention Terry, perhaps?"

"No. Why on earth would she know anything about her?" Mom asked.

I rose from my office chair and worked some of the stiffness from my hips and legs. "She said the day before she died that she'd once seen me with my other mother."

Mom peered over her glasses. "I don't know how she could have. We ran a couple of articles in the paper looking for her and no one said a word. And I know Mabel read that paper cover to cover every day of her life. She would've said something to me."

I searched her face looking for any sign of shift or concern that might hint to a lie. I know Mom would never lie to be cruel, but she'd deceive to protect. "She never said a word?"

She peered at me, her gaze hardening with a hint of annoyance. "Honey, I would have told you about something as important as that."

"I've seen you forget to tell Dad details that he was happier not knowing."

She waved away the comment. "Your father is different. He really is happier not knowing how much I spent on a purse or a new mixer. Or if one of you girls failed a test or got a tiny ding in the fender. I know you like to know things, but Daddy is happy not knowing."

Margaret cleared her throat. "So does anyone want to hear what I've to say?"

My gaze lingered on Mom, and hers on me, until we both reached a silent accord. If Miss Mabel had known about my birth mother, then she had not shared the secret with my mother. And of course, this was all supposing that Miss Mabel wasn't totally senile toward the end and hadn't mistaken old articles she'd read for memories.

Shoving out a breath, I shifted my body toward Margaret. "Yes, please tell us what you have found."

She grinned, glad to have the floor. "I've been doing some digging."

"And?"

"First, let me read you the entries. It won't take long."

"Sure."

Margaret gave me a recap of some of the events in the young girl's life but the entry that stuck with me the most I read for myself:

I saw Emma today at the bakery. She spoke to Seymour, who manages the shop. I overheard her say that her brothers were sold yesterday at Bruin's to a man who owns a plantation in South Carolina. Their mama wept, for she knew she'd likely never see her children again. Emma whispered about taking the railroad, moonless nights, and secrets. It's the talk of runaways.

When the two saw me, neither was pleased. Emma has always been a nervous woman but today her hands trembled as she held her breadbasket close to her chest. Mr. Seymour looked at me with anger, thought that is nothing new. He hates my green eyes and calls me high yellow each time we meet. I don't know what I've done but I fear I'll never see his good side. But today with Emma present, he guards his tongue and smiles too sweetly as if he fears I've heard something that could get him whipped. He quickly fills my order for my mistress and asks me how the new baby fares. We all hope and pray this one survives, I say.

Now as I sit in the attic, it is late and my bones ache from running up and down the stairs and fetching for the mistress and the new baby. Mistress frets over the child and forever worries if the room is too cold or too hot. Mama is not yet home from the bakery. Her hours are long, and she looks wearier each day. It is dangerous to say, let alone write, but I can't contain my thoughts any longer. Like Emma, I dream of us running away from this place to a home in the country where the sun shines and there ain't no master or misses so ready with the switch or threats of the auction block.

To think of freedom, much less talk about it, is to invite the whip. But the thoughts of freedom rattle so loudly in my head, they are all but begging to be released. I have ruthlessly denied them but can do so no longer.

I dream of freedom. Of slipping unnoticed into a crowd and becoming faceless and invisible. I dream of reading in the park, savoring the words without fear of reproach. I dream of making my own money. Buying fancy silks. I dream of living my life freely and without the fear of the whip or being sent away from my mother.

"Wow," I said.

"I know," Margaret said, "Powerful stuff."

"Did you ever figure out who owned Susie?"

"I did." She pulled out a notebook and flipped through pages filled with notes. "Susie mentions him only once, but she and her mother were owned by Dr. Rupert Randolph. He was a local physician who practiced up until his death. He died in 1852 at the age of forty-three. Susie would have been about twelve."

"What happened to Susie after he died?" Mom asked.

"I went to the courthouse to dig through the old wills."

"Wills?" Mom said. "Why on earth would you do that?"

"Because the writer of this journal was a slave. That means in 1852

she would have been considered property, so if she wasn't sold, she might have been listed in the will of her owner."

"That would be Dr. Randolph?" I asked.

"Exactly. So, I went and found the wills of 1852 and sifted through them. And let me tell you, there were more than a few documents to read through. Anyway, I found a will for Dr. Rupert Randolph of Alexandria. He died October 15, 1852."

"How did he die?" I asked.

"I don't know. That will require more digging into the

newspapers, which is next on my list. For now, I can only tell you what he left behind went to his son."

"Susie mentioned the child in her diary."

"Yes. The baby. The doctor left the entire estate to the baby. Trustee for the child was Mrs. Elisabeth Randolph." She flipped. "Here's Susie's entry about the kid."

The baby has lived longer than any of his brothers or sisters and hope is starting to creep into the house. I still fear that the angels will sweep in and take him Home with them.

"I guess the angels didn't take the baby," I said.

"No."

"Well, that's a good thing that he lived," Mom said. "How long did the boy live?"

Margaret held up a finger. "I'm getting to that."

"The doctor left nothing to his wife?" I asked.

"That wasn't uncommon. It would have been his way of ensuring that all his assets went to his child and not to some unnamed man his wife may have married down the road. Husbands still controlled a wife's property in the 1850s."

"What's the boy's story?" I asked.

"I've yet to track down how long he lived or what happened to him. It can take time to find all the pieces. What I can tell you is that among Dr. Randolph's assets were two slaves: one named Hennie, age thirty-one, and one named Susie, aged twelve."

Dr. Randolph might have been the product of his time, but I didn't like him. He'd bedded a slave, married another woman, and then left his ex-lover and child to his son. "Susie mentioned her green eyes. She was called high yellow, a term used to denigrate biracial children."

"What happened to Susie?" I asked. "I mean after she was passed to the son, her half-brother."

"I don't know yet. But you're going to love this."

I leaned forward. "All ears."

Margaret flipped through more notebook pages. "The will stipulated that Hennie could not be sold for a period of three years because she was leased under contract to work for . . . drum roll, please . . . a one Shaun McCrae, the new owner of the Alexandria Bakery, which he renamed the McCrae Bakery. Which became the Union Street Bakery after the Civil War."

"No shit," I said. "Hennie worked here at our bakery?"

Margaret's face brightened. "Well not here, here. Remember, the original bakery was on the wharf by the water, and it burned in 1885. McCrae and his wife Sally moved the bakery here in '86."

"And Great-great-grandfather leased Hennie."

"Yes. My guess is that she made the tea biscuits for the ladies in town. If she simply baked the common man's hard tack or oversaw something menial, McCrae would not have had such a specific agreement."

This glimpse into these past lives stirred an excitement I'd not expected. "Hennie was a master baker."

"Yes."

"So did this also mean that Susie would not be sold?"

The lines in Margaret's forehead deepened as she shook her head. "No. Even though Dr. Randolph's kid inherited Susie, Mrs. Randolph was his guardian and as a result could sell his assets if need be. Mrs. Randolph was free to sell Susie at any time."

Susie had been a little girl who wanted nothing more than to learn to read and write and go to a real school. "Did she sell Susie?"

"Here's the last entry in the journal. It was hard to read because the handwriting looks shaky and rushed. It reads, 'I am to be sold today. I love you, Mama.'"

Mom and I didn't know what to say.

"Now, listen to this." Margaret pulled the tape recorder from her pocket and hit Play.

The little slave girl said that after the master's baby was born . . .

"That's Mabel's voice."

"Remember, I interviewed her?"

Mom nodded. "That's right."

Margaret rewound the tape and hit Play again.

She said that after the baby was born, the mistress kept the girl close and worked her from before sunrise to well after dark, washing clothes, cooking, and fetching. This went on for months and she was about near exhaustion when one day the mistress approached her at her washing cauldron. The mistress had the devil's gleam in her eyes when she looked at her, smiled, and insisted that the girl change into a nice dress, which the mistress supplied, and to wash her face and hands. The girl sensed something was about to change and was so terrified she couldn't enjoy the feel of the new blue cotton twill dress, the nicest she'd ever worn. The urge to pull free was strong but such a show of defiance would mean a beating.

Mistress and her slave hurried out the front door and up King Street. All the while the mistress kept a tight grip on the girl's arm.

The girl hurried to keep pace. They arrived at the front door of an office building housed in a brick building two blocks north on Duke Street. There was no sign out front, but Susie knew where they were. Instinct had her digging in heels. The mistress tightened her hold and jerked the girl forward.

Mistress pushed through the door as if she knew exactly where she was going. They moved down a center hallway to a man sitting at a desk. Mistress gave her name and the two were admitted to an office.

An older man glanced up from behind his desk. He wore round wire-rimmed spectacles on the bridge of his nose. A stretch of rawhide held back a thick crop of dark hair.

The girl knew the man. His name was Bruin, and he ran the largest slave auction house in the city. She tensed at the mention of the man's name. She'd never met him face to face but had heard tales. He bought and sold area slaves and transported them to the Deep South where the demand for labor was always high.

Mr. Bruin was surprised to see the mistress with the girl in November, one of his slowest months. Most slave holders waited to sell until January 1, a day when buyers and sellers all met in the marketplace to trade human flesh.

Mr. Bruin was a clean man, with white cuffs and hands freshly washed. Word was he was also a churchgoing man who could easily quote the Good Book. When Mrs. Randolph said she wanted to sell now, Bruin rose from his desk and came around to inspect the girl. He reached for her bottom lip, pulled it down, and inspected the girl's teeth. "There are no restrictions on her sale?"

When she said no, the trader offered two hundred dollars. But the lady wasn't pleased. "Her mother is training her in the bakery, and she's quite capable of doing laundry and light housework."

"Ah, if she can learn master baking skills then her value will increase." Bruin's gaze shifted to the girl a second time, and he inspected her like a prize colt. He suggested if the lady wanted more money, then she should wait until the girl looked more like a woman.

The girl didn't utter a word as they walked quickly home. Her mistress seemed in unusually good spirits and waved and nodded to several other ladies.

After changing back into her work dress, the girl returned to her laundry. Since she was a small child, she'd never believed that she would ever leave this house. This was her home. Where she belonged. When the master had been alive, she'd always sensed he'd keep her close, not for her sake but for darker reasons she didn't fully understand.

For the first time in her life, she wondered what her mistress would do with her now. And she understood why her mother worried so much.

"Was Mabel talking about Susie?" I asked.

Margaret nodded. "I think she was."

Chapter Twelve

TUESDAY, APRIL 6, 2010, 2:00 PM

For the short time I'd worked in the bakery, I'd had no choice but to keep my head down and work. It had been all about putting out fires. But this afternoon as I sat at my desk and stared at the neat stacks of paper, I knew that I'd put out the major fires. Yes, smoke smoldered all over the desk and if I stayed away too long, I'd once again have a raging inferno but for now each problem was safely satisfied.

A knock on my door had me looking up to find Rachel. She smiled. "Can I come in?"

"Sure."

A week ago, she'd begrudgingly made the cuts to the menu, which we'd implemented. Not only were we making a little bit more money, but also Rachel had more time to work on the popular baked goods. Life was a little less frantic at Union Street Bakery. Rachel and I hadn't spoken much in the last week, however. We did our work but there was no chitchatting, laughs, or quips.

If she thought to punish me by excluding me, she'd hit the nail on the head. The distance between us hadn't been easy. But if keeping clan McCrae together meant dealing with pouty hurt feelings, then so be it. Rachel would come around. Eventually. I hoped.

"What do you need, Rachel?" I'd kept my tone businesslike this last week because I could hide behind it so easily.

She slowly sat in the chair beside me. "I'm sorry. I've been a brat."

I nodded, tempted but not quite willing to put salt in the wound. "Running a business isn't easy. I don't make these decisions because it's fun for me."

"God, do I know that. I know you've given so much, and Margaret has, too, and I was acting like a baby when it came time for me to give."

"Stuff happens. Now we move on."

"You aren't mad?"

Margaret's revelations about Susie had stuck with me throughout the last week and a half. I knew the rift between Rachel and me would ease, and the work would slow. I had choices and freedom where Susie had not. "No."

Rachel started to cry. "You should be."

I tensed. "Why?"

"Because I was a PMSing bitch who couldn't let go of a few lousy menu items Mike added. God, I don't even like the molasses cookies."

I laughed. "We've all been there."

She swiped away a tear. "Maybe you have but I haven't. I'm the nice, reasonable one."

"And I'm not."

She sniffed and brushed away tears with the cuff of her sleeve. "Not usually. I mean, you're but if anyone is going to dig in their heels and play hardball, it's you. Not me."

"You weren't playing hardball, Rachel. More like softball."

"Really?"

"I've dealt with worse."

She rose. "Well, I am sorry."

"No worries."

She held out her arms. "Hug?"

"What?"

"Hug. We need to hug."

"Rachel."

She waggled her fingers. "Now."

"Fine." I rose and stood and stiffened only a little when she wrapped her arms around me and squeezed.

"Hug back, Daisy."

Shoving out a breath, I patted her on the back as she squeezed me tight. "You're the best sister."

"I know."

She released me and stepped back. "You're still a crappy hugger."

"Not my thing. Nothing personal but I just don't hug well."

"Now that we're speaking again, we'll work on that."

"No, we won't."

She smiled. "Yes, we will."

"Fine."

"We're really good?"

"We're great." And we were. The non-hugging policy of mine had more to do with my own quirks rather than any grudge.

She smoothed her hands over her apron. "I must get going. School thing."

"Is Anna in trouble again?"

"I think she's made another unfortunate choice of words again."

Grimacing, I said, "Should I ask?"

"It was the *Sh* word. And the *D* word."

"All together?"

"Apparently." She waved her hand as if shooing away a worry. "Enough about us. What are you going to do?"

"Don't know. This is my first afternoon with no work."

"Ah, freedom! If it were me, it would involve a hot bath, a high-fashion magazine, and a beer."

"Could be a plan."

"Have fun."

After she left, my smile waned. Now that I had free time in the daylight hours and I wasn't exhausted, I considered my options. I could have gone to my room and unpacked the boxes and made my room more habitable, but that didn't quite feel like a celebration of life.

I could have visited old friends, but I flashed to sitting in Tammy's living room balancing a cup of tea or a glass of wine and listening to her tell me how wonderful her life has become. Pass.

As I pulled off my apron and hung it on my back-office door, I thought about tracking down Mom or Dad. I could see what they were about. But hanging with Mom and Dad didn't seem like the thing a single thirty-something woman did. Rachel was with the girls. And Margaret was at the Archaeology Center conducting a tour for third graders.

A movie required driving. Shopping equated to spending money I didn't have, and I had never found a hobby that had appealed.

What the heck had I done with my free time in the past? The only time I remember really kicking back had been during the months that I'd lived with Gordon. We often were just content to cocoon in his apartment and be together. Not much was ever said but that had seemed fine. I guess looking back there'd been a lot to talk about. Maybe if we had talked more, my insecurities and his worries wouldn't have bubbled into the perfect storm. And then it occurred to me, I could stop by his shop and see what he was up to. We weren't exactly friends, but we weren't enemies.

Do you ever think about me?

Well, maybe, like right now. But it was not like I was *pining* for what we had. I just wanted to fill some spare time.

I pushed through the front door of the bakery, double-checked to make sure the closed sign was in place and the door locked, and then headed down the uneven brick sidewalk. I shoved awkward hands in my pocket, then pulled them out and then . . . shit. This wasn't a date, for God's sake, it was a visit. I let my hands fall by my sides as I moved away from the river.

This close to rush hour, the streets were clogged with cars—tourists in for the day, commuters trying to get home, and the miscellaneous police car or delivery truck. As I approached Prince Street and the line of cars waiting at a red light, I ducked down a quiet side street. Lined with old oak trees, the residential street was too small for most commuters.

Halfway down the street, I spotted Florence coming out of a town house. She held a basket of wilted, brown flowers, which she carried down the front steps toward a row of scuffed plastic garbage bins. She wore her blue uniform as if saying to the world that the death of her employer wasn't reason enough to break ranks.

She wrestled with the lid of the trash can and grumbled under her breath.

I picked up my pace and called out. "Hey, Mrs. Tillman."

Before she could answer I lifted the lid free, and she dumped the flowers into the bin. "Thank you, Daisy. That trash can is dancing on my last nerve. And you can call me Florence."

"They can be tricky."

She studied me with a narrowed gaze. "So, what brings you here today?"

"Well, nothing really. I had some free time, so I thought I'd take a walk. I saw you and thought I'd help."

"A walk is the best you can come up with? Young girl like you should be spending time with a nice young man."

The same advice from my mother would have had me bristling, but from Florence, I took it in stride. "My nice young man and I have had our share of issues."

Florence chuckled. "Making up is half the fun."

Gordon and I had never really fought back in the day. And the unspoken emotions had been like a bucket of cold water on our sex life. "I'm not so sure about that this time."

"Well, if you've got a minute, I could use a hand with more dead flowers. The house is full of them, and I need to get them out before they drive me nuts."

"Be glad to help." I followed her inside and hesitated at the threshold as my eyes adjusted to the dimmer light. The interior was a good bit warmer than the outside, a reminder that the ladies who lived here were old and fragile.

I spent the next twenty minutes hauling out all manner of dying or near-dead floral arrangements. There were flowers from the historical society, the library friends, the church, and even the local rotary club. Everyone seemed to have known and missed Miss Mabel and they expressed their grief with flowers. By the last load, Florence was no longer climbing down the front steps but waiting for me inside the door.

"What do you think Miss Mabel would have thought about all these flowers?" I brushed the dirt from my hands as I climbed the brick front steps.

Florence shook her head. "She'd have complained about the waste, but she'd have liked the attention. She always enjoyed the attention."

Florence moved down a long, dark center hallway. She'd not invited me in to stay, but I found myself drawn to this house. I figured she'd tell me to leave if I'd overstepped, so I followed her down the hallway, pausing often to look at the endless rows of framed pictures on the wall. Most of them had been taken at least fifty years ago. There was a picture of a young bride and her groom, which appeared to have been taken in the '30s. A closer look and I guessed the bride was Mabel. I'd seen a similar portrait at the funeral, but it was still odd to see the old woman as a bright-eyed young girl. There was hope and laughter in this girl's face and the way she hooked her arm around her husband's spoke of love and devotion. I didn't want to think how time had transformed such a lovely girl into a withered old woman.

"She was a beauty back in the day." Florence's voice echoed from somewhere inside the house "Come on back here and let me pour you a lemonade."

"Oh, you don't have to do that." I followed, aware I wasn't ready to leave just yet.

"Sure, I do. You hauled those nasty, dirty flowers outside and saved me from having to drag my carcass up and down those stairs." In the background, a gospel singer crooned something about Jesus and eternal salvation.

"Glad to help." As I stared at the older pictures of Mabel, I found myself searching for features like mine. Examining the faces of strangers was something I'd done most of my life. I didn't look like any McCrae but knew I must look like someone. Who?

As a younger woman, Mabel had dark hair; clear, bright eyes; and an odd little crease at the corner of her mouth when she smiled. I raised my fingers to my lips and smiled almost half expecting to feel that same indentation. But the skin was smooth.

"She lived a long and full life." Florence turned toward the counter, opened the can of powdered lemonade, and scooped several spoonfuls in a glass pitcher.

"Looks like it. How many children did she have?"

"None. Only lots of nieces and nephews. She wrote to them often enough."

"They were there for the funeral on Monday?" I moved into the kitchen. The bank of windows to the right of the sink let in a stream of warm sunlight.

"Some were. They sat up front. Several just didn't want to make the trip from California."

"We were standing to the side, and I couldn't see who was in the front row."

She filled the pitcher with water and with an old wooden spoon started to stir. "They didn't stay long. Came back to the house, talked about what furniture they wanted, and then headed back to their hotel. Mabel's oldest brother will be back in the next couple of weeks to close the house."

As Florence stirred the wooden spoon in the pitcher, I watched as the yellow lemonade crystals melted and blended into the water. In a few weeks, the house would be emptied out and all traces of Mabel would be gone. "What are you going to do?"

"Miss Mabel left it in her will that I could stay here until I die. And that is what I'm going to do. It doesn't matter to me what furniture the family takes. Fact, I'm looking forward to it. Will be nice to have a few of my own things in the place. Mabel always said the house was my home, but I felt like a boarder."

"Speaking as an adult boarder living in her parents' home now, I feel ya."

A smile tipped the edge of her lips as she pulled two glasses from the cabinet. She went to an old refrigerator and pulled out an ice tray. She twisted the plastic tray over the sink until the ice cracked free. Fishing out several cubes, she filled the glasses and then poured lemonade.

I accepted the lemonade and took a long sip. The tart sweetness cut through the drying in my mouth. I didn't know Florence and was hesitant to discuss the journal with her, but I had an opportunity to get information that might vanish overnight. "You know that book Miss Mabel left me?"

"I do. She was right to give it to you before her brothers and nephews arrived. They're already worrying about losing something valuable. Meaning, I'd be careful who you tell about the book."

Water dripped down the side of the glass and over my fingers. "Thanks for the tip. I'll watch what I say."

She sat across from me, adjusting her girth on the chair until she found a comfortable spot. "It's your book as far as Mabel was concerned and that's good enough for me."

"Thanks." I traced my finger on the lip of the glass. "I read the book."

Charcoal, dark eyes stared at me. "Did you?"

"It's a journal. Written by a young girl living here in the 1850s. She was a slave."

Florence arched a brow as she sipped her lemonade. "That so?"

"I can't for the life of me figure out why Mabel gave me that book. Margaret is still convinced it was a mistake and that Mabel meant for her to have it. She's the history guru in the family. Did you know she and Mabel spoke for hours and hours about the history of the area and her family?"

"I know Miss Margaret visited and they'd talk."

"We think that Mabel's grandmother might have known the girl who wrote the diary."

"Well, isn't that something." Florence shook her head. "Miss Mabel was as clear as a bell when she told me to give you that book. She knew exactly what she was doing."

Curiosity had me leaning forward. "But why?"

"Honey, I stopped trying to figure out Miss Mabel a long time ago. She does what she does and never had a need to explain herself."

"I barely knew the woman. But she did seem to remember

me. She recalled my last day in the bakery when I was a teenager."

Her nose wrinkled, drawing my attention to a sprinkle of freckles on her nose. "I didn't have to tote her everywhere then, so I wasn't there. I can't say much on that."

I shrugged. "It was not one of my finer moments. I made a real fool out of myself."

She chuckled. "Baby, we've all done that."

I traced my finger down the side of the glass, through the condensation. "Somehow I can't imagine you or Mabel reduced to blubbering tears."

She arched a brow. "That's because all you see is old."

I straightened, ready to protest but she held up her hand.

"You see the wrinkles and the gray hair. You see the slow walks and the bent backs. It's easy to forget that we were both once young girls with more emotion than sense. It's easy not to think that we loved men, giggled like girls, or let foolishness take over our lives."

She was right. I was guilty of thinking just that. I hadn't thought beyond what I saw. "Sorry."

"You wouldn't be the first or the last, honey."

I traced the rim of the lemonade glass, letting it circle several times before I found my voice, which still sounded a little too quiet and weak for my taste. "You never saw this book before?"

"Not until she had me dig it out of the trunk that last night, she was alive. She was quite insistent you have it."

"The book was given to Susie by someone by the name of J. Don't suppose you got any info on J.?"

"Sorry. Maybe Miss Mabel mentioned J. to Margaret in their talks?"

"No, no word. But Margaret is on her trail."

"Then I reckon she'll find her."

Frustration churned in my gut. I'd been given a puzzle

with only half the pieces and was beginning to wonder why I bothered. I already had a real everyday puzzle to contend with: Terry. Maybe it would be best to forget about Susie and deal with Terry. I could call this Terry chick today and ask her what she wanted. A DNA test would answer a lot of questions. I could, should, do a lot of things.

A heavy silence nestled between us, each of us drawn in by our own thoughts and worries. Finally, Florence took a long slurping sip of lemonade. She set the glass down slowly and carefully. "I will say that I got to be cleaning out Miss Mabel's papers over the next few weeks. The brothers don't have much interest in family history unless it can be sold. They offered to pay me extra if I'd start cleaning out her things."

"Are you going to take on the job?"

"Wasn't so sure I wanted to fuss with it. Mabel said everyone could take whatever they wanted after she was gone. She said she'd be far away and not caring so much if people read her old letters. But now that we've had this little chat, I've a mind to sift through the papers. You never know what will be found." She smiled. "But those boxes are gonna be mighty heavy, and it gets hot in that attic. I don't know about lifting so much with my old back the way it is, especially in the heat."

I straightened. "I've a strong back and so does Margaret." It made perfect sense to include my sister on this treasure hunt. "We can lift a good amount of weight. And heat is par for the course in a bakery."

Florence's belly rose and fell as she took a few long, deep breaths. "Well, then, maybe we can help each other. You get those boxes down for me, I earn a little extra money, and we can dig through and see if there's more to be found about that little girl."

A part of me wanted to climb the attic stairs now and start digging, but I could see the dark circles under Florence's eyes and hear the laboring in her breathing. "I have evenings off and Sundays."

"Well, I got my church on Sunday mornings, but we could plan to meet sometime this Thursday and see what we see."

"How long do we have before the brothers roll through and start cleaning out the joint?"

"About two weeks, but maybe a little longer if I tell them I'm sifting through clutter."

"I appreciate this, Florence."

She sipped her lemonade. "Got to say, I'm a bit curious about Susie and J. I'll be sure to keep an eye out for both initials when I start sifting through the papers on her desk tomorrow morning."

I sat down my glass. "Do you know of anyone named Terry in Mabel's family?" An anxious, needy tone that I didn't like slipped into my voice.

"Honey, that family has more cousins and nieces than you can shake a stick at. There could be, but I just don't know. But I don't think there was anyone by that name in the receiving line after the funeral." She sat back and studied me with brown eyes that peered over the top of her glasses.

"We could spend the next couple of weeks digging through old papers. Maybe we'll find Terry. Maybe not. But we can try."

It felt good to talk to someone who didn't study everything I said. "Thanks."

"Go on home and get your rest. I'll be sure to save anything I find, and we'll start doing the real digging on Thursday."

"About six?"

"Sounds good. Now if you don't mind, *Oprah* will be on soon, and I don't like to miss."

I rose. "See you on Thursday."

That night, I fell into bed just before nine. My body ached

and my head throbbed from energy overload. I sensed I was on the edge of something huge. It was something that felt dark and dangerous and like it or not would change my life forever. And as much as I wanted to turn back and run to my old life, I knew that a door had shut, and a deadbolt thrown. I could remain in limbo, churning and fearful, but I was ready to creep closer to the edge.

I nestled in my bed, which my mother had fitted with real sheets and a blanket. The sleeping bag was now rolled up and tucked next to the stack of unpacked boxes. As I slid under the sheets and lowered toward the pillow, I noted Mom had also gathered my dirty laundry today, washed it, and left it folded in a neat stack at the foot of my bed. She loved me. She was doing her best to take care of me. And I loved her for it. If I loved Mom so much, why did I care about Terry? Why wasn't Mom enough?

Because she just wasn't.

The frenetic pace I'd maintained all my life—the boyfriends, the demanding jobs, the trips—they'd all been about filling a hole I didn't even want to acknowledge. And no matter how much I crammed inside my days, nothing was ever quite enough.

I really welcomed sleep tonight. I needed a quiet refuge from the day's demands.

"You're such a baby, Daisy." Susie wore a white dress and dark braids secured with blue bows. She twirled in circles, waving her arms in an odd dance.

"I'm not a baby."

"Then prove it. Jump."

I glanced over the edge of a cliff, which seemed to have no bottom. "I don't have to prove anything to you."

"Baby, baby, baby. Jump. Jump. Jump."

Her teasing stoked frustration and anger. Leave me alone. "Not until you jump!"

Irritated and angry, I gritted my teeth and with my gaze on the girl, I jumped.

* * *

Just after six the next morning, Henri stumbled while he was carrying a tray of unleavened bread. I heard the *woof* of air come from his lungs and turned in time to see him teeter forward.

Thankfully I was close enough to grab the tray, save the dough, and steady him.

He met my gaze, and I saw a worried old man wildly searching the room, fearful that someone besides me might have seen his misstep.

I set the tray on the worktable. "She's out front. She didn't see."

He righted himself and moved a trembling hand through thick, graying hair. For a moment, he didn't say anything. Finally, he said, "She worries."

A half smile tipped my lips. "I worry, too."

"You are different."

"Different? That has been the underlying theme in my life."

"In your case, different is good. You are stronger."

"I don't feel so strong."

He picked up the tray from the counter and carefully carried it toward the ovens. "I have contacted my cousin."

I opened the latch to the oven. He slid the tray inside. "Your cousin?"

"From France." He dropped his voice a notch, mindful that Rachel was just on the other side of the door. "Lyon."

"Does he bake?"

"*Oui.* He bakes."

"Did you tell him about this job?"

"I have not spoken to him yet. I have left word with his sister to call me. Sometimes he is hard to find."

"What does that mean?"

"He travels." His even tone didn't hold the least hint of frustration.

I tried to maintain the same equilibrium. "When do you think he'll call you back?"

"Soon."

"As in?"

"Soon."

I ran nervous hands over my apron-clad hips. "Great."

Henri met my gaze. "He will call."

"Let's hope, because I got nothing on my end when it comes to finding another baker."

By ten a.m., the morning rush had left the store, and we could enjoy a small lull until the pre-lunch crowd showed. I'd grown to expect this quiet time and use it to check the register, restock, or take out trash. When I heard the front bell jingle, I glanced up with more than just a little annoyance thumping in the back of my head.

It was Dad. He wore jeans, a white T-shirt that read Union Street Bakery, a ball cap, and tennis shoes with new inserts ordered by Mom. I knew Dad didn't like the shoes, but he'd relented when Mom told him the shoes would ease the pinched nerves in his feet.

"Hey, Dad."

"Kiddo, thought things would be slow. No matter how many years I work here, this is always the slow time."

"Yeah. It's nice."

"How about you pour me a cup of coffee and give me a few cookies?"

"You're not supposed to eat sweets."

He winked. "I won't tell if you don't."

"Sure."

I filled a mug with hot robust coffee and plunked two sugar cubes and a dollop of cream into the mug. I slid it across the counter. "There ya go."

He took the cup and sipped. "Thanks. I see you made changes to the menu."

"Rachel was not pleased."

"So, I gathered."

"Did she come running to you?"

"No, but it doesn't take much to figure out what's going on in this place."

I grabbed a piece of paper and snapped up two sugar cookies, which I knew were his favorite. I handed them to him. "I told her she could cut whatever she wanted if she cut the line up by 15 percent. She did a good job but kept that pumpkin bread, which never sells well."

"It was one of Mike's specialties."

"Maybe in time she'll learn to let it go."

He bit into the cookie. "You're an angel."

I grinned. "That's not what Margaret called me this morning."

"She can be prickly when you pull her away from her books and broken pieces of pottery."

"I've noticed."

He came around the counter and I had the odd sense that he'd just invaded my domain. I'd made the back office mine almost immediately but wasn't sure when I'd decided the bakery had become mine as well.

"Why don't you sit?" he said.

"I can talk and work."

"You should sit."

"Drives me nuts." I grabbed a bottle of Windex and a handful of paper towels as I moved around the front of the display case. My old friend Tammy had come in again this morning, dragging a couple of kids who'd smeared my clean glass with their pudgy little fingers. "And as I remember, Mom could never get you to sit."

"That was different. I had a family to support."

"So do I." I sprayed the cleaner on the blurry glass.

Dad frowned as he moved back around the counter. "I didn't mean for you to take on all this. I know it's not what you wanted."

"It was never in the plan." I wiped the smudge away with unnecessary ferocity. Maybe if I made the smudges go away, I could make Dad's worried expression disappear. I didn't like seeing him upset.

"But plans change."

He drank his coffee but didn't eat his cookies. "You're doing a yeoman's job here, Daisy. You've stepped up and I appreciate it."

"Happy to help."

"What are your plans once you get this place back on its feet?"

I stopped wiping. "You're the first person who thinks this might not be forever."

"I want you to do what you want to do. Life is too short." He stared into his coffee.

"I never planned on spending a lifetime here. I had dreams of going off to school." He'd never told me this before.

"Why didn't you?"

"My dad died. Someone had to step up and take over. My mother couldn't do it alone. I was the only child." There was no hint of self-pity as he stated the facts.

I'd never really thought of my father as a real person. He was just the guy who worked, who went all out with the Christmas decorations, and the guy who kept us safe. "I always thought that you loved this place."

"I don't love it, but I respect it. And I understand now

that life isn't about doing what you want to do but what you need to do."

"That's what I'm doing."

His expression turned grim. "And that was okay for me, but it's not okay for you. I want more for you."

"If not me, then who? Rachel can't do this alone, Dad. You and Mom have done enough. And Margaret, well, she's a bit of a witch when she stays here too long."

That tickled a smile. "How's Henri holding up?"

It didn't surprise me that Dad had noticed Henri's stooped shoulders and worn features.

"He's leaving at the end of June."

Dad drew in a breath. "I'm not surprised. I know his back has been troubling him the last couple of years."

I brushed a strand of hair away from my eyes with the back of my hand. "He's holding on for Rachel."

His lips flattened. "But now that you're here, he's leaving."

I sprayed more cleaner on the glass and attacked another set of prints. "He says that he has a cousin. He's put a call in to him."

"When will you know?"

"Your guess is as good as mine. But he says soon, and I trust him."

He glanced around the room seemingly cataloging every crack and flaw. "That's the thing about this place, it's never satisfied. Just when you think you've done enough, it wants more."

"I'm starting to see that." I stared up at him. "Did you ever resent this place?"

"Sure. Probably more times than I could count in the early days. But it gave me a life, put a roof over my head and my family's. And I've met a lot of good folks in this community because of the bakery. I met your mother here."

"But it's not what you wanted."

"Maybe not in the beginning, but over time I stopped wondering where it ended and where I started. One door closes and another opens. That's life."

Nervous laughter bubbled inside of me. "I'm starting to feel that way."

"You're more like me than Rachel and Margaret. They're like Mom."

He meant that as a compliment, but it irritated me for some reason. "The non-McCrae is the real McCrae."

A deep frown creased his forehead. "You're a real McCrae. Mom and I never thought otherwise."

"I am, but I'm not. I'm connected to a whole other family." I could never say this to Mom. Her eyes would have filled with tears as her gaze looked away.

Dad, however, was more practical. Life had left him with little patience for shades of gray.

"Then call that woman, Daisy. Ask her what the hell is going on."

"I am."

He studied me as if trying to peel the layers away. "When?"

"Soon."

"Time to rip the Band-Aid off, Daisy, and see what you've got. If you don't, you'll never know."

"What if it's bad?"

"Better to know than spend the rest of your life wondering."

Chapter Thirteen

TUESDAY, APRIL 6, 2010, 7:00 PM

"Oh, you are so not going to believe what I found." Margaret's voice jumped through the phone when I answered it just after seven on Friday night.

I plopped on my bed and kicked off my shoes. I stared at my swollen feet. "What?"

"Pictures. I found pictures of the Randolph family."

I swung my legs over the side of the bed. "As in the Randolphs mentioned in the diary?"

"One in the same." She sounded quite pleased with herself.

I had to concede that when it came to all things historical, Margaret was gifted and driven.

"Really? Where?"

"Digging through tons of files and archives. Are you coming over to see them or not?"

I glanced toward the window. The sun clung to the sky, but it wouldn't hold onto the light much longer. "Where are you?"

"At the Archaeology Center. The front doors are locked now but I'll wait for you. Ten minutes."

"Fifteen." I scrambled swollen feet into clogs and grabbed a sweatshirt. Though the temps had hit the low eighties today, the spring air cooled quickly as the sun set. I moved down the attic stairs softly, not really interested in catching Rachel's attention, which could trigger a Q&A session.

Since Terry's letter arrived, she'd seemed motherly toward me. And right now, the last thing I needed was another mother. Through her door I heard the girls giggling and Rachel singing.

Pausing, I listened as the trio managed a rendition of the "Itsy Bitsy Spider."

The peals of laughter triggered an unexpected tightening in my throat, and I found myself longing for the connection that Rachel shared with her daughters. Their losses had bound them closer, and I knew no matter how bad things got, Rachel would never leave her kids in a café bakery with a couple of cookies and a lousy, "Be a good girl."

Drawing in a deep breath, I straightened my shoulders and headed down the remaining stairs. The cool air outside had me shoving hands in my pockets as I hurried down the uneven brick sidewalk along the waterfront. The orange-red sun had dipped in the sky casting a soft glow over the waters of the Potomac. Scattered sailing boats passed slowly through the shallow waters. Sails low, they searched for a place to dock for the night.

The Archaeology Center was located on the third floor of the Torpedo Factory. The Torpedo Factory earned its name because it had been a torpedo and munitions factory back in the '30s or '40s.

Sometime in the early '80s, it had been converted to an art center and now housed artists on all three of its floors. I hurried north on Union Street toward the factory. Inside the large glass doors stood Margaret, her hands folded over her chest.

Tense fingers drummed her forearms until she saw me, muttered something I couldn't decipher and opened the front door. "That was fairly fast."

"I aim to please." My voice echoed inside the large concrete building and bounced off the center foyer, which stretched up to the third floor. I had never taken the time to stroll through the hallways and visit the artists' shops. It was one of those *really-should-do* things, but it had never climbed far enough up the priority list to require action.

I followed Margaret up the metal center staircase to the Archaeology Center, which took up a better part of the north side of the third floor. The center's glass walls gave passersby a view into the long white tables that held displays of recent digs in the city. A large sign in one corner read Shuter's hill and featured volunteers digging on a side near the Masonic Temple at the end of King Street. Margaret had said Shuter's Hill was the site of an eighteenth-century home that volunteers and professionals were slowly unearthing. On the table were bits of pottery, buttons, doorknobs, and bricks.

There were older displays. One featured Civil War soldiers in Alexandria and another highlighted Jamison's Bakery, which I'd been told had been one of Shaun McCrae's biggest competitors in the 1850s.

Beyond the first set of white tables was a collection of photos that had been laid out in a long, neat row. The pictures varied in size from several inches in diameter to more than a foot in length.

"All those pictures are of the Randolph family?"

"Or people they knew. I've arranged them so that they tell a story." As I moved toward the table, I couldn't help but admire Margaret's dedication. "Damn, Margaret, there must be two dozen photos here. Where did you find all these?"

She hooked her thumbs in her belt loop. "I put a 411 call out to my sources, and they really came through. Some come from private collections, others private museums, the Barrett Library's collection, and, of course, our own files."

Several of the old black-and-white photos were yellowed and had cracked or curled on the edges. Some looked so delicate that I was afraid to touch them. They stood testament to Margaret's cache in the historical world. "You are amazing."

"I know."

Laughter bubbled. "One is never a prophet in their own land."

"Exactly."

Excited, I pushed up my sleeves. "What do we have here? You said a story?"

"A story indeed." She pulled dark framed glasses from her pocket, cleaned the lenses and then settled them on her nose. "Let's start at the photo closest to us."

The man in that daguerreotype had closely cropped black hair parted severely on the right side. He had a high slash of cheekbones and vivid eyes that held no hint of laughter. He stared not directly into the camera's lenses but off to the side as if he has been caught in a daydream. "A young man."

"Not any young man, but one Rupert Randolph while he attended the University of Virginia. He went to the university to study medicine. He received his degree in 1832 and returned to his family home in Alexandria."

I sensed that I'd glanced into those eyes before, and then I remembered the presence I'd felt a week earlier. Anger had radiated from the figure. Could it have been Dr. Randolph?

Margaret moved to the next photo of a young girl. A center part divided blond hair, which had been swept back into a low chignon. A high lace collar teased the underside of a square jaw and drew attention to full lips and large, wide-set eyes. Her features weren't beautiful, but she was pleasant enough.

"This is Elisabeth Stewart who, according to the society page of the *Alexandria Gazette,* in 1840 married Dr. Randolph in a lavish affair. She was nineteen and from a wealthy prominent merchant family. He was thirty at the time of their marriage. It was quite the affair, according to the paper, which reported that the new couple moved into the home Rupert inherited from his father. The marriage did quite a bit to improve the young doctor's struggling practice."

She arched an eyebrow. "And here is the big kicker. Their house is Mabel's house."

"You're kidding."

"Nope. Rupert Sr. passed the house to Rupert Jr., who left it to his only child, a girl, Frances, who married Colin Woodrow. Frances and Colin had one son, Henry Woodrow."

"Mabel's husband."

"Yes. She inherited the house from him when he died in 1946."

"I never would've connected the dots. Florence said that Mabel's will allows her to stay in the house until she dies."

Margaret straightened. "When did you see Florence?"

"A few days ago. I happened by while she was tossing out flowers."

I shifted my attention to the next set of photos. "By the way, Florence says we can dig through Mabel's attic on Thursday."

Her eyes widened. "No shit!"

"Yep."

She sat back, her gaze alight with excitement. "What time?"

"Six."

"Damn. I must work, but I'll switch with someone. I'm not going to miss this."

"I can go it alone," I teased.

Margaret held up her hands. "No f-ing way, Daisy. That attic is my idea of a wet dream."

I laughed. "And I thought my sex life lagged." I glanced at the pictures. "These are the Randolph children?"

She shifted her attention back to the pictures. "Yes."

I leaned in to study the delicate lace gowns the infants all wore. A closer look revealed that each child had been photographed in the same white christening gown. In some photos, the children laid in a small cradle and in the last two an older, a sterner Mrs. Randolph held a baby in her arms. In the image, the mother glanced down at the child but there was no hint of warmth in her eyes.

"She doesn't seem to be happy."

"That's because these first six children were photographed after their deaths."

I backed away from the desk and the photos, which in an instant took on a grotesque aura.

"What? How do you know that?"

"A couple of reasons. According to church records, the Randolph's had seven children and six died in infancy before the age of one. The first six children fit that age range."

"Yes, but how do you know they're dead and who in God's name would photograph a dead child?"

"It was common to photograph the dead in the nineteenth century. It wasn't like today. In those days, death was a very common threat and worry. And in a time when photos were taken only at very special times, it made sense to mark the end of a life, which would have been their final special event."

"But to photograph a dead baby in your arms? That doesn't strike me as healthy."

"It was a different time, Daisy. No doubt Mrs. Randolph also kept snippets of hair from each child and wore them in a locket close to her heart."

This woman buried six children. Even in a time when death hovered constantly, that kind of loss had to have been devastating to a young woman. "How did the children die?"

"That I don't know. There were outbreaks of typhus and smallpox during those years. The house was also on city water until the late 1840s. Bad water could very well have killed the children. I also wonder if it might have been a genetic issue. But I don't think we'll ever know."

I lowered my gaze back to the faces of the children. "They look like they're sleeping."

"I know."

"Mrs. Randolph lost six of her seven children. What happened to the seventh?"

"Rupert Randolph Jr. grew into adulthood. He was the one who inherited Susie. And his survival also supports the theory that bad water killed the first six children. He was born after the family installed a private cistern. Anyway, like I said, he married and had one daughter."

She picked up a picture that had been taken in the 1880s. "Here he is."

Father and son were strikingly similar. "They must have cherished him."

"I suppose Elisabeth did. Remember Rupert Sr. died when Rupert Jr. was just seven months old."

"Crap. I mean I knew that, but I forgot. So much death in one family. Did you ever find out how he died?"

"Heart failure was listed as the cause of death in the *Alexandria Gazette*'s obituary."

"Honestly, it's a wonder Elisabeth could get out of bed in the morning."

Another picture of Elisabeth taken in the 1860s showed a very different woman. Her features had grown stern, her mouth pinched and her eyes sunken. In this photo she didn't stare down at a bouquet in her hands but directly into the camera. Intensity in her eyes made my skin prickle and I resisted the urge to step back. "I can see why she resented Susie so much. Living under her roof was her husband's child by another woman and as she buried her children, that child thrived."

Margaret tapped Elisabeth's picture. "She lived to be forty-three," Margaret said. "She died just before the Civil War ended."

"How?"

"From what I can gather, a sudden illness overtook her. According to the paper, her sister, Joanna, moved from Newport News to Alexandria to raise the boy."

"What happened to Susie and Hennie? You said the doctor left them to his son. And we believe Susie was sold, likely by Bruin."

"I'm almost certain Mrs. Randolph sold the girl. Both mother and daughter were assets, and after her husband's death there were a lot of debts to be settled. Seems Dr. Randolph was good at spending money, but his medical practice never earned what he'd hoped.

"Though the house had been an inheritance to the doctor, its maintenance always seemed to remain beyond the doctor's means. And, by this time, I'm guessing whatever Elisabeth's father had left her had been spent maintaining their lifestyle."

"How do you know this?"

"Filed with the doctor's will is a petition for payment. He was in real debt at the time of his death. Susie and Hennie would have fetched a good price at market."

My voice dropped to a hoarse whisper. "Do you know if both were actually sold or who bought them?"

"That's a question I have yet to answer. I have Elisabeth's and Rupert Jr.'s wills but of course slavery was outlawed in 1863 so Hennie or Susie would not have been listed as assets in Rupert Jr.'s will. But I'm going to see if I can get a hold of the property tax records from the late 1850s and early 1860s. The records are spotty, but who knows? I might get lucky. And then there are the records from Bruin's."

"The slave trader. His house is on Duke Street."

Margaret's gaze sparked with approval. "You do know a little history."

"Hard not to, growing up with you. Didn't you do a paper on him in high school?"

"Two points, grasshopper. I never thought you noticed."

"I'm the one who took the pictures of you standing in front of the house for the report, remember? We used Dad's old Polaroid, and you bought me ice cream for my services."

"Right again. Bruin operated Bruin and Hill in the 1840s and 1850s. He was arrested at the beginning of the Civil War and put in a Washington, D.C., jail." The dancing light in Margaret's eyes signaled she was on the verge of a history lecture.

"What's next?"

She rubbed her palms together. "More detective work." She picked up one last photo. "Have a look at this."

I hesitated. "Please no more dead children."

"No. No more dead children. This is a picture taken of Jenna McCrae and her tutor. Jenna McCrae was Shaun's daughter from his first wife, who I believed died shortly before they arrived in Alexandria from Ireland."

"Jenna? J."

"It certainly backs up the story Mabel told. The young slave girl was sent to tend the baker's daughter. Jenna, by the way, died in 1864 of heart failure caused by an early bout with measles."

"How did you come across her?"

"It just seemed kind of odd that we are descended from a baker, have Mabel's accounts as well as a slave girl's journal."

She unfolded a long piece of paper that looked like an ancestry chart. "Sally married Shaun in 1865."

"Sally Good was Jenna's Alexandria friend who attended school with her in Ohio."

"Right. Sally and Shaun had four children. We are descended from Thomas, the second son. And guess who is descended from their fourth child, Ruth."

I shrugged.

"Mabel. Sally and Shaun were Mabel's grandparents."

"Damn."

I stared at the ancestry chart down through the generations. The line from my parents to Rachel and Margaret was solid. There was a dotted line to my name. "So why give this to the adopted kid?"

"I've no idea."

Studying the browning, faded photo of Jenna and her tutor, I couldn't help but marvel at the girl's serene beauty. "How do you know this is Jenna?"

"Because the tutor's name was Silas Barnard and he lived and taught in the area in the 1840s and 1850s. Remember, Susie mentioned in one of her journal entries that she wished she could again sit in Mr. B.'s classroom."

I leaned back and stared at her, my amazement clear. "Genius."

Margaret puffed out her chest. "I wish I had that on tape." She flipped over the picture and revealed a thick bold script. "Mr. B. was a careful historian. A man after my own heart. See where he's written, "Mr. B. and Jenna McCrae, 1851."

"When did Jenna leave for Ohio?"

"Likely before the war, because Shaun wanted her away from the fighting. Somehow, she hooked up again with her dear friend Sally Good."

"Sally Good. Shaun's second wife."

"Exactly. Sally accompanied Jenna's body home. That's how she and Shaun met."

I squinted and stared at the little blond girl with the bright eyes. So much death.

Standing behind Jenna was another girl. Her face was turned, and she wore a simple dress that appeared a little large for her. Her brown shoes looked well worn. This child had light brown hair and pale skin. "There's another girl in the background."

"I think," Margaret said carefully, "that this girl is your Susie."

I shook my head. "It can't be. She's too . . . white."

"Some slaves did have lighter skin. If her mother was biracial, and she was as well, then light skin could very well have been part of the genetic draw."

"But how do you know she's a slave?"

"Conjecture based on her clothing. Worn, oversized. Also, she's standing behind the other two and holding a fan."

"Damn."

"Virginia law stated that a slave mother's children were her master's property. Sadly, the lighter skin would have increased the girl's marketability. Still need to find the Bill of Sale. That might tell us what happened to Susie."

"Marketability. Bill of Sale. God, we are talking about a *child*." Margaret shrugged. "I don't defend. I document."

I left the Archaeology Center just after nine. Street lamps mingled with a nearly full moon, making it easy to move down Union Street easily. I'd walked these streets all my childhood and a good portion of my adulthood, so I wasn't worried about trouble. My mind was tangled up in the pictures of Elisabeth and Rupert's dead children, who'd been so lovingly coiffed and posed for their final images. And of Susie, the little girl in the threadbare clothes with her face turned partly from the camera.

The restaurants and pubs along the water were alight with patrons. The warming weather would soon pull the tourists into town, and in the coming weeks this whole area would be teeming with people.

Now when pub doors opened, laughter and music flooded out onto the street in a rush. The scents of beer and pizza also drifted past before doors closed and silenced the revelers.

A look into a picture window and I could see people crowded around the bar. The women looked dolled up in heels and designer ware and the men had the lean, hungry look of a man on the make.

I'd never been good with the bar scene. I gave it a try in college and had some fun. The buzz of alcohol combined with the inane conversations of friends had been a welcome distraction from studies and my self-imposed need to succeed. In the bars I could also, for short bits of time, forget about Renee, Mom's latest phone call, or my most current break-up. In the confusion, I found peace.

But as I moved into my early and mid-twenties, the bars lost their appeal. Work became my newest and best distraction —my favorite numbing agent of choice. I shoved hands into my pockets. wondering if I'd be in a better place now if I'd taken the time to make more friends. I'd kept relationships light and easy but perhaps I'd have been better off risking more with a little greater depth.

"Daisy." The sound of Gordon's voice caught me off guard. I turned to see him moving toward me with long, even strides. Moonlight glowed above him, highlighting his light hair, biking-T-shirt, jacket, and jeans. Loafers without socks completed the image.

My stomach tightened, and I braced. In all the years when I'd left boyfriends in the past, I never looked back. I broke all ties. But with Gordon, tangled emotions and past regrets wouldn't untangle or sever. "Hey."

He quickened his pace and caught up to me. "What puts you out on the streets this late? Don't you bakers get up early?"

"We do." I could have used that excuse as my exit strategy but opted to linger. My gaze dropped to his flat belly and flashed to the last time I'd kissed his stomach. Then it had been soft and not so muscled. This newer, sexier Gordon was a bit of a stranger and a little unnerving. Old Gordon wouldn't have minded the extra pounds I'd gained since my return, but I wondered if New Gordon did.

"I'm getting used to the odd hours and the lack of sleep." And that was true. "What has you out?"

He ran long fingers through his hair. "Chamber of Commerce mixer. Trying to drum up support for the new business."

"Grand opening in a couple of weeks."

"Four." He dug in his coat pocket, pulled out a business card, and handed it to me.

"Singleton Bikes. Union Street, Alexandria, Virginia. I like the little wheel logo. Did you design it?"

"Nah. It's stock, just like my website. Working on a shoestring budget these days."

"You and me both." I walked slowly, hoping and not hoping he'd follow.

He fell in step beside me. "I saw you come out of the Torpedo Factory."

"My sister, Margaret, works in the Archaeology Center. She's kind of helping me with a project. Long story."

"A project?"

"A historical thing."

"I thought you weren't a fan of history."

"I'm not normally but this thing just kind of caught my attention. Like I said, it's a long story."

"Right now, I got the time. No place to be until tomorrow."

"That's a switch. You with time. And me with time. Seemed neither one of us had it before."

A weighty silence settled and lingered. "Yeah. And both of us were too busy to notice."

On the few occasions I had shared a bit of myself with him, it had usually been at night in bed. We'd be shrouded in darkness, and I'd whisper rare thoughts to him. He'd always listen as if collecting precious nuggets. I had no reason to open up to Gordon now. We were broken up and finished as a couple. Still...

I sighed. "Margaret is helping me put together the pieces of a girl's life. She lived in the 1850s."

He cocked an eyebrow, and I wasn't sure if he were more surprised by the topic or my openness. "That's out of left field."

I laughed. "If you'd bet me a year ago, I'd be doing what I was doing and talking about history, I'd have taken the bet and raised you."

"Life has really changed for you." He hesitated. "I'm sorry about that."

"You've apologized before. Shit happens, Gordon."

Generally, when he steered us toward emotions, I'd shut down and do my best to squirm out of the conversation. But I was tired of that. "This old lady in town left me a journal that belonged to a kid who lived in the 1850s. It's a long-winded, boring tale that has little interest to most, but Margaret and I are having fun with it."

He touched my forearm lightly. "I didn't say I wasn't interested. Who was this girl?"

I searched his gaze looking for any emotion that would tell me to shut up or perhaps just sock him. But the only light that flickered was one of interest. His body was turned toward me, and his head was slightly cocked, something I remember he did when he really wanted to hear and understand.

So, I explained about the journal, Mabel, even Terry's letter, hesitating every so often to check his expression for any sign of boredom or wandering thoughts. To Gordon's credit, his gaze never wavered. I finished and let out a long sigh, as if I'd just released a lungful of toxins. "Do I sound like I've lost my mind?"

"No. You sounded fine." He watched me as heat rose and colored my cheeks.

"Then why are you staring?"

Grinning, he dropped his gaze to his feet before lifting it again. This time, there was no trace of sadness or regret swirling his gaze. "I think you've just told me more about yourself in the last few minutes than you did in the entire year we were together. I never knew about Terry. It fits, though. When I saw your sisters . . . well, they look alike, and you look different. And I don't mean different in a bad way. Different in a really good way."

"Don't worry, you're not the first to notice that I don't exactly look Irish." My lips flattened. "I never told anyone in D.C. that I'm adopted."

"Why not?"

"I've spent my whole life being different, so I don't go out of my way to be different."

"You always stood out as a ballbuster at work."

I laughed. "Work is different somehow. It's not personal. Or so I thought."

"Tell me about it."

More silence fell between us, and I wished he'd say something to fill it. "I know I could . . . can be aloof, at times. I'm not an easy person."

He nodded. "You live behind a wall of ice, Daisy. The only time we ever came close to connecting was in bed."

It was my turn to lower my gaze. "I remember. And I'm sorry. I just kind of expect people to leave me, and so I invest as little as possible and then do the leaving before they can."

He nodded as if I've told him what he knew all along. "This Terry woman has really shaken you."

"My life turned upside down when I was fired, but I thought I was dealing okay. It's only since I've been back at the bakery that all the emotions have started to churn."

"I'm sorry about that." He drew in a breath. "My deal with management was that none of the investment team would be fired. I left hoping you, and the others, would keep their jobs."

I'd blamed Gordon for the screw-ups. He'd been CFO. He'd made the decisions that had led to the catastrophic losses and eventual firings. "I didn't realize you'd tried to save our jobs."

Pain deepened the lines around his eyes and mouth. "I should have tried harder."

The fact that he'd tried at all meant something to me. I'd always thought he'd walked away without a backward glance toward anyone. "In the end we were all adults, Gordon. We knew that investments could go south and that the red-hot market of the last decade could not last forever."

"I should have seen it coming, but I was in so deep." His last words were little more than a hoarse whisper.

I shoved out a sigh. "Honestly, that job seems a million miles away right now. And as much as I missed it a month ago, I'm not so stressed about it now."

His gaze telegraphed skepticism. "Just like that?"

"Not just like that. But it's where I'm slowly heading."

We meandered down the brick streets. To our left the Potomac drifted past. The stars twinkled above, and a cool breeze drifted off the water.

The tension in his shoulders eased. "What are you going to do about Terry?"

"Dad says to rip the bandage off and be done with it. He told me to call her." I hesitated. "What do you think?"

He shook his head. "A year ago, I was black-and-white on most subjects. Now, after seeing a billion dollars vanish, I realize I don't know much."

"The words are humble. You get points for that. But I know you. Even if you got hit by a Mack truck, you'd have an opinion."

He grinned. "I'm trying to embrace shades of gray."

That prompted a smirk. "Okay. Sure. Whatever you say."

His smile deepened the creases at the edges of his eyes. "I'm trying to be more open."

"That's a lovely thought but right now I need black-and-white. What would you do if it were you?"

"Call her. Get your answers and put the deal to rest." The crisp, direct words were from the Gordon I'd known.

Nervous laughter bubbled. "Just like that."

"Answers. I'd want to know why the hell she bolted on a three-year-old. I'd want medical information. I'd want every detail I could squeeze out of her."

"Yeah, but . . ." His eyes gleamed with the old intensity.

"Just do it, Daisy. You might have been a lot of things but wishy-washy was never one of them."

"You're right. You're right."

He cocked his head. "So why the wait?"

I stared up at the sky. I felt so lost. "I'm scared."

"Of?" He'd softened the edge in his voice.

Tears tightened my throat. For a moment I can't speak. "That she'll worm her way into my heart and dump me again."

He laid warm fingers on my shoulder. Strength radiated from him to me. "You're an adult now. She can't hurt you."

"Oh, she sure can. A part of me wants her to love me just as much as three-year-old Daisy."

"You aren't three. You're thirty-four. You're educated. You can take care of yourself."

"Logic, Gordon, you're hitting me with logic. None of what I'm feeling is logical."

"You want me to contact her? I've got no skin in the game and I could be like an intermediary."

"You'd do that for me?" I'd left him. Hurt him. And he was willing to be my knight. I was humbled more than I'd ever been in my life.

A wave of his hand dismissed the suggestion as no big deal. "Consider me Switzerland or your emissary."

"My sisters have offered the same."

"Your sisters and parents can't be unemotional about it. But I can be. I can talk to her. Feel her out and make sure she's on the up-and-up."

More sharp emotions tightened around my throat. For a moment I was just overcome by the generosity, and I couldn't speak. Finally, I cleared my throat as a tear ran down my cheek. "That's very kind of you."

"I care about you, Daisy. That has never changed. If I can help, let me." The tenderness in his voice was nearly my undoing.

"I appreciate the offer. I really do. But as much as I'd like to run and hide on this one or send you in to do the dirty work, I'm going to have to be the one to deal with Terry."

"You'll call her?" There was no missing the challenge in his voice.

"I will." My back straightened a little as if readying for attack.

"When Daisy?"

"Soon."

He leaned toward me a fraction. "Which means?"

I shifted back a step. "Why do you care about this so much?"

"As private as you've been about your entire life and feelings and now you mention something like this to me. Let's face it, it's not only chewing on you, but it's colored your entire adult life."

"You're pushing."

"I know," he said, with no hint of apology.

I should have been offended that he was backing me into a corner.

My family still tended to treat me as a fragile piece of crystal, whereas Gordon was treating me as just me. Other than the backing-into-a-corner thing, I appreciated feeling normal, if only for a few minutes.

"Tomorrow."

He lifted his hand a fraction as if he wanted to take my hand in his but instead, he slid long fingers into his pockets. A part of me was sorry he'd not taken my hand. I wanted him to touch me. But I was also relieved that he'd kept the distance. The very last thing I needed now was romance with a guy I'd never really stopped loving.

"You're going to call Terry tomorrow."

My stomach knotted. "Yes."

He arched a brow. "You're going to stick to that deadline?"

"Like glue."

Chapter Fourteen

THURSDAY, APRIL 15, 2010, 7:00 PM

If you had to guess whether I called Terry or not, what would you have guessed? I mean I had promised to Gordon and myself that I'd "take care of business."

I did take care of business. Bakery business. And I didn't call Terry. I wanted to. In fact, a half-dozen times I picked up the phone and started to dial. But before I could get past her area code, I'd chicken out. Every time I entered a room now my family would study my expression as if searching for hints that I'd taken the plunge. When it was clear I'd not made a move, they'd quickly talk about something that had nothing to do with anything. And yet each time I looked at any one of them, I heard all the unspoken words from my family: *weak. coward. baby.*

By the following Saturday, the bakery and the business all but rolled over me like a steamroller. Bank statements, which had sort of recovered, had taken a hit when I'd paid quarterly taxes. Minutes after I'd mailed the check, the bakery's water heater blew, and I had to find a plumber to install a new one. Did you know they charged triple time on Sundays?

Monday morning brought in an irate patron who'd

ordered a flag-draped cake filled with Bavarian cream from Rachel. My sister had warned the woman that the cake needed refrigeration. Rachel had even called the day of the event to check on the cake's reception at the Army Officers Club. When she'd discovered the woman hadn't cut the flag-shaped cake's center and instead stowed it in the trunk of her car, Rachel had shouted Code Red and we'd all scrambled to find the woman and warn her the cake, if left unrefrigerated, would make people sick. The woman had turned her cell off, and we'd been forced to call her office, friends, and family. Three hours later we'd tracked her down through a friend of hers who'd told her about the problem before she'd served the center filled with cream. She'd been pissed. When she marched into the bakery and demanded a refund, I'd reminded her of Rachel's warnings. She'd said it was not her fault that the cake had been too pretty to cut.

Then there'd been Tuesday's bride who'd ordered 100 apple-shaped cakes to serve at her wedding. She and her fiancé had met in an apple orchard and the entire affair had an apple theme. Four days before the wedding, bridezilla had realized the wedding was too expensive and was forced to make cuts. She'd come by the shop, cancelled her order, and demanded her five-hundred-dollar deposit back.

I wiped powdered sugar from my hand before I extended it to bridezilla. "Is there a problem here?"

Rachel, her face flushed with anger, gave me a recap.

I looked at bridezilla, a petite girl with large breasts and rounded hips. "I can't afford the cake so I shouldn't have to buy it. This woman here told me I could cancel at any time."

"Union Street Bakery contracts allows for cancellation up to one week before an event." That was a clause I planned to change, but for now we honored the seven-day window.

"She told me any time," Bridezilla snapped.

"I didn't," Rachel countered. "I told her about the seven-day policy."

"Let me get the contract."

Rachel looked at me, a little afraid. I knew what she was thinking: You'll never find it. But any contract that had been on my desk had been filed in alphabetical order.

"What name did you place the order under?"

Bridezilla didn't bat an eye. "Walker. Samantha Walker."

"Be right back, Ms. Walker." I went to my office, dug out the contract and came back out front. Rachel and Ms. Walker's gazes remained locked in battle. I flipped to the back page of the contract. "Is this your signature, Ms. Walker?"

She glanced down. "Yes."

"And your initials?"

"Yes."

I nodded. "It appears your initials and Rachel's are right next to the cancellation clause. You agreed in writing to cancel seven days before delivery. It's three days before, therefore no refund."

"That's bull." Gold bracelets jangled on her wrists as she waved French manicured hands around. "I'm going to sue."

Business confrontations made Rachel want to weep. I loved them. "You go right ahead. We'll see you in court. Though I can promise an attorney is going to cost you a couple of grand just to review the case. And then I'm going to countersue for court costs, time, and aggravation."

"This is bull!" She stamped her feet. "I want my five hundred back."

"We've already used the money to buy supplies for the cakes. No refund."

Ms. Walker cried. She stamped her feet again, but in the end, she had nothing to bargain with. She left, angry and deposit-less.

When the bakery door slammed closed, Rachel shook her head. "She's going to bad mouth us."

"Let her. We may have the deposit, but we're out the one-thousand-dollar balance and left with one hundred square cakes."

Disasters like bridezilla and the water heater kept dropping out of the sky and none could be ignored. I had to choose between the smoke on the horizon and the raging infernos at my feet.

Thankfully, by Thursday life had settled to a dull roar and Margaret, and I were able to slip away and visit Florence. We arrived on Florence's doorstep just after six p.m.

"I got a friend coming to help with the heavy lifting," Margaret said. "I figure since we don't have much more time, if Hugo can get the big stuff out of the attic, then we might be able to get to the good stuff faster."

I rang Florence's front bell. "Margaret, I've never seen you so focused."

She all but glowed. "Never ever get between Margaret and her history."

"Speaking in the third person. You haven't done that since middle school. This must be important."

She grinned. "Margaret thinks this is very serious."

We were both smiling when Florence opened the front door. The older woman wore her blue uniform, light-colored hose, and white orthopedic shoes. She smelled of Dial soap and oranges.

"Well, you smiling girls are a sight for sore eyes. Glad you could come."

"We wouldn't miss it," Margaret said.

Florence chuckled. "Don't know what's got you all riled up, honey. It's just a pile of junk in the attic."

"Are you kidding?" Margaret said. "This is like the best

treasure hunt I've ever been on. This is even better than the Greek ruins."

It was hard not to smile seeing Margaret so excited. "If you haven't guessed, she loves history."

"Well, come on in. We got boxes of it in the attic."

We moved past Florence into the foyer. The house smelled of cooked green beans and fried steak. "I hope we haven't come too late in the day."

"Oh, no. Timing is perfect. Fact, if you get hungry, I can fry up a few steaks. Miss Mabel wasn't eating so much toward the end, and she couldn't stand the smell of food, so I didn't cook so much. These last few days that's all I've done. Even baked a couple of cakes this morning."

I'd eaten three bagels today and five cookies. Now fried steak and more cake. At the rate I was going, I was going to have to surrender my jeans and change into sweatpants. "That sounds good. You mind if we check the attic first?"

"No, not at all. Steaks won't take but a minute to cook."

"I invited a friend," Margaret said. "His name is Hugo. He's a big hairy dude and he looks rough but he's a great guy and can lift anything. He's a grad student looking for help on his thesis. I said I'd trade my vast knowledge and a bag of bagels for a little labor. He was all over it."

"So, he'll be hungry?" Florence said. There was no missing the hopeful hint. She was enjoying the excitement of company. No doubt the last years with Mabel had been quiet and a bit isolated.

"Hugo will be thrilled with any food you put in front of him," Margaret said.

The old woman grinned. "Then maybe I'll whip up a batch of biscuits."

I shrugged off my jean jacket. "Sounds awesome. How about we see you about six."

Florence clapped her hands together. "Perfect."

The front doorbell rang, and we all turned to see a tall man with broad, stooped shoulders hovering on the porch outside. Through the glass I could see a twenty-something-year-old guy who had shoulder-length hair and wore a leather jacket and jeans. A gold earring winked from his left year.

"Hugo," Margaret said. She moved to the door and opened it. "Hey, dude."

"Hey," he said, his voice a deep baritone.

After quick introductions and a promise to meet for dinner (which thrilled Hugo) the three of us left Florence to her biscuits and climbed into the attic. We moved up the wooden stairs and past the now familiar unfinished walls, where insulation was haphazardly stuffed between the wallboards. The steps moaned and creaked their complaints as we climbed to the landing. Just enough light leaked in through the slats in the eaves enabling me to spot the string dangling from the lone sixty-watt bulb on the ceiling.

Margaret clicked on the overhead bulb. The attic was so full of boxes, clothes, and furniture, there was barely room to walk.

"Whoa," Hugo said. He pulled a flashlight from his back pocket and swept the light across the room. "Lots of stuff."

"I knew this would be so awesome," Margaret said. She switched on her light and crossed her beam with his.

"Totally," he said.

I felt a little out of sync because I'd not come with a flashlight. "Do all history buffs carry a flashlight?"

Hugo nodded. "Always."

Margaret looked at me. "You didn't bring one?"

"Never crossed my mind."

She reached in her oversized pocket and pulled out another. "What am I going to do with you, Daisy?"

"I don't know, Margaret," I teased. "I'm just hopeless, I suppose."

"Turn your light on. Let's get digging."

Over the next hour and a half, we sorted item after item. A 1950s phonograph, LP records, dresses from the '30s and '40s, a cradle, a rocker, and items I could not identify. Margaret worked with laser precision, inspecting and then delegating either Hugo or me to remove an item from the attic. After a while, my back ached from lifting and stooping, and a fine layer of grit coated my skin. My stomach grumbled and I was ready to call it a day and dive into Florence's fried steaks and biscuits.

"Hey, dudes," Hugo said. "I found a hatbox. It's got pictures."

"Approximate dates?" Margaret said.

"Civil War, give or take five years."

Margaret's gaze met mine. "That's our time period. Let's have a look?"

The three of us sat cross-legged and shone our lights onto the brown box spotted with water stains and patches of mold.

Margaret pulled off the lid and studied the contents before she removed anything. I'd learned throughout this process that she always surveyed the item in question carefully before she touched it and possibly damaged it. The image on top was of a mother and her three children. The woman appeared to be in her mid-twenties. Two of the children were boys and maybe about eight or nine and they were dressed in fine twill jackets and knickers with white socks and polished buckled shoes. The girl, not more than a year, wore a long white gown, which draped over her mother's full velvet skirt. The mother's expression was serene; the boys looked the picture of austereness and the baby stared wide-eyed into the camera.

Margaret lifted the picture out and carefully turned it over. All that it read on the back was "1902." She handed the picture to Hugo who pulled a magnifying glass from his front pocket and studied the picture.

"What other equipment are you two carrying?" I quipped.

Margaret ignored me but Hugo answered in all seriousness, "I'm just carrying a screwdriver, gloves, and a backup light. I left my toolbox in my truck out front."

"I hate to ask what's in the toolbox."

"Really, Daisy," Margaret said. "Would you go into an audit without a calculator and computer? Would Rachel ice a cake without a cake wheel and an offset spatula?"

"No."

"These are our tools of our trade." She peered into the box and removed more pictures, which seemed to go in reverse chronological order. There were pictures of the woman with just the boys who were much younger. Then there was a photo of the woman standing next to a man. She wore a white dress and cradled a dozen white lilies in her arms. She smiled directly at the camera and looked radiant; a truly happy bride ready to embark on her life.

Tension suddenly rippled through my body, and I looked up toward the shadows. The presence that had visited me at the bakery was here and he was staring at me. My breath caught in my throat. His bold, dark gaze had me leaning back and struggling to take a deep breath.

"What's wrong?" Margaret said.

What was I supposed to say, that the ghost who was haunting me was in the corner? "I think I'm just hungry."

"Really? You don't look hungry. You look like someone just walked on your grave." She flipped the picture over. "Ruth and John Samson, 1902, on their wedding day. They must be Mabel's parents."

I took the picture from my sister and studied the stern line of John's face. Mabel looked a good deal like her father. She had his firm jaw.

Setting the picture aside, I pulled another picture from the box. This time it was a very old photo of a man. In his mid-thirties, he stared directly into the camera, his gaze hard and defiant as any prizefighter's. I traced the line of his jaw and the bridge of his crooked nose, which appeared to have been broken a couple of times. His clenched hands rested in his lap, and his back was ramrod straight.

My breath caught in my throat, and I glanced toward the shadows. Whatever had been there was gone . . . and he was also the guy in this photo. "Who is this guy?" I flipped over the picture but there was no inscription.

"I dunno," Margaret said.

The more I stared at it the more certain I was that he was the ghost who wasn't happy with me. But why the heck should he care about me? What the hell had I done to a dude who had been dead for more than a hundred years?

"This guy gives me the creeps."

"Why? He's been dead over 150 years."

"If I told you he might be haunting our house, would you think I'd gone off the deep end?"

"Seriously?"

"Totally."

Her eyes brightened. "Then I'd say way cool, and I'd start digging into mystery man's past ASAP."

Hugo nodded. "So cool."

Within the half hour, we three were exhausted and hungry (me more than the other two), and we found our way into Florence's kitchen. After washing our hands and faces, the four of us sat down to a feast of fried steaks, mashed potatoes, biscuits, and green beans that looked like they'd been cooking since yesterday. There wasn't a fresh vegetable or lean protein in sight, and I'd faint if I analyzed the fat grams.

But it was a hot meal, something I'd not had in weeks, and I was so hungry I promised yet again that tomorrow would be different as I bit into my first creamy bite of potatoes.

The dinner conversation started with Hugo, who after

some prompting said he was working on a dissertation on George Washington. Margaret argued that he should have picked a topic that hadn't been covered so extensively, but Hugo remained steadfast and determined to shed light on our country's first president.

Florence turned the conversation to Margaret. "Baby, you ever find a use for those conversations you had with Mabel?"

"For the longest time I had no idea what to do with them. And then you gave Daisy Susie's journal, and we embarked on this historical adventure. I'm not sure how all the dots connect, but I think I've got the makings of a great dissertation." She poked her fork in what remained of her fried steak. "I really thought this dissertation was the end of me, and I'd never get it right. Now I just know that I'm on track."

As Florence piled another heaping spoon of mashed potatoes on her plate, she said, "Well, you kids can dig in this house as much as you can until the nephews arrive. There just might be more stuff up in the attic."

"That would be great," Margaret said.

Florence spooned mashed potatoes on my plate. "And how do you like working in that bakery, Miss Daisy?"

"It's not bad. I'm getting the hang of it. Like Margaret, I've got an idea sparking. A website. An online store. More catering. There's so much I can do, it's just a matter of time and money."

Margaret stared at me with a mixture of shock and admiration. "I didn't know you were getting into the business thing so much."

"If you're not moving forward, you're falling back," I said.

She nodded and pushed bits of steak around her plate. "So, Florence, we found these pictures of Mabel's parents, John and Ruth."

Florence sipped her sweet tea. "She didn't know her folks

so well. They died when she was young, and she was raised mostly by her grandmother."

"Do you know anything about them?"

"No. I asked her a couple of times, but it seemed to pain her. Seems they were madly in love and when Ruth died, John couldn't hold on. He died about a year later."

Margaret set her fork down. "Could we come back on Sunday?"

"Sure," Florence said.

Hugo had to beg off, something about a trip to Virginia Beach. But when Margaret's gaze locked on mine, I grinned. "Wouldn't miss it for the world."

Chapter Fifteen

SATURDAY, APRIL 17, 2010, 2:00 PM

By Saturday afternoon when we flipped the open sign to closed, my body and head throbbed. We'd had very brisk business the last few days, and though we weren't even close to paying off my loan, hitting breakeven would count as a victory in my book.

As Rachel cleaned out the cases, I retreated to the office to tally the money. An hour later, she was in my doorway. Her apron off and draped over her shoulder, her hair hung loose around her shoulders. "How does it look, boss?"

"Better. And please don't call me 'boss.'"

She strolled into the office and took a seat by my desk. "You are the boss, babe. Own it. Love it."

A small part of me resented being the one thrust into the leadership position. Why me? "We covered our costs this week."

Rachel shoved her hands in the air and gave out a hoot of laughter. "Score!"

"That's hardly getting rich," I cautioned.

Her eyes danced with excitement. "No, but it's better than sliding into the depths of financial hell, as we had been."

"True. But we're going to have to start generating more dough. No pun. Have you considered catering?"

"Sure, I've thought about it a lot. The corporate sector pays well. But I've just not had the time to market. The extra wedding cakes have been about all I can handle."

"We're going to have to make the time." I glanced at the calendar on my desk; it was the same one that had sat on my desk at Suburban Enterprises and was my record of everything —including the very empty months of February and March. Flour and sugar distributors had replaced investment committees and conference calls, but the white boxes marking the days were again filled with notes and meetings. "Tuesdays are our slow days."

"I'd agree."

"Good. Then next Tuesday, we're hitting the streets with trays of cookies. There are several large office buildings on Duke. If we could drop off samples with cards, we might get lucky."

She sat back and threaded her fingers together in her lap. "Mike had just started marketing before he died, but afterward I'd never had the nerve or the time."

"I've got more than enough nerve." I was good at sales and hearing no from strangers didn't bother me.

"After lunch is a great time. People are craving that sugar fix and it's our slow time of day."

"Cookies?"

"Why don't I make some magic with my apple cakes. I froze them after bridezilla left. They are just waiting to be iced and eaten."

"Good thinking. Are they all apple flavored?"

"Chocolate, vanilla, and apple spice. Flavors to tempt all taste buds."

It felt good to be planning and not just reacting. "We hit the offices next Tuesday at two."

She rubbed her hands together. "I'll ice them with something sinful."

"Make it extra sinful. I'm looking to create a full-on addiction with these folks."

"That I can do. I've got a chocolate icing that's very, very good."

"I'll leave that to you. My job is to scrounge up a brochure or card. The quick-print place can help me out."

She pressed her hands together. "What about Mom and Dad? They could help cover ground."

"I thought about them. But since this is our first time, we'll go it alone. Just to test the waters. We'll get them to hold down the fort here."

She tucked a stray curl behind her ear. The gesture was pure Mom, and it struck me how much she'd inherited from Mom not just in looks, but also in mannerisms. But I had Mom's mannerisms, too. Our hardwiring was different, but we both shared a love of a good kosher pickle.

We both were a little OCD about making sure the back door was locked at night. And we both weren't afraid to do whatever it took to care for this family.

"Point taken. Mom can talk way too much."

"Just a little."

She pressed her long fingers against her thighs and pushed up to a standing position. "What are you doing tomorrow afternoon?"

"Running errands and then digging through Florence's attic again with Margaret."

"You two are a regular Thelma and Louise."

I shrugged. "It's kinda cool seeing a more human side of Margaret.

"You can come with us if you like."

"Thanks, but Sunday is my day with the girls. We're going to the park. Then it's our favorite DVD of the month, *Beauty and the Beast*, and ice cream. A kick back, no-agenda kind of day."

"Enjoy."

"Why don't you call Gordon? See if he's up for an attic adventure." She wagged her eyebrows in such an obvious and goofy way that I had to laugh.

"Maybe I will."

"Really?"

"Yeah, sure."

She cocked her head. "You're not going to call him."

"I might." But I wouldn't. Not because I didn't want to see him, but because I didn't want to get into why I hadn't called Terry.

"Well, all right, sister." She tossed a last grin and left. In the silence of the office, I thought about Gordon. I wanted to see him. In fact, I'd thought about him a lot in the last few days. No, I'd not called Terry but why should that get in the way of me seeing Gordon? I'd put enough of my life on hold because of my birth mother and it was time I broke the habit. Before I overanalyzed the situation too much, I pulled my cell from my back pocket and fired off a text.

Rachel just pulled out a batch of chocolate chip cookies. Any takers?

The cookies had come out of the oven two hours ago, and they really were sinful. I hit Send and set the phone on my desk, determined not to stare at the screen like a fool.

When a message blinked back seconds later, I grinned, more pleased than I should be. "Can't. HUGE deadline. Rain check?"

Typical Gordon. Business first. And as an admitted workaholic, I couldn't fault him for that. "Yes."

"Terry?"

"Not yet."

"Bad girl."

"TRUE. BUT STILL EATING CHOCOLATE CHIP COOKIES."

The cursor blinked once and then twice.

"HAVE A FEW FOR ME."

Smiling, I texted, "WILL DO."

I rose and pulled off my apron. As I hung it on the back of my office door, a cold burst of air shot across the room and swirled around me. For a moment, I stood very still as goose bumps puckered the skin on my arms. A glass of water on my desk tipped to the floor and shattered. Images of mystery man's stern gaze flashed in my mind, and I had the distinct sense he was really pissed.

Since we'd left Florence's on Thursday, Margaret hadn't had time to do much historical digging. Her two-day jobs had taken up most of her waking moments, but she'd promised to dig up what she could early next week.

"Hello?"

My heart pulsed in my chest as I waited for what I didn't know. When nothing happened, I felt just a little damn foolish. I was talking to thin air. Ghosts, no less. Chuckling at the absurdity of the moment, I turned to leave when my cell phone rang. I jumped, startled by the sound. "Union Street Bakery."

"Daisy?"

"Yes." I'd answered my personal phone as if it belonged to the bakery.

"It's Brad Foster."

I released a breath. "Brad. How did those carrot cake cupcakes go over at your party?"

"A huge hit. In fact, it got us all to talking about you. Were your ears burning?"

"Like an inferno." I laughed. "I hope it was all good stuff."

"Absolutely. In fact, Ralph Denton was there. He worked with us, and now he's at United Capital."

"Got himself a sweet deal. Closed End Funds, right?" I liked Ralph and was glad he'd landed on his feet.

"Not much gets past you."

That information was over two months old. Ask me what had happened in finance last week and I'd have been at a loss. "So why the call?"

"Ralph wants to talk to you about a job. He's looking for a marketer. He'll have his hands full managing the fund, but he'd like someone who knows the business selling his product."

"Really?" God, but I wanted out of this bakery and this life right now.

"Got a pencil and paper?"

I grabbed a pen from my desk and uncapped it. "Shoot."

Brad rattled off Ralph's new information and I scribbled it down.

Ralph was looking to move fast, according to Brad. I was to give Ralph a call and set something up for next week.

"You're going to call him?"

"Sure, why not, sounds great."

"Good. Let me know how it goes."

"Will do."

I hung up the phone and sat down to my computer. I switched it back on and waited for it to reboot and then searched out Ralph and United. I could feel the blood pumping in my veins as I read through the company information. God, this gig sounded like it would be perfect for me. I could so take this company to the next level.

My mind still buzzing, I called Ralph. We exchanged pleasantries and set a date for Tuesday evening. It was one of the rare moments during the week that I had off, and Ralph said he was working just about twenty-four/seven these days, so the late time worked for him.

I hung up the phone, my hands tingling. My chair

squeaked as I leaned back and stared at the ceiling. This kind of job would pay good money. I'd get benefits. A paycheck every two weeks and not have to worry about water heaters and old mixers. It was all perfect.

Except. I'd made a promise to my family to run this business. Suddenly, I felt like a creep and a traitor and every variety of pond scum. How could I leave Rachel and Margaret? Weren't they depending on me? They needed a manager.

If I got the job at United, I'd be living in a less emotionally charged place, but I'd be making good money and I could hire a manager and pay them out of my own pocket. My heart raced faster. Maybe we could have our cake and eat it, too.

Chapter Sixteen

TUESDAY, APRIL 20, 2010, 11:00 AM

"Hurry up," Rachel yelled into my office. "We got us some marketing to do."

"Right." I dashed up the back stairs, passing Mom and Dad, who made their way to the bakery, ready as all agreed, to man the shop for the remaining two business hours. The last few days had been insane.

Not only did I have my everyday routine, but I was making a website for the bakery and putting together cards and a brochure. No one would ever accuse me of being a graphics expert, but the work was simple, informative, and would do the job for now. And in my very spare moments I was in my office online and reading all I could about United. Each time I searched for information on the company, I felt a gnawing guilt. I'd not told anybody about the job interview, knowing it would not go over well.

I focused on getting the United job, garnering a great salary, setting up sales contracts for the bakery, and then pitching my manager idea to the family.

Dad glanced at his watch. "Hurry up, kiddo."

"I know. I know."

I was pulling off my flour-dusted, sweaty-stained T-shirt as I moved toward the bathroom. Turning on the shower, I kicked off my shoes and pushed my jeans to the floor. Last night I'd dug out my interview clothes for my meeting with Ralph and hid them in my closet. The plan was to slip out the back with my clothes in hand and change somewhere else. There was no sense raising questions until I had answers.

Jumping under the spray, I intended to be done in seconds. But the rush of warm water felt so damn good. And so, I stood under the shower, savoring the hot steam and the beads of water as they hit the tense muscles in my neck.

With regret, I finally shut off the tap, toweled off, and dressed in dark pants and a chef's jacket that had once belonged to my mother. When we'd told her of our marketing plans a few days ago, she'd dug out the jacket, washed, and pressed it. I'd tried to explain that I wasn't a chef like Rachel, but Mom said none of that mattered. I ran the Union Street Bakery and I'd earned the right to wear the jacket. I smoothed my hand over the jacket's smooth worn cotton and thought about the thousands of times I'd seen Mom wear this when I was a kid. Pride welled inside me, and my throat tightened with emotion.

I cleared my throat. "Stop it."

With no time to dry my hair, I combed it out and tied it back at the nape of my neck in a neat bun. A little lip gloss and a touch of blush and I was ready, if you could call it that. I feared I'd never be the neat, buttoned-up old Daisy, and for the first time wondered if I had still had the chops for United.

"Shit." I headed down the stairs and found Rachel surveying our trays of cookies and looking clean and as fresh as spring.

"How the hell do you do it?" I asked.

She glanced up. "What?"

"You look great. Always."

"Thanks, I think." She cocked her head. "Was that a compliment?"

"Yes. Damn it. How do you always look so pulled together?"

A hint of color rose in her cheeks. "Glue and spitballs and prayers."

I laughed. "Say again?"

"Don't be fooled, Daisy. It's all smoke and mirrors. Now, are you ready to hit the road?"

"Ready and willing."

We found Mom and Dad in the café, standing behind the display case. Seeing them in their Union Street Bakery T-shirts and white pants really took me back to when I was a kid. When I was in elementary school, I'd come home in the afternoons, snag several cookies, and sit behind the counter while I did my homework. Margaret and Rachel always headed to their rooms, but I liked being around my parents and the day's last burst of activity. Back then, I thought my parents could do just about anything, and they'd be around forever.

Now, as I stared at Dad's stooped shoulders and the streaks of gray in Mom's hair, I realized that forever wasn't as long as I'd first thought. Hell, I was reading the journal of a girl, who even if she went on to a full life, has been dead over a hundred years. Time waited for no one.

"Daisy." The edge in Rachel's tone had me turning.

"Yeah?"

"Grab a platter." Annoyance snapped in Rachel's eyes. The cheerleader did have a temper. Good.

"I'm coming." I lifted a tray filled with little cakes covered in chocolate, vanilla, lemon, and what I thought was apple-flavored icing.

Rachel had carved the plain squares into triangles and dusted them with sparkling sugars. The display was a work of art, and I could tell Rachel had put her heart and soul into the confections. "You didn't sleep much last night, did you?"

"Why do you say that?"

"This is fabulous, and you're in a foul mood. And I believe your foundation is a shade thicker under your eyes."

The compliment coaxed a hint of a smile. "I'll get to bed extra early tonight."

"You girls look as pretty as pictures." Mom pointed the digital camera I gave her for Christmas and snapped. "Now, stand together really quick and let me shoot a picture."

"Mom, we've got to go," I said.

"Smile," Mom warned.

Dad glared at us. "Do what your mother says."

We stood side by side, our platters waist high and grinning into the camera. Mom snapped a picture and then a second and, yes, a third for luck.

We started for the back door and Dad looked as if he wanted to follow.

"Don't you dare, Frank," Mom said. "This trip is the girls' job."

He grunted and winked at us. "They're prettier than me."

"Where are you going today?" Mom asked.

"Duke Street, to the 1212 Building." Remembering Brad's comment about Simon Davenport I'd also researched his company last night. Davenport was hiring and gearing up for a big development. Developments required meetings and openings and ribbon cuttings. And all those events were more palatable with baked goods.

Dad frowned. "I thought no solicitation in that area."

"I'm banking on the fact that no one is going to stop us once they see Rachel's creations."

"They might throw you out," Mom said.

"So be it."

We loaded up our trays in the back of the bakery's delivery

van and drove the ten blocks to the city's business district. Tall twenty-story buildings, built in the last twenty years, were stacked end to end within a few blocks. These buildings were home to endless associations, nonprofits, and other businesses that I was sure could have used a good dessert caterer. We were less than a couple of miles away but none of the folks who worked here would make the trek to us. Until we got a website, if we wanted them, we had to travel.

We parked and unloaded the trays. As we approached the first glass tower, Rachel nodded toward a no soliciting sign on the front door. "They're going to kick us out."

"Maybe. Maybe not."

Worry creased her forehead. "Yeah, but the sign reads 'No Soliciting.'"

"Please. If I were afraid of the word *no*, I'd never have earned a living in my past life."

"I hate 'no.'"

"I welcome 'no.' It's a challenge for me." Why I couldn't translate that sentiment to Terry escaped me. "Just follow my lead and smile."

We shoved through the front door. From the directory, I snagged a few names of companies I'd remembered from my finance days and then walked up to the security desk. The guard, an older balding guy in his fifties, lifted his gaze from a *National Enquirer* magazine. "What can I do for you ladies?"

"We're here to see Simon Davenport." I couldn't say for sure if Davenport had a meeting today, but chances were, he did. He was a bit of a control freak and stayed on top of his employees' work.

"No one goes directly to Davenport."

Good, because I really wanted the office manager or the gatekeeper, or the one who wielded the company's food purchasing power. Simon was just a name to get us past the guard.

The old man's gaze flickered over the dessert trays as if it were a juicy bit of porn. "Are they expecting you?"

I held the tray up so he could get a better look. "Cakes are for his meeting."

"He's never ordered food before."

Rachel shifted uncomfortably.

I grinned. "Hey, in this financial market, wouldn't you want something sweet to eat while you heard the latest news?"

A half smile tipped the edge of his mouth. "Yeah. Yeah."

Rachel pulled out a napkin and plucked a cake from the tray.

"Would you like a snack?"

He glanced from side to side. "We're not supposed to take anything."

Rachel, taking her lead from me, set the cake in front of him. "I won't tell."

Like an errant child, he snatched the cake. "Fancy."

"Melts in your mouth." I was the devil, recruiting another sinner.

He pinched a piece of icing and then took a bite. "My God."

Chalk another one up to the dark side. "I know, I know. Sin."

People could talk for hours about low-fat, high-protein, or fat-free, but in practice few stuck to it. Americans spent billions on diets and all kinds of devices to give them rock-hard bodies, but the reality was they wanted the gooey, sweet, fattening stuff that they knew in their heart of hearts was bad.

The guard shoved the rest of the cake in his mouth. "Davenport Property is on the sixth floor."

I set another cake in front of him. "Thanks."

When the elevator doors closed, Rachel's nerves bubbled up in giggles. "I can't believe we made it this far."

Elevator music hummed above our heads. "Stick with me, kid."

"Who is Simon Davenport?" she said.

"A dude we really have no intention of seeing. Chances are, he's locked behind closed doors, and we'll never see him. We're going to tell his secretary he placed an order with us. When the secretary announces he placed no order, we'll feel bad and leave samples behind."

"And cards?"

"You're catching on, grasshopper."

"What if they throw us out?"

Of all the things Rachel had endured in the last year and a half, and she was afraid of this. "Then they throw us out."

"How did you get so brave?"

Once your mother left you on a patio at age three to fend for yourself, the rest just didn't seem so bad. "Genetics."

The doors opened to chrome, glass, and muted tones of blue and gray with accents of black. All very tasteful. The cool, clean lines coupled with sleek furniture, and the gentle hum of fluorescents took me back to Suburban Enterprises. It had been less than three months since I'd worked in a place like this, and yet it felt like a million miles way. Were United's offices this nice? I hoped they would be but would have been happy with a cubicle at this point.

"Can I help you?" The question came from an efficient woman sitting behind a tall receptionist desk. She wore an earpiece that connected to a phone bank, which must have had thirty lines.

Suddenly, the bravado wilted a fraction. I'd been a part of this world, and now I was the outsider. Shit. I hated being the outsider. Feeling defensive quickly morphed to anger, which motivated me to speak. "We have a delivery for Mr. Davenport's quarterly meeting."

Plucked black eyebrow rose. "That is not until tomorrow."

"Really?" I tried to look confused. "You sure? The delivery slip says today. The twenty-first."

She drummed manicured fingers on her desk. "Wrong day. And I can promise you that I didn't order any refreshments for tomorrow's meeting."

"Wow." I nibbled my lip. "We goofed."

"I never placed an order."

I shook my head. "Hey, it's not my job to sort the mysteries. Only to deliver the goods." I glanced at the tray. "We're here. And the boss will flip if I bring these back. Would you like them?"

"I'm not paying."

"Free of charge. A gift from Union Street Bakery." I set the tray on the receptionist desk along with a few dozen cards. "Enjoy."

She rose and inspected the confections. Rachel was an artist, and her creations were hard for even a hard-core purist to resist.

"Take just one." My voice was soft and inviting as the Serpent's was to Eve. "You won't be sorry."

She smiled a conspirator's smile and took a chocolate cake with vanilla icing. She bit and her eyes closed in pure pleasure softened her features. She couldn't speak.

Bingo. Hooked.

"Well, we better get going," I said.

She opened her eyes as if she'd just enjoyed a great round of sex.

"Perhaps we can drop the tray in the break room."

"Sure, fine."

The door to the conference room opened and a tall, lean man with eyes the color of coal appeared. He wore a dark suit, white tailored shirt and gold cufflinks that caught the light.

His gaze landed on Rachel, and then me and then, back on Rachel. "What's this?"

The receptionist hid her remaining cake behind her console. "They're with the Union Street Bakery. They had a delivery on their books for your quarterly meeting."

"That's tomorrow. And I don't order food." He surveyed our wares and frowned, clearly in no mood for any distraction. "I don't have time for this. I need the financials on Morrison on my desk in five minutes."

Davenport and I had attended the same meetings over the years. We'd shaken hands and spoken to each other. Once he'd even complimented me on an observation I'd made about a particular bond. But now his assessment of me had stopped at the uniform. I should be grateful that the receptionist loved our stuff and that we had made real headway. I just needed to stay quiet and leave. But common sense had not been my best friend lately.

I moved toward Davenport, my hand extended. "Mr. Davenport, Daisy McCrae."

He glanced at my hand but didn't take it. "Who?"

"Daisy McCrae. I used to be with Suburban Enterprises."

The dark gaze narrowed before recognition flickered in his gaze.

"You worked with Gordon Singleton."

"I did."

"The firm blew up. Your team was fired."

I tossed him a bright smile. "Yes, we were."

"Is this a ploy to get a job here?"

"As the uniform suggests, I'm no longer in finance. I'm working at my parents' bakery."

"Quaint. Good for you."

I wasn't accustomed to being dismissed. Who was he to look down on my family and the family business? Sure, I'd looked down on them at times, but they were my family, and I had the right. He did not. My smile widened to the point of brittleness. "Would you like a cake?"

"No."

I thrust a napkin and cake in his hand. "Why not? They're great."

"I don't eat sugar." He made "sugar" sound as if it were a dirty word.

"You and Barbie Baker need to leave."

"What did you call my sister?" I asked.

Davenport glared at his receptionist. "Why are we here having this conversation?"

She paled. "I'll call security."

"No need," Rachel said. "We're going."

"Right," I said. "No need to call a man in to do what you can't. Take care, Davenport. Oh, and too bad about the Waterford property. I read a few weeks ago that the banks are calling in the loan."

As the elevator doors closed, Davenport glared at us as if we were something the cat had thrown up. I waved. So did Rachel.

"Call us if you need a bakery."

The doors dinged closed, and Rachel shook her head. "Way to go, Daisy."

"The guy's a dick."

Laughter erupted from Rachel. "Daisy!"

Later that evening, thoughts of Simon and the other nine business calls we made today dug at me. All in all, the visits had been good. Everyone loved the cakes, and I was sure we'd see orders. But Simon's sneer still tugged at my ego.

Ass. Dick. Jerk. I was just as good as I was a year ago. Hell, I'd argue I was better and smarter about finance and life in general. And my sister was a goddess in the kitchen.

"You look like you could kill." Margaret peered over the top of a buttercream cake that I was desperately trying to crumb coat before I had to leave for my eight-p.m. interview. My clothes were in a green garbage bag, and I knew if I could get out of here by six thirty, I had time to change.

But I was so annoyed I was ruining the cake with my crumb coating. All crumb coating required was a thin layer of icing to seal in the crumbs. It took a delicate touch, something that didn't come naturally to me, so I had to concentrate. Tomorrow Rachel would come behind me and smooth out my rough patches and cover the cake with a white layer of icing smoother than glass. She'd have been here now but had a thing with the girls.

"What?" I glared at Margaret.

"You look murderous. I mean, more murderous than usual. Did your ghostly friend reappear?"

"Maybe."

Her eyes widened. "Really?"

"He didn't say anything, just knocked a few things over. You found out anything about the guy? I think he still wants me to leave."

"Word's out on the street."

That made me laugh. "You put a word on the street? What is this, *Cops*?"

She grabbed a tasting spoon and scooped up some icing. "We history geeks have our mean streets just like everyone else. If there's something to be found on mystery man, I'll find it." She sucked on the icing spoon. "So how was your marketing adventure?"

I tried to smooth more icing on the cake but found I was excavating more crumbs than sealing them. "Oh, it was good."

"Then why so glum?"

"Guess the whole adventure was too much of a reminder of where I was and where I am."

"Sucks to see what you want and know you can't get it."

The tone of her voice caught my attention. Was there a hint of sadness there? "Everything all right?"

She brushed away my concern with a causal wave. "Yeah, of course. It's just since I didn't get that job at Tulane or Boston, I've been a little out of sorts."

"What jobs?"

"I asked Mom not to tell. I was up for two full-time teaching positions. Neither panned out. But I've got more irons in the fire."

"I never put much stock in a job because I'd always had the one that I wanted. I get now what it feels like to lose a job you love. It kind of sucks."

Margaret shook her head. "It sucks balls."

We both burst out laughing.

"You think you could get another job in finance?" she said.

A knot formed in my stomach and for a second I wondered if she'd guessed I had an interview. "I went a long way to pissing off a big fish today. It's a small community and word spreads."

Margaret snorted. "Rachel told me about Barbie Baker. I think I'd have punched him."

"It did cross my mind."

I couldn't decide if I was a traitor, a sneak, or a savior as I hustled down the back stairs of the bakery, my hefty bag of work clothes clutched close. I stopped in a local fast-food place and changed in the ladies' room. As I struggled with panty hose for the first time in three months, I really had to question my sanity. Real women didn't have to go through this kind of BS to sit in on a job interview. But apparently women who were afraid of disappointing family and losing their love did.

Shoving swollen feet into heels, I winced and then smoothed down my skirt. I hustled out of the stall to the mirror and applied my makeup. Smoothing my hands over my skirt again, I looked in the mirror. For a moment I just stared a bit befuddled by the person looking back. It was the Old Daisy—or at least as close a version as I could manage in a ladies' room. I liked what I saw and that went a long way to calming my nerves.

A quick cab ride later and I was standing in the lobby of United Capital on Duke Street. My heels clicked on the marble floor as I moved toward the elevator and hit the Up button. Butterflies gnawed at my stomach as I thought about what I was going to say. I'd done my homework. I knew Ralph. I could make small talk, even regale him with stories from the bakery. It was all good. I felt great. Pretty much.

When the doors dinged open, I stepped inside the car, hit 20, and rode up in silence as the car rushed past the floors. Twenty arrived, the doors opened, and I crossed plush carpet to a receptionist desk, where a young woman sat. She smiled up at me. "Ms. McCrae."

I was expected. A small detail that I'd taken for granted in my old life—but not now. "Yes. I'm here to see Ralph Denton."

"He's waiting for you in the conference room."

"Thank you." My portfolio tucked under my arm, I followed the receptionist down the hallway. I moved deliberately slowly, shoulders back and chin tilted up. She stopped, nodded to an impressive door and left me alone. I knocked on the conference room door and Ralph, head bent over spreadsheets looked up. He grinned and motioned me inside.

I entered and smiled as he rose. "Ralph. It's good to see you."

He was a tall, lean man with thinning red hair and a ruddy complexion. One of the smartest guys in the industry, it didn't surprise me that he'd landed a job after Suburban's crash.

"Daisy. You're looking great." He extended his hand. "Brad tells me you're managing your folks' bakery?"

"I am." I learned long ago, less was more. Ralph didn't

need to know I'd been drunk when I said yes or that I'd no longer able been able to make my rent payment when Mom had called.

"And it's going well?"

"It's been great. Kind of takes me back to the days when I was a kid." He nodded. We made a little smaller talk. I gave him my resume and a bakery card and then we discussed the particulars of the job: lots of travel, client servicing, long hours. And though we didn't discuss salary, he hinted that it would be in the six-figure range.

"I like you, Daisy. I've always had nothing but great respect for you and if it were up to me, you'd have a job offer now. But I've got partners and I'm going to need to talk to them."

I'd have been shocked if I had walked out of here with a job. "That's reasonable."

"I'll call you in a couple of days."

"Great."

"And if you're wondering about timetables, be ready to start in a week or two."

Next week: the Kushman wedding cake, the meeting with the oven mason, and the health inspector. And after that, Henri's replacement, finding a manager who didn't mind Dad's hovering, Mom rearranging cookies, Margaret's tardiness, and Rachel's inability to remember where she put the latest receipt. "I'll need time to wrap up bakery details, so I'll need some notice."

He grinned. "That's what I always liked about you, Daisy. You never leave a loose thread."

"Thanks, Ralph." I rose, shook his hand, and made as dignified exit as I could. As I stepped onto the elevator, I smiled at the receptionist and watched the doors *ding* closed in front of me.

Ralph had said he'd call within a couple of days, but he

didn't. It really wasn't surprising, I kept telling myself. He was swamped. He was setting up a whole new company and he didn't have time for every personnel issue. Whereas days could pass before he even thought about me, I thought about him every hour on the hour.

In the days since my interview, I had gone from excited to guilt ridden too anxious to be pissed. And by the time I met Margaret at Florence's at precisely two p.m. on Sunday, I had decided Ralph wasn't going to call. It was business, I told myself. It wasn't personal. It was karma. I was willing to leave the bakery and my family. Damn.

Unlike me, Margaret was grinning from ear to ear and her cheeks were flushed. Her aura buzzed with excitement, and I had to admit it felt good to see my sister happy.

Florence greeted us at the door as if we were old friends. "Well, isn't this nice."

She wore a white dress that gathered at the neck and then opened over her large breasts and full body. From a gold chain, a long thick cross dangled at her neckline.

Stockings remained in place, but she'd kicked off her shoes. "Excuse me, ladies, I'm running a bit late from a church luncheon. The deacon wanted to hold a prayer session for Miss Mabel, and it wouldn't have been right for me to leave early."

"Is this still a good time?" This was my attempt at politeness; in my heart of hearts, though, I didn't care if the time was good or not. I wanted to go up into the attic and dive back into the past, which for now felt like the safest place to be. And I could sense by Margaret's shifting stance behind me she was just as anxious. We both smiled, waited patiently just as Mom has raised us.

"The time is fine." She peered around me at Margaret. "And seeing as you brought your sister again, you won't need me climbing up in that attic to help. That young man coming again?"

Margaret grinned. "No. Hugo had some other gig today, but he wished us luck. Daisy and I have strong backs and can manage the dirty work, Miss Florence. Why don't you sit and rest a bit?

We'll give a shout if we find anything."

"Suits me just fine, girls. My butt is still too fat and old to climb those stairs anyway. Care for some lemonade before you go up there?"

"Maybe after?" I suggested.

"Sounds good, baby. You two know the way." She moved up the stairs to the second floor and opened the door that led to the attic staircase. "Call out if you need me. Oh, and you may want to do some of your hunting in the back right corner. For some reason, I'm thinking that's where you'll find stuff of interest."

"Thanks," I said.

The instant the door to the attic was opened, a rush of musty, warm air washed over us. I didn't get the sense of being greeted but of being warned that I don't belong up here. The sensation almost made me smile. If something was up there looking for a fight, I was more than ready to mix it up.

We climbed the stairs, and I jerked the chain and the bulb flickered on. Margaret reached in her knapsack and pulled out two scuffed silver flashlights. "I assumed you forgot your light again."

"Guilty." I accepted the light. "Two points to the history geek." She clicked on her light. "I want to start digging."

"Will do."

A quick pass with the flashlights revealed the area that we'd cleared out the other day and then the other side that remained stuffed. We'd stayed away from that side the other day because the area had barely enough clearance for our heads. Clothes hung from the rafters and boxes, trunks and old furniture ate up just about all the floor space.

My light skimmed over more boxes. "You think we'll find more pictures?" I asked.

"Worried about old Simon?"

"Not worried but curious."

"No more woo-woo stuff at the bakery?"

"Not really."

Margaret pushed past me and weaved through the boxes toward the back wall. "It would be so cool if he showed today. So cool."

She'd yet to feel the thickening of the air, the rush of adrenaline and a racing heart as she pulled in a breath. "Yeah, cool." Crouching, I followed. "So where do we start this time?"

"Like all good archaeologists. The top layer." She sat her light down on a box and opened the one next to it. "We'll start with a general sort. See what's in the boxes. If it's of general interest, we'll dig a little deeper. If it makes the cut, we'll haul it downstairs."

It was a plan, and I could do anything if I had a plan. Logic. Numbers. Plans. That was me. "Tell me what to do, boss."

Margaret raised her head and smiled. "Boss. I do love the sound of that." There were only a few times in my life that I'd really appreciated.

Margaret. She had, after all, been put on this earth to torture me. But in this moment, I did appreciate her. I'd be a little bewildered without her. And life was never quite as interesting when she wasn't around.

"Don't let it swell your head."

"No. Never." She dropped her gaze to the box and began to plow through what looked like clothes. Not ancient clothes but like a couple of decades old. "This box is a no—1960s stuff. We want much older." She handed me the box. "Put it on the other side of the attic. We want to be methodical about this."

I took the box. "Margaret and methodical. I never would have thought I could use those two words together."

"Hey, you see me at my worst every morning. Most nights I'm up till two doing real work, and then I drag my carcass out of the bed to ring that register. Not my best time."

"It's a paycheck."

She snorted. "Believe me, there are better ways to earn a living."

I raised a brow. "Then why do you do it?"

For a moment, her hands stilled. "Same reason as you, Rachel, Mom, and Dad. You and I are more alike than you realize." An uneasy knot formed in my gut.

"Please."

"We've both given up lives we loved to work in the bakery."

"I lost my job."

"Don't bullshit me or yourself. If you'd really wanted to stay in the industry, you could've gone to another city. There's work out there, but you're not willing to relocate. You are tied to this area, like it or not." She rummaged through the next box and closed it. "This is a no. More '60s shit."

I put the box aside. "I'm not saying you're right about me. But you're not exactly wrong, either. If ever I got back into the industry, I'd stay local."

"If ever?" she said.

"Just saying."

If not for the attic's treasures, she might have picked up on the guilty tension rising in my body. Interviewing with Ralph was feeling akin to adultery. After about thirty minutes, I could feel the sweat trickling down my back and the dense, dusty air clinging to my skin.

"So how is it that Mabel would have had Susie's diary? I haven't seen the connection."

"Remember, this is the Randolph house. More than likely, Susie hid the diary and someone along the way found it. Maybe it was Mabel."

"Okay. Then what is the connection to us? It's got to be more than she liked the bakery's sweet buns."

"I think that is the puzzle Mabel has left for us."

I brushed my hair out of my eyes with the back of my hand. "Why not just tell us?"

"Where is the fun in that?"

"Would she really do that? Turn this into a game?"

"Maybe. Maybe she figured you wouldn't sit and listen to what she said but you'd care more if you had to dig. Maybe she just couldn't remember as well as she used to. Who knows?"

Despite it all, the search grew boring for me over the next hour. My back hurt and I was getting hungry. Margaret, on the other hand, was energized despite the mountain of mess. If I'd been alone, I'd have given up by the third box, but with her I was willing to stick it out—if not for my sake, then for hers.

Twenty minutes and five boxes later, Margaret let out a low whistle that had me turning. "What does that mean?"

"It means I just found a box of letters that date back to the nineteenth century. They are from a woman named Sally Good, and she's writing the letters to Shaun McCrae."

"Our Shaun?"

"It's addressed to McCrae Bakery."

"Sally Good, the woman he married."

She tapped her finger on the side of the wooden box. "That is correct."

"How did they get here?"

"I don't know. Yet." Gingerly, she thumbed through the collection of yellowed envelopes. "I don't think I can get back to my office fast enough to read these."

"Don't forget that Mabel's nephews are rolling into town this week. This might be our only chance to dig and get what we can. Is there anything else in this area? That might be the first of several items."

"Good point. You're thinking like an archaeologist now. Very good."

"I like to think I can adapt." My energy returning, I held out my hands for the box. "Give that to me and keep digging."

We rummaged for another two hours but most of what we found was furniture, knickknacks, lanterns, and picture frames.

When we came down the attic stairs after too many dusty hours, we'd hauled down all the boxes we'd inspected and then found Florence sitting at the kitchen table sipping her lemonade. She'd changed into a blue housecoat and traded her white low heels for house slippers. A small television on the kitchen counter blared a televangelist's sermon. When the floorboards creaked under our feet, she glanced up from the screen.

With a groan, she pushed to her feet. "I was thinking you two might have gotten lost up there."

"Lots of stuff up there," I said. "We hauled down a good many boxes and left them in the hallway."

"Good. Got to be a lot. There's a lifetime or two of memories." Florence's gaze dropped to the box in Margaret's hands. "Looks like you found something."

"We did," I said. "A box of letters from a woman named Sally Good."

Florence shook her head. "Can't say as I know that name."

"We've not had time to read them," Margaret said. "But we think she was the woman who married our great-great-grandfather."

Dark brows rose in interest. "That so?"

Margaret's blue shirt was covered in dust and sweat. I glanced in the glass-paneled door and caught a hint of my reflection. Like Margaret, I looked like I'd been dragged through the mud. My hair stuck up and my shirt was covered in dirt smudges. We resembled Thelma and Louise after their lives had gone wrong.

"I was hoping you would allow us to take them back to the center so we can read them properly," Margaret said.

"Keep them for all I care," she said. "Those nephews are gonna toss or sell what's in this house, and I'd rather know that they went to someone who cares about them."

"Thanks," I said. I thought about all that was up in that attic. "When did you say the boys were coming?"

"Tuesday."

"I don't think we'll be able to get by again," I said.

Margaret knitted her hands as if in prayer. "Yeah. Darn."

"Well, if they happen to haul anything down of interest, I'll pull it aside."

"Thanks," Margaret said.

"I do appreciate it."

"Mabel wanted you digging for a reason, so it seems right I should help if I can." She clapped her hands together. "Now, let me get you girls lemonade and sandwiches. You've got to be hungry. Maybe you could read me one of those letters."

My stomach grumbled.

Florence laughed. "Sit yourselves down."

As Florence poured the lemonade, I watched as Margaret gingerly pulled out a letter. The faded ivory envelope was yellowed around the edges and the pages crinkled when she pulled out the first page.

"I really shouldn't be touching this," she said. "I should have gloves."

"I got my white church gloves," Florence offered as she stirred the lemonade in the glass pitcher.

"Actually, that would be great," Margaret said.

"In my handbag, by the front door. They're lying right on

top." Margaret glanced at me as if to say, *Do it*. My knee-jerk response was to argue but she'd earned big-time brownie points so headed down the hallway. I spotted the white patent leather purse on a small mahogany table by the door and the gloves draped over it. As I snatched up the gloves, I happened to glimpse a picture of Mabel taken with a young man. The photo looked to have been taken in the early '60s. Mabel stood straight, and her dark hair was teased high on her head. She wore funky catlike glasses and a flowered dress. She would have been in her mid to early fifties when the photo was snapped. My gaze drifted to the guy who was in his mid-twenties, wore a checkered short-sleeved shirt and short hair parted on the right. Tall and lanky, he had his arm around Mabel and was grinning.

I'm not sure what it was about him that caught my attention, but I found myself leaning in for a better look. His hair was as dark as mine, and his skin had an olive tint. As I looked at him, I had the odd sensation that I was looking at myself. This wasn't the first time this had happened to me, so instantly my guard rose. I didn't want to start daydreaming about how another stranger might somehow be related to me. I didn't need that drama.

Irritated, I turned from the photo and carried the gloves into the kitchen. Impatience and annoyance snapped in Margaret's eyes. "Did you get lost?"

I had, when I'd stared into eyes that had reminded me of me. "Sorry."

The weak attempt at an apology grabbed Margret's attention. "Everything all right?"

"Yeah, sure." Florence handed me the lemonade and before I thought to ask, I said, "Who is in that picture with Florence by the front door?"

"The young man with that checked shirt?"

"Yeah." Today the lemonade tasted bitter.

"That's one of her nephews. Thomas. He was one of her favorites."

"Was Thomas in for the funeral?"

"No. Thomas passed about twenty years ago. Had a heart attack, I think. He has a sister, but she didn't come to the funeral."

Disappointment slammed and bounced around my chest. I had never met this guy, and I still felt as if I'd lost something. Stupid. "So, let's have a look at that letter."

Margaret seemed to understand that something was up, but she didn't say a word. Instead, she slipped on the far-too-large gloves, pulled the letter out of the envelope, and gently opened it. Paper creaked and cracked.

Dear Mr. McCrae,

I've decided that I am not well suited for boarding school. The girls here continue to be far too silly, and I've no desire to sit and stitch for hours on end. I am doing as you advised and keeping my thoughts to myself but my frustration bubbles when the other girls giggle at my cross-stitch patterns. The world is full of far more important issues than the petty dramas that erupt in dance or French lessons.

Jenna continues to thrive, and she seems to love her art classes the most. I do worry about the spring cold that she caught. Though she's mended now, it took her some time to recover. Do not tell her I've told you this. She does not want you worrying about her.

How does work at the bakery progress? Will you be buying that new oven? How is Hennie doing? Does she still miss her Susie? My heart goes out to her. Tell her I understand her loss, and that I too miss my own mother terribly. Send her my love. Please send word of real news soon.

Your friend, Sally

April 3, 1856

"Sally knew Susie and Hennie," I said.

Margaret laid the letter down. "Remember Mabel said her grandmother told her stories about a young slave girl?"

Keeping all the family connections straight was a challenge. "Sally was Mabel's grandmother, and Mabel is a distant cousin of ours."

"I don't know," Margaret said. "She never said a word to me about family connections. And Mom and Dad never said anything, either."

"Well, Dad never talks about family. Losing his dad was painful so he just avoided the whole family tree thing all together," I said. "And if Mom knew I was a bit touchy when it came to discussing past relations seeing as I didn't know mine."

We both reread the letter. "It sounds like Sally lost or had been separated from her mother, and that she understood what Hennie might be feeling."

Susie. Jenna. Sally. All girls who'd lost their mothers. Like me.

Their losses made me take a hard look at my situation. I could contact mine. She'd written me a letter—and I hadn't done a damn thing about it but whine and worry. It was time to stop and rip the Band-Aid off. There was a woman out there who had answers, and I was ignoring her because I was afraid. Suddenly, my fear smelled like a big load of bullshit.

An hour later, I left the letters with an excited Margaret in her apartment and made my way back to the bakery. After a quick check of inventory and supplies, I headed up to my room and dug Terry's letter out of the box where I'd stashed it weeks ago.

It wasn't like me to run from trouble. In fact, I was the kid who ran *toward* it. My coworkers at Suburban often said Daisy never met a problem she didn't like to ratchet up. And here I'd been acting like the small child on the bakery patio eating her cookie and waiting desperately for her mother to return.

As carefully as Margaret opened Sally's letter, I opened Terry's. My hands trembled and my breath grew shallow as I read the words: *Thirty years ago . . .*

Tears burned my eyes, and I felt sick. Like it or not, I had to talk to this woman. She might be bogus. She might have answers. But one way or another, I needed to know.

Picking up my cell, I dialed the contact number in the letter. My heart hammered in my chest as the phone rang once. Twice. Three times. And on the fourth ring, voice mail picked up. "*This is Terry Davis. I'm unable to answer my phone right now but leave a message, and you know I'll get back.*"

You know I'll get back. I wanted to say that I do not know that. I wanted to say that I hated her for leaving and turning me into such a goddammed basket case. I also wanted to tell her I loved her, and I wanted her to say the same to me.

But instead of going into a long explanation, I let my breath trickle and leak slowly from my lungs before I said, "This is Daisy McCrae. I believe you sent a letter to my mother, Sheila McCrae." Pause. Crap. Now what do I say? "I'm familiar with the little girl you mentioned. We might be able to help each other."

I left my number, and then quickly hit End. I held the phone to my racing heart, wondering how long it would take her to return my call. What if she never called me back? What if she was a con artist who'd dug up old newspaper articles? What if she missed me all these years and was sorry?

I had no idea what to expect. "Damn."

Chapter Seventeen

FRIDAY, APRIL 23, 2010, 2:00 PM

I obsessively checked my voice mail every morning . . . oh, hell, I checked it on the hour, every hour for several days, hoping to hear from Ralph or Terry. There was no message or text from either one. Nothing. Nada. Two simple phone calls could have made my life so much easier and yet neither came.

I did check in with Florence and learned Mabel's nephews were indeed in town. They'd hired an appraiser and were trying to figure out the value of the furnishings. Neither nephew was happy about the fact that the house couldn't be sold but for now they'd accepted the terms of the will. I told Florence to call me if they got nasty. I knew attorneys. Margaret went through the letters one by one and had reported it was slow going. Time had faded the ink, and the attic heat had left many of the pages brittle. Many crumbled in her hands when she tried to open them, so she'd contacted a preservationist.

As much as I wanted to care about the letters, I couldn't sum up any real interest. Even my interview with Ralph had faded to the background. My thoughts stayed glued on Terry.

I did multiple internet searches. I got a few hits on the name, but with no pictures I really couldn't tell definitively who was who. I even pulled up Facebook and searched through every Terry Davis shown, thinking I'd spot someone who looked like me. I got nothing.

Frustrated, I shut off the computer, annoyed that I was sacrificing good sleep to chase down this woman who was only a brief letter and a voice on an answering machine. *You know I'll get back.*

And through all my emotional crap, the bakery business, unmindful of me, moved on as it always did. Customers. Orders. Deliveries. Repeat. Rachel and I dropped off more samples at the office buildings on Duke. We gave out quotes for parties. We booked two more weddings.

By Friday, I'd still heard nothing from Terry or Ralph, and my nerves surrendered to anger. Ralph owed me a damn call as did Terry, who had dropped a freaking grenade in my life and hadn't bothered to return the call. Just my luck.

So, I decided to take the bull by the horns. I went out to the back alley behind the dumpster and called Ralph, the lesser of the two evils. I got his secretary first, who put me on hold. I wasn't sure if she was going to put the call through when Ralph got on the line.

"Daisy," he said. "I'm so sorry I've not called you. It's been a damn nightmare here."

I forced a smile in my voice. "Hey, I know you've got to be swamped, but I'm at the point where I either commit to you or the home business." And that was true. I couldn't keep accepting orders and marketing if I intended to bolt.

"It's been a bitch getting the board of directors together so we can look at your resume."

The committee hadn't even looked at my resumé. I'm not sure why that would have caused me to snap but it did. I was damn tired of being ignored and though I couldn't do anything about Terry, I could handle Ralph. "Ralph, take my name out of the hat. I don't want the job."

"Daisy, it's just a matter of days."

Maybe. Maybe not. "Either way, I appreciate the effort, but I'm staying put."

"You're sure?"

No. "Yes."

"If you change your mind . . ." His voice trailed off.

"Thanks."

Carefully I closed my phone and kicked the Dumpster in a rush of frustration. "Damn. Damn. Damn."

"You interview for a job?" Margaret's voice echoed through the alley.

I started and turned and found her holding a bag of trash. Her expression was a mixture of shock and disbelief. "I just took my name out of the hat."

"Why?"

I pressed my phone against my temple. "Because I have lost my mind."

"Did you have a shot at it?"

"Yeah."

"Why?"

I shoved out a breath. "Because the guy I interviewed with was supposed to call me back and he didn't and I just kind of decided if he didn't have the manners to call, he could bite it."

Margaret crossed to the Dumpster and tossed in the trash. "Let me guess. You called Terry and she didn't call you back."

"How did you know?"

"You can't get a hold of her so you're going to hammer the next closest person—interview guy."

I shoved fingers through my hair. "Crap. I just gave up a dream job."

"Dreamier than this place?" she said with a smile.

"If the Smithsonian came to you with a curator position,

would you take it?"

"Hell, yes."

"Well, I just passed on a job like that."

Worry creased her forehead as the analogy took root. "Maybe if you call him back, you could tell him you went insane for a minute or two."

"I thought you wanted me to stay."

"If it's the Smithsonian of the finance world, I can't keep you from that."

"Thanks. That means a lot." I swallowed a lump in my throat. "But I'm supposed to be here. I don't know why, but I am."

We stood there for a few minutes, saying nothing. Around the rumble of car engines, the blare of a police siren and rush of wind swirled around us.

"On a lighter note," Margaret said, "I've been reading Sally's letters."

I softened the edges of my voice. "What have you found?"

"You're probably not going to like it."

I sighed. "Try me."

"In the earliest letters, the girl mentions missing her mother often. She wishes she could see and hold her mother again. She was homesick for Virginia."

My stomach burned with frustration. I didn't want to feel so awful. "Sally was from Alexandria."

"She never said exactly where, and I've found no record of her." Margaret leaned against the brick wall of the bakery and folded her arms over her chest. "But that's not a huge surprise. Lots of people vanished into history."

"Anything else?"

"She speaks of her studies and of Jenna's health, which improves and slides with the seasons. No more mention of Susie."

"Why would she talk more about Susie?"

"I don't know. Just thought she would. The trail on Susie went cold shortly before Sally's first letter."

"And the trail on Terry is cold." The irony of the whole mess was not lost on me. I couldn't connect with a birth mother or a damn kid from the past.

"Have you talked to Mom? I mean, she's been cool about this whole Terry thing."

"I know I should. She's chomping at the bit about the whole thing. But I need neutral. I need Switzerland. A place without drama or emotion."

A breeze teased the wisps of hair framing her face. "I can see that."

"I don't have too many options."

"Florence?" she suggested.

"The nephews have arrived."

"I saw movers hauling furniture and boxes out. And when I caught glimpses of her in the front window, she was always talking to someone."

I thought about the photo of Mabel and her nephew Thomas, who had eyes like mine. Dead Thomas. I wondered if there was another nephew who looked like me. Maybe I should go back and introduce myself.

That's when I decided I was losing it.

"You got any friends?" Margaret asked.

I laughed. "You mean other than Tammy?"

She rolled her eyes. "Right. I forgot. You didn't make that many friends in high school."

Perhaps it was my lack of choices that made me think about Gordon. "Mind if I take a break? I've mixed all your icings, so you have all you need for the cakes."

"I got this," she said.

"Rachel should have the girls settled from school in the next half hour, and she'll help finish up."

"Thanks."

"Sure."

I walked quickly up Union Street but slowed my pace when I saw the new bike shop sign dangling above the brick building's door. Through the big picture window now displaying bikes, I could see Gordon standing behind his counter surrounded by dozens of half- opened boxes. He was talking on his cell phone and gauging by the frown wrinkling his forehead he didn't look happy. Good. We were a matched set.

I pushed through the front door, wincing as a doorbell jangled.

Two rows of bikes took up a good chunk of the room. A neon sign in the back blinked race. A poster on the wall featured a Tour de France rider blazing through a field of sunflowers.

He lifted his head. He winked and some of the ice in my chest melted. I flexed my fingers; aware I'd arrived empty handed. I wished I'd brought something. Cookies. Cupcakes — something to give me an excuse for being here. Pushing my hands into my jean pockets, I wondered why I felt like a teenager. As he spoke on the phone, I pretended to care about a bike hanging from the wall.

When he hung up, he ran long fingers through his hair. "Hey."

"So, who's chewing on you?" I asked.

He rubbed the back of his neck. "What makes you think someone is chewing on me?"

"You run your hands through your hair when you are upset. And right now, your hair is standing on top of your head, Gordon. What gives? And don't lie, I know you."

That coaxed a grin. "Attorneys."

"Good ones or bad ones? And yes, there are both kinds in the world."

"Good ones, for now. They represent Suburban in a

lawsuit from a former client."

It made sense that some of Suburban's clients would eventually sue.

Billons had been lost while Gordon had been at the helm. "Do they represent you?"

"That was my question."

"And?"

The frown returned. "Still waiting on that one."

"Who's suing?" And then I held up my hand. "Let me guess. Consolidated, Travers, or Carpone." I'd just rattled off the three biggest losers in the market crash.

"Travers. And they want a pound of flesh."

I sighed. Everyone had been advised of the risks and still they'd kept their very big bets on the table. They'd known that Gordon's lucky streak, like even the best poker players', could end. But they kept letting their bets ride. "The president at Travers is trying to save face with his board."

"You were always clear with him about the risks, and you stayed within the client's investment guidelines." Which was true. Gordon had never sugarcoated the fact that he was a high-stakes gambler.

"Thanks for saying that. It's good to hear. Sometimes it's hard to get past all the losses."

"The market went sour. A lot of people got burned." I'd been one of those who'd been burned and yet here I stood, consoling him.

"I might have talked about risks, but I was arrogant. A decade of winning made me believe I was flameproof, and I got scorched."

Talking about Suburban three months ago would have really ramped up my blood pressure. The losses, the work, and the people were all still so fresh in my mind. The time at the bakery, however, had given me some distance. I'd transformed from a fast-burning fuse into a slower version. "You and half the industry. Yep, you fucked up, Gordon. No secret there. You took risks and lost. But it's time to come down off the cross."

He frowned. "I'm not on the cross."

"Oh, please. You are so up on the cross. If that winter bike trip wasn't penitence, then I don't know what is. Let's face it. You've been up there for a couple of years."

He frowned. "Not true."

I'd cracked open a door that I'd wanted to open for a long time. Even if I could have taken back my last words and slammed the door closed, I wouldn't. "All those nights you worked late. The missed meals. The weekend dates we had that always fell apart. When I tried to talk to you about all that, you called me ungrateful and childish. Once, you even said that if I really understood, I'd back off."

His brow furrowed as if he recalled the incident. "You left shortly after that comment."

I was surprised he'd even remembered. "I did understand. I wanted to help. But you were determined to go it alone. I felt rejected." Tears pooled in my eyes. "And if you haven't noticed, I don't do rejection well."

For a long, tense moment he stared at me. "I never wanted you to leave."

"I couldn't stay. I felt so useless."

"You were never useless."

I swiped away a tear. "Yes, I was."

"No, you weren't, Daisy. If not for you, I'd never have made it that last year. I'm sorry."

"Are you?"

"Yeah. I really, really am."

I'd had dozens of reasons that rationalized our breakup. Now it seemed they all could have been neutralized with a simple conversation.

I should have just pushed and used this moment of openness to air out all our past grievances. But I did what I did best: I backed away from the problem. "Well, that level of deep was not what I expected when I came today. Honestly."

The darkening in Gordon's gaze told me he recognized my familiar retreat tactic. "I'm not sure I want to change this subject."

"Why not? I've got a ton of other things I can talk about."

"Not me. This is the first time I even halfway understand how things got screwed up between us. I want to understand."

"Hey, it's troubled waters under the bridge."

"You know, I thought you'd met another guy."

Now that threw me for a loop. "There was no other guy. Did someone tell you that?"

"It was the abruptness of the breakup. One day you were there and the next you were gone."

"No other guy. Just me snapping."

He cocked his head. "You left because I was gone all the time?"

I pressed fingertips to my temple. "Basically, yeah. Frankly, you left me long before I moved out."

"I was trying to save billions of dollars." Frustration rattled around the words.

"My adult brain gets that. But the kid in my soul is an immature shit. I have a history of impulsive actions that just dig me into holes. Frankly, Gordon, I did you a favor by leaving. I'm not designed for the long haul."

Blue eyes narrowed. "When did you decide that?"

Frustration, anger, and fear bubbled up like a perfect storm. I almost shouted, *When she left me.* "I don't know. I just know."

He came around the counter and moved within inches of me. Heat radiated from his body. "I always thought we had a real shot at the long haul."

I swallowed, wondering how this can of worms had gotten

wedged open. "I never knew."

"Liar."

"I don't lie. I run, but I don't lie."

"You knew I wanted more." The words were softly spoken but still felt like a right hook.

"You never said so."

He shoved long fingers through his hair. "I tried to show it. I mentioned kids, a topic you always skidded around. And I did propose."

"It felt a little like desperation when you asked."

"Maybe I was desperate. You did all that at first, but then you stopped trying."

"I could say the same."

Unshed tears clogged my throat. "I've told you there's a layer between me and the world. And like it or not, it will always be there." He placed his hands on my shoulders and the warmth from his fingertips moved through my body like a soothing balm. "Have you called her?"

I nodded. "On Sunday night."

"And?"

"I haven't heard a word from her. Which is driving me insane, because I am finally ready to get a few answers and now she's MIA. I keep compulsively checking my voice mail and the mailbox and every time the stupid front door to the bakery opens, I jump."

"Call her again." An edge of anger sharpened the words.

"I am not calling her again. God. It took me four weeks to get up the nerve to call her the first time. A second call requires at least two months of second-guessing and worrying."

My lame attempt at humor didn't sway him. "I'll call her."

"No!"

He opened his phone. "I'm not going to spend the next two months watching you suffer."

"Fine. I'll do it in silence."

He shook his head. "I'm perfect for this. I have no dog in the fight. Besides, what if she didn't get the message or was on vacation?"

"Or space aliens abducted her?"

He glared at me. "I think there are a lot of regular reasons. Let me call her."

My heart thumped one, two, three times. What did I have to lose?

I could say everything, but I'd lost that already when she left the first time, so what did it matter if I lost it again? Before I could think, I fished my phone out of my back pocket and handed it to Gordon. "Her number is in my directory. Davis, Terry. But I've already left her a message."

"Now it's my turn." He pushed a couple of buttons and then held the phone to his ear. "It's ringing."

I tried to back away, but he grabbed my hand. His skin was rough, calloused and warm. This close, I could hear a masculine voice on the other end say, "Hello?"

"Hi, this is Gordon Singleton and I'm calling for Terry Davis." There was no hint of apology in Gordon's voice. In fact, his tone hinted that he had every right to speak to anyone he chooses. He tilted the phone toward me.

"Terry is out of town. She forgot her cell phone. Can I take a message?"

"I'm a tour guide in Alexandria, Virginia, and she'd arranged for a bike tour. I just wanted to confirm the details."

God, he was so smooth. I squeezed his fingers, and he winked at me. "Terry didn't say anything about a bike tour, but she flew out this morning for D.C."

I thought my knees would give way. "Then I'll bet she catches up with me when she lands. Just didn't want to hold the four road bikes past today until I confirmed. Tell you what, if she calls in could you have her call me?"

"Sure."

Gordon rattled off his number, said his good-byes, and hung up. "She's headed this way."

I smoothed sweaty palms down my jeans. "Do you think she's coming to see me?"

Gordon brushed a lock of hair from my eyes. "That's a safe bet."

"Yeah, but why would she forget her cell phone? If she wants to call me, she won't have a phone."

"Hotels still have phones, Daisy."

"Yeah, but . . ."

"Stop analyzing. You'll see her soon enough."

* * *

Rachel was icing a cake for a birthday party that the girls were attending. Money was tight, and Rachel didn't have the thirty bucks to drop on the kid's present, so when the mom had mentioned ordering the girl's birthday cake, Rachel had offered to make the cake as the girl's present. The mother had jumped at the idea.

The afternoon was slow, so she'd called up to her mother and told her to bring the girls downstairs. She knew they'd be excited about the party and wired. She thought (foolishly) that they could play in the bakery while she piped the finishing touches on the princess cake.

When the bakery closed at three, the trio, cake in hand, would head out to the party. The perfect plan.

Neither Anna nor Ellie seemed to care about helping, however. Both had found long wooden spoons, decided they were pirates, and that a sword fight was in order. When the noise reached ear-shattering levels Rachel ordered silence, directed them into the kitchen, and gave the girls paper and pencil. Their assignment was to draw a birthday card for their friend.

Rachel set down her piping bag and glanced through the oval window into the kitchen door. The girls lay on the floor, coloring and giggling. When the twins were like this, she had to concede that they were more angel than devil and that she was so lucky to have them. Losing Mike had nearly killed her, and if not for the girls she wondered where she'd be now.

She understood adoption and surrendering your child to the loving arms of another, but to just abandon a three-year-old? For her own selfish reasons, she hoped Daisy did get to meet Terry. She wanted to hear the woman's explanation directly.

The bell rang again. She didn't want to deal with this new customer and found the interruption more than annoying. But she forced a smile and turned. Her smile froze. Her jaw dropped before she snapped it closed. Simon Davenport stood at the door.

She crossed and opened the door. "Can I help you?"

Simon Davenport wore a crisp dark suit, white linen shirt, red tie, and polished wingtips. Sunlight danced on his gold cuff links.

"I need a cake." The deep voice sharpened each word.

In his office, he'd looked like the captain of his ship, tall, intimidating, and ready to bark orders and send heads rolling. But here he looked just a little lost. Daisy said he'd brokered billion-dollar deals, but she doubted he had ever handled daily mundane tasks such as dry cleaning, paying a parking ticket, or buying a cake.

She was oddly pleased that the man who had ruffled her just days ago and made her feel like a babbling idiot, was now on her turf. "We can do just about any cake you'd like. Can you tell me the occasion."

He took a step forward into the bakery, drawing confidence with each breath. He was the type who adapted quickly.

"Birthday. Fiftieth." She wiped the remnants of pink icing from her hands. "A milestone. So, something special."

"Yes."

"What kind of cake?"

"I was hoping you could tell me."

From the kitchen, childish peals of laughter drifted into the front shop. "My girls," Rachel said.

When he didn't show the least bit of interest, the snap of irritation returned. She cleared her throat. "Chocolate or vanilla or something denser, like a carrot cake."

"Do you have a specialty?"

"Two. Chocolate espresso and carrot. Both are to die for."

An eyebrow arched. "No lack of confidence there."

In most things in life, she worried, fretted and second-guessed.

But in the kitchen, she was at home and blissfully sure of herself. "This is what I do. And I'm good at it."

The thread of confidence seemed to intrigue him. "I'll leave the decision up to you."

She brushed long bangs out of her eyes. "The cake is not about me. Who's it for?"

"My secretary."

"The cake should reflect her tastes. What does she like?"

"I don't know."

It didn't shock her that Davenport didn't know much about his secretary. Mike, God bless him, could have listed her favorite books or movies without prompting. "How long has she worked for you?"

"Ten years."

"Does she put sugar in her coffee?"

He frowned and thought for a moment. "No."

"Cream?"

"No. She drinks it black."

"When she orders food for a meeting, does she choose

donuts or bagels?"

"Bagels. Fruit." He hesitated. "She keeps chocolate in her desk drawer. I saw it the other day when I was searching for a pencil."

"Dark or milk?"

"Dark."

"Okay, she likes a touch of sweet but leans toward savory. We'll do the chocolate espresso." She made a note on her order pad. "How many people?"

"One hundred."

She blinked. "One hundred."

"I want all the employees to have a slice."

He didn't strike her as a giving man. "We can do that. When do you need it?"

"Monday by eleven o'clock."

To her credit, her jaw didn't drop. "That's a quick turnaround." Normally she allowed three days for a big cake. Day one, bake; day two, crumb coat; day three, ice. To make this schedule work she'd have to bake the cakes tonight before she went to bed.

He didn't look concerned. "Can you fill the order or not?"

Immediately she thought through tomorrow's baking schedule. "It'll take all hands-on deck."

"I'm willing to pay expedited charges."

She dropped her gaze to the pad. What the hell did that mean? Twenty? Fifty percent? A hundred? God, where was Daisy?

Quickly she calculated the cost of the cake and manpower, and then, channeling Daisy, added a 30—no, 60—percent rush charge fee. She wrote down the final cost, circled it and tore off the page. She handed it to Mr. Davenport, ready to apologize for the extra charge

and backpedal.

He glanced at the sheet and then back at her. Amusement

sparked behind gray eyes. "Pricey."

Ellie laughed, and Anna's voice grew louder. Pots clanged and dropped. Any second, they would burst through the door and start running around the café like wild animals.

Apologies danced on the tip of her tongue, but she swallowed them all. "It'll be the best cake you'll ever eat." And she knew it would but saying it out loud sounded so brash.

"All right."

All right. Crap. If she could pull this off, the bakery just might stay in the black another week.

"Just initial the order, give me a 20 percent down payment, and we're good to go."

He handed her a credit card. She rang it up, half expecting him to change his mind. But when she put the slip in front of him and handed him the pen, he signed a quick efficient signature.

"Give it back," Anna shouted.

"I hate you!" Ellie said.

There was a loud crash, and Rachel guessed the girls had just fallen into the stacks of metal mixing bowls on the counter. The bowls she'd just washed.

Rachel smiled, wondering how she could love her children so much and still have fantasies about selling them to the gypsies. "Thank you for your order, Mr. Davenport. What time would you like this delivered?"

Another crash pulled his attention to the window into the kitchen. "Is there a problem back in the kitchen?"

Rachel didn't bother a glance back. What kind of disaster was she going to discover? "Nothing out of the ordinary." In the next instant, the swinging door between the front and back swung open. A quick glance over her shoulder revealed two five-year-olds standing in the doorway, each covered in white flour. When each blinked, white flecks fell from their eyelashes.

Davenport stared at the children as if they were space aliens. "You're sure you can fill this order?"

She thought about the charge she'd just run on his card. It would pay the electric bill, which she knew Daisy had been holding. "Your cake will be on time and perfect."

"Mom," Anna said.

Rachel kept her gaze on Davenport, but her hand shot up in warning to her child. "What time did you need the cake?"

"Eleven. Monday."

"Mom," Ellie said.

Rachel's pulse throbbed in her neck as her smile widened. Executive pastry chefs in D.C., New York, or Paris didn't deal with children tearing apart their kitchens. They had staff that helped them and told them that they were wonderful. "We'll have it there. Thank you for your order."

Davenport glanced at the children and then back at Rachel. She'd been told she didn't look old enough to have children, and she imagined that was what he was thinking. "See you then."

She kept her back to them as she stood calmly and quietly until he left through the front door. He looked back through the large windowpane. She waved. Only when he walked away did she dare ask, "What does the kitchen look like?"

The girls looked at each other. "Bad," Anna answered.

"Real bad," Ellie said.

Rachel pushed an unsteady hand through her hair and glanced at the clock. Three p.m. She rushed to the front door and locked it, fearing Davenport would change his mind and return for a refund.

As she moved back across the bakery, she noted the girls' faces were filled with worry. As much as she dreaded the mess, she didn't have the heart to yell. "So, we have some cleaning up to do?"

Anna nodded. "Yes. I got the broom out of the closet."

"And I got the dustpan," Ellie said.

"Then let's get to work."

A knock at the front door had her tensing. Mr. Davenport had returned, no doubt rethinking the high cost of the cake. So much for paying off the electric bill.

A closer look and she was relieved to see that her latest visitor was not Davenport but a woman. The closed sign blocked her face, but it was clear she was tall and lean. Rachel had never turned a customer away no matter how tempting . . . but it was so tempting now. She had a cake to deliver and girls to drop off at a birthday party.

But customers were money and money were a very necessary fact of life. "Girls, wipe off your hands and faces. We're going to need to hustle to get to the birthday party."

"What about the mess?" Anna says.

"I'll get it later." She crossed and opened the front door. The bells above her head jingled and danced as the woman in profile stared at the street, a curtain of dark hair obscuring her features. She was nicely dressed in a cream-colored suit and suede high heels. She wore a thick gold bracelet on her wrist and sported a huge diamond band on her ring finger.

"Can I help you?" Rachel said.

The woman turned and offered a chilly smile. "I hope so."

Rachel took immediate note of the woman's trim figure, smooth olive skin, and angled chin. Gray streaks at her temples suggested she was in her fifties. But what struck Rachel the most was the woman's gray-green eyes. How many times had she seen those same eyes filled with sadness, anger and, on rare occasions, laughter?

She knew those eyes because they were Daisy's eyes. Her sister, who had never looked like anyone in the family, who had been the odd duck, the fish out of water, now had a doppelgänger.

Anxiety clenched Rachel's spine. "You must be Terry."

Chapter Eighteen

FRIDAY, APRIL 23, 2010, 5:30 PM

I was surprised to see a customer in the store a half hour after closing. I knew Rachel had a birthday party with the girls, and she'd been adamant about closing on time. The instant I pushed through the front door and saw the strain on Rachel's face, I knew something was wrong. Her expression mirrored the one she had at Mike's funeral. It was one of grief, anger, and dread.

My gaze flickered to the threat: the tall, nicely dressed woman who stood with her back to me. Instantly, fire stoked in my belly as I drew in a breath ready to battle this woman, whoever she might be. "What's up, Rachel?"

The woman turned and for a moment my mind didn't register what I saw.

"Daisy." Rachel's voice held the controlled calmness that had soothed many a family row.

"This is Terry Davis."

Renee. Terry. The author of the letter. My birth mother. The woman who had abandoned me on the patio so many years ago. I'd rarely been at a loss for words in my life, but they failed me now. What the hell did someone say in a situation like this? *How's it going? Nice you could stop by? So, what's been going on the last thirty years?*

Terry took a step toward me. Tension rippled through her body. "Daisy is still your name."

"Yes." Her fingers, I noticed, were just like mine. Long and lean with deep nail beds. And her face mirrored mine.

Even as I stared at a mid-fifties version of myself, I felt like a small child. For an instant, I flashed back to a moment when I sat in my birth mother's lanky lap trying to relax into her tense arms as she rocked back and forth. I was crying, hungry for comfort. She was also crying, seemingly just as starved for comfort.

The child in me was selfish indeed and had little care for the young mother who'd birthed her. That little girl wanted her mother—this woman—to take me in her arms and whisper words of apology as she sought forgiveness and explained everything. God, there was so much I wanted . . .

"Daisy." Rachel's calm voice cut through the tension. "I just put on a pot of coffee. I thought you two might like a cup. Mom's run the kids to the party. I can stay if you want."

I couldn't take my eyes off Terry. Growing up, I'd never looked like anybody and now I stood face to face with a near twin. "No, that's fine, Rachel. You go."

The eerie calm in my voice had Rachel staring closely at me. "Are you sure?"

"Yes. I'm fine."

"Okay. But Mom will be coming back here soon." I didn't miss the warning or the extra emphasis on "Mom."

"I've got my cell. I'm only ten minutes away."

"Go. Please."

Terry rubbed her thumb over the top of her Prada purse, which she held close to her cream jacket. A white silk blouse, fitted pants, and sleek suede shoes told me life had treated her well. So much for all the dreams I'd had of a poor, destitute Renee.

When Rachel left, I moved toward the counter, needing a task to buy me a little time. "Would you like a cup of coffee?"

"Sure. I've not reached my ten-cup quota yet." Her smile was stiff and forced.

"You and me both." In a family of tea drinkers, I'd never imagined a coffee junkie had birthed me. I poured two cups in USB mugs and nodded toward the back. "I've an office back there. It's quiet."

"Sure."

"Oh, cream or sugar?"

"No. Black is fine."

Aware only of the coffee's heat warming my fingers and the click of Terry's heels, I made the short trek to my office. I set the mugs on the edge of my desk and then cleared bank statements and invoices from the one spare chair I had. I positioned it closer but not so close that our knees touched.

As I stared at the face that looked so much like mine, I thought about the lifetime of dreams I'd had about her. As much as I thought I knew her, I realized I didn't know her at all. She was a stranger. And I didn't warm up to strangers easily.

My chair squeaked and groaned as I settled and then debated the merits of leaning back, which denoted casual, then fearing that would appear indifferent, I thought about sitting forward and crossing my legs. Did that show interest or over eagerness? In the end, I didn't really move in either direction. I remained straight, feet flat on the floor.

Terry nestled her purse in her lap. Her long fingers traced and retraced the triangular Prada logo. "I wasn't sure if you'd talk to me when I didn't hear from you after I wrote the letters. I was just going to let the whole reunion thing go but then you called."

I tugged at a loose thread on my jacket. "Yeah. I left a message on Sunday."

A long, shuddering breath filled her lungs. "It took me a few days to arrange a getaway. I thought a face-to-face might be more effective than a call."

"Honestly, a call would have been better. It would have given me a little more time to digest this whole thing. I had a friend of mine call your cell. I guess your husband answered." Color drained from her face. "What did your friend say?"

"He owns a bike shop and he inquired about your upcoming rental. We didn't want to blow your cover."

A breath eased from her. "Thanks."

"Your husband doesn't know you're here."

"No." She crossed and recrossed her legs. "I'm kind of an all-or-nothing person."

"I've noticed." The words bit more than I'd intended. "Sorry."

Why was I the first to utter an apology?

She frowned. "I brought pictures for you. They are of you when you were born." She fished the photos out of her purse and handed them to me.

I took them and slowly thumbed through them. There was a half dozen in all and the first featured me as a newborn swaddled in a pink blanket. I had a scrunched face and from the looks, I'd been crying. In next picture, I was a few months old. Terry held me close to her face, and we both were smiling. In this photo, we looked so happy. I leaned into the pictures, studying her face. There was no hint of fear. No hint that she would run.

"Until now, my earliest pictures were taken when I was three. Can I keep these?"

"Yes, they're for you. I'm sorry there aren't more, but I didn't have a camera then. These were all taken by friends and roommates." She tapped her foot. "I know you've got to have questions for me."

"I do." I sipped the coffee but found it far harsher than Rachel's usual fare. Carefully, I set it on the desk, noting Terry had not touched hers. "But honestly, I'm not sure where to start."

She sat back in her chair. "I suppose the day I left might be a good place."

A numbing stillness settled in my chest. "That does top the list."

For several moments, she didn't speak as if she were flipping through a script written and rewritten over the years. "I was a different person then. I was very young and was on a bad path. I was only seventeen when you were born. I wasn't married and my parents could not accept that I'd had an out-of-wedlock baby."

So, I had grandparents who also had not wanted me. Wonderful. "Who's my father?"

"His name was George. When we met, he wasn't even old enough to have a driver's license.

There was only the one night between us."

"Wow." Product of a one-night stand. "Did you tell him about me?"

"No." She released a breath. "It wouldn't have worked even if I had told him. He was so young. From what he told me that night, he didn't get along with family either and I feared they'd take issue with a baby. I didn't want to end your life before it began."

For that I was grateful. She'd given me what no one else on the planet could have: life.

"You didn't consider adoption?"

"I thought I could raise you by myself. But I had no idea how hard it would be to raise a child."

Emotion tightened my throat. "Where was I born?"

"Baltimore. Do you have children?"

"No."

"Well, in case you do, you might like to know that you were an easy pregnancy and delivery. Just a couple of pushes and you were out."

Fertile stock. Great. "Did we stay in Baltimore?"

"Yes. I was living with cousins and then later, friends. And for a while it worked well. I worked nights while you slept. My friends watched you at night and I took care of you during the day."

"What went wrong?"

"I woke up on my twentieth birthday and looked in the mirror. I looked twice my age, and I felt so old. You were so full of energy and light, and I did love you. But I realized we just weren't good for each other."

"You just said I was doing well."

"*I* wasn't."

"What you're saying is that I wasn't good for you." My voice remained low and controlled but sharp edges bracketed the words.

Her lips flattened. "I'm here to explain, not to justify or apologize. I don't expect you'll like everything I have to say, but I believe you have a right to know."

I leaned forward. "I'm thirty-four years old. Why now?"

She eased back in her chair. "About time, don't you think?"

I wasn't sure what it was that set my senses on alert. Was it the quick downturn of her gaze or the shift in her energy? Whatever it was, I knew she wasn't telling me everything. "Mabel Woodrow was an old lady who lived here in town. She died two weeks ago at the age of ninety. She swore she saw us together before you took me to the bakery. Did she see us together?"

Her gaze widened. She opened her mouth. Closed it. And then finally said, "She did."

I sat back in my chair, annoyance shattering the shaky reserve I clung to. "So, all these years she knew who you were, and she never came forward."

"I don't know anything about that. I haven't spoken to Mabel in thirty years."

The image of the young boy standing next to Mabel flashed in my head. Now I knew why he'd looked so familiar to me. He looked like me. He looked like Terry. "So, she must have been your aunt or something?"

Her complexion paled. "How did you know?"

"There's a picture hanging in her hallway. She's standing next to a boy. I was there last week, and the picture caught my attention. He looked like me. I'm guessing he was your dad."

"Daddy was her favorite nephew."

"He died."

"Ten years ago. Heart attack."

"Sorry." Shit. *Stop apologizing.*

"Thanks."

Silence settled between us, and I found myself again facing the question that had haunted me for thirty years. "Why did you just leave me?"

Terry moistened her lips. "I didn't just leave you."

"You left me in a bakery, alone." The calmness in my voice amazed me. In fact, the entire tone of this conversation was a wonder. So civilized. So, contained. "I was three years old."

"There were plenty of people. And I watched the lady running the bakery for a good half hour before I made my decision. She looked kind."

My heartbeat so loudly I folded my arms over my chest. "She's kind. She and her husband adopted me."

"Really? I didn't know that. I only contacted the bakery because this was the last place, I saw you."

"Right." I was trying hard to find something to like about her. I wanted a good reason for her abandonment.

She nodded, and I sensed if she'd had any lingering guilt over my desertion, it vanished. "Then I made the right decision leaving you with her."

"She could have been a serial killer for all you knew."

Her gaze hardened. "That's not fair. I watched her for over a half hour."

"That's right. A whole half hour. I heard that. What led you to the decision to walk?" The question was soaked with anger.

"I went to see Mabel to ask her for money. I needed help." She flexed her fingers. "I had a drinking problem then. I wasn't doing well. She'd given me money before and I thought she'd do it again. When she wouldn't return my calls, we took the bus to Alexandria, so I could see her. I thought if she saw me —and you, especially—she'd give me money."

"Mabel didn't give you a dime."

"She gave me two dollars and told me to go to the bakery. She said to feed you and to think about my life."

She shook her head, as if the memory of Mabel's rejection had stalked her for years. "She told me that two dollars was the last bit of money I'd ever see from her again."

"And you went to the bakery."

"I bought you cookies."

"Sugar with red sprinkles."

"You remember?"

"I remember that and the scent of peppermints."

"I ate a lot of candy then. The drugs made me crave sugar. They gave out peppermints where I worked, and I was always snagging some."

"Okay."

"Daisy, I really did think you'd be better off. I believed Mabel had sent me to the bakery because she knew the lady who ran this place was a happy, giving person. And when I saw her, I thought she was the kind of mother I wanted for you."

"You never spoke to her. You didn't ask her if she knew anything about kids. You didn't know if she could afford a child. You only watched her for thirty minutes."

"But Mabel sent me here. Mabel did everything for a reason."

"What if she'd sent you to the Dairy Queen or McDonald's?"

Her grip on her purse tightened. "Don't be flip."

"Don't be flip? I'm feeling like I've got a right to a lot of emotions.

After thirty years of questions, I think I'm entitled to a little anger and frustration."

She tapped her foot. "I came here in good faith. I didn't come to be attacked."

"Why did you come? After all these years, it's clear you're doing well. Why now, after so much time?"

"Maybe I thought you had a right to know about your past." I sensed that Terry had rewritten much of what had happened. Somehow in her version, she'd not really done anything wrong. In fact, she'd been more than a tad virtuous when she sat in the café for a whole thirty minutes before walking out of my life.

"Or maybe Mabel contacted you and told you to call me. She knew she didn't have much time, and I'm guessing it bothered her just a little I didn't know the truth."

Terry's jaw tensed, and I knew I'd hit a nerve.

"Did she promise to upset that nice, neat world you have now? Did she threaten to call your husband?"

"She said it was time for me to clear my conscience. Time for me to make peace. She told me to get in touch with the bakery and find out what had happened to you."

"And here you are."

"Yes." She leaned toward me. "I'm trying to do the right thing. You have a right to know where you came from and what's going on in your life. You have a right to know I had uterine cancer two years ago."

That caught me short and drained some of the fire from my belly. "I'm sorry."

"Cancer is no walk in the park, but I'll be fine. But it's something you need to watch out for, though, when you get into your forties."

"Okay."

She pulled a file from her purse. "This is a complete medical history. There's also a copy of your original birth certificate."

I opened the manila folder but didn't really focus on the words. I'd had precious morsels of my past over the years and had jealously guarded them. Now I had a feast to review but found I didn't know where to begin.

"So where do you live now?" I asked.

"New York."

I closed the file. I'd sift through it later but not now. "You look like you've done well for yourself."

"After I left here, I went home. My parents forgave me and helped me get my act together. I got my degree and a job in advertising. I'm married now. I have two boys, ages sixteen and seventeen."

"Did your parents ask about me?"

"I told them I gave you up for adoption. They accepted it without explanation." And so, Daisy the mistake had been brushed under the carpet and forgotten. "I've got to tell you, Terry, in all the years I've fantasized about this moment, this is not what I expected."

She stared at me but didn't apologize.

I knitted my fingers together and set them in my lap. "So where do we go from here?"

"I'll be in town until the end of next week. I'm staying at the Armistead in Alexandria. This is your time to ask your questions."

"And then?"

"Then I go home. You go back to your life, and I go back to mine."

"Just like that?"

"Yes." She rose. "Look, I think we've covered a lot today."

Standing, I couldn't help but smile at the absolute insanity of this day. "You're never going to tell your husband and sons about me, are you?"

"No."

"Did you know child abandonment is a class-six felony?"

She pulled in a steady breath. "My attorney is willing to argue that the bakery was safe harbor."

Of course. "You've covered your bases."

Her lips thinned. "I've got to protect my family."

And yourself. I had always received unconditional love from Mom and Dad. They'd sacrificed a lot for my sisters and me, and I'd never once heard them complain. It was their love that made it so very hard for me to understand how a mother could put herself so easily before her child. Or how she could reject one child and adore others. I'd look back on this moment and wish I'd said a million other things, but I could not summon another word from my stunned brain.

"Call me at the hotel if you want to talk more," she said.

"Sure." I could barely think straight right now and hoped I could calm myself enough to see her again.

I followed her down the hallway into the bakery and to the front door. She unlocked the dead bolt and opened the door. The bells jingled. For a moment, I thought she'd say something else but then she left, vanishing around the corner just as she'd done thirty years ago.

Numbly, I closed the door and locked it. I didn't know whether to laugh or cry or call Mom. I just couldn't move.

Finally, I crossed to the door that led to my apartment. I wanted nothing more than to lie down and curl up into a ball.

When I opened the door, I nearly screamed when I discovered my entire family huddled on the stairs. Dad was at the top, then Mom, then Margaret and Rachel. They made no effort to hide their eavesdropping.

"Honey, are you alright?" Mom asked.

"I'm fine."

Margaret stood. "I hate that word. *Fine.* What the hell does that mean? *Fine.* You look like a truck hit you."

"I'm fine."

"You can't be *fine*," Mom said. She threaded her way through my sisters so that she stood on the step above me, which put us at eye level. "I heard what she said. And I know I wouldn't be fine. I'd be so pissed I'd be throwing pots and pans."

My knees wanted to buckle, and I wasn't sure how much longer I could stand here. Depressing emotions clawed at my insides, and I knew they were going to burst forth like the Hulk. And I didn't want an audience present when the green monster tore its way out of me. "I just need a moment alone."

Mom laid her hands on my shoulders and the gentleness made me flinch. "No more alone time for you, Daisy. I let you sulk in that room of yours far too much when you were a kid. We are going to do this together."

"Together? How can we do this together? You can't know what it feels like to be left. You had your parents. You've got Dad and your kids. Everyone in your life is here."

Tears filled her eyes. "Everyone who is important in your life is here, honey."

"I know what you're saying. You are here for me. And I love you for it. But right now, I just want to go to my room."

"You need us," Dad said.

"I know that. I do." Without warning tears spilled down my face. "But the fact is that the woman who gave birth to me just left me again. Shit. What does that say about me?"

Mom traced a tear from my cheek. "It doesn't say anything about you. This is about her and her shortcomings. You did nothing wrong." Margaret swiped a tear from her face. "Mom's right, Daisy. Don't carry her shit on your back."

"I get that, in my head. I really do."

"Then, what?" Rachel asked.

"Did you hear her say she had two boys? She's raising her boys. She's being a mother to them. But not me."

"As angry as I am about what she did, I do feel sorry for her," Rachel said.

"How can you feel sorry?"

"She made a bad choice thirty years ago. And no matter what she says, she feels it every day. You can't be human and not feel that kind of mistake."

"I don't think she does feel—at least for me."

"She's here, isn't she?" Mom said.

"Because Mabel threatened her."

"She could have rolled the dice on that one, Daisy," Dad said. "We knew Mabel didn't have much time. Terry strikes me as a very clever girl. She'd have figured a way around Mabel."

"I wish I could believe that."

"Honey," Mom said, "Terry fucked up big time when she walked away from you. But I've got to say, the selfish side of me is glad that she did. Otherwise, I wouldn't have had you in my life."

I laughed and swiped away another tear. "Mom, you just said 'fucked up.'"

"Yes, I did. And I meant it."

"I've driven you crazy."

"And so has Margaret and so has Rachel. You each have your own set of issues."

The logic of her words didn't connect with the emotions. Maybe one day. But not today. "Okay."

"Okay what?"

"I hear you. I do. But I just can't think anymore. I just can't. I'll see everyone in the morning."

I climbed my way through my family and up the stairs to my room and went to the window that overlooked the café below. I wonder if Terry had paused and remembered leaving me on the patio when she'd arrived today or had simply breezed past the chairs and tables outside.

I leaned my head against the cool glass of the window. "Shit. Now what?"

And as if by providence, my cell in my back pocket rang. I dug down and glanced at the number, half hoping and half dreading it was Terry. It was Henri.

I cleared my throat and hit send. "Henri."

"I'm in the bakery. We need to talk."

"About?"

"Not on the phone. In the back alley."

I closed my eyes. "I'll be right down."

I moved down the stairs, gave a quick easy wave to everyone and then cut through saloon doors. In bright light of the alley, Henri's wrinkles looked deeper and his skin sallower. I knew I'd be lucky if he made it out the month.

"Henri." I drew in a measured breath, oddly grateful to have a problem that could be solved. Losing Henri would take a toll on us, but we'd survive. The bakery would continue.

He reached in his pocket and pulled out a packet of cigarettes.

Instead of waiting for me, he moved down the alley away from the bakery. I followed. He flipped a lighter open and lit the tip of his cigarette. White smoke curled around his squinting eyes.

"Your father knows, I believe."

"Yes, he knows. I didn't say anything. He guessed."

"He is a smart man. I've always respected him."

"Me, too."

He studied the glowing tip of his cigarette held between his gnarled thumb and index finger.

"Has anyone said anything to you? Has Dad said something?"

"He understands I will come to him when I'm ready."

"No offense, Henri, but you're looking pretty ready."

He smiled . . . a first in my lifetime. "Perhaps I am."

The smoke curled around his face then rose in the air. "So, what is the deal with your cousin?"

I leaned against the brick wall and watched as he took a long drag on his cigarette, savoring the way the smoke rolled out of his nose and lungs. I'd watched him smoke since I was a kid and he made it all look so exotic. When I was fourteen, I'd even stolen one of his cigarettes and lit it up. I'd felt so grown up and so sure. Until I inhaled a lungful of smoke. So light-headed I had to sit down, I'd coughed and sputtered for an hour. Henri had seen me coughing but had never said a word.

"He said he would work for you for two months. If he likes it here, he will stay. If he does not, he will leave."

"Not exactly the solution I was looking for."

"He will like it here."

"How do you know?" A good old-fashioned guarantee would have been nice now. *"Je sais."* I know.

"How old is he now?"

"Thirty. Maybe more."

"Where did he study?"

A grunt told me he didn't think much of my question. He

inhaled again. "He is like me. He worked in a bakery and learned as he went."

No formal training. Of course. But customers didn't care about degrees and certificates. They cared about food.

Choosing the bakery's primary baker was not a decision to make lightly. I was literally allowing Henri to perform a heart transplant for this place. Without the bread baker, we'd die. Two weeks ago, I'd have insisted on a resumé. I'd have worried about immigration paperwork. Work visas. Did the guy even speak English?

But now, I could only run my fingers through my hair and ask, "When will he be here?"

Chapter Nineteen

MONDAY, APRIL 26, 2010, 9:30 AM

My phone rang a lot over the next three days. Most of the calls were from Gordon. A couple calls were from Ralph and Brad. I let all of them go to voice mail. I just didn't have room in my head or heart for anything emotional or troublesome. Gordon wanted more from me; I could hear it in his voice. And Brad, well, he would want to know why I'd walked away from a great job. But I had no answers for anyone.

Noticeably absent from my message bank was a call from Terry. She'd said she was in town all week and I could call her. But it hadn't taken long for hurt feelings to sour into anger. Why should I have to chase after her? She was the one who should be coming to me, hat in hand.

And just like the little three-year-old who'd waited for nights and nights for her mother to return, I waited for Terry to call me.

Rachel stepped out of the kitchen, her gaze a little wild. "The cake is done."

I continued to count the change in the till. "For Davenport?"

Rachel blew out a breath. "I feel like I just gave birth."

I grinned. "You look like it."

She pushed her hair away from her face. "Thanks."

"Anytime."

She plucked a sugar cookie from the case and bit into it. "God, I hope Davenport loves that cake."

"I've never known you to doubt your cakes. What gives?"

"Something about the guy screams, *Prove to me you're good enough*. I hate that."

"Your cake will be good. You've nothing to worry about. Is the cake loaded in the van?"

"It is. Can you drive me?"

"Where's Margaret?"

"MIA."

"Shit."

"I'd drive myself, but someone has to sit in the back and steady the cake."

"Right. Fine. And because Margaret is not here, we'll have to close the bakery." I yanked off my apron and tossed it in the corner.

"Boy, you're in a lovely mood today. In fact, I think you've been an all-around delight since Terry's visit."

"Sorry."

"Why don't you just call her? Talk to her more. Maybe there's more to learn."

"She pretty much said what she needed to say." Rachel pulled off her apron, neatly folded it, and laid it on a nearby chair. "I never figured you for a victim, Daisy. You always seemed so strong."

"I am strong."

"Marshmallow."

"Stop it."

"Then get over yourself and call."

Margaret pushed through the front door. "You'll never believe what I have."

"Where have you been?" I shouted.

"And good afternoon to you, darling." Margaret wore her hair down and a blue peasant blouse that billowed when she moved.

"Bite me."

"Ah, there's my Daisy."

"Look, as much as I'd love to stand here and watch you two argue, I have a cake to deliver. And might I add the client is paying a fortune and please don't forget the fact that I was up all night working on the damn thing!"

Margaret and I had never heard Rachel yell. And it caught us both off guard. I closed the register and really looked at her. Face flushed, eyes bright blue, she looked ready to explode.

"I'll get my keys," I said.

"Doesn't anybody want to hear what I have to say?" Margaret protests.

"Got to drive Rachel across town."

"Fine, I'll come with you."

"You have to babysit the shop."

Margaret went to the door leading upstairs. "*Mom!*"

"What?"

"We have phones, Margaret," I said.

She waved me away. *"Can you work the bakery for an hour? We have a delivery."*

"Sure, honey."

Margaret smiled. "Let's go."

Five minutes later, I was behind the wheel of the truck that Dad bought in the early eighties. The buttons on the radio had broken at least a decade ago and duct tape covered several cracks and splits in the front seat. Margaret rode shotgun while Rachel sat in the back, guarding her cake as if it were a child.

"So why are you here?" I asked Margaret. The engine started on the first.

She twisted in the seat and faced me. "You're going to be sorry for your attitude, missy."

"Right. Sure." I pulled out of the alley and onto a side street.

"I found out what happened to Susie."

Susie had hovered behind my thoughts of Terry, but she never quite made it to the front of my mind. "Great."

"You don't look impressed," Margaret said.

I put on my blinker, turned onto Duke Street and wove into traffic.

"I am. Really. Really," I added with more meaning. "Tell me."

"I found out she was sold at Bruins in January 1853 to a man named Murdock. I started doing a little digging on Murdock and discovered he owned a house of prostitution in New Orleans."

I gripped the wheel, feeling a sense of injustice for the girl. "Basically, she was sold as a sex slave."

She twirled her hair around her finger. "'Fancy house' makes its sound nicer but yeah, that is exactly what happened."

"That just breaks my heart," Rachel said softly from the back. "I think of my girls, and it makes me sick."

Hearing of Susie's bleak life shook away some of my own melancholy. "So, what happened after she got to New Orleans?"

"Well, here's the thing. There was no record of her arriving in Murdock's cathouse."

"What do you mean?"

"Susie was put aboard the ship called the *Diamond*. Murdock bought six slaves that day and he was using the ship to transport them south. The trip by water took a third of the time as it did by land and I guess the way he looked at it, time was money."

I rounded a corner and had to brake suddenly when the car in front of me stopped to let someone off. Rachel held onto the cake while I honked the horn. "So, what happened?"

"Well, I went to the archives and found the manifest for the *Diamond.* Sure enough, six slaves were loaded onto the ship. But only five were delivered to New Orleans."

I glanced at her. "They lost one along the way?"

"She was listed as lost at sea," Margaret said.

"Maybe she jumped overboard and swam to shore," I said.

"It was January. Even if she did jump and even if she could swim, she'd have frozen in the waters."

Before I could answer, we arrived at the office building, and I parked out front in a no parking zone. While Margaret sat behind the wheel, Rachel and I yanked out the folding stainless steel delivery cart and set it up. We loaded the cake on top and pushed. Rachel then grabbed a pink makeup bag, which was chocked full of all kinds of cake repair tools. She also stuffed a piping bag full of icing in her pocket.

As we pushed the cart, the front wheel wobbled and squeaked. This was the part I hated the most: the long walk up the service ramp to the elevators. We'd never lost a cake in my memory, but Dad always told the tale of the time he dropped a cake. *Splattered into one holy goddamn mess.* I'd heard the story a thousand times. And it had left its mark on me.

"You know this fee is going to really help," I said.

"Good." Rachel gritted her teeth as we moved along the concrete. "It damn near killed me."

The wobbly wheel stuck in a crack in the sidewalk and the cake lurched forward. Rachel caught it but judging by the paleness of her face, the near-miss shaved years off her life.

"Damn." I shook my head. "There are easier ways to earn a buck, Rachel. You know that, right?"

She blew a blond lock out of her eyes. "I've heard rumors."

"So why are we doing this?" Why did I give Ralph the big kiss-off? "You've got to admit, there's never a dull moment. You know what you need to do in the morning, and you know if you've done it or not by night."

I laughed. "My paper-pushing days were never clear cut."

"Or satisfying." She hesitated. "Margaret told me about the job offer you turned down."

I wasn't surprised. There were no secrets in the bakery. "It's already ancient history."

"Well, for the record, I'm beyond glad you're staying. You're the heart of USB now."

"You're the heart. I'm the legs and maybe the hands." The smell of cake swirled around me. There was a time when I adored the smells of confections. But lately I been around it so much I'd lost my taste. "This year for my birthday, I know what I want."

"Cake?"

"God, no. I want a bag of chips, a cheese pizza, and a day of dull moments."

"At the rate things are going for us, you might have to settle for cake. We ain't going to be earning big money."

"Don't I know it."

When we arrived on the eighteenth floor, the elevators opened to the quite sterile environment of Davenport Property. There wasn't the rush of customers coming and going, the *clang* of pots, or the gurgle of the espresso machine. I'd longed for this clean sterility just a month ago and now found it flat and dull.

A secretary, sleek and tall with smooth blond hair, rose from her station. "Union Street Bakery?"

Rachel, who'd been on fire in the kitchen, seemed to wilt under the woman's icy stare. She opened her mouth to speak and then glanced at me.

"That's us," I said as cheerfully as I could manage. "We're here with Mr. Davenport's cake."

"In the conference room. Follow me."

As we followed, I glanced at Rachel and wagged my eyebrows. I mouthed the name *Cruella Deville*, which coaxed a little smile.

A long bank of windows, with its views of the Potomac River, dominated the room. It was impossible not to stop and stare at the stunning view. I was only sorry it was a cloudy day. No doubt on a sunny day, the views extended down to the river plantations nestled on the fingers of land jutting into the river.

Rachel carefully pulled the box off the cake and together we lifted it onto a credenza. The cake weighed a good fifty pounds and was a bit unwieldy. But when in place, it was a sight to behold. Rachel had outdone herself.

Even Cruella lifted an eyebrow as she picked up a phone receiver. "As soon as Mr. Davenport gives his final approval, I'll cut you a check."

"Great."

Rachel pulled a small digital camera from her pocket and snapped several pictures. "For our website."

"Which I've got to do this weekend." The to-do list only seemed to get longer.

Davenport appeared minutes later, cold, stern and distant. Gordon had been much like Davenport when he'd worked at Suburban. Tight, controlled, and like ice. I'd liked that about him at the time. Untouchable had suited me just fine then. Now, I thought about Gordon's sun brushed hair and easy smile. He was now so approachable, touchable . . . and frightening.

"The cake appears off center," Davenport said. He must have been six or seven inches taller than Rachel. And his broad frame dwarfed her size.

Rachel tucked her camera in her pocket and studied the cake. "It is perfectly straight."

He moved closer to her to study the cake from her vantage. "It tilts."

She folded her arms over her chest. "It's not a skyscraper. It's a cake. And I promise you when you bite into it, you will feel as if you'd died and gone to heaven."

"Doubtful." He reached in his pocket and handed her a check. "But I've no doubt that it will do."

"It. Will. Do. My cakes will do better than just do. They will make your event."

Her tone had me straightening. You go, Mama Bear.

"I'm sure you believe that," he said. "But it is just a cake."

I really thought Rachel's eyes were going to pop out of her head, so I hooked my arm in hers. "I promise you, Mr. Davenport, Rachel is an artist. You will not forget this cake."

He checked his watch. "I'll forget the cake."

I glanced at Rachel's face. His indifference had not only stunned her, but it had also offended her. She'd put her heart and soul into this cake, and it was a masterpiece. And this guy didn't think it was much more than a Hostess Twinkie. I took the check from Rachel's clenched fist and tossed a fleeting look at the $1,400 windfall. This check was going to solve more than a few problems. It was hard cash we could really use.

"Take the check back," I said.

He frowned but didn't reach for the check. "I pay my debts."

I laid it on the credenza next to the cake. "If that is not the best cake you have ever eaten in your life, then don't pay us."

"That's a lot of money, Ms. McCrae."

"It is. But the way I see it, my money is safe."

Rachel's eyes widened as her gaze darted between the check, Davenport and me. For a moment I thought she'd cave and take the check, but her voice was clear and strong when she said, "And when you discover that that cake is the best you've ever had, I expect you to make us your exclusive caterer."

Amusement danced in his eyes. "You're quite confident."

"About my baking, yes."

"Deal. "I'll call you in the morning with my verdict."

An exclusive deal with Davenport could mean tens of thousands of dollars. We left the offices feeling courageous for as long as it took us to reach the elevator and for the doors to close behind us.

"What have we done?" Rachel buried her face in her hands.

"I just turned down fourteen hundred dollars."

"Fourteen hundred frickin' dollars." She sounded a little hysterical.

"I should have grabbed the check and run."

My heart hammered in my chest. "It'll be okay."

The doors *ding*ed open and a couple of men in suits stepped onto the car. I lowered my voice. "Because that cake is a masterpiece."

"I know that. You know that. But what if he hates the cake? What if he reneges on the deal?"

I laid my hands on her shoulders. "Rachel, he will love the cake and thanks to your throw-down, we just might land a great catering gig. And I know Davenport. He never reneges."

"I shouldn't have said that. You said so yourself: When it comes to business, I'm not so talented. And what if he hates the cake? Do you know how much it cost me to make it?"

"I've seen the receipts."

"The specialty chocolate and organic eggs tipped me over budget, but I just really wanted to blow his socks off."

"You will."

"How do you know?"

"Because I know you and your talents. You're a genius. Not in the office, but in the kitchen, there's no one better."

Her eyes filled with tears. "That's the nicest thing anyone has ever said to me." She hugged me, unmindful of the suits staring at us.

For a moment, I stiffened before relaxing into the hug. "I do have my moments."

"If you can believe in me so much, why can't you believe in yourself?"

"I believe in myself."

She shook her head, fished a tissue from her pocket, and blew her nose. "No, you don't. You have about as much confidence in yourself as I do in business."

"I'm super confident."

"You're a marshmallow."

"I am not."

"Then go see Terry again. Talk to her. Get to know her."

"I don't need Terry to feel good about myself."

She tucked the tissue in her pocket. "That's the thing. You do."

Tears stung my eyes and for a moment I tipped my head back so that I could corral them. "I don't need her."

"Not on a day-to-day basis. But you need to make peace with her so you can make peace with yourself."

"This is bullshit."

Rachel, who had never uttered a harsh word in her life, met my gaze head on. "Life is full of shit we don't want to deal with. I'm living proof. Now put on your big girl pants and go see Terry before she leaves town."

We got into the truck and Margaret fired up the engine. "So, where's the big money?"

"We didn't get paid," I said.

"Did that cheese dick stiff you?" Margaret said. Her bracelets rattled as she turned the corner.

"No. I kinda got pissed when he dissed Rachel."

Rachel leaned forward between the seats. "That's not important. You need to take Daisy to Terry's hotel."

Margaret slammed on the breaks, narrowly missing the BMW in front of us. "I can do that."

"No," I said. "Take me home first. I need to shower and change first. Provided I don't die in a car crash first."

"Sure. But if you don't leave within the hour, we're tossing you into the street," Rachel said.

"Fine."

Margaret hit the accelerator and the van lurched forward. "Guess this isn't the best time to tell you the rest of my story."

"Birth mother. Rejection. Financial ruin. Maybe later."

As promised, I showered and dressed for another meeting with Terry. I lingered in the shower, washing my hair twice and shaving my legs. I dug a clean pair of jeans out of a garbage bag of clothes and an olive-green blouse, which was one of my favorites. I dried my hair and applied makeup.

This was the most pulled together I'd looked in months and that included my interview with Ralph after my quick change in the fast-food ladies' room. I'd done my best to look my best—all for Terry. "So, like she'll like you better if you wear mascara? Pathetic."

As I headed downstairs, Anna's and Ellie's giggles drifted out from their rooms. The sound was so pure and joyful that I had to stop and listen. They were whispering to each other and laughing.

I rounded the corner and found the two sitting cross-legged on the floor around a picnic blanket. A child's plastic tea service was set. The cups were filled with milk and the plates filled with Oreo cookies. There were three place settings.

"Store-bought cookies, ladies?"

Anna laughed. "Mom said we could have real cookies if we were good."

"Real cookies do not come out of a box."

Ellie's eyes widened. "They do! All the girls at school have them."

"I wish we had more real cookies instead of that homemade stuff," Anna said.

"Don't tell your mother that. What are you two doing?" I asked.

Ellie smiled. Her neck was draped in bright, colorful beads. She'd lost her front tooth last week and now whistled when she talked. "We're having tea. Can't you see?"

"I can see you've set a lovely table." Rachel had liked tea parties when we were little, but I'd never had much patience for them once the cookies and milk were gone.

Anna had a boa around her neck and the feathers tickled her nose, making her sneeze. "Ellie won't let me eat my cookies until we've finished."

"Finished what?" I sat between the girls in front of the untouched tea setting.

"Our discussion. And you're sitting in her spot," Ellie said.

I stared at the single Oreo and full cup of milk. "Is Mama coming?"

"No." Ellie giggled. "She's taking a nap."

"I don't think she slept much last night."

"Baking a cake," Anna said.

"So, who is the setting for? Grandma?"

"No," Ellie said. "She's at yoga."

"Grandpa?"

"No," Ellie laughed. This was turning into a game for her. "He's at Roters."

"You mean Rotary?"

"I guess."

I rubbed my chin. "Is Aunt Margaret coming?"

"No. She's at the center. She's got a tour this afternoon."

I shrugged. "Well, I give up. Who is your mystery guest?"

The girls looked at each other and giggled.

I waited, starting to wonder what I was missing.

Anna leaned forward, cupping her hand over her mouth, and whispered, "It's for Susie."

Susie.

For a moment I froze. "You have a friend named Susie?"

"Yep," Ellie said. She picked up her teacup carefully and raised her pinky as she sipped. "You have to drink tea like this."

"So where is your friend?" I said, peering around.

"She comes and goes," Anna said.

"Where is she now?"

"I dunno. Around," Ellie said.

"What does she look like?"

The girls looked at each other as if they didn't know how to answer.

"She looks like Susie," Ellie said.

I didn't want to describe my Susie because I wanted to make sure I'd not put answers in their heads. "What does she wear?"

"A white dress and white stockings," Anna said.

"A white dress with black ankle boots," Ellie offered. "And she has ribbons in her braids."

I glanced down at the untouched cookie. Nerves had me picking it up and taking a bite.

"Hey!" Anna said. "That's for Susie."

"If we're talking about the same Susie, she doesn't eat."

"Why not?"

Because she's a ghost, and she's dead. "I dunno."

"She might want a cookie," Anna said.

"If she comes and wants a cookie, I'll get her one."

That satisfied the girls enough so that they let me eat the cookie. And so, we sat, eating our Oreos and drinking lukewarm milk. I was also careful to keep my pinky elevated as I sipped.

"She knows you," Anna said.

"She does?"

"And she wants you to do something," Ellie whispered.

"What is that?" I whispered back.

"She said you have to talk to Terry."

I swallowed wrong and for a second coughed and struggled to catch my breath. I'd never mentioned Terry to the girls and knew they'd been out of the bakery during her visit. "Terry?"

"The lady who looks like you," Ellie said. "Don't you know anything?"

"I don't think I know so much anymore." I looked down at the dark crumbs sprinkled on my plate and lap. I was tempted to search out the remaining Oreos and polish them off alone in my room. "Did she have anything else to say?"

"She misses Hennie," Ellie said.

"And sometimes she argues with the mean man," Anna added.

"Who is the mean man?"

"She won't tell us," Anna said.

"But," Ellie said in a whispered, "He really doesn't like you."

* * *

I passed a few lively and fun-looking bars as I walked up King Street toward the Armistead. I could have ducked in any one of them, ordered a few beers, and eaten chicken wings until I was sick. I could have even rounded the block and gone to the center and hung out until Margaret returned from her tour.

Instead, I kept putting one foot in front of the other and found myself standing in front of the mahogany desk in the Armistead's reception area. The lobby had an old-world feel with Persian carpets, leather chairs, and a large stone fireplace still sporting the charred embers from last night's fire.

"I'd like to ring Terry Davis's room," I said to the receptionist. "We announce all guests to our visitors. May I give her a name?"

"I'm Daisy McCrae." I hesitated and then added, "Her daughter."

The clerk, a young girl with straight blond hair and clear skin, nodded. She dialed the room and announced me.

I pictured Terry receiving a message that her daughter was downstairs. Not Daisy. Not a friend. But her daughter. A part of me wanted the announcement made to the entire lobby just to upset her . . . a little payback, I guess. But a bigger part of me wanted her to feel some sense of joy or happiness that her own child stood in the lobby waiting for her.

I moved away from the desk, shoving trembling hands in my jean pockets, and took a seat at a baby grand nestled in a corner. Mom had signed me up for piano lessons when I was a kid, but I'd had no interest in learning. The eight weeks' worth of lessons in Mrs. Grover's house had been living hell and I'd been sure to let Mom know all about it each time she picked me up. As a result, the best I could manage on a keyboard was "Chopsticks" and I didn't think the lingering guests wanted to hear that. I traced the black and white keys lightly with my fingers, marveling at the worn softness of the ivory.

"Do you play?" Terry's raspy voice jostled me to my feet.

"No. I tried when I was ten, but I didn't have the patience. Both my sisters play."

Terry wore a black long sleeve T-shirt, black jeans and heels. She'd swept her dark hair back into a ponytail bound at the base of her head with an ebony clip. She wore almost no makeup but that gave her a natural attractiveness. With luck, I'd at least age gracefully.

"Why don't we have a seat by the fireplace? I'll order coffee."

"Sure." She was polite and formal when all I wanted was a hug. But when we sat, she ordered our coffees, scooted back on the full cushions of a red couch, and stared at me. "I'm guessing you have questions."

"Terry, I don't know where to start." Though I'd called myself her daughter at the front desk it never occurred to me to call her "Mom." Sheila McCrae was "Mom."

"I'm still trying to wrap my brain around everything."

She sat back on the couch. Though we were both tense, at least this time it wasn't the paralyzing fear that had made it tough for us both to breathe. "It must be confusing."

"Confusing is on a different scale from what I'm feeling. Confusing is equivalent to a brush fire. I'm standing on the surface of the sun."

"Okay." She crossed and recrossed her legs. "Maybe I should start with the questions."

"Sure." Our coffee arrived, and we both passed on the sugar and cream. "Everyone in my family took cream, but I've never had a taste for it."

"I've never cared for milk in my coffee." A half smile tipped her lips. "Genetics is a crazy thing."

"You're telling me." I sipped the coffee, grateful to have something to do with my hands. "Thanks for the medical information. I've not had a chance to look at it, but it will come in handy one day."

"Sure." She studied me. "So, have you been working and living at the bakery all these years?"

"No, it's a recent thing." Pride had me avoiding the topic of my job loss. "Rachel . . . my sister . . . needed a hand and since the timing was good, I came on board."

"That's good."

"So, I have two half-brothers?"

The apprehension in her eyes faded a fraction and she nodded. "Kyle and David. They're a lot like you. Like me. Both are math minded and like sports."

I'm not sure if she cared but I decided to offer, "I played soccer in high school and majored in business and finance at the University of Richmond."

"You were always a smart kid. Always asking questions."

"What else was I like when I was a baby?"

"You weren't much of a sleeper, and you hated being in the crib alone. You always wanted to sleep with me." Her gaze softened as if a hint of a memory had returned. "When you were two, I took you to see Santa at the mall. All the other kids your age screamed, but not you. You stared at Santa as bold as you pleased and then you pulled his beard off."

"Is that why you left me? Did I ask too many questions? Was I just too demanding?"

I sensed if she could have melted into the cushions she would have. "As I said before, none of this had anything to do with you. I just wasn't ready to be a mother."

"I'm still trying to wrap my brain around the fact that you walked away from your own kid."

She set her cup down. "I know you have a right to be angry, but I'm not interested in sitting here and getting beat up."

"As tempting as that is, I really don't want that either." Odds were my anger would return, but for now it was quiet. "I just want answers."

She fiddled with her wristwatch. "Look, you were a good kid. You were cute. Everyone loved you. I just couldn't hack it."

"But you're hacking it with your sons. I can see that you love them."

"I'm older. I'm in a better place and ready to be a mother.

Frankly, Daisy, I wouldn't wish teen motherhood on my worst enemy."

"My timing was just bad." Bitterness tightened my throat.

"Yes. I suppose."

My stomach clenched. "You said my birth father's name was George. And he was too young to drive. What was his last name?"

"I don't know. He never told me." She held her hand to silence my next comment. "It was a one-night thing at the fair. I only knew about the driving thing because he asked for a ride home."

"That's all you know about him."

She sighed. "I'm not proud of what my life was like when I was younger. I made a lot of big mistakes, both before and after you were born."

This was just getting better and better. "You've no idea who he was?"

"No."

"What did he look like?"

"Short. Reddish hair. Blue eyes. He had a thing for baseball."

"That's not much."

"No." She threaded her manicured fingers together and nestled them in her lap. "I'd doubt I'd even recognize him if he walked into the room right now. And before you ask, you look nothing like him."

"Where did you two meet?"

"Here."

"In Alexandria?"

"Yes. My dad had sent me here to spend a week with Mabel. At the time it felt like punishment, and I was looking to get back at him."

I sat back against by chair. For a moment I simply stared at the ceiling. As much as I wanted to rant and rave, I just couldn't seem to summon the energy. I was the product of teen rebellion.

"When is my real birthday?"

"May 12, 1977."

"May 12?"

"You never knew your real birthday, did you?"

"I didn't."

"What date did you celebrate?"

"That's the kicker. Mom and Dad chose May 12."

"Really?"

My head felt like it was pounding, and I didn't have the reserves to figure out how they'd landed on the correct day. "So where do we go from here?"

She frowned. "I'm here to give you pieces of your past. But . . ."

All the background noises in the room vanished, and all I could hear was the rush of wind in my ears. "You don't want to see me again."

She rubbed her palms together. "Look, if you ever have questions— medical questions—I can try to help, though you'll find most of what you'll need in the file. But no, as far as a mother-daughter thing, I just can't go there."

"I'm not really in the market for a mother. I have a great one. But I thought if we could just correspond." My voice sounded far away, as if it belonged to someone else. "It would be nice to have some kind of connection."

"I don't think that's such a good idea. There's no sense in it."

"No sense?" I laughed.

She raised her chin, the one that looked so much like mine. "I don't see what's so funny."

"You don't? Well, I do. I find it somewhat hysterical that the lady who abandoned me when I was three doesn't want anything more to do with me. Again. God, I thought after all this time something would have changed. I'm not a high-maintenance toddler, and you're not an overwhelmed teenager."

Stress sharpened angles on her face. "I'm sorry. I really am sorry."

"Me, too." As much as I wanted something between us, I wasn't going to beg.

"Best of luck to you, Terry."

I rose and left.

I was not sure where I was going after I left the Armistead, and for a while I walked around, circling the block over and over. Finally, I thought about Mom. She was the one to talk to about Terry. She knew me better than anyone. But Mom also had a dog in this fight, and I was afraid she'd get wound up. Margaret and Rachel would parrot Mom.

Gordon again was the logical choice. But I'd spent the better part of the week ignoring his calls and was not sure if he'd be pissed or glad to see me.

Feeling like it all couldn't get much worse, I walked to his shop, and I pushed through the front door. I wove down the rows of bikes and found him in the back working on a mountain bike.

"Hey."

He glanced through the spokes at me. "Daisy."

"Am I interrupting?"

"I'm putting a new derailer on this bike. The owner needs it in the morning, but I've got a few minutes to spare. What's on your mind?" His tone was clipped, direct, and not the least bit welcoming.

I deserved that. I'd been rude. "I'm sorry I didn't call back."

He fitted his wrench on a bolt and tugged until it loosened. "What can I say?"

This was like removing a Band-Aid. I could peel it off slowly or just let 'er rip. I ripped.

"What is it about me that makes people leave me?"

He cocked his head as tension rippled through his body. "Say that again?"

I folded my hands over my chest. "People leave me. What do I do to drive them away?"

He shoved out a deep breath as he set down his wrench and grabbed a rag. He wiped the grease from his hands. "You left me."

"Because you had left me. I mean, not physically but you'd checked out mentally. Your life became all about work and there didn't seem any room for me." I picked up some of his business cards and then set them back down in a neat stack. "I was trying to save us both grief."

He shook his head. "That plan didn't work out so well. At least for me."

"I know. I'm sorry. And if it helps, I didn't do myself any favors by leaving."

He tossed the soiled rag aside. "Want to know something? I thought if I moved back to Alexandria and put myself in your way every chance I got, you'd eventually start talking to me."

"And here I am, which brings me back to my original question."

Blue eyes narrowed. "No question is simple with you, Daisy. Ever. What happened?"

"I went to see Terry. I won't bore you with all the details, but basically, she doesn't want a relationship with me."

The lines on his face deepened with sadness that heightened my edginess. "She said that?"

"She was quite clear. Several times. So, what is it about me, Gordon? Why do I drive people away?"

He came around and stood so close I could smell the bike

oil mixing with his scent. "I didn't leave you, Daisy. At least, I didn't see it that way. I was trying to work as hard as I could so things would turn around in the company and we could stay together. Your mom and dad and sisters haven't gone anywhere. Fact is, I think they'd all kill for you."

I dropped my gaze and shook my head.

He shoved out a breath. "You're a hard, exasperating woman with strong opinions, a mouth like a trucker, and the work ethic of a sharecropper."

"Those are my good points?"

"You're funny. You make a great grilled chicken. You can play chess, and you're one of the best investment bankers I know."

"But there's something wrong, Gordon. Otherwise, we'd have done a better job. And Terry wouldn't have left me in that damn café all those years ago."

He laid his hand on my shoulder, and I absorbed the warmth while resisting the urge to lean into him and cry.

"I could see how shitty the investment numbers were, Daisy. I knew I was going to put a lot of people out of work." His voice was barely above a whisper, but the words were as rough as sandpaper.

"I was fucking up, and I couldn't stop it. And I couldn't be with anyone."

Tears burned my eyes. I heard the words, but they didn't satisfy me. "I thought we were friends."

"We were. We are." His fingers tightened on my shoulder. "I just couldn't deal with anyone."

"Not even me."

"I'm sorry I pulled away. And I'm sorry Terry doesn't see what she has in you. You really are special."

Tears trickled down my cheek. "Special. Right. That doesn't exactly answer my question."

"You've had the unfortunate luck to be surrounded by damaged people, starting with Terry and, more recently, me."

He captured my hand in his and pulled me toward him. He wrapped his arms around me and held me close. The dam of emotions cracked, letting the sorrow leak and then flood free. I clung to him and started to weep.

Finally, when the tide ebbed, I was able to pull free. I felt foolish standing there all red-faced and weepy. "I better go."

"I want a second chance, Daisy."

"What?"

"It's why I came back. I want to try again."

"I don't know, Gordon. I don't have it in me to endure another breakup."

"There you go again."

"What?"

He brushed a strand of hair away from my eyes. "Assuming the shit is going to hit the fan."

"It always does."

"Not always."

"It's happened enough to scare the shit out of me."

A hint of frustration snapped in his eyes. "Doesn't sound like you have a lot of trust in me."

"Or myself."

"So where does that leave us?"

"I don't know."

His jaw tightened. "I'm trying to be patient, Daisy. But I can't wait forever."

"I know."

He stepped back. "Well, when you do, let me know."

With as much dignity as I could muster, I walked out of the bike shop and back to the bakery. Instead of going to my room, I went to Mom's place and knocked on the door. Only seconds passed before the door snapped open. Mom stood there in her *Runs with Scissors* T-shirt and her knitting in her hand. One glance and she set the knitting aside and took me in her arms.

Tears welled and before I could stop them, I cried.

For several minutes, Mom didn't say anything but held me close. She patted my back and whispered, "I know, I know, my dear."

Finally, when my throat ached and my eyes burned, I pulled back and rubbed fingers over my swollen eyes.

Mom studied me. "You went to see her again."

"Yes. At her hotel."

Mom ushered me inside and closes the door behind me. "Come in the kitchen. I'll make you something."

"I'm not hungry."

She squeezed my hand. "Neither am I, but it'll give us something to do."

"Okay."

I settled into a chrome chair at her kitchen table. I'd sat at this table for as long as I could remember. I'd not only eaten but I'd colored, done homework here, learned to paint my nails, written my college applications as I wished for a different life. And now here I was again. Older. And not so much wiser.

Mom opened the fridge and pulled out luncheon meats, cheeses, and a loaf of bread from the bakery. With her back to me, she got her cutting board and serrated knife. "So, what did she have to say?"

I watched as Mom sliced the bread. "She wished me the best." Mom glanced over her shoulder at me, her brow cocked.

"Really?"

"I thought our first meeting was just too much and that maybe if she

had time to think it over she'd want to get to know me. But she doesn't." I could see it was taking a lot of control for Mom not to unload.

"Did she say why?"

"She's married and has a family. She doesn't want to remember the past. And I'm the past. Nothing has changed since the other day." Mom dug her knife deep into the bread and into the cutting board beneath.

"She did say if I ever had any medical questions that I could contact her."

"How generous."

I traced circles on the table. "She doesn't know who my birth father is. He was a young kid she met at the fair. His name was George. And I was conceived in Alexandria."

"Really?"

"Terry is Mabel's great-niece."

"Did Mabel know about you all along?"

"She did. Terry came to town with me looking for money. Mabel gave her two dollars and told her to come to the bakery and think over her life."

Her mom frowned. "That was the summer of 1980."

"Yeah."

Mom's frown deepened into a scowl. "She showed a lot of interest in you. She encouraged us to keep you. She even suggested we pick May 12 as your birthday."

"Which, as it turns out is my real birthday, according to Terry."

Mom slapped slices of meat and cheeses on the freshly sliced bread and squirted spicy mustard on it, like I preferred. She cut the sandwich on a diagonal, set the plate in front of me, and pulled up a chair across from me. "That crusty old broad knew all along and never said a word."

I reached in my pocket and pulled out the photos of me as an infant. "She gave me these."

Mom studied the photos. Her eyes lit with joy as if she stared at a great treasure. "My goodness. You were a serious little thing even as a baby. See the way your mouth curves down? You do that when you are worried."

"Rachel and Margaret are always smiling in their baby pictures."

She took my hand in hers. "You had a lot on your plate, even as a little thing. My guess is that you understood things were not great even then."

She squeezed my hand. "Daisy, I know you. You've been carrying Terry's problem since you were a child. It's time to let go. Forgive her. And remember that you deserve all the love that is waiting for you to accept."

"I hear you."

"Do you?"

"Sure. Hey, don't worry. I will be fine."

"I want more for you than fine." She studied my face. "What about that Gordon fellow?"

"What about him?"

"He likes you."

I rolled my eyes. "Mom, we had a good thing going but it's over."

"I don't think that it is."

"How can you say that?" Anguish coated the words.

"Honey, he's in town. No one made him come here. He wants to be here near you."

Chapter Twenty

MONDAY, MAY 18, 2010, NOON

Three weeks had passed since I'd seen Terry at the Armistead. She'd left town and I'd not heard anything from her. For a few nights, I'd half expected, half hoped she'd contact me, but she never did. Slowly I stopped obsessively checking phone and email messages.

I was sad and angry by her rejection. It wasn't like I was expecting a fairytale ending but I'd thought she'd want me on some level. Christ, she gave birth to me. But she didn't want me. She had her perfect family in New York, and I didn't fit.

After too many restless nights, I begrudgingly accepted that she was gone. A part of me still hoped that maybe one day she'd reconsider, but most of me knew she wouldn't be calling.

Rejection like that hurts like a bitch, but I'd learned it doesn't kill.

And so, I did what I did best. I tossed myself into work. I'd traded financial statements for pastries, but the result was the same. I worked so I wouldn't have to think.

The happy result of my workaholic ways was that the bakery was starting to thrive. The cake Rachel made for Simon

Davenport was a hit, and we not only got our check for $1,400 but received a couple of corporate orders from the company. Yesterday, I'd been able to sit down with Dad and truthfully tell him we were doing okay. We were in the black, just barely, but it was a good place to be.

I'd not seen much of Gordon, but he left me a message and this time I did call him back. We talked and though we didn't make a date to see each other, we both agreed the talking was good. I don't know if I could welcome an ex-lover into my life now, but a friend might be all right.

Just as the midday lull began, Margaret rushed into the shop. "I have news."

I glanced up from the register and counted out the change for a customer. "Thanks for visiting us at Union Street Bakery."

The woman smiled, accepted her bag of sweet buns, and barely glanced at a grinning Margaret as she left the store.

Margaret hesitated as she waited for the woman to leave and then hurried to the front door and locked it. She flipped the sign from open to closed.

"Hey," I said. "We aren't closed."

"You're gonna want to hear this."

"I can listen and work. Open the door. Those customers keep us in business."

"God, when did you turn into Dad? I mean, grow a paunch and lose some hair and you two will be twins."

"Bite me. Now, open the door."

She opened it. "Now, I'm not so sure I'll tell you what I found."

For reasons I didn't understand, I simply laughed. "You had something to tell me a couple of weeks ago, but it kind of got lost in Terry-gate."

She waggled her brows. "This is even better. I mean, the other stuff was interesting, but this is better."

Seeing Margaret dance of excitement made me laugh. Just to tease her, I made a show of turning toward the cappuccino machine and cleaning the milk dispenser. Whatever Margaret knew, not telling was killing her.

"You're doing this on purpose," she said. "You think I have to tell you, or I'll bust."

I wiped the milk spout on the machine. "I know you'll bust."

"I will not bust. I don't have to tell you anything."

"One. Two . . ."

She groaned her frustration. "Okay, okay, big-time business gal. I'm caving. I can't hold this in another minute."

I didn't turn immediately, but carefully folded the damp towel first.

"What's up?"

"Okay, okay. The trail on Susie went cold."

"You told me."

I knew Margaret had been methodically digging through wills, documents, and papers, but I'd not paid much attention. She had also been digging through Sally's letters. The search for Susie had been an entertaining distraction but the reality was that I needed to worry about my own life, not the girl's tragic, short one.

"What I didn't tell you is what became of her."

Despite my best interest not to be pulled back into this mystery, I found myself turning.

She smiled. "The girl did get on the ship but there's no record of her getting off it."

"Margaret, if she jumped, you said it yourself, she likely drowned. I mean, the ship was in the middle of the Chesapeake Bay in January, wasn't it?"

"I know. I know. But something about the whole thing kept bugging me." I started to protest but she waved her hand.

"So, I went to the ship's inventory log. Turns out McCrae crackers filled the *Diamond*'s storerooms."

"Yeah, I remember Dad saying old Shaun made good profits feeding sailors."

"Then I decided to see what I could find out about Sally Good McCrae. The wife of our illustrious ancestor."

Our ancestor. I didn't see the point in making an issue. "Why look into her past?"

"There was something about her letters that kept bugging me."

"How so?"

"I kept getting the sense that everything she said was double speak."

"What do you mean?"

"There's a line in her first letters to Shaun. It's something like, *'Please tell my Hennie that I so enjoyed the tin of her biscuits. I remember standing back home in Alexandria at my own mother's side making and forming the dough that we sold at market.'*"

"Her mother worked in the bakery, too?"

"She could have been a home baker." Margaret ran her fingers through her hair. "But it is kind of a strange coincidence that both mothers baked and sold goods."

Interest sparked in me, and I leaned into the counter, my arms folded over my chest. "Keep going."

"I searched birth records. I searched wills. Marriage records. Nothing. There's no record of Sally Good until the letters to Shaun begin. And then in 1864, she arrived in Alexandria accompanying Jenna's body. Shortly thereafter she became Mrs. Shaun McCrae. She was twenty-four and he was forty-eight. She becomes an active member of the community. She was a big supporter of education and funded the local schools. If you ask me, I'd say Susie changed her name to Sally Good."

It made sense. "If Susie was Sally, she'd have mailed her letters to Shaun, and he'd have passed them on to Hennie, who lived in the Randolph house until Elisabeth died in 1864. And the journal?"

"My only guess is that Hennie found it. Anyone else would have destroyed it."

"What else do you know?"

"I found a picture of Sally." Her eyes danced with such excitement I couldn't help but get involved.

"And you have it."

"I do. It's a wedding portrait taken of her and Shaun." She opened the folder and held it out to me.

I studied Sally's pale eyes, brown hair, and lovely smooth skin. "Holy shit. Is that Susie?"

"It's hard to tell. We only have the one grainy picture of Susie as a child. But it does look like her, doesn't it?" She pointed to the groom. "Now take a look at Shaun."

I studied piercing eyes, a nose that had been broken several times, and a stern jawline.

"Mystery man."

"Bingo."

"Shaun is haunting me. But why?"

"No one would have figured out the Sally-Susie connection if you'd not come back to Alexandria."

I stared, transfixed, at the couple. "So how did she get off the slave ship?"

"That I don't know."

"Do you think anyone knew her heritage?" I asked, staring at the picture, searching for anything that might confirm our thoughts.

"Doubtful. Her marriage to Shaun McCrae would never have been considered legal if her heritage was discovered. In fact, she could have gotten into serious legal trouble if anyone knew she'd passed herself off as white. And it may have started as her protecting herself, but when Sally and Shaun had children, she would have been worried about them."

"Mrs. Randolph died at the end of the war?"

"From what I understand, Mrs. Randolph got sick right around the time Sally wrote home and said she was returning to Alexandria."

"That's coincidence."

"Maybe Hennie decided she needed to protect her daughter."

"Poison? She poisoned Mrs. Randolph?"

Margaret shrugged. "Who's to say?"

"And her son wouldn't have remembered Susie. He'd been just a baby when she left."

"Others must have known."

"By all accounts, no one guessed that Mrs. Randolph's slave was the beautiful woman who became Mrs. Shaun McCrae."

"So, Sally lived her life with a secret."

"A huge secret. I suspect she had to always be on guard." Had Terry spent most of her life guarding a secret she always feared would be discovered? "That is so sad."

"Read this last letter."

November 30, 1920

My dearest granddaughter,

I so enjoyed your visit to the bakery this morning. When you walked into the bakery today, I was drawn back to the precious days I had with my own mother. It has been fifty years since I've seen my mother, but not a day passes that I don't walk through the bakery *and remember her sweet face. As I watch our bakers knead the dough, I remember her baking lessons, and I realize all that she tried to teach me in those brief years we had together.*

It is my greatest regret that my age may keep us from

standing in my kitchen. I so want to teach you to bake as my mother taught me and I taught your mother. I want to talk to you of a past filled with tales of an auctioneer's block, the putrid hole of a slave ship, a savior hiding me in a cracker barrel, and a frightening trip to Ohio. Fear kept me from telling such tales to your mother, but age has made me bold, and I did so want to share them with you.

I sit now in my chair, fashioned by my dearest Shaun, and stare at the river I love so much. The spring thaws have arrived and the fishing boats, dormant this winter, have resumed their daily treks into the bay. My bones ache more with each day, and I no longer have the desire to mix my dough, which makes me believe my time is nearly past, and I will never be able to tell you or anyone my stories. So, I have assembled my letters and placed them in this box so that you or your children may one day read the history of your family.

All these years I've lived a lifetime pretending to be someone I'm not. The last months spent with my dying mother were done in secret. When people I knew from my true past stared too long, I'd worry and fear, not for myself but for Shaun and our children.

Shaun always labeled the lies necessary if we were to remain together and as much as I understood his reasons, I never totally accepted the deception. I'm a woman of two worlds, who was forced to deny one to live in the other.

The wind grows quite cold now and my toes have gone numb from the still chilly ground. Regrets will always linger in the shadows waiting to unleash melancholy, but it is important, dear Mabel, that you never let past regrets rob you of life's blessings.

Your loving grandmother,
Sally Good McCrae

I glanced up from the letter. "Are you thinking what I'm thinking?"

Margaret nods. "Shaun helped Susie escape to Ohio."

"And the two just started corresponding?"

"It would have been a way to get news to Hennie. Remember, if Shaun's actions had been discovered Mrs. Randolph would have gone out of her way to see him arrested and ruined."

"And when Jenna died, Sally or Susie returned with the body?"

"Despite a twenty-year age difference, she and Shaun must have developed a bond."

"Mabel was their granddaughter. You are their great-grand daughter."

"So are you. We are descended from their second son Robert, and you come from their daughter Ruth's line."

"Which means we are biologically related." My head was spinning with the intertwining connections.

"Second or third cousins, or something like that. But the bottom line is we were both descended from Shaun and Sally McCrae."

I laughed. "I'm a real McCrae."

"Imagine that."

When I climbed the steps to the attic that night, I felt different. Not exactly happy and buoyant but not weighed down and lost as I'd felt so many nights before. There was a sense of acceptance. I understood that my life was not perfect, that Terry and I weren't finished. She might believe that I was a part of her past, but something in me said that we'd meet again. I didn't know when, but right now didn't care, but I knew we had more in store for us.

I wanted to believe that Susie had escaped and had been able to not only remake herself in Ohio but had returned home to live a full and happy life. As I stepped into my room, the sun hung on the horizon and cast orange and gold lights into the room. I turned on a lamp and pulled off my USB T-shirt and flour-caked jeans and shrugged on an oversized T-shirt. I craved a hot shower and change of clothes and maybe even heading down the street to the pub and getting a burger.

As I reached for the shower's tap, the light I'd just turned on flickered once, twice, and on the third blip went out. I stood waiting, knowing someone had come.

"Shaun."

Of course, no voice answered. That would have been too simple. Instead, there was a steady thickening and souring of the air. The lightness around me vanished, and in its place came the dark anger, which I'd felt a couple of times before. My heart beat a little faster as I clenched my hands at my side.

"The secret's out, Shaun. We know Sally is Susie. And it's okay. No one is going to hurt her. She's safe."

The books stacked on the floor toppled over, and the light on the nightstand flickered. A glass on the sink in the bathroom rattled, fell to the floor, and shattered.

Leave.

The message was as clear as if it had been spoken.

Leave.

"Sorry, pal," I said in a stern voice. "I'm here to stay."

Leave.

"No."

I stood tense and waiting as the energy swirled around me. Sensing I was in some battle of wills, I mentally dug in deeper. "Like it or not, Shaun, I'm stuck here for the duration. I've got a family to look after, just as you looked after yours."

For a moment the sour air swirled, but my heart slowed, and my palms didn't sweat. Shaun and I weren't so different. We would both do what it took to take care of our own.

And then just as quickly as the presence came, it vanished.

The air cleared and the light on the nightstand flashed

back on. Releasing a tense breath, I moved into the bathroom and gingerly picked up the broken glass. A shard caught the tip of my thumb and nicked the skin. A trickle of blood oozed out.

I cursed and grabbed toilet paper from the roll and wrapped it around my thumb. Life at the bakery would never be easy. This place would always require something. Dad had said it was never satisfied and he was right. But I was okay with that for now.

“I am here to stay.”

Epilogue

SATURDAY, MAY 29, 2010, 11:00 AM

I'd never given a guy flowers. I'd received my share, but I'd never given. Buying the yellow sunflowers had seemed like a great idea at the time, but now as I stood outside of Gordon's shop on this lovely early May Saturday morning and watched the passersby go in for the grand opening, I was feeling a little foolish. We'd not spoken much in the last couple of weeks, and I wasn't sure if he'd really welcome me.

"Buck up, Daisy," I whispered. "Don't be a baby."

With those words rattling in my head, I crossed the street and walked into the shop to find a crush of people who'd gathered for his opening. I spotted several of my customers as well as a couple of folks from Suburban.

I caught sight of a group of women and knew I'd found Gordon. The ladies in town who came into the bakery had not been shy about gossiping about the new hot bike guy.

As I wove through the crowd, I bumped into a tall guy wearing a Tour de France T-shirt. He had suntanned features and a dark hair. "Hey," he says. "Love the flowers. Tour de France, right?"

"Very good. The tour cuts through the sunflower fields of southern France."

"I know my bike races."

He shifted a water bottle from his right to his left hand and extended his hand to me. "I'm Sam. Gordon and I rode bikes together back in college."

"Daisy McCrae. I manage the Union Street Bakery." The words no longer tripped on my tongue but flowed easily.

"I've seen that place. Very cool."

"We like to think so. So, you in town for long?"

"Maybe." Twin dimples appeared on his cheeks when he smiled. "I'm starting to like Alexandria a lot."

The gaggle of women parted, and Gordon caught my gaze. He smiled.

"Hey, let me go wish Gordon good luck," I said.

"Yeah, sure. Maybe I'll come by sometime and buy a cookie."

I laughed. When I reached Gordon, I'd forgotten about feeling awkward about bringing flowers or even coming. It was just good to see him. "Hey."

"Hey, yourself." He glanced at the sunflowers. "For me?"

"For you. I thought about a cake or cookies but that seemed too predictable."

He took the flowers. "Thanks."

"You're very welcome. And I wish you many years of good business."

"Back at you."

"Hey," I said before I lost my nerve, "want to grab dinner and a lecture next Saturday?"

"Lecture?"

"Margaret is giving it. It's about our family and kind of cool."

"I'd like that." For a moment we just lingered, only inches apart.

The crowd around me faded, and I had the urge to kiss him. "Hey, Gordon!" Sam called. "I got someone you need to meet."

"He's interested in investing in the shop," Gordon says.

"I've got to go."

"Saturday, then."

"Yeah."

Smiling, I tossed him a final wave and made my way out of the shop. The air outside was cool, but the sun was warm enough to make this a perfect spring day.

As I reached the bakery, I could hear yelling. It was Rachel. And I'd never heard her so angry. I pushed through the front door and found her standing by the front register sporting a glare that bordered on wild.

"What the heck is wrong?" I asked. Illness, death, fire, you name the disaster, and it flashed in my mind.

"There's a man. A horrible man who smokes and rides an old Harley."

I didn't see anyone. "Where is this man?"

"The kitchen. He left his nasty, beat-up backpack right by the register and is rearranging my kitchen. I told him to get out. He told me to call Henri."

"Did you?"

"Yes. But he's not answering his phone." Her flushed cheeks made her eyes look all the bluer. "I'm out here to call the police."

I moved behind the counter and took the phone from her hand. "I don't suppose he speaks with a French accent, does he?"

"How did you know?"

"You just met our new bread baker."

What Came Before

MONDAY, JANUARY 19, 1852,
MIDNIGHT

A man who stuck his neck out was a fool. A wise man kept his head low, worked hard and never drew the attention of the authorities.

Shaun McCrae had learned this lesson well in Ireland as a boy. His dad had objected to rising land rents and had been organizing the other farmers in protest when English soldiers had showed up at their cottage in the middle of the night. As his mother screamed and his little sister cried, the soldiers had taken his father away. He'd returned seven years later, but he was never the same.

These warnings from the past rumbled when two big men from Bruin's came to his bakery to fetch the girl. The instant she saw them, she'd clung to her mother. When the men had dragged her to a waiting wagon, she'd screamed as if Satan himself had grabbed a hold of her hair.

He'd stood by and watched, and even when her pleading gaze had met his, he'd not said or done anything that gave a hint that the scene troubled him deeply. After the girl was gone, he'd gone to Bruin's and found out that the girl had been auctioned to a New Orleans man, Murdock, known for his exclusive fancy houses. He could see the girl's fate as plain as day.

The girl was being kept in Bruin's holding cells for several more hours, and then she would be transferred to the *Diamond*, Murdock's slave ship bound for New Orleans. He returned to the bakery and kept working as if nothing had happened.

At midnight, he drove his wagon down to the docks and stopped in front of the *Diamond*. The vessel was being loaded, and she would be ready to leave on the morning tide. He set the brake on his wagon, tied off the reins and jumped down.

In the soft glow of lantern light, as Shaun unloaded a biscuit barrel, he caught the gaze of the sailor guarding the ship's entrance. The bloke, known to him from the gaming tables, was called Joey One-Thumb because he'd lost his right thumb in a ship's rigging when he was a lad. Joey had a good bit of muscle, a lacking brain, and he owed Shaun a good bit of money from the previous Saturday night's poker. Joey's presence was a sign from the Lord.

Shoving out a breath, he moved slowly and carefully as if he were a man only about the business of delivering sea biscuits to a ship readying to leave port. He'd done the task a thousand times before and with luck would do it a thousand more times in the future. He unloaded two more barrels and loaded all sideways onto a hand trolley he kept in the wagon bed for such deliveries.

With a grunt, he tipped the load back and pushed it up to the plank. "Good evening, Joey."

Joey straightened. "If you've come about your money, I'll be paying you when we return from New Orleans. I told you I'd not have it until then."

Shaun's biceps bunched against his shirt as he balanced his weight. He glanced from side to side down the dark, quiet dock. "I've a proposition for you, Joey-One-Thumb."

Joey rubbed his right snubbed thumb along the stubble of his chin. "What is it, Shaun?"

Grinning, Shaun again glanced from side to side and swallowed the knot in his throat. "Lend me your keys and give me ten minutes on your ship and I will forget your debt to me."

"What did you say?"

"You heard me."

"I could land in jail for that!"

"Aye, and I could for asking it. But two hundred dollars is a nice bit of change to have lost at the poker tables. Would be nice to keep it, don't you think?"

The stench of the human cargo below deck clung to Joey's tattered jacket. "Why would you give up that kind of money?"

"That's not for you to wonder. Are you interested in my offer?"

"What do you plan to do on that ship?"

"Just delivering a bit of biscuits to your captain. I've heard he has always favored them."

Joey moistened cracked, dried lips like a man half-starved placed in front of prime beef on a spit. "You'll forgive it all?"

"Aye, every bit of the debt. But you must act right now, or the deal is off." Shaun dug a loaf of bread from his pocket and handed it to the man.

Joey hesitated a moment and then fished a ring of iron keys from his coat pocket. He slipped the keys into Shaun's rough hands as he took the bread. "Just ten minutes."

Shaun nodded. He pushed his burden up the gangplank lit only by a few swaying deck lanterns. The ship under him creaked and swayed as he pushed toward aft section doors. He'd delivered sea biscuits to *Diamond* before and knew its general layout. The male slaves would be kept in the hole of the ship, chained to the floor, but the females and children were locked away in a cell just belowdecks and across from the captain's quarters. The captain rarely chained the women and children unless they caused trouble.

The ring of keys bit into his fingers as he wheeled toward the port that led to the lower levels. Several sailors, dozing against a mast, waved a weary greeting to him. They'd seen delivery people here before, so he wasn't out of place and in the fading light they'd not be able to tell who he was or what he was delivering. Only Joey One-Thumb could say for sure that Shaun McCrae had boarded the ship and his greed would keep him silent. He backed his load down a few steps and descended into the lower deck. The holding area was a deck below, but the foul smell had permeated the floorboards and burned his nostrils.

He'd arrived in this country with his young daughter and the clothes on their backs. In those days, there had been little work for a poor Irishman. But years of backbreaking work on the docks coupled with his talent for cards had won him a bakery and respectability.

"And you risk it all now, boy-o." He lowered the barrels down and unloaded the first two, full of biscuits. And then he unloaded the third empty and hollow, as it had been the day it had arrived from the cooper.

Fumbling in the dim light with the keys, he moved to the last door on the right, glanced through the barred window, and saw several older women huddled by the porthole where cold, fresh air drifted in from the river. One woman held two small sleeping children and a few others stared sightlessly into the dark.

He pulled in his breath. "I've come for Susie. Is she here?"

The women turned and each frowned their fear and frustration. For a moment, he thought they might rally around the girl and make a scene but in the next instant, one of the women nodded to a silent figure in the corner. She sat on the floor, alone, her knees drawn up to her chest and her head ducked.

"Susie, you are to come with me now." He could say no more without creating a fuss. They had but minutes before someone would wonder why he'd lingered too long belowdecks.

She lifted her head and stared at him. For a moment, she blinked as if she didn't believe her eyes. He nodded as if to say, *Come here, girl.*

Rising, she moved toward him. He could see that her dress was torn, and a bruise darkened her cheek and shoulder. Anger burned hot and quick in his gut, and he knew one day he'd collect his own pound of flesh from the man who'd harmed her.

He fumbled with the keys, found the right one, and opened the door as she rose and moved toward him. Many of the women stared at him, angry and hostile, as if they assumed he was taking the girl for a few minutes of pleasure. He tugged her roughly from the room and locked the door.

When she started to speak, he raised his finger to his lips and bade her to be silent. In a few quick strides they reached the barrels, and he pried the top off the empty vessel. He hefted her thin form and set her in the barrel.

"Not a word to anyone about this. Ever," he said. "This must be our secret."

She glanced up at him, her face so pale and stricken. A bit of his heart broke when he looked into eyes drained of fight and filled with fear.

She nodded.

He capped the barrel and then set it back on the dolly. With a grunt, he put the barrel on the dolly and backed up the stairs with his burden. He pushed across the deck and down the gangplank where he found a nervous Joey glancing from side to side.

Shaun returned the keys to Joey. "I was not here, boy-o."

The seaman's gaze narrowed. "They will ask.

"Aye, they will, and you didn't see me." He paused. "The two hundred dollars is your reward for the help. Two broken legs will be your reward if you talk."

Even in the flickering lantern light, he could see the man pale. "I won't talk."

"See that you don't." He paused. "And boy-o, when they go looking for anything that might be missing, it fell overboard. You hear me?"

"Overboard?"

"You heard a loud splash."

"A loud splash."

Shaun patted him roughly on the cheek. "There's a good lad."

And without another word, he hefted his barrel into the bed of his truck and whistling drove into the night.

Union Street Bakery Recipes

Sugar Cookies

During my years away from the bakery, I never ate these sugar cookies. I knew their buttery softness with the hint of lemon would transport me back to that day Renee and I sat on the patio at Union Street Bakery. They would remind me of the warmth of the sun on my face, the smell of the honeysuckle, and a happy moment that would soon be punctuated with terror.

A few Christmases ago, however, I asked Mom for the recipe. She reduced the portion from twenty dozen to two dozen. I baked the recipe as Mom taught me, but still I never ate the cookies. Instead, I'd pass the little confections out at the office or give them to neighbors. I enjoyed the look of pleasure on their faces when I presented them with these little wonders. The trick, I tell anyone who will listen, is to use ingredients that are the purest and highest quality.

I'm hoping one day to once again sit and eat the cookies and not have any memories attached to it. For now, I'm satisfied that they make others happy.

Sugar Cookies

1-1/2 cups sugar
2/3 cup butter (Mom uses pure Irish butter)
2 eggs
2 tablespoons whole milk
1 teaspoon lemon extract
3-1/4 cups all-purpose flour
2-1/2 teaspoons baking powder
1/2 teaspoon salt

Preheat oven to 350F.

Cream together the sugar and softened butter until fluffy. Add the eggs, milk, and lemon extract. Mix well.

Into another bowl sift together flour, baking powder, and salt. Slowly incorporate the flour into the butter mixture. Refrigerate dough for at least an hour before baking. Spoon evenly sized dollops of batter onto a parchment-lined baking sheet. Bake at 350 degrees for 12 to 15 minutes, until golden.

Rachel's Carrot Cake Cupcakes

Rachel came up with this recipe when she was in high school. She'd been on a vegetarian kick about that time and had started working vegetables into as many confections as she could. There'd been a lot of recipes that had just been too healthy for our customers. "When the customers come through the bakery's front door, they have sin in their hearts," Dad used to say. "Not vegetables."

But this little confection/vegetable hybrid had passed muster and been added to the menu. From day one it had been a customer favorite. Rachel insists that the cook always hand-shred the carrots. She concedes using a grater takes longer, but the carrots retain more moisture when they aren't chopped in a food processor.

These cupcakes can be dusted with powdered sugar but that

was just never decadent enough for Rachel. This cream cheese icing is the perfect topping. Makes 12 cupcakes.

Cupcake Base

3 cups shredded carrots 2 eggs
1⁄2 cup sugar
3⁄4 cup brown sugar
3⁄4 cup vegetable oil
2 teaspoons vanilla
2 cups all-purpose flour
1 teaspoon salt
1 teaspoon cinnamon
1 teaspoon baking powder 1 teaspoon baking soda

Cream Cheese Icing

1⁄2 cup cream cheese (room temperature)
1 teaspoon vanilla
2 cups powdered sugar 1–2 tablespoons milk

Preheat oven to 350F.

Mix carrots, eggs, sugars, vegetable oil, and vanilla and mix well. Sift together flour, salt, cinnamon, baking powder, and baking soda. Add to carrot mixture and gently mix, just until combined. Divide batter evenly between muffin cups. Bake at 350 for 20 to 25 minutes until golden, and a tester inserted into the middle of a cupcake comes out clean. Cool cupcakes completely.

To make cream cheese icing: Cream all ingredients together until fluffy. Frost cooled cupcakes.

Shaun's Seaman's Biscuits

This simple biscuit/cracker is simple. When fully cooked, it's dry almost to the point of hard, but it's stands up to long sea voyages and is perfect for dunking in a hot soup.

3 teacups flour
1 cup water
1 pinch salt

Preheat oven to 250 degrees.

Mix the flour, water, and salt in a large bowl and knead until smooth.

Roll out the dough until it is as thick as your index finger (1 inch) and then cut into squares the length of your pinky finger (2 inches). With a fork poke, holes in the dough and bake for 1 hour. Turn crackers over and bake for another hour. Store in an airtight tin.

Mike's Chocolate Espresso Torte

This cake is not a Union Street Bakery classic. It was brought to the bakery when Rachel married Mike Evans, a Paris-trained pastry chef. Rachel will tell anyone who asks that she fell in love with Mike's cake before she fell in love with him. Its blend of bitter and sweet is fitting for Rachel and Mike's life together. For almost a year after Mike's death, she refused to make the cake at all. But in the last couple of months, she has started to make the recipe again.

Chocolate Espresso Torte
¾-pound butter
¾ cup sugar
¾ cup strong coffee
¾-pound semi-sweet chocolate- chips or chopped up
6 eggs

Pre-heat your oven to 350 degrees.

Melt the butter and chocolate together in a double boiler. Mix the eggs and sugar thoroughly but not to the point that they are frothy. Slowly mix the chocolate/butter mixture into the egg/sugar mixture, add the coffee and stir well. Pour this into a greased 8-inch spring-form pan coated with cooking spray. If you don't have a spring-form pan, any 8-inch pan will do if the sides are 2-3 inches high. Bake the torte at 350 degrees for 15 minutes then turn the oven down to 300 and bake for one hour.

There's no way to tell if the torte is done by looking at it or sticking a knife into it. Just take it out of the oven after an hour. It will be high, like a soufflé at first but will sink down in a few minutes. Let it sit until it thoroughly cools and then put it in the refrigerator overnight. Once it is solid take it out of the pan. If using a spring-form pan this will be simple. If not using a spring-form pan dip the pan into boiling water for about 15 seconds, then dump the torte out onto a plate. This takes a little practice. If the torte breaks it molds back together like clay. Once you have it out of the pan pour the ganache over the top.

Ganache

1 cup milk

1⁄2 cup cream

1 1/8-pound semi-sweet baking chocolate

Melt the butter and add the milk and cream. Do this in a double boiler because this mixture scorches easily. Once the liquid is very hot, but not boiling, add it to the chocolate and stir until the chocolate is thoroughly melted. Pour it into a container and let it cool for a several minutes before pouring over torte.

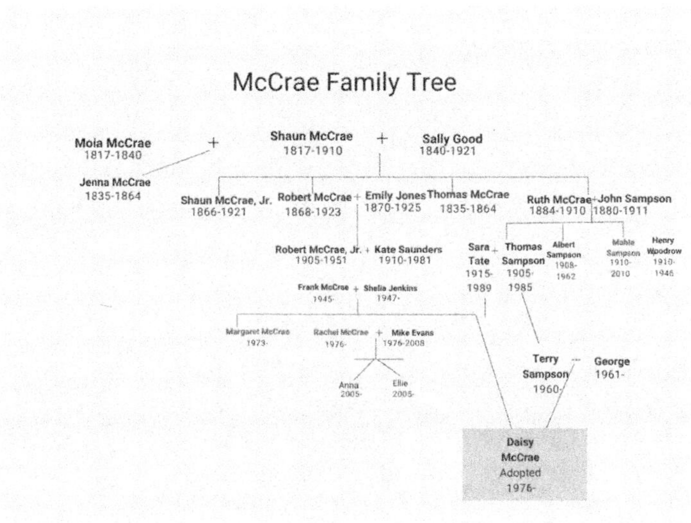
McCrae Family Tree
Moia McCrae
1817-1840
Jenna McCrae
1835-1864
Shaun McCrae
1817-1910
Sally Good
1840-1921
Shaun McCrae, Jr.
1866-1921
Robert McCrae
1868-1923
Emily Jones
1870-1925
Thomas McCrae
1835-1864
Ruth McCrae
1884-1910
John Sampson
1880-1911
Robert McCrae, Jr.
1905-1951
Kate Saunders
1910-1981
Sara Tate
1915-1989
Thomas Sampson
1905-1985
Albert Sampson
1908-1962
Mahle Sampson
1910-2010
Henry Woodrow
1910-1946
Frank McCrae
1945-
Shelia Jenkins
1947-
Margaret McCrae
1973-
Rachel McCrae
1976-
Mike Evans
1976-2008
Anna
2005-
Ellie
2005-
Terry Sampson
1960-
George
1961-
Daisy McCrae
Adopted
1976-

About the Author

Amazon Charts bestselling author, Mary Ellen Taylor's love of history and fiction is evident in her novels ***The Brighter The Light*** and ***When the Rain Ends***. For more about Mary, visit www.maryellentaylor.com

Also by Mary Ellen Taylor

The Union Street Bakery Series

The Union Street Bakery - Book 1

Sweet Expectations - Book 2

At the Corner of King Street - Book 3

The View from Prince Street - Book 4

Printed in Great Britain
by Amazon

33855719R00198